Crown Prince
Challenged

Other Books in the
Brookmeade Young Riders Series

Crown Prince

The Brookmeade
Young Riders Series

Crown Prince
Challenged

Linda Snow McLoon

TRAFALGAR SQUARE
North Pomfret, Vermont

First published in 2012 by
Trafalgar Square Books
North Pomfret, Vermont 05053

Printed in the United States of America

Library of Congress Cataloging-in-Publication Data
McLoon, Linda Snow.
  Crown prince challenged / Linda Snow McLoon.
    p. cm. -- (Brookmeade young riders series)
  Summary: Sarah Wagner dreams that she and her former racetrack rogue,
Crown Prince, will someday reach the highest levels of equestrian competition
and with help from trainer Jack O'Brien they are on their way, but first they
must face hostility from other Brookmeade Farm riders.
  ISBN 978-1-57076-545-2 (pbk.)
  [1. Horsemanship--Fiction. 2. Race horses--Fiction. 3. Interpersonal relations--
Fiction.] I. Title.
  PZ7.M478725Cro 2012
  [Fic]--dc23
                        2012024423

Book design by Lauryl Eddlemon
Front cover design by Jennifer Brandon
Cover artwork and points-of-the-horse illustration by Jennifer Brandon
(www.jachestudio.com). Copyright and all reproductive rights to the artwork,
inclusive of complete ownership of the physical artworks themselves, are the
property of and reserved to the artist.
Typeface: Palatino

10 9 8 7 6 5 4 3 2 1

Dedication

To the generous and loyal horses
I was privileged to have in my life —
good friends all.

Contents

Contents *(Continued)*

CHAPTER 1

End of Summer

SARAH WAGNER TAPPED HER FINGERS on the desk as she waited for her homeroom class to be excused. It was nearly the end of the first day of school at Yardley High, and her eyes were riveted on the classroom clock. When the bell sounded, she grabbed her tote bag and joined the swarm of students hurrying out of the building. She went straight to the Ridge Road bus, where Kayla Romano was saving her a seat. With her curly red hair, cut short, and pancake freckles, Kayla was easy to spot.

When Sarah plunked down beside her best friend, Kayla slid over to give Sarah more room. "How'd it go, kid?" Kayla asked. Kayla liked to remind Sarah she was two months her senior.

"I got Mr. Rawlins for Geometry. Everyone says he's totally cool. I like my other teachers, too. How about you?"

"Okay, I guess," Kayla replied. "I'm glad we're in English together, but I wish I had a different teacher for World History. I've already got a ton of homework." Both girls grabbed the seat in front of them as the bus lurched around the sharp corner coming out of the parking lot. "Enough about school. Are you going to ride this afternoon?"

Sarah's thoughts turned to Crown Prince, the beautiful, dark bay horse she had gotten off the racetrack at the beginning of the summer. Today would be the first time she hadn't been at the farm in the morning to feed the horses, which was part of her job that paid for Prince's board. Lucas, the young worker who was back after having the summer off, would have made the rounds feeding grain and hay. She hoped he remembered to turn Prince out for a few hours, but of course the barn manager, Gus, would have reminded him. Gus might be a total grouch, but when it came to running an efficient barn operation where the horses got the best of care, Sarah had to admit he was on top of everything.

Sarah raised her voice over the laughing and commotion on the bus. "It's going to be tight. I definitely want to ride, but I've got to have time to clean Prince's stall before I do the night feed. You have your lesson today. Will it be a mad rush to get Fanny to the farm in time?"

"Mom will have the trailer hooked up and everything ready, so we should be okay," Kayla said. She raised an eyebrow. "We've had plenty of practice."

Kayla had been bringing her chestnut Quarter Horse, Fanfare, to Brookmeade Farm for weekly lessons ever since she'd gotten the mare a few years earlier. They'd done well in several horse shows over the summer, and she gave a lot of the credit for how well Fanny had performed to her lessons with the farm's trainer and chief instructor, Jack O'Brien.

"I miss riding with you guys," Sarah said, thinking of the talented group of young riders Jack taught on Wednesday afternoons. "It's been great having private lessons with Jack, but I wonder when he'll think Prince is ready to ride with a group. We're still doing a lot of gymnastic jumping, tailor-made for Prince, so I guess it'll be a while."

"How's he doing?" Kayla asked.

"Oh, Kayla, he's awesome! He likes jumping, and his flatwork is coming along. Jack says that for a big horse, he's very well balanced. The only time he got a little upset was when one of Mrs. DeWitt's Jack Russells chased a chipmunk right in front of us. He half-reared and then spun around in the opposite direction." Sarah adjusted the heavy bag, laden with books, on her lap. "Do you know what you guys will be doing today?"

"I'm not sure. But Jack told us to work on transitions this week, so we might do a lot of flatwork. Tim and Paige have two more events this fall, and they'd love to do better in the dressage phase. Rita always likes an opportunity to show off how superior Chancellor is on the flat," Kayla said, putting a heavy accent on *superior*.

Sarah couldn't resist a laugh. "Oh, come on—she'd not as bad as she used to be."

When the bus stopped at her house, Sarah bounded off and hurried to the back door. Her younger sister, Abby, wouldn't be home yet, and her mother might still be at work. Alison Wagner hadn't recovered sufficiently from a serious car accident she'd survived the year before so she could go back to teaching fourth grade, but she'd found a part time bookkeeping job. It was always hard to predict what time Sarah's father might get home from his teaching job at the local community college.

Sarah took the back steps two at a time and immediately went to her room. She wasted no time changing into barn jeans and a T-shirt before picking up her brush and pulling her long dark hair back into a ponytail. As she fixed her hair, she considered her image in the mirror. A somewhat narrow face with long-lashed dark eyes, a high forehead, and an olive complexion gazed back at her. *Nothing there a guy would ever be attracted to,* she thought.

Back downstairs, she grabbed a few carrots from the fridge and stuck them into her jeans pocket before putting on her paddock boots in the mudroom. Minutes later she was heading to the barn on her bike. She had ridden this route every day since Crown Prince had come to Brookmeade Farm back in June, and she knew the bumps and curves by heart, including the half-mile entry road into the farm. This was the part she liked best, where she could see the three broodmares and their foals turned out in the green fields along the way. On this warm, early September afternoon, she was thankful for the stately elm trees that formed a leafy shaded canopy over the gravel road. She pedaled hard, crossing the bridge over the wide brook and flying by the bungalow where Jack and his wife, Kathleen, lived.

Finally she was coasting down the final hill to the parking area. Tim Dixon's car was already there, which meant he had come to the barn directly from school, and he'd probably given his girlfriend, Paige Vargas, a ride. Sarah envisioned them getting their horses ready for the lesson right now. Sure enough, when she entered the barn, she saw Paige, a striking girl with gorgeous blonde hair and deep violet eyes, in the aisle. She was grooming her dappled-gray Thoroughbred, Quarry, who didn't appear very happy. His ears were pinned back, and he tossed his head in annoyance as Paige rubbed his underside with a curry comb.

Hi, Paige," Sarah said. "I guess Quarry isn't crazy about being groomed."

"Actually he only hates it when I curry his tummy. Last week he asked Gus to fire me."

Sarah laughed, something everyone did when they were around Paige for very long. Sarah stopped to look more closely at Quarry. "But seriously, he's looking better and better. He really filled out this summer."

"Thanks," Paige said as she flipped the curry comb back in her grooming caddy and pulled out a dandy brush. Quarry's eyes softened as she ran it in quick strokes along his neck. "It's taken him a while to lose that off-the-track, skinny look. I think that does help us a bit in the show ring. But handsome is as handsome does. I still have to work on keeping him from rushing his fences."

"I've gotta check on Prince," Sarah said," as she ducked under one of Quarry's cross-ties.

When she rounded the corner leading to the two new stalls in the back of the barn, Prince was looking out through the bars of his stall door. His head came up and his ears pricked forward when he saw Sarah. Hurrying to her horse, her heart warmed when she heard his low welcoming nicker. She slid the door open enough to slip through.

"You're glad to see me, aren't you, boy," she murmured. He lowered his head so she could hug his face close to her chest. She stepped back to pull the carrot he had come to expect from her pocket, and he eagerly bit off a big section.

Sarah's eyes ran over her horse. She never tired of looking at the beautiful dark bay with the white star in the center of his broad forehead. His finely chiseled head had large intelligent eyes and a delicate muzzle, and it blended into a long arched neck and well-angled shoulder. A lovely topline continued to powerful hindquarters on the tall Thoroughbred, and his sleek coat gleamed like China silk. Crown Prince was one handsome dude!

So much had happened over the summer, and so fast that memories raced through Sarah's mind like a movie on fast-forward. That Saturday in June when Jack and her dad had taken her to the racetrack to pick out a horse of her own seemed like yesterday. Before Brookmeade's owners, Chandler and Dorothy DeWitt, came up with their generous plan that enabled her to get Crown Prince, acquiring a horse had always seemed an impossible dream. Her mother's car accident and a mountain of medical debt had long ago squelched any possibility her parents could buy her a horse, so Sarah had settled for lessons on school horses at Brookmeade Farm.

From the minute she saw the big dark bay, Sarah knew the horse was the one she'd been waiting for, despite his reputation as a racetrack rogue. The two of them had bonded immediately. After Crown Prince came to the farm, the road had been filled with challenges. Sarah had fought to keep him when his rich owner tried to rescind his offer and take him back. Then, in a thirty-day trial period, she had to convince her parents that Crown Prince was safe to ride, despite his earlier bad behavior at the racetrack. With Jack's help, Sarah and her horse had triumphed over every obstacle in their path.

Now here she was getting ready to ride her very own wonderful horse. It seemed that whether she was on the ground or on his back, she and Prince shared a special connection. Under saddle, he responded to her lightest tweak of the reins and the slightest pressure of her legs against his sides. When she spoke softly to him, his ears flicked in her direction, and whenever she walked away, his gaze followed her until she was out of sight.

Leaving the stall, Sarah hurried to the boarders' tack room to get her things. By putting on her helmet and half chaps and looping her bridle over her shoulder, she had one arm free for her saddle and one to pick up her grooming caddy. Making just one trip saved time. After she got back to his stall, she led Prince into the aisle and put him on cross-ties. She had just started to brush him when she heard the sound of quick boots clicking rhythmically on cement.

They had to belong to Jack, her riding instructor. A clean-shaven man with black hair tinged with gray, Jack's square jaw, snapping dark eyes, and no-nonsense demeanor announced a man who took his job seriously. In his younger days, Jack had ridden for the Irish Olympic Team, and as he strode toward her, his slightly bowed legs spoke to the many hours he had spent in the saddle.

"I'm glad you're here this afternoon, Sarah," Jack said. "'Tis a surprise I have for you. Your horse is doing well enough in his flatwork that I think he's ready to leave the stable area and go for a hack on the trails. 'Twill be good for him."

Sarah hadn't expected this so soon. Up until now, she'd been limited to riding Prince in the indoor arena or the enclosed outside ring, all the while looking forward to the day she could ride him on the miles of trails around the farm. For weeks she'd longed to see how he would react to a trail ride through the woods and fields. She smiled broadly. "Awesome!" was all she could say.

"But you shouldn't go out alone," Jack continued. "For the first hack he should be in company. When their class is over, Tim and Paige usually ride up to the old orchard on the ridge to cool out their horses. And perhaps Kayla and Rita will go along. I'd be thinking 'tis time you joined them."

Sarah felt her excitement rising. "Should we stay at a walk?" she asked.

"The other riders will be cooling out their horses after working hard in the lesson, so walking will be the order of the day. Just use your aids as you would if you were riding him in the ring. When you're climbing up the steep part of the ridge, be sure to let him stretch his head and neck down, so he can best use his hindquarters. Under saddle, the hill might be strange to him, so on the way down, keep him straight and support him in front with your hands. Let me know how it goes." Jack turned abruptly and strode off toward the indoor, in a hurry to set up some jump combinations for his Young Riders class.

This threw a wrinkle into her game plan. Glancing at her watch, Sarah did some quick math. She decided she'd have time to clean the stall now, and Prince could go into one of the paddocks while she worked. With this delay before she rode, Sarah removed her half-chaps and helmet and set them down near the stall. She ran the chain from her lead shank over Prince's nose, clipped it onto his halter, and led him toward the side door, his shoes ringing evenly on the cement.

Sarah waved to Tim, who was saddling Rhodes Scholar, his handsome blood-bay gelding. Rhodes had come from Canada, where he'd been fox hunted before Tim got him. In addition to being athletic and exceptionally sound, Rhodes also had an amazing temperament. He never got rattled, regardless of what was going on around him. Rhodes' good qualities had helped them do well when they'd competed in several events over the summer.

Once outside, Sarah looked over to the gravel parking lot where Rita Snyder's van with the green Pyramid Farm lettering was parked. The Snyders' hired groom, Judson, was helping Rita get her horse ready for the lesson, and Sarah could hear Rita's commands to the balding, ruddy-faced man as they worked. Rita was being Rita, at least to Judson. So much for her pledge to change her ways after the tragic accident at the beginning of the summer. You'd almost think she'd forgotten she'd been responsible for the death of one of Mrs. DeWitt's dogs. But in all fairness, she didn't brag about her horse quite so much, and she'd even found a few good things to say about the other horses in her class.

Riding Chancellor, her black Dutch Warmblood, Rita had mopped up at a number of shows over the summer, winning four championships and two reserves. To celebrate, the Snyders had hosted an end-of-summer pool party for the Brookmeade riders at their estate, Pyramid Farm. The instructors and Brookmeade's owners, the DeWitts, had also been invited. Sarah had been to the Snyders' mega-mansion with pillars like a Southern plantation house before, but she still couldn't believe a teenager lived there. Equally impressive was the large barn with a chandelier hanging in the foyer, many white-fenced paddocks, and a trout pond. The crowning touch was a spectacular view of the ocean beyond the sweeping lawns on the property. An indoor riding arena was being constructed on a level area behind the barn—Rita was truly going to have it all.

The pool party had been a hit. Rita's father wasn't away on a business trip, for a change, and with help from their housekeeper, he had cooked burgers and steaks on the grill. Sarah and her friends from the barn had a blast swimming in the large pool and making do-it-yourself ice cream sundaes. Rita had even arranged to have some classmates in a band liven up the party with a few sets.

The Romanos' pickup and horse trailer were parked near Rita's rig, and Kayla and her mother were getting Fanny ready for the lesson. *I'll wait to talk to Kayla when she isn't so busy,* Sarah thought. She led Prince to the only vacant paddock, turned him out in it, and then said a silent prayer that he wouldn't roll in the muddy area at the far end.

Hurrying back to his stall, Sarah grabbed a manure fork and an empty wheelbarrow on the way. While she cleaned out the dirty bedding and manure, she could think of nothing but the trail ride to the old orchard with Paige and Tim. She could live without Rita's presence, but it would be great if Kayla could ride with them. After emptying the loaded wheelbarrow into the manure bin, she filled it with fresh shavings and spread them in her horse's stall.

On the way back to get Prince, Sarah stopped to watch the lesson going on in the indoor. The class was working at canter, crossing the diagonal and briefly coming back to trot before changing leads in the center of the arena. Sarah's gaze was immediately drawn to Chancellor, Rita's Dutch Warmblood. What a magnificent horse! His black coat gleamed, and his long tail swung from side to side as his powerful strides propelled him forward as if on springs. Despite his large muscular body, he was light on his feet and moved with the grace of a ballet dancer. Rita, as always, was impeccably dressed, wearing new custom black boots, buff full-seat breeches, and a polo shirt with the Pyramid Farm logo.

Fanny was going well for Kayla. The red chestnut with a white diamond on her forehead and four tall stockings was balanced and forward. Fanny's coat color and Kayla's hair were almost identical —they were the "twins" all right, as Paige had dubbed them. Sarah watched Kayla bring Fanny off the track and follow a straight line across the diagonal. She brought Fanny to trot in the center for a simple change of lead, and after only a few trot steps, made a balanced transition back to canter. As they rode by, Sarah shot Kayla a thumbs-up and called softly, "You go, girl!"

Quarry was being a little quick, as usual, and Jack directed his comments to Paige. "Sit tall in the saddle, Paige, and steady your horse with occasional half-halts. If need be, ride a small circle." He watched the horse and rider intently. "'Tis important you be relaxed—take deep breaths." Paige's brow furrowed as she concentrated, her lithe, willowy body moving gracefully with her horse.

Jack made the exercise more difficult. "Now I want you to turn down the centerline of the arena at C," he called out in his Irish brogue, "and again do a simple change of lead at X in the middle of the arena. At A, you'll continue in the opposite direction on the new lead."

Jack turned to watch Tim and Rhodes Scholar attempt the new

challenge. Rhodes certainly was handsome, with more substance and bone than the full Thoroughbreds in the barn, probably from the influence of his Cleveland Bay grandsire. While moving with good impulsion on the bit, he executed a simple change of lead at just the right spot. Jack clapped his hands as he called out, "Brilliant, Tim! That was very good indeed."

Sarah thought of the many great lessons she'd had with her friends. Would she ever be able to ride Prince in the Young Riders class? Right now everyone here was so far ahead of her and her "greenie!" She wished she could stay longer and watch more of the class, but she needed to retrieve her horse and get him ready for their first hack.

When she got to his paddock, Prince was grazing along the fence line, reaching under the lower fence board to crop the thicker grass on the other side. She was relieved that he apparently had been too busy grazing to roll. He brought his head up as she approached, watching her with large intelligent eyes as he chewed a mouthful of grass. He stood quietly as she attached the lead shank to his halter and pressed her face against the side of his muzzle, loving the strong aroma of horse and newly clipped grass. "Come on, boy. We've got an exciting ride ahead!"

CHAPTER 2

On the Loose

SARAH GROOMED HER HORSE quickly and efficiently, beginning with picking out his feet and ending with combing his mane and tail. She put on her half chaps and helmet, and after tacking up, led him down the barn aisle and outside. His highly polished dark bay coat shimmered in the late summer sun as they walked to the enclosed sand ring near the main entrance to the barn. Once inside, she closed the gate and brought Prince to the mounting block. She was thankful it was there—her horse was over a full hand taller than any of the school horses she'd ever ridden, and mounting him from the ground wasn't easy.

The minute Sarah swung her leg over and sat in the saddle, Prince tried to walk forward, but she made him halt. "No, Prince, don't move out until you're asked," she said, as she slid her right paddock boot into the stirrup. "You've got to wait." After walking around the ring once, inviting Prince to stretch his head and neck forward and down, Sarah checked her watch. She would have at least ten minutes before Jack's class ended, enough time to do a little schooling before the trail ride. It would be good to work off some of Prince's pent-up energy.

Sarah pressed her horse into trot. She was always pleased with the steady feel she had in the reins when he went forward from her leg aids into the bridle. Thank goodness his mouth had never become hard from heavy-handed riding, like some of the school horses she'd ridden. He energetically moved forward, seeming to enjoy his work as they walked, trotted, and cantered in both directions in the ring.

They were practicing bending on circles when Sarah saw Jack's wife, Kathleen, come out of the barn followed by two beginner riders leading the farm's two ponies. As they got closer, Sarah could see the straw-colored braids of Grace, the DeWitts' five-year-old granddaughter—she was leading her chestnut pony, Pretty Penny. A boy slightly older than Grace was following right behind them with Snippet, a larger black pony.

Jack's lesson must be over, Sarah thought. *Time to head over to the indoor.* She brought Prince back to walk and was standing by the gate when Kathleen reached the ring.

"If you were hoping to have the gate opened for you, your timing is perfect," Kathleen said, with a smile. She wore riding breeches, tall stockings pulled up over her calves, and turquoise Crocs. With no helmet hiding her shoulder-length auburn hair, it was obvious she wasn't planning on getting on a horse right away.

Sarah grinned as she nodded. "Saves me getting off and mounting him again!" She looked down at Grace and her pony as they walked by. Crown Prince towered above them. "Want to swap?" she asked.

Grace giggled. "He's too big for me!"

"Yes, and Pretty Penny is *just right* for you."

Sarah walked her horse through the gate that Kathleen held open and headed to the indoor. Prince's head was high, his ears alertly flicking back and forth as they approached the main entrance to the indoor arena. The four riders in the class were lined up in the center while Jack spoke to them. Sarah took a deep breath and attempted to control her nervousness. So far Prince had always been well-behaved under saddle, and there was no reason to suspect he'd be any different on a hack. But how would he react to being on the woods trail, climbing the ridge, and going through the old orchard on the height of land? Before Prince came to Brookmeade, all he'd ever known was the racetrack and the breeding farm in Florida where he was raised.

Sarah brought Prince to a halt where she could watch through the doorway. After standing for a few minutes, her horse became anxious and wanted to move on. He pulled against the bit and tossed his head impatiently. Sarah reached down to run her hand along his arched neck as she spoke softly to him. "Good boy, Prince. Just a few more minutes." She circled him a few times until the onlookers who had been watching the lesson from the bleachers finally began to file out of the arena by way of the main entrance.

Four horses and their riders followed the spectators out of the arena. As the horses stepped into the sunlit afternoon, still bright and warm, their heads and necks were stretched low. They had worked hard in the lesson, and their bodies glistened with per-spiration. Sarah called to the riders. "Hey, guys. Jack said you might be up for going to the old orchard to cool down your horses. Would you mind some company?"

"Quarry won't care as long as he can be up front," Paige said. "I guess that's his racehorse instinct." Her almond shaped eyes crinkled as she smiled. "He thinks even a trail ride is the Belmont Stakes."

Tim turned to Sarah. "Prince has never been out on the trails? This might be interesting."

"How about you, Kayla," Sarah asked. "Can you come?"

Kayla looked to where her mother was cleaning out their horse trailer in the parking area, readying it for their trip home. "I wish I could, but Mom will want to get going. One of these days I'll see if she or my dad will drop Fanny off here on the weekend, so we can go for a long ride together. Maybe we can ride the trails that start on the other side of Ridge Road."

"That would be awesome!" Sarah said, already excited at the prospect of a ride with her friends on a cool autumn weekend.

"Are you coming with us?" Paige asked Rita.

"Sure," Rita answered, with a shrug. "Chance was a star today, so I guess he deserves to go for a hack."

As the horses started to move off, Paige twisted in the saddle toward Rita. "Do you want us to wait while you let Judson know?"

"Naw," Rita said. "He'll figure it out."

Sarah guided Crown Prince behind the other three horses as they made their way across the parking area toward the trail leading to the old orchard. Before they reached the opening in the trees, Sarah saw Mrs. DeWitt walking down the driveway from their nearby farmhouse on the hill. Her two Jack Russell terriers—the older dog Spin and the puppy Cameo—led the way. The older woman with plump cheeks, cheery blue eyes, and silver hair twisted into a bun had on navy jodhpurs and paddock boots, so she was probably on her way to the barn to ride her gray Arab mare, Medina. The riders waved to Mrs. DeWitt.

"Have a good ride!" she called out in reply.

The woods were thick where the narrow trail went off from the parking area, a mix of hardwood and evergreen trees. Prince snorted and hesitated a moment at the entrance, but when Sarah reassured him with her legs and voice, he moved forward. He didn't want to be left behind, and once in a while he jigged a step or two. *It's not surprising he's a little nervous*, she reminded herself.

But he'll come to love hacking on the trails. He's just never done it before.

Quarry led the ride, with Rhodes following closely behind and Chancellor next in line. Crown Prince brought up the rear. He chomped on the bit, constantly flicking his ears back and forth, listening to her and the sounds of the forest around them. The trail surface was smooth, for the most part covered with a bed of pine needles, although the horses had to step over some large tree roots and occasional rocks. As they moved farther away from the farm, the woods fell into a deep silence, with only the sounds of the horses' footsteps on the path breaking the stillness. On this warm afternoon, the pine trees gave the forest a fragrance of old world spice.

After they had ridden a few minutes, Tim turned in the saddle to call back to Sarah. "There's a tree down across the trail before we start climbing the ridge. It's a pretty good size, but we've been jumping it. Do you want to try it? You can go around. Our horses have jumped it so many times they don't think twice about it."

Sarah gulped. With the other horses in front of them, Prince would probably be motivated to jump the log so he could keep up with them. Besides, he'd been doing quite a bit of jumping over low obstacles in the lessons with Jack. But when Tim said "pretty good size," just what did he mean? The tree must have come down since she had ridden here the last time.

"Even Quarry doesn't get excited by this jump, Sarah," Paige called back. "It's decently inviting." A few minutes later, she said, "We're almost there. I'm going to pick up trot and pop over the log."

"Me too," Tim said.

Before Sarah could get a good look at the downed tree, Quarry was trotting away from them. He put in one canter stride before jumping the log easily. Tim and Rhodes immediately followed, and in classic form, Rhodes made jumping it a piece of cake. Now Sarah had a better look at the log, and she began to worry. It had been a pretty big tree, and resting on the ground it was probably large enough to challenge a green horse like Crown Prince.

"Here we come," Rita called out, as Chancellor broke into trot, heading for the log.

Seeing Chancellor trot away from him, Prince began to prance, pulling hard on the reins. He neighed shrilly. After Rita was over the log and moving down the trail, Sarah eased her hold on the reins and pressed Prince forward with her legs. But instead of obediently picking up trot, Prince suddenly bolted forward, racing toward the log. He soared over it and continued galloping toward Chancellor, just as the Dutch Warmblood was coming back to walk.

"Whoa!" Sarah shouted. She pulled hard on the reins and braced with her seat, but Prince was on top of Chancellor before she could stop him. Unable to avoid contact on the narrow trail, Prince banged heavily into the black gelding's hindquarters. Chancellor was knocked sideways, and he reacted to the assault by kicking out with both hind legs, narrowly missing Prince and throwing Rita forward in the saddle. She pulled herself up, shaking and furious.

"Get that lunatic away from us!" she shouted angrily at Sarah. "Don't you know how to ride?"

Sarah was mortified by what had happened. "I'm so sorry, Rita. He just took off. He didn't want you guys to get away from him."

Rita was not appeased. "He could have hurt Chancellor! If you're going to ride with me, you'd better do a better job controlling your horse."

Tim, farther down the trail with Rhodes, had turned back and was approaching them. He heard the loud words and saw the angry look on Rita's face. "You guys okay?"

"This off-the-wall horse crashed into Chancellor!" Rita cried out, motioning accusingly at Sarah and her horse.

Paige had also returned, and she interrupted Rita's rant. "We'd better get going. We have a climb ahead to get to the orchard."

Rita glared at Sarah. "You go ahead of me. I don't want your horse barreling into us again." She turned Chancellor off the trail, giving Sarah room to pass.

As the riders proceeded without further conversation, Sarah felt jittery after the incident with Rita. *I've got to be careful I don't telegraph my nervousness to Prince*, she told herself. She could feel tension remaining in his body, and she frequently reached down to stroke him. A little farther along the trail, their path wound around a grove of pine trees with green limbs that reached across in front of them in places. On a horse as tall as Crown Prince, Sarah had to duck a few times, but the branches didn't seem to bother her horse. He moved along at a fast clip, intent on keeping up with Rhodes.

Gradually the forest thinned out as the trail turned steeper, with patches of tall orchard grass growing beside the trail. The horses had to push hard with their hindquarters to make the ascent. As Jack had suggested, Sarah gave Prince more rein so he could stretch his head down while marching up the hill. A few times he tried to break into trot, but she brought him back to walk. Finally the trail reached a plateau with tall grass and an orchard filled with gnarled and weathered apple trees. It had been many years since the orchard had been pruned and sprayed, and while some of the trees had small apples ripening, most no longer bore fruit.

Sarah glanced back to see the Brookmeade barn below them, looking small and far away. From the top of the ridge, they could see the valley stretch all the way to the ocean in the distance, where the cottages at the beach looked like dollhouses.

A soft breeze felt cool and refreshing. *This is one of my favorite places,* Sarah thought. *Prince will come to love it too.* Without a trail to follow, the horses spread out as they moved through the lanes separating the rows of apple trees. Rhodes jerked the reins hard, trying to put his head down into the grass, but Tim kept him moving behind Quarry, who walked quickly, his dark gray ears pricked forward. Chancellor was calm and collected, happy to follow the other horses. Sarah wasn't sure what to expect from Prince, and she kept a short rein. He became more animated as he looked in all directions, his head high and his ears moving constantly.

"How's Prince doing?" Tim called back to Sarah. "He looks like he's done this a hundred times."

"He's a little nervous, but except for his charge to catch up with Chancellor, he's been awesome," she said. "Rhodes looked really good jumping that log. He tucks his knees up high no matter the size of the jump."

They had gotten about halfway through the maze of ancient trees when Rita halted Chancellor. "I'm ready to go back now," she announced. "Chancellor has had enough." She turned her horse around. "You go ahead of me, Sarah. I don't want your horse to land on top of us when we're heading down the ridge."

Sarah thought for a minute. No way did she have to obey Rita's orders, but this was probably long enough for Prince's first hack. "Okay, let's go" she said, turning Prince back in the direction of the trail.

Tim and Paige swapped glances. "We always go to the far end of the orchard," Tim said. "We'll catch up with you."

Prince watched Rhodes and Quarry walk away, but he seemed content to stay with Chancellor. Rita circled her horse to let Sarah take the lead back to the woods trail. As Prince passed him, the black horse pinned his heavy ears flat against his head, warning Prince to keep his distance. *You can't blame him,* Sarah thought. *Prince hit him pretty hard.*

The walk down the steep ridge was far different from coming up, but challenging in another way. To stay in balance and keep from hurtling forward down the hill, the horses had to shift their weight back to their hindquarters, braking themselves with their hind legs. Changing his balance going down a steep hill was something Prince had never learned—he'd grown up on flat terrain and trained on the racetrack. At first he tried to turn sideways as he moved downhill, but Sarah insisted he remain straight as he adjusted to the steep terrain. She leaned slightly back in the saddle, steadied her horse with the reins, and with her legs asked him to reach under himself. She had ridden up to the orchard many times on her favorite school horse, Lady Tate, and that experience helped now.

Rita could see that Crown Prince was having a hard time going down the steep grade. "It looks like your horse can't figure out how to go downhill," she said. "I guess he's not so great after all." Glancing back, Sarah saw the smirk on Rita's face—the girl wasn't just joking. *The old jealousy is still there,* Sarah thought, surprised that Rita was still holding a grudge.

The two horses had gotten nearly to the bottom of the ridge before Sarah began to relax. Prince was doing better with the terrain, and she hoped he was learning a lot on this ride. Soon they'd be on the more level part of the trail, with the log jump just ahead. And this time Prince would jump it *first.*

Then it happened.

Sarah felt her horse react before she actually heard the sound of large flapping wings and saw the flock of wild turkeys take flight from the side of the trail. Prince catapulted forward, racing down the trail. Sarah instinctively grabbed his mane and clung to it desperately while her horse galloped forward at a breakneck pace. *Oh, my God!* she thought, as she let go of his mane and frantically pulled on the reins. *Prince will hurt himself galloping on this trail! I've got to stop him!*

The pulley rein! She had used it to stop Gray Fox when he ran away with her not many months before, and now, as they flew toward the grove of pines, she gathered her reins to try it again. Speeding around the ring of trees, Prince plunged under their outstretched limbs. Sarah had no time to drop her body low in the saddle before one of the boughs caught her across her chest. She felt herself being swept from her horse's back, crashing downward, and then she was lying on the trail with the wind knocked out of her. She struggled to catch her breath and call out to her horse as Prince continued running, streaking down the trail and out of sight. With a sickening feeling, Sarah heard the sound of his galloping hoofbeats grow fainter in the distance, and then only a deathly quiet.

Sarah couldn't move right away, as she struggled to catch her breath and find her strength. Before she could move, she heard more hoofbeats. It had to be Chancellor, and from the sound, he was trotting fast. On a curve in the trail, Rita and her horse probably wouldn't see her lying there until it was too late! It took a gigantic effort, but Sarah willed herself to move and began to inch toward the underbrush on the side of the trail. Just as Chancellor and Rita came upon her, she rolled over, narrowly avoiding the horse's hooves. Her movement caught Rita's eye, and when she saw Sarah lying on the ground, Rita pulled Chancellor up as quickly as she could and looked back. "Sarah, are you all right?" she called out.

Sarah managed to get to a sitting position, and then tried to stand up. "I got the wind knocked out of me, I guess," she said with a gasp. "But I've got to get Prince! He's loose, running back on the trail. I've got to catch him before he gets hurt!"

"If you think you're okay, I'll go ahead," Rita said firmly. Sarah nodded and Rita asked Chancellor for his big ground-eating trot. Soon they were out of sight.

Sarah staggered to her feet, and with adrenalin pumping, she began running as fast as she could in pursuit of Crown Prince. She felt shaky, but concern for her horse propelled her forward. She ran her fastest until she was out of breath and was forced to slow down. After walking a short distance, her chest heaving, she was off again, running faster than before, not easy in her paddock boots that slipped on the pine needles.

Soon Sarah came to the downed log. Prince must have jumped it—what about the reins, which would have been hanging loose? Perhaps he'd gotten his front legs tangled up in them! She scrambled over the log and ran on, the blood hammering in her chest.

Sarah ran until it seemed her lungs would burst, all the while imagining coming upon Prince brought down by with any number of tragic injuries. Maybe she would find him sprawled across the trail! At one point she tripped over a large root and hit the ground hard. With tears streaming down her face, she picked herself up and ran again. It seemed like she had run forever when finally she saw a glimpse of the parking lot ahead.

CHAPTER 3

Injury

BURSTING OUT OF THE WOODS, Sarah scanned the area, desperately searching for her horse. She caught sight of him near a side door to the barn. Judson was trying to lead him in a circle while Mrs. DeWitt and Rita, still astride Chancellor, watched. Prince was animated, prancing in place. Sarah ran toward them. "Is he okay?" she called out, gasping for breath. As she got closer, she could see her horse was completely sweated up, with white lather on his neck and flanks. The whites of his eyes showed prominently, and his nostrils were dilated as he took quick breaths.

"Are you all right, Miss?" Judson called to her as she got closer. "We were worried you'd come to grief out there."

Mrs. DeWitt hurried to Sarah and gave her a hug. "Look at you," she said. "From the dirt on your jeans and T-shirt, I can tell you hit the ground. Are you sure you're all right?" When Sarah nodded, still breathing fast, Mrs. DeWitt said, "When Crown Prince came galloping across the parking area, my first thought was that something terrible might have happened to you. I was about to summon Jack and Gus when Rita arrived on the scene. She told us that you had a fall but were okay."

Sarah frantically scanned her horse for any sign of injury. "Do you know if Prince hurt himself?" she asked.

"He appears to be walking sound," Mrs. DeWitt said, "but one of your reins is broken."

"Maybe that happened when he jumped the tree that's down across the trail," Sarah said, running a hand down her horse's neck.

Rita's lips drew back in a thin smile. "Chancellor might have tried to take off, too, when those turkeys flew out of the grass by the trail, but he's too well trained." She turned to Sarah with a look that was more gleeful than sympathetic. Her green eyes below thick, dark brows twinkled in amusement. "Do horses you ride always try to run off with you?" she asked.

"Prince was racing down the trail where it takes that sharp turn by the grove of pine trees. I was shortening my reins to use the pulley rein when a branch scraped me off. The wind got knocked out of me when I hit the ground." Sarah looked to Judson and Mrs. DeWitt. "Did you have any trouble catching him?"

"I was about to bring Medina out of her stall to groom her when I heard the sound of galloping hooves approaching the barn," Mrs. DeWitt said. "I ran out here just as Prince was coming toward the side door. I think he was headed for his stall. I was able to grab his reins without any trouble. Judson was a saint! He rushed over to help."

Just then the burly and slightly bent frame of Gus Kelso, the barn manager, came out of the door leading to his apartment over the barn, his disheveled gray hair topped by his ever-present red baseball cap. He took one look at Crown Prince and then glared at Sarah. "What have you been doing with this horse?" he demanded. "Don't you know better than ride a horse crazy-like and bring him back to the barn all lathered up?"

Mrs. DeWitt came to Sarah's defense. "Sarah didn't ride her horse hard, Gus. A flock of wild turkeys spooked him out on the trail, and she was thrown," she said calmly. "Prince ran back to the barn, that's all. He seems to be all right."

Gus paused to take this in, still scowling. "Well, she needs to take care of him proper. He needs to be hosed down and then walked dry. And she better be ready to feed the horses on time!" With that he strode into the barn, grumbling under his breath.

Sarah hung her head. Just when she thought she was on better terms with Gus, the grumpy man was on her case again. She had no choice but to work for him if she was going to continue to board Prince at Brookmeade—that was part of the deal the DeWitts had offered her months before—but right from the beginning Gus had been difficult. He'd never had a girl work for him, and he was still having a hard time getting used to the idea.

Sarah took Prince's reins from Judson. They had been buckled together, but now the reins were in two distinct pieces, one far shorter than the other. "It's okay, Prince, it's okay," she said, reaching up to stroke his neck again.

"It's time for me to take off," Rita said, dismounting. She turned to Judson and handed him her reins. "Untack him and get him ready for loading," she instructed the hired man as she ran up her irons. Judson obediently walked Chancellor toward the Pyramid Farm van, but Rita stopped when she saw Paige and Tim emerge from the woods trail.

As they got closer, Paige and Tim noticed that Prince was sweated up and prancing. They picked up trot to hurry over. "What happened?" Tim asked, obviously concerned. Sarah continued walking Prince in a circle while she told them the whole story.

"Wow!" Paige exclaimed. "You didn't get hurt?"

Sarah reached down to feel the place on her hip where she'd hit the ground. It was sore, and from the looks of some scratches on her arm, a branch must have whipped against her when she went off. Only now did she notice her arm was stinging. Her helmet had stayed secure, thank goodness.

"I'm fine, except for freaking out about what might have happened to Prince."

"Well," Tim said, "let's take a look." Both riders dismounted, and Paige held their horses as Tim bent down to inspect Prince's legs. "Here's something," he said, maneuvering to get a better look at Prince's left front leg. "There's a lot of dirt and gunk on there, so it's hard to tell, but it looks like he's bleeding on the inside of his left front."

Mrs. DeWitt and Sarah got closer to check out the injury. "I'd better hose him down now," Sarah said. She raised an eyebrow. "So much for our first trail ride." She led Prince into the barn and down the aisle to his stall to remove his tack. She checked her watch. *His lesson will be over soon, and Jack will want to hear about the ride,* she thought. She didn't look forward to that conversation one bit. *He'll probably be disappointed I fell off. At least when Gray Fox ran away with me, I managed to stay on! And stop him.*

Prince seemed glad to be back in his stall. As soon as Sarah had swapped his bridle for his halter, he went immediately to his water bucket. She let him drink a few swallows before removing it from the stall. He was still too hot to drink all he wanted. Prince had calmed down after his frantic run through the woods, and even though he was covered with sweat and in need of a bath, Sarah hugged his head and held him close. "Good boy," she said softly as she caressed his white star and tugged his ears gently. "You had some bad luck. Birds, big birds…." His large dark eyes softened, and he lowered his head as she stroked him gently.

All at once the seriousness of what had happened hit her. She envisioned Prince running wildly down the woods trail, riderless with his reins hanging loose. The story could have had a tragic ending. He could have gotten his legs tangled in the reins and taken a devastating fall. What if he had broken a leg and had to be put down? She pressed her face against his neck as the tears flowed freely.

Finally Sarah raised her head. She needed to get it together and get her horse cleaned up so they could get a good look at the injured leg. This was Prince's first injury since she had gotten him, and she was worried. What if it got infected?

Sarah was unbuckling the girth on her saddle when Mrs. DeWitt came around the corner with Spin and Cameo. She was carrying a stable bandage, a quilted cotton wrap, a jar of antibiotic ointment, and a box of large gauze pads. "Sarah, I don't suppose you have these in your collection of horsey things, and I suspect you're going to need them. See what Jack says."

"Oh, wow," Sarah said, coming out of the stall. "And thanks so much for catching Prince." She couldn't resist leaning down to stroke the two small dogs as they jumped up on her in their eagerness to be petted. The terriers never failed to cheer her up. Cameo was not-quite-four-months old, but she was fast catching up to Spin in size.

"Horse people always stick together, my dear," Mrs. DeWitt said, with her usual warm smile. She put the items beside Sarah's grooming caddy. "I've included a salve that prevents infection and really helps healing. It does wonders." She saw the look of worry on Sarah's face. "This appears to be a minor injury, Sarah. Your horse isn't lame, and I suspect you'll be riding him again in no time. But let me know if Jack thinks Prince needs the veterinarian. And now Medina and I are going to take these little beasts for the trail ride I promised them." She started back to her mare's stall with the dogs trotting behind.

Sarah removed the saddle and led Crown Prince to the wash stall. Once he was clipped to the cross-ties, she turned on the hose and adjusted the water temperature. After letting cool water run over the dirty, bloody area on his leg, she took a closer look at the wound. It wasn't bleeding much, which was a relief, but the surrounding area was already swollen. She was letting the water cascade over his neck, back, and down his legs when Jack appeared at the door of the stall. He looked tense.

"I just spoke with Mrs. DeWitt. She tells me your trail ride to the orchard was rather exciting. And how would you be feeling after your fall?"

"I'm fine, but Prince cut himself. It's on his left front." She turned off the hose, and Jack immediately went to look at the leg. "I thought you'd want me to hose it clean," she said.

Jack didn't reply right away. Prince flinched when he pressed his hand near the injury. He examined the other front leg, and then leaned down to check the horse's hind legs. Finally he stood up. "He must have interfered from behind when he was running. It looks like he has just the one cut, though, with some bruising. There's already heat there, but I don't think the injury is severe enough to warrant a visit from Dr. Reynolds. Just keep the area clean so it doesn't get infected. Cold water will help keep the swelling down, so try to hose that leg for twenty minutes as often as you can."

"Mrs. DeWitt thought I'd need to wrap his leg, but she wanted me to check with you."

"Yes," Jack said, "'Tis not an infection you'll be wanting. After you've cooled him out, you should apply some antibiotic ointment, and wrap the leg. Then we'll see how it looks tomorrow."

"Mrs. DeWitt lent me the things I'll need, but I've never bandaged a horse before. Will you have time to show me how?"

Jack nodded. He paused and seemed to be deep in thought. His next comment made her stiffen. "Your folks, Sarah. They will have to be told."

Of course. She should have thought of that right away. Her

mother had voiced concerns for her safety right from the start. She remembered the conversation with her parents the night she had turned down Hank Bolton's incredible offer to "buy back" Prince. Her mother's words were: "Unless Crown Prince proves to be a reliable and safe horse for you to ride, he will go back to the race-track faster than you can snap your fingers!" Sarah began to feel a knot in the pit of her stomach.

"I know your horse's trial period is over," Jack said, "but in the beginning I made a commitment to your parents that I wouldn't let you be in harm's way." He crossed one arm and stroked his chin with the other while deep in thought. "Perhaps I should have gone along on the hack riding another horse. It was Price's first time on the trails. Perhaps I should have ridden him myself."

Then he shook his head. "No, for your horse to bond with you as his partner, you must be the one in the saddle. You must be the one he learns to trust and respect. I'd not be helping you if I took over on the important milestones."

"But what happened today was, like, totally weird," Sarah said. "There were lots of turkeys, big ones, and they were in tall grass close to the trail when they took off. What are the chances of that happening again?"

"Whenever you ride, there will always be the chance of some-thing spooking your horse. Not just wild turkeys—a deer in the woods, a honking truck on the road, a dog that chases you, a motorcycle speeding by. That's the reality. You and your horse must be prepared for the unexpected, and you must be ready to deal with it if your horse bolts off."

"But a branch swept me off his back!" Sarah exclaimed. "Otherwise maybe I could have stopped him with the pulley rein, like with Gray Fox."

"I'll grant you that trees don't usually prove the villain. I've noticed those pine branches need to be trimmed, and now I could kick myself that I didn't ask Gus to have it taken care of long ago. But remember, there will be other such situations. 'Tis lucky that neither you nor Prince were badly hurt." Jack turned to go. "Come get me in the office when you're ready to bandage him."

Sarah finished rinsing Prince, and after using her sweat scraper to remove water from his coat, she led him to the courtyard, a good place to walk him dry. He was subdued and content to move quietly by her side. As she walked, Sarah thought about how she would break this news to her parents. Maybe she would change into a long-sleeved shirt to cover up the scratches on her arm, and of course she would definitely *not* complain about the soreness on her side where she'd fallen.

Perhaps I can convince them it was an unusual accident, and that falling off a horse is no big deal, she thought. *I'll just die if Mom freaks out and brings up the subject of sending Prince back. I've got to talk to Kayla.*

Sarah dug her phone out of her pocket and speed-dialed Kayla's number. She would have gotten home from her lesson some time ago. Kayla picked up on the second ring. "What's up, kid?"

"Kayla," Sarah began, "you'll never guess what happened."

"I don't believe it!" Kayla said, after Sarah filled her in. "I've gone on a zillion trail rides, and I've never come close to being knocked off by a tree branch. We've seen plenty of wild turkeys, though. They're everywhere these days. You're lucky Prince came out of it with only a cut. Can you still ride him?"

Sarah took a deep breath. "I didn't think of that, but I'll ask Jack. He's going to help me bandage Prince. And something else, Kayla. Prince stepped on his reins when he was loose, and one of them snapped. I need to get to Atlantic Saddlery or order some new ones online, but do you have an extra set I could borrow in the meantime?"

32

"Sure. I have the reins from my old bridle and another extra pair. They're not fancy. I'll bring a set to you at school tomorrow—you can keep them."

"Cool—thanks so much! But here's my biggest problem," Sarah said. "I'm worried about how Dad and Mom will react. They might even want me to give Prince back. Mr. Bolton would love that!"

"Chill out," Kayla said. "I know you're totally upset, but remember—you didn't get hurt, and Prince got only a minor cut." She paused for a moment. "For that matter, do you really *have* to tell your parents?"

Sarah thought on the question before answering. "Yeah, I do. Jack thinks so, too. I can just see myself getting into more trouble if I don't."

"Listen, I've got to go finish cleaning Fanny's stall," Kayla said. "Keep me posted."

Sarah closed her cell. When she touched Prince's neck, it was dry. He was cool enough to take back to his stall. A good thing, since it was almost time to feed the horses. She led him into the barn and walked him to the back of the barn. She was glad that earlier she had bedded his stall with lots of fresh shavings. It looked clean and inviting.

Prince was drinking from his bucket when she headed to the office to find Jack. A few parents of riders from the four o'clock class were talking to the instructor when Sarah got there. Not knowing how long he'd be tied up, she decided to find Kathleen to ask about the pony lesson while she waited. Sarah found her chatting with the farm's owner, Chandler DeWitt, while Grace was in Pretty Penny's stall running a brush over the pony's face. Mr. DeWitt turned toward Sarah as she approached.

"So it was another runaway for you this afternoon," said the tall man with a full head of thick white hair and a trim mustache.

He looked at Sarah closely through his steel-framed glasses. "I hear you're none the worse for all the excitement, but how is Crown Prince?" he asked.

"He has a cut on one of his front legs, but other than that, he's okay," Sarah said. "Jack's going to show me how to bandage it."

"Is there a chance the cut should be stitched?" Kathleen asked.

Sarah shook her head. "Jack doesn't think so."

Mr. DeWitt saw the worried look on her face. "My hunch is this will be just a temporary setback. I've seen you riding Crown Prince in the ring a few times, and he was very impressive. You should be proud of the job you're doing. Do you think he's made a good adjustment to life here at Brookmeade?"

"Oh, yes," Sarah said, her face brightening. "He looks really healthy. He's gained some weight, and his coat looks great. He even has some dapples. Mrs. DeWitt says that's a sign of good health. I think he likes to be ridden, too."

"Hank Bolton will be pleased to hear that," Mr. DeWitt said.

Sarah became more serious. "The only thing is, I'm worried we could run into wild turkeys again on a trail ride. I can't let him run away like he did today, but I don't want to be stuck riding him just in the ring or the indoor."

"Perhaps a stronger bit would help," Mr. DeWitt replied. "I think I told you about the time a horse fresh off the racetrack ran away with me on a fox hunt. It was the wildest ride I ever had. After that, I never rode him in anything but a Kimberwicke, and he never took off with me again."

"I'm sure Jack will have some thoughts on that," Kathleen said.

Just then they saw Jack walking toward them. He beckoned to Sarah. "Let's take care of your horse," he called, heading in the direction of Prince's stall.

CHAPTER 4

Warning!

ONCE PRINCE WAS ON CROSS-TIES in the aisle, Jack liberally applied some of Mrs. DeWitt's furozone salve to the area around the wound. A large gauze pad stuck to it, conveniently covering the injury. "The pad will keep the ointment directly on the cut, and also prevent it from soiling your stable wrap," Jack said. Next he deftly wound the white quilted wrap around Prince's lower leg, and followed with the blue stable bandage, showing Sarah how to apply it so it wouldn't place excess tension on the tendon. He worked efficiently, but slowly enough so Sarah would remember how to do it.

"Will I be able to ride him right away?" she asked.

"Not until we're sure there's no heat or swelling there. And no turnout tomorrow—hand walk him instead, after removing the bandage. If there is heat and swelling there when you arrive at the barn tomorrow, it's important to hose the leg for twenty minutes with cold water right away, and repeat just before you leave. Do it more often on the weekend, if the swelling persists. And another thing. When you roll a bandage after removing it from his leg, roll it tight. Rock hard. It will roll on better that way." Jack looked at his watch. "I think Gus might be wanting you to feed some hungry horses now."

During the time it took to make the rounds feeding grain and dropping hay into every horse's stall, Sarah thought about what lay ahead of her that evening. She would have to tell her parents about her fall. She knew they would hear about it sooner or later. Before leaving for the day, she went back to see Prince one more time and check his injured leg. The bandage was staying in place, and from the way Prince was going at his hay, he was feeling fine. While he ate, Sarah stood close to his shoulder and stroked him softly.

As she pedaled home from the barn, Sarah thought about what she would say to her parents. With the extra time she had spent with her horse, she was running a little late. That would automatically put her mother in a bad mood. Sarah had thought about calling her, but decided it would be best to explain what had happened in person.

When Sarah arrived home, tantalizing aromas told her dinner was ready and reminded her how hungry she was. She quickly removed her paddock boots and washed her hands in the half-bath. She stepped into the kitchen and found her mother near the stove, facing her with hands on her hips. Sarah recognized the look—her mother wasn't happy. Mrs. Wagner brushed past her to call into the den, her words clipped: "Dinner's ready."

Sarah quickly sat down at the table. She held her left arm close to her side, hoping no one would notice the scratches. Mr. Wagner and Abby appeared at once. The family usually dined promptly at six, and everyone was hungry for the dinner that was twenty minutes late. Mrs. Wagner brought a steaming chicken and rice dish out of the oven and placed it on a hot pad on the table.

Sarah decided to get it over with. Before Abby could start her usual nonstop chatter about her day at school, Sarah took a deep breath and launched into her explanation while the others were still settling into their chairs.

"I'm sorry I'm late, but I took Prince on his first trail ride today," she said in a voice she hoped sounded casual. "Something totally weird happened. A flock of wild turkeys flew up and spooked Prince. He took off down the trail where the trees are thick, and a branch knocked me off. I'm fine, and except for a small cut on his leg, Prince is too. But I had to walk back to the barn, and it took extra time. Then I gave him a bath and walked him dry. I'll try hard not to be late again. I am *so* hungry!"

Mrs. Wagner abruptly put down the large spoon she was about to dip into the serving dish. For a moment the family just stared at Sarah, and then everyone started talking at once, firing questions at her like drill sergeants.

"Are you sure you're all right?" her mother wanted to know.

"Where did Prince run after you fell off?" Abby asked.

From her father: "Does Jack know this happened?"

Sarah told them as much as she could. Her parents occasionally looked solemnly at each other as she spoke, and once her father interrupted her story. "You were able to stop Gray Fox with a pulley rein when he ran away with you at the beginning of the summer," he said. "Didn't that work with Crown Prince?"

"I didn't have time. The pine trees were too close. I went off Prince before I could even try to stop him. It was just a fluke accident that will never happen again." Her dark eyes pleaded for understanding.

"You were lucky this time," her mother said, "but you might not be as fortunate in the future. I've been concerned all along that you might be in danger riding a horse as large and strong as Crown Prince. Now I'm even more worried. You were thrown off him on your very first trail ride!"

Sarah's face darkened into a scowl. "More like *knocked* off him, Mom. You make it sound like Prince bucked me off, like he *wanted* to dump me!" she protested. "It was totally an accident, for crying out loud. The branch was right over the trail."

"Just a minute," her father said. "There's no need to overreact. While Crown Prince was on trial, Jack oversaw everything you did with him. Now things are different. It's to be expected that you'll be acting more independently and riding the horse on your own, but does the lack of supervision put you at risk? That's what we need to know."

Sarah felt her temper rising. "Dad, do you want me to, like, live in a bubble, where I'm totally safe but away from the whole world?" She shook her head. "I could have an accident just riding my bike to Brookmeade! Abby could get hit by a broken bat when she's playing softball. You can't expect me to stop riding my horse just because a freaky thing happened!

"Sarah, calm down," her father replied sternly. "Your mother and I put a high priority on your safety. We don't want to someday have to ask ourselves why we permitted you to be in a hazardous situation. I think I will have a conversation with Jack about this. It's all about risk, and how much risk you're exposed to riding that horse."

Mrs. Wagner was frowning. "And remember, our position hasn't changed one iota. If that horse is dangerous, you cannot keep him. He will have to go back to Hank Bolton." Her mother picked up Abby's plate and began spooning from the serving dish. "In the meantime, let's have dinner. This was the first day of school, and I'd like to hear how it went for both of you."

Later, after the table had been cleared and the dishes loaded into the dishwasher, Sarah decided to get started on her geometry homework. She picked up her school bag and headed for the desk in her room. Before she got to the stairs, the telephone rang. As usual, Abby jumped up to answer it. "It's for you, Dad," she said. Abby gave no indication who the caller might be, but Sarah decided to hang around a moment to see.

Her father was only on the phone for a short time, and with his back to her, Sarah couldn't hear what he was saying. After he hung up, he turned to face Sarah and her mother. "That was Jack O'Brien. He and Kathleen have been out to dinner and would like to stop by on their way back to the farm. They should be here soon." Mr. Wagner looked at his wife. "He didn't say what he wants to talk to us about, but I think we have a pretty good idea."

For Sarah, all thoughts about homework were gone. This would be the first time Jack had ever come to their home. He must be worried about her fall. What was he going to say to her parents?

Abby went into the family room to watch *America's Got Talent*, but the rest of the Wagner family sat in the living room waiting for the O'Briens to arrive. So many thoughts ran through Sarah's mind. Could Jack have decided that Prince was not the right horse for her? Was he planning to tell her parents he'd made a mistake in approving the horse at the end of the thirty-day trial? Sarah gripped the arms of her chair a little tighter. She would just die if she had to give up her horse!

It wasn't long before the O'Briens' SUV turned into their drive-way, its headlights lighting up the yard. When the doorbell rang, Sarah went to answer it. Her eyes met Jack's, but no words were spoken as she ushered the O'Briens into the living room. Kathleen looked so pretty, dressed in a green skirt and matching top that complimented her dark auburn hair, a change from the riding pants she always wore when she worked at the farm. It seemed strange to see Jack wearing casual clothes.

Sarah retreated to her chair while her father welcomed the O'Briens. "May I offer you some coffee or a cold drink?" Mrs. Wagner asked, as they sat down on the sofa.

"Thanks, but no," Kathleen said. "We just had dinner at that new Thai restaurant at the beach."

Jack looked serious when he began to speak. "We won't be stopping with you long, but I suspect Sarah has had a chance to tell you what happened earlier today." He looked inquiringly across the room at Sarah and her parents. She nodded slightly to let Jack know his news would not be a surprise.

"Yes, Jack," Mrs. Wagner said. "Sarah told us about coming upon the wild turkeys on the trail and how she fell off her horse. You should know that we're upset to learn that happened. We thought that Prince had proven he would be a safe horse for Sarah to ride."

"The trial period was over weeks ago," Mr. Wagner said, "but that doesn't mean we're not following Sarah and her horse closely. What happened today is disturbing. It makes us worry that Sarah is in a risky situation riding that horse. What's your take on the accident?"

There was a long pause before Jack spoke, and his words were measured, as he chose them carefully. "Yes, things went well after the wolf tooth was removed, leading us to believe pain from the bit banging up against the tooth had been the cause of Crown Prince's bad behavior at the racetrack. And since that time, the horse has demonstrated an excellent attitude in his training with Sarah. Things couldn't have gone better—until today."

Jack shifted uneasily on the sofa while they waited for him to continue. "I have to be honest with you. What happened this afternoon was the kind of riding accident that could happen to almost anyone, myself included. There's no guarantee that a horse will never be spooked and never bolt, or that a rider will never fall. I think that would apply to training and riding *all* horses. But there are things we can do to lessen the odds that such an incident will happen with Prince." He paused.

"The first thing is to have a strong foundation of training in the horse, so he will trust his rider and be more likely to respond to the aids in a stressful situation. Another is to introduce new experiences slowly, in small increments, like starting with a short ride and gradually expanding it. That should give him more confidence if a spooky situation arises."

"You say riding will always have an element of risk," Mrs. Wagner said, leaning toward Jack as she spoke. "But wouldn't there be less danger for Sarah if she were riding an older, more reliable horse, one that would be less likely to bolt with her? She always loved riding Lady Tate, and nothing ever went wrong."

"But I don't want another horse, Mom!" Sarah blurted out. "Prince is the only horse in the world for me. Please don't think about taking him away from me!"

"Sarah," her father said, "your safety comes first, and we have to look at all the options."

"Wait a minute," Jack said, raising his hand. "To answer your question, 'tis true that a quieter horse might be less likely to bolt off, but there's no guarantee it won't happen with *any* horse—unless he has only three legs." The laughter that followed seemed to lighten the mood in the room, although Sarah's mother remained stone-faced.

"Crown Prince has so much to offer, and Sarah is becoming a talented rider," Jack continued. "It would be a shame to throw away their bright future. I'd like to suggest a few things, the first being to trim back those pine limbs that extend over the trail. I'll mention it to Gus in the morning. We have a number of riders who go up to the old orchard, and while none of the horses are anywhere near as tall as Crown Prince, we don't want to take any chances.

"I'd also like to suggest that Sarah continue taking her horse onto a woods trail," Jack said, "beginning with a short distance and gradually increasing the time she's out. The more good experiences they have, the more confident Crown Prince will become. As I told Sarah earlier, I think 'tis best to let her remain in the saddle, because my riding him will not really smooth the way for her. Sarah is the one Crown Prince must come to trust and respect. He's got to listen to her, and they must become a team."

Sarah studied her parents' faces, wishing she could read their minds. They appeared far from convinced.

Jack had one more card to place on the table. "I also think it's time for Sarah and her horse to ride in one of my classes. They would fit into my Wednesday afternoon class that goes immediately after the advanced Young Riders. So instead of continuing to have private instruction, Crown Prince will be in a class with other horses."

Sarah's eyes opened wide and she sat up straight in her chair. The four o'clock class was the one Nicole Jordan and Kelly Hoffman rode in using their horses they boarded at Brookmeade. They were no friends of hers. *Ouch!* she thought. *This might not be cool.*

Her father's voice brought Sarah back from her own thoughts. "I want to commend both of you for not trying to hide what happened today. You were open and honest, and I appreciate that. And I expect you will always be straightforward with us should anything else go wrong."

Mrs. Wagner looked intently at Jack. "I think we need to repeat something that has always been our policy on Crown Prince from day one. If he's a dangerous horse for Sarah to ride, then we need to know about it. And if she's at risk riding him, she can't keep him." She held her arm out in Sarah's direction to stifle the expected protest. "But we sincerely hope the steps you've proposed will make a difference, Jack, and it won't come to that."

Jack nodded, and he and Kathleen stood up. "Thanks for your willingness to see us on short notice," Jack said. "I felt this was something we should talk about."

"That feeling is mutual," Sarah's father replied, reaching out to shake Jack's hand. "Don't hesitate to contact us anytime."

After the O'Briens left, Sarah turned to her parents. "I know Prince still needs to prove himself to you, and I just know he will. You don't know him like I do. He's as safe as any horse at Brookmeade Farm, and someday you'll believe in him like I do."

"We want to think Prince has left his bad behavior at the racetrack," her father said. "We only hope the facts will bear that out."

Sarah went to her room to start on her geometry assignment. It was due the next day, but however much she tried, she couldn't concentrate on angles or intersecting lines. Her mother's words kept coming back to her. She knew if her parents became convinced Prince was dangerous, he would be taken away from her. No way could she let that happen!

CHAPTER 5

The New Boy

WHEN THE BUS CAME to a stop by the Wagners' driveway the next morning, Sarah got on and threaded her way to the fourth row to sit with Kayla. After sliding over to make room, Kayla pulled a plastic bag out of her tote. "See what you think of these," she said, handing it over.

Sarah withdrew a pair of dark-brown laced reins from the bag. "Awesome! These are perfect."

Kayla was pleased. "Maybe you'll be using them this afternoon."

"I hope so," Sarah replied. She sighed. "It all depends on how Prince's leg heals. If there's heat and swelling there when I get to the barn, there's no chance I can ride."

"So, what did your parents say when they heard about your taking a fall off Prince?" Kayla asked. She leaned closer to hear Sarah's reply over the din on the crowded bus.

"You can probably imagine," Sarah said. "Dad wondered if riding Prince is too risky, and Mom went on a tear about him being dangerous because he's so big. But get this! After dinner, Jack and Kathleen came to our house to talk to my parents." She went on to tell Kayla the details of the conversation, concluding with the most important part. "Here's the biggie—Jack wants me to start riding in the class that follows yours on Wednesdays."

Kayla thought a minute before responding. "Kelly Hoffman and Nicole Jordan's class?

Sarah nodded, as they both braced for a stop the bus made further down Ridge Road. "I'm not sure if you knew that Nicole's horse, Jubilee, injured a tendon early in the summer and couldn't go out of her stall for a while except for hand-walking. A few weeks ago Paige told me the vet finally gave Nicole the go-ahead to ride her mare if she took it easy. While I was waiting for you guys to come out of the arena yesterday, I saw Nicole leading Jubilee in for the lesson. So I guess the horse is sound again."

"I'm not at Brookmeade as much as you are" Kayla said, "but it seems like those girls always hang out together. Talk about being joined at the hip! They ride together all the time, and I've seen them grazing their horses near the outside ring. You never see one without the other. With all that mascara, they even look a lot alike."

"Last year, when I was riding with them in one of Jack's classes, they wanted to be moved up to the advanced Young Riders class," Sarah said, "but Jack said no. They were peeved when I got to ride in your class using Lady Tate. Anyway, I just wish they would knock off having a grudge against me. It's not going to be cool riding with them."

"I've seen Kelly riding a bay horse lately, one I don't recognize. What's the deal with him?" Kayla asked.

"That's her Quarter Horse, Midnight Jet. I heard he was shipped in from the West. Kelly just walks away when I ask her anything about him. Maybe you should see if her horse and Fanny have any of the same bloodlines."

Kayla sniffed and raised an eyebrow. "She's such a snob— forget it!"

When the bus finally came to a stop at Yardley High, the girls got off and separated to go to different home-rooms. "See you in English," Sarah said. She was glad she had a second period study hall, where she'd be able to finish her geometry homework. She'd hate to be late on homework her second day of school! But doing her best that day wouldn't be easy. Her mind kept drifting to her horse. Would his injury be better when she got to the barn, or—she shuddered to think of it—infected, hot, and swollen? And without his usual morning turnout, would Prince be a little crazy?

When school let out later that day, the sky had filled with ominous dark clouds, and by the time the bus dropped Sarah off at home, a steady, warm rain was falling. She quickly changed her clothes and grabbed a few Oreo cookies before pulling her poncho from the mudroom closet. She stuffed Kayla's extra set of reins deep in one of her pockets and started pedaling for the farm. Her bike splashed through puddles along the way, and occasional bursts of wind blew rain into her face. The foul weather brought back her nagging worry of what it would be like getting to the barn during the winter. She would have to depend a lot on her parents or friends for rides—her bike just wasn't going to cut it.

The parking area at Brookmeade Farm was crowded, which, on this rainy afternoon, meant the indoor would be mobbed. Sometimes in bad weather the large indoor arena was divided so two lessons could run concurrently. Sarah wheeled her bike into the shavings shed to park it out of the rain before heading for Prince's stall.

When she turned the corner at the end of the aisle, Sarah saw a well-dressed man and woman she didn't recognize standing near Prince's stall. They were looking into the large stall across from Prince that had remained unoccupied after Rita's horse, Chancellor, had abruptly left the farm on Mr. Snyder's orders early in the summer. Rita's week of intensive private lessons with Jack, before her show season went into full swing, had come to a grinding halt when Rita's father learned of the reckless driving prank that had ended in tragedy.

Sarah walked faster, curious to see what was going on. As she got closer, she saw a big-bodied, light bay horse in Chancellor's old stall. He was attached to a stall tie, and a guy around her age, she guessed, was leaning down to remove the horse's shipping boots. When he had finished, he released the horse and stepped back to observe him closely.

"He shipped really well," the boy said, turning to the couple standing outside the stall. "He's not tucked up at all. The driver told me he polished off lots of hay in the van, and he drank plenty of water when they stopped along the way." When the boy came out of the stall, he noticed Sarah standing in the aisle and walked toward her. As he got closer, he displayed an even smile, flashing perfect teeth.

"Hi," Sarah said, feeling her cheeks warming as she noticed how good-looking he was, with a closely trimmed haircut, deep-set blue eyes, and that amazing smile. She shook some rain off her poncho, shyly returning his smile, not quite sure what to say next. "Are you boarding here now? My horse is right across the aisle. I'm Sarah Wagner."

"Derek Alexander," he said, grinning. "Pleased to meet you, Sarah Wagner. Yep, we're moving in." His gaze shifted to Crown Prince. "That's a good-looking horse you've got there." He stepped closer to read the info tag attached to Prince's stall door. "What breed is he? He looks almost too big to be a full Thoroughbred. Is he a Warmblood?"

The tall woman, who was made even taller by black hair piled high on her head, stepped toward them. She spoke to Derek in a chiding tone. "I've told you that Thoroughbreds come in all shapes and sizes." She pointed at Crown Prince. "This horse is your classic Thoroughbred, or the moon is made of green cheese!"

Derek looked inquisitively at Sarah. "And the answer is….?"

"Yes, Crown Prince is a full Thoroughbred." Not comfortable with the conversation focused on her, Sarah changed the subject. "And your horse?"

Derek gestured toward the stall. "This is Bismarck. He's a Holsteiner, six years old, and we imported him from Germany about six months ago. He just made another long trip by commercial van to get here from Chicago. He's pretty easygoing, which helps make him a good traveler." Derek suddenly looked embarrassed as he glanced at his parents. "I'm sorry—I should have introduced you. Sarah, meet my mother and father."

"Hello, Sarah," Mrs. Alexander said. "Since Derek is new here, I hope you can show him around and introduce him to the other riders."

Derek rolled his eyes. "Mom, I'll be fine."

At that moment Jack came around the corner. He offered his hand to each of the Alexanders and welcomed them to the farm. Jack walked over to look in at Bismarck, instantly recognizing a quality animal. He seemed very pleased. "I understand our stable manager, Gus Kelso, checked in with you about feed and what your horse has been fed prior to now," he said to Derek. "Gus will gradually wean him off that onto the excellent grain combination we feed here, along with high-quality hay. It's a Timothy and alfalfa mix."

"We've been looking forward to meeting you," Mr. Alexander said. "Derek has wanted to ride with you ever since he read you were coming to this country. It took a transfer to my company's office in Winchester to make it happen, though."

Mrs. Alexander laughed. "Derek wasn't totally happy with his father's promotion and the move to Winchester until he learned we would be close to Brookmeade Farm. How soon can he begin a lesson program with you, Mr. O'Brien?"

"Call me Jack, if you please," Jack said. "New riders start out with a private lesson so I can evaluate them, particularly when they have their own horses. Then we decide where to place them in our lesson program." Jack turned to Derek. "I believe I'm booked up this week, but stop by the office so we can schedule something. Gus has made a place for your tack and equipment in the boarders' tack room," he said, gesturing down the aisle. "Let me show it to you."

Jack swiveled to face Sarah. "I'll be wanting a look at your horse's leg before my next lesson starts," he said. "I'll be back after I show Derek the tack room. Could you please remove the bandage?"

"We'll be off, Derek," his father said, as they started down the aisle. "Your mom and I have lots of unpacking to do in the new house."

Sarah turned to look at her horse. She had never failed to go to him first when she arrived at the barn, and now he stood at his stall door, tossing his head, his eyes fixed on her. When she slipped into the stall, he pushed his slender muzzle toward her. She stroked his face while he tugged at her jacket and nuzzled her coat sleeve. She fished his carrot from her pocket and offered it to him. "I'm sorry I made you wait, Prince," she said softly. "I guess I've spoiled you." She gave him a quick hug before slipping his halter on and bringing him out to the cross-ties in the aisle.

Jack had done a good job putting on the stable bandage—it hadn't slipped down at all. Sarah's fingers worked quickly to remove it and the cotton wrap, anxious to see the injury it covered, and gently pulled off the gauze pad. She was studying the injured area just as Jack returned. He leaned down to look closely at the wound, now twenty-four hours old, before gently placing a hand in back of the cannon bone to check for heat and swelling.

Jack looked pleased when he stood up. "'Tis coming along well," he said. "The area around the cut is only moderately warm, consistent with healing. The only thing you have to work on is keeping the cut from getting infected, and it will soon be scabbed over. Cold water, wrapping the leg, and stall rest have taken care of any minor stress to the tendon area." Hearing Jack's words, Sarah felt a wave of relief. The injury would soon be a thing of the past! She noticed a second shadow on the aisle's cement floor, and realized Derek was behind them, also looking closely at Prince's leg.

Jack stepped back and rested his hand on Prince's hindquarters. "I suggest both of you hand-walk your horses in the indoor today. 'Tis too bad we have the rain, but just stay at one end while the lessons are going on. Bismarck has had a long van ride and needs to stretch his legs." Jack shifted his gaze to Sarah. "Crown Prince hasn't been out of his stall today, and proper circulation from light exercise will promote healing. Afterward just slather on a goodly amount of the Furoxone ointment and wrap his leg for one more day."

Jack started off to his next lesson, but paused and turned around. "Prince's cut isn't very deep and should heal over in a few days. By Saturday you can probably get on him again. If you don't have any polo wraps, best to pick up a set before then. Wrap his front legs only. Paige will show you how to do it, and if she's not around, Tim and Mrs. DeWitt are also good with polos." Jack smiled. "And perhaps Derek, too."

After Jack left, Derek walked around Prince, looking at the horse up close. "He's pretty tall," he said. "How do you manage to get your foot in the stirrup?"

"Only with a mounting block," she said, and they both laughed.

"Maybe you should take some rock climbing lessons, just in case you're without the block one of these days." His face became serious. "What are you planning to do with him?"

"I haven't gotten that far yet. He's my first horse, and I've only had him since June. I might event him and do some small shows."

Derek walked over to look out the window. "I think it's only sprinkling outside now, so before I walk Bismarck, I'm going to bring in some of the things that are jammed into my truck. I didn't realize I had so much horse stuff until I had to pack it all up."

Before Derek could leave, Tim and Paige appeared, eager to meet the new boarder. When Sarah introduced them, she mentioned that Derek lived in Winchester.

"The vets that take care of the Brookmeade horses are from the Winchester Equine Clinic," Tim said, "and a girl who rides in our class goes to Winchester Academy."

"I'm going to be a junior there, a day student. Most of the kids who go to the Academy are boarding students, though."

"Have you met Rita Snyder?" Paige asked. "She would also be a junior. She's thin with long black hair. She drives a green Mustang convertible."

Derek shook his head. "Our classes don't start until next week."

"What do you do with your horse?" Tim asked.

"Before I got him, Bismarck was a show jumper in Germany," Derek replied. "When we get our act together, that's what I hope to do with him. I really love doing the jumpers. I wasn't totally thrilled with my instructor in Chicago, though. I'm hoping Jack can help us. What kind of riding do you do?"

Paige and Tim looked at each other, as if not sure who should answer the question. Paige jumped in first.

"I have a gray Thoroughbred, Quarry, and both Tim and I started eventing our horses this year," Paige said. "Quarry is off the track, so it's taken some time to get him retrained. He's quick, and likes to rush his fences." She grinned. "At the Maple Crest event in July, there was a huge rock pile on cross-country called Titanic. Quarry was a little intimidated, and he didn't know whether to rush it or suck back—so he was just right."

Like the others, Derek laughed. "You'll have to tell me more some time, but I've got to move my stuff into the tack room before it starts to rain hard again."

"I've got some time," Tim said. "Want a hand?"

"Sure," Derek said, as the two left for the parking area.

When they were out of earshot, Sarah spoke softly to Paige. "What do you think of the new guy?"

"I think he's totally cool!" Paige said. "You'll probably see Kelly and Nicole stopping by here a lot now, like they do around Tim's stall."

"I hope not," Sarah said. "They've had it in for me ever since Jack moved me into your class last winter. They don't speak to me, and I have a feeling they would stab me in the back if they got a chance."

"I'd ignore them if I were you," Paige said. "They're just jealous. Maybe you'll be back riding with us one of these days."

"It can't be soon enough for me," Sarah said, "but Prince is still green. I saw some of your lesson yesterday, and all of you guys looked awesome. Next year you'll be long-listed for the Olympic eventing team."

"Yeah, right before I win the New York Marathon," Paige said, rolling her eyes. She turned to leave. "I've got to get back to Quarry."

Sarah looked at Crown Prince standing patiently on the cross-ties. He didn't appear to be jumping out of his skin after being cooped up in his stall all day. Maybe he wouldn't be too rambunctious if she tried to hand-walk him in the indoor. *I can clean his stall later,* she thought. She left for the tack room to get her grooming caddy. When she returned, there was a pile of tack and horse care equipment near Bismarck's stall. It looked like Derek and Tim had gone back for more.

After going over Prince quickly with a soft brush, Sarah grabbed a hoof pick out of her caddy. A thorough grooming could be skipped on this day when she wouldn't be riding, but his feet needed to be picked out at least once a day. The farrier said his feet were healthy, and she wanted to keep them that way. When she had finished, she attached his lead shank to his halter, unclipped the cross-ties, and led him toward the indoor, his shoes ringing on the cement floor.

CHAPTER 6

Trouble Brewing

THE INDOOR ARENA was wall-to-wall horses when Sarah and Prince approached it from the stable entryway. To allow more than one class to ride simultaneously, cavalletti had been placed across the arena to divide it into two working areas. Jack was instructing a group of adults in the far end, while in the closer section, Lindsay worked with a class of intermediate riders. A few well-placed cones marked a boundary that reserved a small portion of the arena for boarders' horses.

Sarah scanned all the activity. Along with a number of horses that had trucked in for lessons, it looked like every one of the Brookmeade school horses was in the arena. With so many horses going in all directions, Prince became anxious, pulling on the lead shank. He might have some extra energy after all!

Kelly and Nicole were walking and trotting their horses in the tight space reserved for the boarders. This was where Sarah was headed, and the last thing she wanted was trouble with those girls. Having a problem with Rita the day before was bad enough. Maybe she should just take Prince back to his stall and forget this.

No! she thought. *I'm not going to let those two keep us out. With the rain, the indoor is the only place we can walk, and Prince needs to get some exercise.* When she saw the entrance was clear, she called out, "Gate!" and walked him into the arena.

Thankfully Kelly and Nicole were tracking left. Sarah led Prince close to the rail in the same direction so horses could pass her easily. From the tension on the lead shank, even at walk, she could tell Prince was tense, particularly when a horse came close to them. *Just let them keep their distance!* she thought. Prince moved with his head high, and his ears flicked in all directions as he took in the activity around him. It seemed like there were horses moving everywhere, and riders in Jack's class were cantering through a short gymnastic jumping line. When Prince pulled on the shank to go faster, Sarah had to give frequent short tugs to slow down his walk and keep him listening to her. She was glad for the chain shank over his sensitive nose that helped regain his attention when necessary.

Sarah glanced around to check on the riders, hoping they wouldn't come too close. Kelly Hoffman on Midnight Jet was not far away, and when their gazes met, Kelly gave Sarah a dark look before turning away and almost immediately putting her horse into a brisk trot, making as large a circle as space allowed. Glancing over her shoulder, Sarah saw that Kelly and Jet were approaching them closely from behind. To give Kelly's horse as much room as possible, Sarah pushed her arm against Prince's shoulder, and with the shank, asked him to move closer to the wall. When she looked again, Kelly and her horse were directly behind Prince, coming up fast. It looked like Midnight Jet might actually brush up against her horse!

"Watch it!" Sarah called out, but it was too late. Crown Prince was also aware of the other horse moving quickly toward his rear, and as the bay Quarter Horse came upon him, Prince kicked out in warning with his left hind leg, causing Jet to shy hard to the left to avoid the blow. Kelly wasn't prepared for the unexpected swerve, and she lurched partially out of the saddle, making her horse shy even more to the left. With a cry of frustration, Kelly fell from her horse and landed hard on the arena floor. Midnight Jet cantered away, his reins hanging loose and stirrups flapping.

Someone shouted, "Loose horse!" and all the other riders in the arena quickly brought their horses to a halt. Lindsay left her class and immediately walked toward Midnight Jet, who had stopped by the gate. He didn't attempt to move away when she reached for his reins. By then Kelly was on her feet, her face twisted in anger as she hurried to retrieve her horse. Without saying a word, she snatched the reins away from Lindsay.

"Are you all right?" Lindsay asked her. When Kelly nodded, Lindsay said, "Would you like to get back on?"

"I'm not riding in here with that crazy horse!" Kelly snapped. "Let me out."

Lindsay held the gate open so Kelly could lead Jet away. Nicole quickly dismounted and followed them with her buckskin mare, Jubilee. Sarah watched them go, relieved that at least it appeared Kelly hadn't gotten hurt.

Prince didn't like standing still and was getting antsy, tossing his head and pulling harder on the lead shank. Now that she and her horse had the boarders' area all to themselves, Sarah resumed walking Prince. He continued to be distracted by the many horses in the arena, jigging occasionally and pulling on the shank, but she was able to get in the fifteen minutes of walking Jack had pre-scribed. It wasn't pleasant dealing with a totally uptight horse, but Sarah realized the experience might make Prince calmer on another, similar occasion. When she finally turned him toward the gate, she was glad to be leaving the hubbub behind.

Once they were back in his stall, Sarah stood close to her horse, talking softly and stroking his neck. Gradually she felt the tension leave him. She thought about what had happened in the indoor, knowing the humiliation of falling from her horse would make Kelly even more resentful. *Would it help if I apologized?* Sarah wondered. She decided to bite the bullet and give it a try.

At the other end of the barn, Midnight Jet was on cross-ties in the aisle with Kelly and Nicole standing beside him, deep in conversation. Kelly's gray riding pants had a large dark stain on her right side where she had fallen. The girls saw her coming and turned to face her, silently glaring. *Ugh!* Sarah thought. *Two against one.*

"Kelly, I'm really sorry for what happened," Sarah said. "I hope you're okay."

Kelly put her hands on her hips. "You've got some nerve, bringing that crazy Thoroughbred into the indoor arena when it was crowded. He's an accident waiting to happen!" she said, glowering.

Sarah wasn't surprised by Kelly's words, but that didn't make them any easier to take, especially when Kelly's riding had caused the incident. There was no doubt in Sarah's mind that Kelly had purposely tried to frighten Prince. Sarah took a deep breath and shook her head. She'd been an idiot not to realize this conversation would be a waste of time. She turned to walk away.

"And don't even think of riding him in our class, either," Nicole called after her. "Your horse is a menace!"

Sarah winced. She stopped short and spun around to face them. "Excuse me?"

"It's all over the barn that you're supposed to start riding in our class," Nicole continued with a sneer. "After what your horse did today, we don't want him anywhere near our horses. He's dangerous!"

Sarah bit her lip and decided not to argue. She started back to her stall, her mind racing. *How do those jerks know Jack wants me to ride in their class?* Perhaps Paige had mentioned it to someone, and then the boarding-barn rumor mill had kicked in. *I wonder if Kelly and Nicole plan to use what happened today against me,* she thought. *Will they try and convince people Crown Prince is vicious because he kicked out at Jet?*

Sarah needed to share this latest incident with Kayla, and she texted her friend. *Call me ASAP. Important!* She put her phone in her pocket and went to get a wheelbarrow and manure fork from the shavings shed, dodging rain drops along the way. With Prince on cross-ties, she got to work on his stall, but it wasn't long before her cell vibrated. It was a text message from Kayla. *"What's up, kid?"*

Sarah called and told Kayla the whole story, ending with the choice remarks the girls had made to her after she apologized. "This totally freaks me out!" she said. "I can't have people saying my horse is dangerous—what if my parents hear these rumors?"

"They're dorks!" Kayla said. "Your horse isn't vicious or dangerous! But you've got to be careful. If those losers are trying to keep you out of their class, they're going to complain to Jack. I wouldn't put it past them to make up some crazy story."

Sarah shut her eyes and gripped her phone tighter. "You're right, Kayla. They're going to exaggerate what happened and blow it all out of proportion."

"You know, it's a no-brainer that those two jerks are jealous of you. If they really want to ride better, they should think about losing a few pounds. Did you give them a piece of your mind when they opened up on you with both barrels?"

Sarah was quiet for a moment. Kayla had a point. When Kelly and Nicole were spewing all their venom, she should have set the record straight. Instead she'd just walked away. "You know I'm not good at that. I'm not fast on my feet, and I never know what to say."

"Well, I wouldn't have let them get away with it. I'd have told them off and then some. You're going to have to grow some backbone, kid. But Mom's yelling for me—gotta go. Don't forget. You need to tell Jack what's going on before they do!"

After Sarah had finished cleaning Prince's stall and returned the wheelbarrow to the shavings shed, she met Derek and Bismarck on their way back from the indoor arena. She studied the horse as Derek led him by. Bismarck had a lot of Prince's refinement, plus other qualities that would serve him well, specifically as a show jumper. His legs had substantial bone and a larger foot, and like Chancellor, he had massive hindquarters for pushing over large fences.

"It was a zoo out there!" Derek complained. "Is the indoor arena always this busy?"

"No, thank goodness," Sarah said. "They usually don't hold two classes at the same time. How did Bismarck handle the mass confusion?"

"He was a little nervous, but not bad." Derek led Bismarck into his stall and removed the lead shank from his halter. "If only people wouldn't ride so close. We're not dealing with bicycles here."

"Tell me about it," Sarah replied. She considered revealing what had happened with Prince in the arena earlier to Derek, but decided against it. *Derek's new here. He doesn't need to hear about all the drama.*

"Bismarck's been exposed to a lot," Derek continued. "The shows in Germany can be really big. After doing that a couple years, it would take something pretty wild to get him totally unglued."

"You probably can't wait to show him," Sarah said.

"I love doing the jumpers and sailing over big fences. We have a few wrinkles to work out, though. That's where Jack comes in."

Sarah watched him head for the tack room with his box of grooming equipment. *What a cool guy!* she thought. *But why would he ever be interested in me? Anyway, I've got more important things to think about right now.*

Sarah left to give the horses their evening feed, and after making the rounds distributing the grain and filling the plastic pails with the next morning's rations, she climbed the stairs leading to the hay loft. She was lost in thought as she picked up flakes of hay with the pitchfork and tossed them down into each horse's stall. After her confrontation with Rita, now she had to deal with Kelly and Nicole. Why couldn't things just go smoothly? All she wanted was to ride and care for her beautiful horse. If Kelly claimed that Prince had maliciously kicked out at her horse, would Jack believe her? *I know what happened,* Sarah thought. *I saw the whole thing.* She had to tell Jack her side of the story before Kelly and Nicole got to him.

When every horse and the two ponies had been fed, Sarah started down the stairs from the loft to return to her horse. She needed to reapply his bandage before she headed home. She had almost reached the foot of the stairs when she saw Jack approaching.

"Hello, Sarah. I was just coming to find you," he said, his voice carrying a somewhat steely edge. "When you have a moment, I'd like to talk to you in the office."

For a moment she froze, her hand gripping the banister. "Sure. I can come right now," she said. With a sinking feeling, she followed her instructor the short distance to the stable office, which was unoccupied. Jack closed the door and turned to face her.

"Are you aware of what's going on with Kelly Hoffman?" he asked.

Sarah took a deep breath. "Yes, I am. I think she's upset with me because she fell off Midnight Jet in the indoor this afternoon. Prince kicked out at her horse. When Jet swerved sharply to miss the kick, Kelly lost her balance and hit the dust."

Jack's face was serious. "So Prince *did* kick out at Jet?"

Sarah nodded. "I know that's bad, Jack. But Midnight Jet was coming up behind Prince very fast, and it seemed like he would miss us only by inches, if at all." Sarah clenched her fists. "Prince was just trying to protect himself!"

"Well, Mrs. Hoffman called here a little while ago. She's upset. It's her understanding that Prince actually *kicked* Midnight Jet, and she doesn't want Prince in the same class with her daughter." Jack hesitated a moment, looking at Sarah sharply, and asked again, "Are you *sure* Prince didn't hit Jet?"

Sarah stood tall, her expression resolute, and looked Jack straight in the eye. "I was looking back when it happened. I saw the whole thing. Kelly's horse was coming up behind Prince very fast, and I think she was doing it on purpose, trying to make Prince totally freak out. But his kick didn't touch Midnight Jet."

Jack stepped past her and opened the office door. "Let's go have a look." Together they walked to Midnight Jet's stall. Most of the riders had gone home, and the barn was quiet except for the sounds of horses eating, some rattling their feed tubs as they cleaned up the last kernels of grain. Jack picked up a lead rope from a hook beside the door to Jet's stall.

"He's not going to like leaving his hay, but I'm going to bring Jet out into the aisle where the light's better. You can hold him while I check him over. Mrs. Hoffman said he was kicked on his side, and by now there would be some heat and swelling at the point of impact."

Jack led Midnight Jet from the stall and handed the lead rope to Sarah. She studied the bay horse with a snip of white on his muzzle. After being around Crown Prince, the 15.2-hand gelding seemed small. Except for a slightly Roman nose, he had a pretty face and seemed pretty easygoing. Jet nuzzled her sweatshirt looking for treats, and Sarah stroked him lightly. *Kelly should realize she's lucky to have such a nice horse,* she thought. *She needs to find better things to do than give me a hard time!*

Jack moved to the horse's right side and scrutinized the area near where a saddle would sit. Not a hair was out of place. Next he ran his hands gently over the entire area, searching for any place that might feel slightly warm or swollen to his touch. He repeated the process on the opposite side, before inspecting the horse's legs and chest for any sign of injury. At no time did Jet flinch or show any sensitivity to pressure from Jack's hands.

When Jack straightening up and spoke to Sarah, his words were clipped. "There's nothing wrong with this horse. Let's put him away." He took the lead rope and led Midnight Jet back into his stall. Jack looked troubled when he stepped back into the aisle. He slid the stall door shut, and without another word, headed back to the office. Sarah stayed for a few minutes, watching Midnight Jet. The horse was content, eating his hay and occasionally going to his water bucket. He certainly didn't act like a horse experiencing any discomfort.

Why do some people have to go out of their way to make trouble? Sarah thought. She headed to her own horse's stall, where Prince was also busy eating. Derek must have left for the day. She felt a twinge of disappointment as she walked to the tack room to get the things from her trunk she needed to wrap Prince's leg. Upon returning, she put him on the cross-ties in the aisle and brushed the injured area lightly with a soft brush. The cut was lightly scabbed over, and following Jack's instructions, she dabbed it with

Furoxone ointment before applying the bandage. She stepped back to survey her work, noticing that her bandaging job didn't look nearly as good as Jack's. *I hope it won't slip down,* she thought.

Sarah suddenly remembered that Mr. DeWitt had suggested she try riding Prince in a different bit. Maybe someone in the barn had one she could borrow just to try it out. She decided to call Jack.

His phone rang twice before Jack answered. "Sorry to bother you, Jack, but there's something I forgot to ask you," Sarah began. She told him about her conversation with Mr. DeWitt and his suggestion of switching to a stronger bit. "What do you think, Jack? If it's a good idea, I could try to get one before I take Prince into the woods the next time.

There was no hesitation in Jack's response. "Sarah, a stronger bit is not the way to go with your horse. You want him to respect the bit you put in his mouth, and he must respond to what you ask, but at the same time he needs to go forward into that bit, to take it willingly. Do you understand what I'm saying?"

"I think so," she said, feeling her cheeks warm at the correction. "You've told us it's bad for a horse to be behind the bit. Is that what you mean?"

"Exactly. When a bit makes a horse uncomfortable, he'll bring his head back too far in an effort to evade it. You certainly don't want that. I believe training and experience are the keys here."

"Thanks," Sarah said quickly. "I thought I should ask, and thanks for explaining it to me. I've got so much to learn!"

Biking home from the barn, Sarah's thoughts were on her horse. As soon as his leg healed sufficiently, she'd be able to ride him again, and not just in the indoor or sand ring. They were going on another trail ride, and she and Prince would have their chance to convince her parents and everyone else that her horse was as level-headed and well-behaved as he was beautiful.

CHAPTER 7

Enemies

SATURDAY DAWNED MORE LIKE SUMMER than fall, with a warm breeze skimming over the grass in the fields at Brookmeade Farm. As Sarah biked along the farm road that morning, she watched the three Thoroughbred foals with their dams turned out in the acres of green pasture on her left. The two colts and a filly had grown a lot in the last month, and before long they'd be weaned from their dams and shipped to Hank Bolton's farm in Florida. If all went well, someday their speed would be tested on the racetrack.

As she pedaled up the hill toward the O'Briens' bungalow, Sarah thought about her new fall schedule at the farm. Now that school had started, she would have much more work to do on weekends. Not only would she feed the horses in the morning, but on Sunday, which was Gus's day off, she would also scrub clean and fill all the water buckets. On Saturdays, she'd be doing a lot of sweeping—both aisles, the two tack rooms, the feed room, and the lounge—and it would be her responsibility to clean her horse's stall every day. Somewhere in between she would find time for her top priority: Crown Prince.

Braking to a stop in front of the barn, she felt a tingle of excitement. It would be like old times to connect with her horse at the beginning of the day. After parking her bike by the side door, she hurried to his stall, where Prince was standing by his window looking out at the turnout paddocks. He swung around when he heard her approaching, voicing a low nicker. She opened the stall door enough to slide through and went to her horse.

"Hi, buddy," Sarah said, as she stroked Prince's face and gently pulled his ears. He nuzzled her pockets for the carrot he'd come to expect, and made short work of it when she held it out to him. She hadn't wrapped his leg the night before, and now she leaned over to check on it. A substantial scab had formed over the cut, and she felt no heat when she pressed her hand against it. *Awesome!* she thought.

Sarah spent a few extra minutes with her horse before heading to the feed room. It was off limits to everyone except the regular barn staff, and she closely guarded the key Gus had given her. It always hung on a sturdy chain necklace she wore to the barn. She remembered the dire warning Gus had given her when he first presented it to her. *If a horse ever got into the grain room, there'd be hell to pay. Most would eat so much they'd colic and die.* She slipped the chain over her head and fingered the key as she approached the grain room's extra-large door, wide enough to accommodate the grain cart that was pushed through it twice a day.

After she fed the horses their breakfast and refilled the grain pails, Sarah tossed down hay from the loft. Her mind kept coming back to her planned ride on Prince in a few hours. After working in the ring, they'd go part of the way up the old orchard trail. She tried to quell the butterflies she felt already starting.

With most of the paddocks unoccupied at that hour, Sarah decided to turn Prince out once he'd finished eating his grain. It would give her time to clean his stall and possibly get a head start on sweeping. On her way back from the paddock, Sarah saw Tim with Rhodes in the back aisle and considered stopping to say hello. But she wrinkled her nose when she noticed Kelly and Nicole standing close by while Tim groomed his horse.

Sarah decided to avoid that scene. She would check in with Paige instead. She found the blonde girl in Quarry's stall leaning over picking out her horse's feet. Sticking her head through the partially open door, Sarah said, "Hey, Paige. What's up?"

"Oh, hi." Paige released Quarry's near hind leg and stood up. "Tim and I are going to ride to the beach. I think the summer tourists are gone, so we can actually ride right on the beach."

"Cool!" Sarah said. "It must take a while to get there, though. Which trail do you follow?"

"There's an old path on the other side of Ridge Road that skirts around Quimby Farm. We discovered it by accident. Want to come with us today?"

"Hey, I don't really think you want me coming along when you're going on a beach ride with your boyfriend, do you?" After they both laughed, Sarah said, "Anyway, I don't think Prince and I are ready to go that far. I'm going to take him up part of the old orchard trail again."

"Are you still planning to ride in Kelly's class next week?" Paige asked, as she picked up Quarry's near front leg and began picking packed bedding and manure out of his hoof.

"I guess," Sarah said. "Have you heard anything about that?"

Paige hesitated a minute. "You should know that Kelly is telling people Jack won't let Prince in a class with other horses because he's a kicker." Paige put down Quarry's leg and looked at Sarah to gauge her reaction.

Sarah swallowed hard as she felt a rush of anger. This is what she'd been afraid of! Kelly and Nicole were bad-mouthing Prince, and what they were saying was totally false. Apparently they didn't have a problem telling a flat-out lie.

"Paige, I think Jack would tell me first if he thought Prince couldn't be ridden in a group. I hope you didn't buy that ridiculous story."

Paige threw her head back and laughed. "If I believed everything I heard around here, I'd really be a dumb blonde!" Sarah's grin turned into a scowl as she turned to go. "Look, Sarah," Paige said, "don't let them get under your skin. Crown Prince will be able to tell you are tense and angry. Have a good ride, and stay away from the wild turkeys."

"Yeah, I know. Thanks, Paige," Sarah said, as she walked slowly away toward the shavings shed to get a wheelbarrow. The smut campaign against her and her horse was in high gear. She just had to shake it off.

Later, after finishing Prince's stall, Sarah swept the two tack rooms and feed room. She'd do the aisles and lounge after she rode. She was leaving for the paddock when she heard the sound of paws skittering down the aisle behind her. Looking back, she saw her favorite Jack Russells bounding toward her, with Mrs. DeWitt not far behind. Sarah laughed and leaned over, clapping her hands to the dogs. Spin got to her first and jumped up to be petted. Cameo caught up to them a few seconds later. The puppy didn't know Sarah very well, but her tail was wagging just as furiously as Spin's. Sarah laughed as she stroked their backs and rubbed their ears.

"Good morning, Sarah," Mrs. DeWitt called out, smiling warmly. "And how is that handsome horse doing these days?"

Sarah stood up. "His leg is healing great. I don't have to wrap it anymore, so I'll put the things you loaned me by your stall. Jack says I can ride Prince this morning, but I'm going to start using polo wraps on him in front."

"It's wonderful that you can ride him again!" Mrs. DeWitt said, coming up to her. "How about polo wraps? Do you have any?"

Sarah nodded. "Rita gave me a box of things she didn't need when I first got Prince. The polos are a little tired, but they'll do." She couldn't help laughing again when Spin approached her with a towel he'd grabbed from a tack box. He was ready for a tug-of-war. She grabbed the end of the towel and held on while Spin pulled on it with all his might, growling furiously. Cameo didn't need any encouragement to join in when Sarah offered the puppy her end of the towel. Turning back to Mrs. DeWitt, Sarah said, "Are you getting ready to ride?"

"Yes, as a matter of fact, I'm expecting my son to drop Grace off any minute. We're going to ride on the meadow trail. We have to go early because Grace has a piano lesson right after lunch."

I wonder if I should ask her about Kelly and Nicole? Sarah thought. She desperately needed some advice on how to handle those girls, and there was no one better to listen and help. Telling her parents anything negative that involved Crown Prince was out of the question.

"Mrs. DeWitt, can I ask you about something?"

Mrs. DeWitt's face clouded. "Of course, Sarah. What is it?"

Sarah shifted uncomfortably, not sure how to begin. Finally she told Mrs. DeWitt the whole story as quickly as she could. "I wish I could just concentrate on Prince and his training, but Kelly and Nicole are going to make trouble for us in that class. I just know it."

"It's not an easy situation, Sarah," Mrs. DeWitt said. "Sometimes as hard as we try to get along with other people, it just doesn't work. In this case, I suggest you try to stay away from those two girls as much as possible. When it comes to your class, you know Jack will be objective. He'll not be drawn into a false story about your horse, and he won't put up with any pettiness. Just ride into that class with the intention of learning all you can from Jack. He'll bring Crown Prince along in his training like no other instructor can."

Mrs. DeWitt turned when she saw a tan Toyota Camry pulling into the parking area. "Here's my precious Grace, coming now." Sarah embraced Mrs. DeWitt with a quick hug. "Thank you," she said. "Talking to you always helps so much!"

Later, while she groomed Prince on cross-ties, Derek arrived at the barn. Dressed in rust breeches and brown field boots with his helmet under his arm, he was clearly planning to ride. Bismarck came to his stall door when he saw Derek and quickly devoured the large apple the young man offered him. After a quick greeting to Sarah, Derek went to the tack room to get his grooming tools and tack. He returned a few minutes later.

"How's your horse's leg?" he asked, as he walked Bismarck from his stall to cross-ties further down the aisle.

"Much better," she replied. "He hasn't been ridden since our crazy ride on Wednesday, so I don't know what he'll be like." She laughed. "It might be another wild ride. What are you doing?"

"Now that the rain has cleared out, I want to explore some of the hacking trails around here," Derek said as he curried Bismarck's muscular neck. "I heard there are quite a few. Do you know where they are?"

"You're asking the wrong person," Sarah admitted. "Prince and I have had one trail ride, and that one was pretty much a disaster. Check with Tim or Paige after they get back. They left about fifteen minutes ago on a trail to the beach." She saw the look of disappointed on Derek's face.

"I think it's important to hack show horses a lot," Derek said.

"They can become ring sour if all they do is work. I'm not a jump, jump, jump kinda rider."

Sarah hadn't noticed Kelly and Nicole show up, so she was startled when she heard Nicole's voice from the other side of Bismarck. "Kelly and I can show you some of the trails if you want," Nicole said to Derek. "We were just getting ready to groom our horses. Then we're going on a hack." Sarah continued brushing Prince, fighting a surge of annoyance while she listened intently.

"Sure, thanks," Derek said, in a voice that thankfully didn't sound too enthusiastic. "How long will you be out?" he asked.

Kelly replied quickly. "We can be out for as long as you'd like." Then the two girls made a beeline for the other end of the barn. Derek was quiet, focused on getting his horse ready for the ride.

Crown Prince stood fully relaxed on the cross-ties, one hind leg drawn underneath him. When Sarah was nearly finished grooming him, she lovingly went over his face with a soft brush and used her comb on his mane, trying to get all of it to fall neatly on the right side. She gave a sigh of exasperation when, as soon as she was finished, he gave his head a deliberate toss, sending his mane flying in all directions.

Now it was time to wrap his front legs. Sarah reached for one of the green polos Rita had given her. If only she could remember the video she'd watched in the lounge the other day that demonstrated how to put them on. It was different from the stable bandage she'd used to dress his wound. A few minutes later she discovered that wrapping it wasn't as easy as the video had made it seem. Several times she removed the polo wrap to start over, only to be just as frustrated on the next try. She finally had to admit to herself she needed help.

"Hey, Derek," she called out. "Do you have a minute? I'm not doing so well here."

Derek left his horse and came to take a look. A grin flickered on his face as he pointed to the front of the polo wrap. "Sarah, you've got to run the wrap so the bandage forms an upside-down V in front. Otherwise your horse won't be able to flex his ankle joint very well." He bent down and took the wrap from her. After removing it from Prince's leg and rerolling it tightly, he showed Sarah the right way to run the polo wrap around Prince's leg, not so snug it might cut off circulation, but with enough tension so it would stay in place. "Now *you* try the other leg," he said.

Sarah got down on one knee and started winding the bandage around Prince's foreleg, trying to follow Derek's example. She was nearly finished when out of the corner of her eye she saw Kelly and Nicole coming back. Sarah hastily did the final loop of the bandage and used the Velcro fastener to secure it. Nicole glared at her, slit-eyed, before shifting her gaze to Derek. Her face became sugary sweet. "Our horses are all ready to go."

Derek rose to his full height and turned to the girls. "I'll be along in just a minute. I'm just helping Sarah get these polo wraps right." This was not the answer Kelly and Nicole were looking for, and the girls huffed away.

Turning back to the polos, Derek said, "They look okay, and they'll keep him from reopening that cut." His gaze followed Kelly and Nicole. "Time to obey my marching orders," he said to Sarah with a grin before he went back to Bismarck. After putting on his horse's bridle, he buckled the chin strap on his riding helmet and led Bismarck away.

Sarah stood for a minute, deciding what to do. No way did she want to meet up with those two girls and Derek on the old orchard trail. Derek would probably suggest she ride with them, and even with Derek there, Sarah would prefer a date with a serial killer. She would just have to wait until they got back.

Then it dawned on her. Since Prince hadn't been ridden for several days, this was an ideal time to longe him in the ring before she rode. Sarah went to the tack room for her equipment. She saddled and bridled her horse and then fixed the stirrup leathers so they held the irons in place and secured the reins around his neck. With her longe line attached to his bridle and carrying her longe whip, she led Prince to the sand ring outside.

While Prince was trotting smartly around her, she thought ahead to their ride in the woods. It was a perfect day to go on the old orchard trail, even if they didn't go very far. The air was warm, and the sun shone brightly, with only occasional fluffy, cumulous clouds showing against the cobalt sky. After longeing Prince in both directions, Sarah gave him the voice command for halt. She was pleased when he remembered and obeyed. She quickly went to him and stroked his neck. "Good boy, good boy," she said, removing the longeing equipment and putting it outside the ring, where she could pick it up later.

Sarah mounted her horse and headed for the trailhead, her fingers crossed that she wouldn't meet up with the girls and Derek. As she and Prince walked near the barn, Jack stepped outside and beckoned to her. When she got closer, he asked, "So is it a wee bit of trail riding for you and Crown Prince this morning?"

"Yes. I hope he'll be quiet. He's had a lot of stall rest this week, so I longed him in the ring first to take the edge off."

"Excellent," Jack said.

Prince suddenly raised his head to look across the parking area, his ears pricked. When Jack and Sarah followed his gaze, they saw Derek, Nicole, and Kelly coming toward the barn. "It appears we have riders returning," Jack commented. Sarah noticed how strikingly handsome Bismarck looked under saddle. He dwarfed the two other horses.

"Howdy," Derek called out, as the group neared.

"Good morning," Jack said. "I know Nicole and Kelly have ridden their horses to the old orchard before, but I'm thinking this might have been your first visit. 'Tis a great ride, is it not?"

Derek flashed his even smile that made Sarah's heart beat a little faster. "The girls were nice enough to show me the way."

Kelly had come up behind Derek. "It was a great ride," she said. "Our horses totally get along. No kicking out, and not once did they pin their ears." She paused to give Sarah a mocking look before turning back to Jack. "Nicole and I were wondering if Derek could join our class. The horses would be, like, perfect together!"

There were a few moments of silence as four faces watched Jack for his reaction. He looked directly at Kelly, his expression stern and uncompromising. "I place riders of similar riding ability together, as much as possible, and if they have their own horses, I try to put those with a similar level of training together," Jack said in a clipped voice. "I certainly don't make up classes based on the horses' social relationships ... or the riders', for that matter."

Sarah turned her head to hide a smile, but Derek couldn't stifle a laugh. From the stony looks on their faces, it was obvious Kelly and Nicole were not amused.

Jack remained serious as he continued. "There *is* someone who will be joining your class on Wednesday, and that rider is Sarah. If you have any concerns about how well her horse behaves with yours, then I recommend you keep a safe distance, a rule you should *always* observe on horseback."

Holy schmoly! They're going to freak out! Sarah thought, as she looked at the ground to avoid meeting Nicole's glare. *Time for me to make an exit,* she thought. She couldn't help thinking about her next conversation with Kayla. *She'll be in hysterics when she hears about this!*

CHAPTER 8
Chance Encounter

SARAH GUIDED PRINCE toward the parking area and the dark opening in the trees that marked the head of the old orchard trail. A shiver of excitement tinged with a touch of nervousness ran through her. This would be an adventure she and Prince would share, just the two of them. They were going on the old orchard trail by themselves, and that's how she wanted it. Just her and her horse. If they met wild turkeys, this time she'd be ready. She vowed that no matter what happened, she would be in the saddle when Prince got back to the barn!

Approaching the narrow trail entrance, Sarah sensed some tension in her horse. He knew where they were going, all right. With her legs she assured him that yes, they were going onto the trail. In response, he stepped onto the path and moved rapidly over the pine needles. With his head up and ears flicking in all directions, Prince took in everything around them. She felt his powerful muscles working, even at walk, moving them along at a quick pace. *He's loving this!* she thought. And, as her butterflies calmed, so was she.

The quiet of the forest was broken only when Prince snorted at a squirrel leaping from one branch to another above the trail.

When Sarah felt him hesitate, she immediately reassured him by pressing her legs firmly against his sides. "It's okay, Prince," she said softly, and he resumed his energetic walk. *So far, so good,* she thought.

Minutes later, Sarah recognized the group of trees ahead that signaled they would soon be in sight of the fallen log. She brought Prince to a halt and stroked his glossy neck. They should probably turn around at this point and head back to the farm. Jack had made it clear she was to go only a short distance the first day, and to gradually increase the length of the ride over the next few days. But Prince had been walking so fast. She'd probably gone too far already.

When she asked him to turn around on the trail, Prince braced against the bridle. He wanted to go farther! He wasn't ready to go home. Perhaps they could just jump the log ahead and then turn back. He had done it so effortlessly on their first ride, and there was no reason to think things would be any different today. Besides, she had been on this trail so many times with Lady Tate when they hadn't seen even one wild turkey. She envisioned being totally in sync with her horse as he lifted her over the jump. *Okay, Prince,* she thought. *I know what you want. Let's do it!*

Sarah shortened her reins and gathered her horse before asking him to trot. He pushed off eagerly, as if remembering the jump ahead. As they rounded the curve in the trail, the big log came into view. Prince's ears went forward, focusing on the jump, while Sarah concentrated on looking through his ears ahead to the trail in the distance. In no time, Prince was rising off the ground, carrying both of them over the downed tree and leaving it behind them. He floated along the trail in a relaxed canter, not hurrying or pulling to go faster. His gait was so smooth, so perfect. Sarah didn't want to stop! They continued cantering until they passed through the narrow section where the low overstretched limbs had been removed by Gus and Lucas.

Sarah was in heaven! This is what she had dreamed of for so long, riding such a magnificent horse, *her own horse,* and leaving all her problems behind. Now Prince grabbed the bit as he quickened his pace and extended his stride into a gallop. As they raced by the tall thin grasses where the turkeys had been, he ran even faster. In no time, they were at the base of the ridge and beginning the climb toward the old orchard. Sarah felt the strength generated by Prince's powerful hindquarters as he galloped up the steep incline. At the same time, almost by instinct, she leaned forward and extended her arms to allow him more rein. The trail whizzed by as his gigantic strides devoured the ground. Horse and rider were moving as one! Higher and higher they climbed, and soon they were galloping through the thick, green grass of the orchard in the midst of the old apple trees.

Sarah sat back in the saddle and asked her horse to slow his pace. At first Prince resisted pressure from the reins. He shook his head, loving the run that had gotten them there and not wanting to stop. Sarah was insistent, and after a few strides he came back to her, first to trot, and then to a walk. The gallop up the steep ridge had been strenuous, and his breathing was quick, his nostrils red and dilated. She reached down to stroke his neck—it was warm and moist. She turned him to take in the view of the farm below, and in the distance, a few cottages in miniature with a glimmer of the ocean beyond. For several minutes they stood still, catching their breath and taking in the world.

Sarah felt on top of the clouds, her heart beating fast from the excitement of the ride. But the spell was broken when she checked her watch. She gulped. They needed to get back to the farm before anyone was concerned! She hoped no one was keeping track of how long they'd been gone.

Sarah turned Prince toward the trail that would take them down the ridge. As on their last visit, she asked him to carry with his hindquarters while she tweaked the reins to keep him light in front. Prince had learned something about negotiating hills on their first ride, and now he moved down the ridge in a more balanced frame, containing his forward movement without attempting to turn sideways.

As they proceeded slowly down the steep trail, Sarah's conscience began to bother her. There was no question she had failed to comply with Jack's wishes. How could she have done that? He had helped her so much. Without Jack's support, she would never have gotten Prince in the first place. From the beginning, he had convinced her father to let her take Prince on trial, and Jack had gone the extra mile to provide help whenever she'd needed it. And yet today she had clearly disregarded his instructions.

Excuses ran through her mind. *It isn't as if I'm riding a Brookmeade schoolie,* she thought. *Prince is my horse, and I should be able to do whatever I want with him, like the other boarders do.* But deep down she knew she shouldn't have ignored Jack's advice, and the place where the turkeys had swooped out of the tall grass was still ahead of them. She clutched the reins a little tighter and scanned the trail ahead.

When they reached the bottom of the ridge where the trail leveled off, Prince suddenly stopped and twisted sharply to look to his left. His body was rigid and he snorted loudly. Sarah had been focusing on the tall grasses close to the trail, searching for signs of the turkeys, but now she turned to see what Prince was looking at in the thick woods. Standing close to one of the mammoth pine trees that grew in this section of the forest stood a massive moose! With its huge rack of antlers, it looked enormous. Prince was riveted to the spot and snorted again. The moose didn't move, its eyes fixed on them.

Sarah felt a chill run down her spine. Perhaps they had invaded the moose's territory. What if it charged them? She wanted to get out of there fast! She kicked Prince hard with both legs while pulling his head around, sending him flying down the trail. After they galloped through the trail's narrow section, she twisted to look back. There was no sign of the moose in pursuit. She sat deeply in the saddle and asked Prince to slow his pace. The large log wasn't far ahead, and she didn't want to meet it at a full gallop.

Sarah was happy when Prince slowed his pace when she asked, and as the log came into view, he was back to trot. After steadying him a few strides, Sarah applied enough leg pressure so Prince knew they were committed to jumping it. He trotted to the base of the log and then lifted over it, cantering down the trail toward home. With little resistance, he came back to trot, and then willingly walked when she asked him.

"You amazing horse!" Sarah exclaimed, stroking his neck. She noticed that he was still quite warm, and a new worry flashed across her mind. No way did she want to bring him back to the farm hot and sweaty. If they ran into Jack, he would know in an instant she had done more than just walk Prince a short distance on the trail before turning back. Prince was walking at a fast clip, for now he knew he was headed back to the other horses at the farm, but he responded when she used half-halts to ask for a slower walk. Occasionally she halted him for a few moments, and frequently reached down to feel his shoulder. She was relieved that as they approached the parking area, Prince was nearly dry to her touch.

As had been the case when she left earlier, there were a lot of cars in the lot. Saturday was a busy day at Brookmeade when people who were in school or worked during the week could ride.

Earlier she and Prince had been the only ones in the sand ring, but now there were half a dozen horses there. One of them was Bismarck, and Kelly and Nicole stood at the rail watching Derek's every move. *They probably never take their eyes off him,* she thought. *I wonder how Derek likes his new bodyguards.*

Her mind came back to Jack with a jolt. What would she say when he asked her about the trail ride? She was dying to tell him how totally awesome Prince had been. She wanted him to know her horse hadn't freaked out when they encountered the big moose. But she had ignored his advice and had gone on a longer ride then she should have. He would have every reason to be upset with her. Could he understand that she and her horse had just gotten carried away? She was torn between regretting her actions and glorying in how Crown Prince had galloped up to the old orchard. It was a day she would never forget! She and her horse had been as one, his powerful strides eating up the trail as he flew up the ridge.

Sarah guided Prince directly to the barn's side door, dismounted, and led him down the aisle toward his stall. Once he was on the cross-ties, she removed his polo wraps. They had done their job—the cut on his leg had been well protected and was still firmly scabbed over. After untacking Prince and going over him with a soft brush, she led him into his stall, where he drank deeply from his water bucket before starting on his noon hay ration.

Sarah leaned on the back wall of the stall and reached for her phone. She needed to find out what was up with Kayla. Her friend answered right away. "Hi," Sarah said. "I just remembered you have a show coming up. Is it tomorrow?"

"No, the Fairmont Farms show is *next* weekend. Want to bring Prince?" she teased.

"I wish I could," Sarah said. "Maybe someday, although the way Nicole and Kelly see it, Prince should be banned from all horse shows and group lessons for the rest of his life." She paused to change the phone to her other ear. "I've got a Kelly and Nicole update for you," she continued. "They're following Derek around this place like stalkers, and this morning they got him to go on a trail ride with them. When they got back, right in front of me Kelly asked Jack if Derek could join their class. Kelly said they should ride together because their horses don't kick and totally get along."

"You've got to be kidding!" Kayla cried. "What a stupid reason for someone to join a riding class."

"Isn't Kelly a piece of work? Jack told Kelly he doesn't make up his classes based on the horses' social relationships."

Kayla was laughing so hard she couldn't speak right away. "That is priceless!" she squealed. Becoming more serious, she said, "It would be nice if those two dufuses would get off your back, but somehow I don't think you've heard the last from them."

Sarah stepped aside as Prince turned in the stall, brushing up close to her, and then put the phone back to her ear. "Here's another thing, Kayla. Promise you won't tell?"

After Kayla pledged herself to secrecy, Sarah began to describe her trail ride to the old orchard. "It was awesome! Prince was loving it!" she said. "And we had some excitement coming back. We didn't see any wild turkeys, but after we'd come down the steepest part of the ridge, there was a huge moose beside the trail."

Kayla gasped. "What did Prince do? Try to cut and run?"

"He was amazing! He just snorted, frozen to the ground. I was afraid the moose might charge us, and I knew we needed to get out of there fast. I gave Prince a kick and we left the moose in our dust. Later, when I asked Prince to come back to walk, he was perfect!"

"This all sounds great," Kayla said. "Why don't you want me to tell anyone?"

Sarah frowned to herself, then confessed. "Jack told me to go a short distance on the trail, but we went all the way to the top. How will he feel if he finds out I ignored his instructions? When it comes to working with horses, he's pretty strict."

Kayla was quiet, thinking. Finally she said, "The trouble with stretching the truth is the cover-up never ends. You just get drawn in deeper, needing to tell more lies to keep your secret. If Jack ever found out, you'd worry he didn't trust you anymore, and the truth is, he might not. It would be better if you tell him what happened. You need to come clean, just like you decided to do with your parents when you fell off."

Sarah thought a minute. "I guess you're right, Kayla. Thanks. Hey, listen ... I gotta go. I'll call you later though."

Sarah put her phone back in her pocket and went to her horse. When Prince raised his head from his hay pile, she hugged his neck. Kayla was right. It would be best to talk to Jack right away. She swallowed the lump in her throat and headed to the office. Lindsay was sitting at the desk with a sandwich and a Coke when she walked in. "Hi, Lindsay. Is Jack around?" she asked.

"He was just here," Lindsay said. "He's got a class in the indoor this afternoon. You might find him there setting up a course."

"Thanks, Linds," Sarah said, leaving the office. She hoped Jack was alone in the indoor. What would she say? How could she keep him from being angry and disappointed in her? She walked down the aisle that led to the indoor, hesitating as she approached the gate. Jack was dragging standards and rails into place for his afternoon class. A quick scan of the arena showed that except for him, it was deserted.

I hope he won't mind being interrupted, Sarah thought, as she pushed the gate open and walked toward Jack. He stopped what he was doing when he spotted Sarah and watched her approach. His face sobered when he saw her serious expression.

"Have you good news to tell me about your ride?" he asked.

Sarah remained quiet until she got closer. "The good news is that Prince was a star today. He couldn't have gone better."

Jack smiled. "You had no problems in the woods? No wild turkeys to cause him fits?" Sarah shook her head. "Then why the long face?" Jack asked, studying her thoughtfully.

"I have something to tell you." Sarah paused and looked down at the ground. When she could bring herself to meet his eyes, she went on. "Right from the beginning, Prince was perfect. He was striding out, and we quickly got to the big log. I should have turned him around then and headed back, like you told me. But Prince wanted to go on. And I let him." Jack was quiet, listening, as a frown spread over his face.

"We jumped the log and kept on going. I didn't stop him. He was cantering so beautifully, loving it. When we got to the ridge, he galloped even faster. We went all the way to the top." Sarah paused, looking for Jack's reaction. She went on to tell him about the moose and how she had asked Prince to take off down the trail before it could charge. "Then when I asked him to stop, he did. He didn't fight me. He didn't panic. He listened." Sarah searched Jack's face for the slightest indication he understood what she was sharing—that for those minutes she and her horse had become one creature, and *that* was why she kept going.

Jack didn't reply right away, but his stern expression spoke volumes. Sarah's heart sank. Finally he spoke, his voice clipped. "It sounds like you had a thrilling ride, but it might not have turned out so well. You're fortunate the moose didn't charge you, because we're into rutting season, and a bull moose is quick to charge anything he thinks is challenging his territory. You were wise to get out of there fast. 'Tis also possible there may be negative impact from letting an unfit horse gallop up that long, steep ridge. His muscles could tie up, which would be serious. You'll have to watch him closely for the next hour."

Sarah looked at Jack in alarm. In disregarding his instructions, she might have hurt her horse. She hung her head, unable to meet his gaze. "Prince was so good. And now I feel awful, not just because I might have hurt him, but because I didn't listen to you. I guess I've let you down."

"Your horse's care should always come first," Jack said, all business. "Make sure he has plenty of water and cut his grain in half tonight. Hand-walk him when you get back to his stall. If you notice any stiffness to his walk, or if the muscles in his hindquarters feel hard to the touch, call me at once. 'Tis a vet he'll be needing and fast."

Jack went back to setting up the jump, but paused to make one final comment. "I am disappointed in you, Sarah, because I thought you took your horse's training more seriously. But I do appreciate your being forthright and honest. From now on, *you* need to make the decisions, not your horse. Use your head and don't take chances on a whim of the moment."

Sarah rushed back to Prince's stall and immediately attached the lead shank to his halter and walked him to the courtyard. Thankfully he seemed fine. A wave of relief passed over her. On the way back to Crown Prince's stall, they passed Gus in the midst of cleaning Wichita's stall. Sarah halted her horse in front of the open door.

"Hi Gus." She waited for the craggy older man to pause in his work. When Gus turned her way, Sarah said, "Prince had a pretty demanding workout, and Jack says there's a chance he might tie up. He seems fine right now, but Jack told me to cut tonight's grain in half. I'm going to walk him again later to see if he's okay. I just thought you should know."

Gus jammed the manure fork into the bedding and glowered at her. "You rode him too hard again! When are you going to learn anything?" Sarah hung her head and walked away, not surprised at Gus's reaction. But she'd *had* to tell him. This way, when she left for the night, he'd be sure to keep checking on her horse. Once Prince was back in his stall, she went directly to the feed room, unlocked the heavy door, and removed half the grain ration she'd dished into his pail for the night feed. He would know he'd been shortchanged, but it couldn't be helped. After she had walked him again a short time later, she thought about heading for home. Prince seemed perfectly fine, thank goodness, with no change in his walk or the muscles in his hindquarters.

As Sarah swung onto her bicycle and started up the farm road, she thought about the important business on her to-do list at home. She needed to tackle the essay Ms. Dunlop had assigned—it was due Monday morning—but more importantly, she wanted to tell her mother how good Prince had been on the trail ride, of course leaving out the part how she'd ignored Jack's instructions. When she turned into the driveway, Sarah was glad to see her mother's SUV in the garage. The Creamery was still open on weekends, which meant her father and Abby were still at work. Sarah found her mother reading in the family room.

Mrs. Wagner closed her paperback when Sarah came to sit beside her on the plaid loveseat. "How was your day at Brookmeade?" her mother asked.

Sarah took a deep breath before starting. "Mom, you don't have to worry anymore about how Prince is going to behave in the woods. We went by ourselves on the old orchard trail, and he was amazing. And guess what! While we were on the trail, we met a bull moose, a big one with huge antlers. Prince just stood there, staring at him. I was afraid the moose might charge, so I asked

Prince to get out of there fast. He did, but then he came right back to me when I asked him to walk. He didn't make one mistake the whole ride. He's such a totally fantastic horse!"

"I'm glad to hear that," Mrs. Wagner said, putting her book down on the table. "And now you're also going to tell me a flock of wild turkeys flew up in front of you, and Prince chose that moment to take a quick nap. Right?" She looked at Sarah pointedly, waiting for an answer.

Sarah's heart sank. Every good thing that happened on the trail that day wasn't going to make any difference to her mother. It all boiled down to turkeys. "Actually, we didn't see any turkeys," Sarah admitted.

As she always did when making a serious point, Mrs. Wagner spoke evenly, not in a rush. "Then we both know that the jury is still out on the safety question, isn't it? I'm happy things went so well today, but you have to know I'm still concerned about you riding that big horse. And your father is, too." Mrs. Wagner picked up her book when Sarah got up to leave. "Thanks for sharing your day. I hope you'll have many more good rides on Crown Prince."

Sarah went to her room, pulled out her desk chair, and turned on her laptop. As it booted up, she tried to think of ideas for the essay that was due in English class, but her mind was blank. Her eyes scanned the posters of the great race mares, Rachel Alexandra and Zenyatta, on the wall near her desk. She closed her eyes and relived Prince's incredible gallop up to the old orchard. Even if her mother wasn't impressed, it had been an unbelievable day for her and her horse. Suddenly she knew. Of course. She'd write about her day's adventure with Crown Prince!

CHAPTER 9

Moving Up

SARAH GOT TO THE FARM on Wednesday a few minutes after the Romanos arrived. Fanny was already off the trailer, and Sarah parked her bike near where Kayla was grooming her horse. Sarah went to Fanny's head and ran her fingers lightly over the perfect diamond on the mare's forehead. "Fanny looks great," she said. "Her coat shines like a new penny. I hope I'll be able to watch some of your lesson today, before I get Prince ready to ride in the four o'clock class. You think you'll be mainly jumping?"

"Yeah, Jack said we might go out on the hunt course or maybe school on a few cross-country obstacles in the meadow," Kayla said, running a dandy brush down Fanny's legs. The galloping boots, which Kayla put on Fanny's front legs when she jumped her, lay on the grass close by. "Paige and Tim are doing the Hobby Horse Farm event pretty soon, so they'll love that."

Mrs. Romano stepped out of the trailer's dressing room carrying Kayla's tack. "Hi, Sarah," she said. "I understand you had some excitement when Crown Prince was spooked by wild turkeys on the trail. I hope he's okay."

"Hi, Mrs. Romano. Yes, thanks. He got a cut on his leg, but nothing serious. He's fine now."

Hearing the sound of a large rig coming down the farm road, they turned to see Rita Snyder's van approach. They looked at each other and smiled—it was a good time for Sarah to leave. She pushed her bike to the side door of the barn, eager to see Crown Prince. She could clearly envision his finely sculpted head, large, intelligent eye, and black forelock falling to the brink of his white star. Prince's welcoming nicker when he saw her come around the corner had become a regular occurrence, and today was no exception.

But Sarah wasn't pleased when she got closer. Prince must have been turned out that morning in a wet paddock, because his right side was caked with dried mud.

"Ugh!" she said, as she hugged his head. "You're a mess! How could you do this to me, Prince?"

After he finished his carrot, Sarah decided she'd better get to it. Grooming was sure to take a lot longer than usual. She rushed to the tack room to get her things before putting Prince on cross-ties. Billows of dust were rising as she curried his dirty side when Derek arrived on the scene.

"Hey!" he said, laughing, as he got closer to Prince. "Are there dirt bombs going off in here?"

Sarah stopped currying for a minute and stepped back from her grimy horse, waving dust away from her face. "He picked a good day to do this! I'm riding in the four o'clock class."

"Lucky you," Derek said, as the corners of his mouth turned up in a grin.

"How did your lesson with Jack go?" Sarah asked, as she got busy again with the curry. "Did he place you in a class?"

"Actually I'm going to stick with privates with Jack, because no one else in the barn does jumpers. But that's cool. I really like Jack's instruction. He has a nice way of gradually increasing the difficulty of what we're doing, so Bismarck isn't overfaced."

Derek turned to go to his horse while Sarah continued grooming Prince. She spent a lot of time with the curry comb and brushes until his coat got back its usual shine. As a final step, she dampened a grooming cloth and ran it lightly over his coat to pick up any remaining dust. She stepped back to appraise his appearance —the difference was amazing! She left him on the cross-ties while she went to get a wheelbarrow and manure fork for cleaning his stall. It would be nice to have that chore out of the way before she warmed him up for their lesson.

Sarah hadn't ridden in a group since the ill-fated ride several months before when Gray Fox had run away with her. She considered what the lesson today would be like. She'd made up her mind she would take Mrs. DeWitt's advice and totally ignore Kelly and Nicole. In fact, she'd stay as far away from them as possible. If they were looking for a confrontation, she was determined not to give it to them.

After Sarah finished cleaning Prince's stall, she checked her watch. There was still time to sneak out to watch some of the Young Riders class. She put Prince away and hurried down the aisle. The indoor arena was vacant, so she looked out on the hunt course. No one was riding there, either. They had to be in the meadow, which had a few cross-country obstacles.

When Sarah stepped out of the barn, she could see Tim cantering Rhodes toward the vertical-to-bank obstacle. The bank, a substantial earthen mound rising several feet above the field, was reinforced with railroad timbers and had a vertical telephone pole jump two strides in front of it. Jack stood near the bank while the other riders and their horses stood under some shade trees on the edge of the meadow.

"Keep that rhythm," Sarah heard Jack call to Tim. "Eyes up

and wait for your horse. Don't get ahead of him." Rhodes got into the jump perfectly, which set him up nicely to do the bank in two strides. Rhodes easily leaped to the top of the bank, and after one stride, jumped off on the other side. Tim was grinning as they cantered away, knowing he'd ridden it well. He gave Rhodes a hearty smack on his neck. "Good job, Tim," Jack called after him. "After such a good effort, it's time to stop."

From the corner of her eye, Sarah noticed Derek coming out of the barn leading Bismarck, tacked up and ready to ride. Derek walked over to stand beside her, and together they watched the riders in the meadow. "Tim rides well," he said, "and he's got a nice horse."

"He sure does," Sarah said. "I need to get on Prince pretty soon, so I won't be able to watch much longer. I hope Kayla will ride next." She was disappointed when Jack signaled to Rita.

"Who's that?" Derek asked, nodding toward Rita and her black horse.

"That's Rita Snyder and Chancellor. He's an imported Dutch Warmblood. She does hunters and equitation shows with him, but she also wants to try eventing."

They watched as Rita asked Chancellor for canter and then made a large circle in the meadow before coming straight toward the obstacle. Unlike show jumping fences, where the rails sat in cups attached to the jump standards and fell down if a horse rapped them with his feet, the telephone pole jump was built solidly and designed not to give. A mistake could be costly.

Rita rode the combination perfectly, keeping Chancellor at a steady pace in his approach while using enough leg so he knew they were committed to the fence. He jumped the vertical in good form, his body basculing with his knees tucked up high, followed by an easy lift onto the bank and a jump off it a stride later. It was the usual excellent performance by Rita and her expensive, well-trained horse.

"They're good. Chancellor's a great mover." Derek said. "Maybe you can introduce me some time." Sarah was surprised at the stab of jealousy she felt. It hadn't occurred to her that Derek might show some interest in Rita. But they went to the same school, and maybe Derek found her attractive. Sarah should have expected it.

"Sure," Sarah said, looking down at her watch. She really couldn't stay a minute longer. The last thing she wanted was to show up at Prince's first group lesson with an overly energetic horse. "But right now I've gotta go!" She hurried back to Prince's stall.

Her first stop was the tack room, where she pulled on her tall black boots. Her paddock boots would do for trail rides and regular schooling sessions, but for lessons, Sarah always wore her tall boots. She put on her riding helmet and grabbed a jumping bat before picking up her tack. From the beginning, Jack had insisted she ride Prince with a crop, even though she didn't feel she needed it. Prince was so willing to do as she asked, and the thought of hitting him was repulsive to her. But she carried it because Jack said she should. She dreaded the time she would ever have to use it.

After saddling and bridling her horse, Sarah led him toward the indoor. Coming closer to the arena gate, she saw two horses already being ridden there. Kelly and Nicole were trotting around the track. *I think we'll warm-up outside,* she thought.

Sarah turned Prince around in the aisle and started back just as two riding students Sarah didn't know approached her. They were leading the schoolies, Gray Fox and McDuff, to the indoor, and would probably be riding in the four o'clock class, too. Sarah asked Prince to walk close to the wall so the horses could pass easily, and she displayed a friendly smile as the girls came closer. She was puzzled when the first one just looked straight ahead as she steered Gray Fox as far from Prince as she could as they passed. When the second girl got nearer, she suddenly pulled McDuff sharply away from Prince. "Don't let him kick me!" she cried. Sarah just shook her head. *I guess I know who's been brain-washing them!*

Derek had left on his hack, but the cross-country school for the Young Riders was still going on when Sarah led Crown Prince out of the barn toward the outdoor ring. The class had finished with the jump-to-bank obstacle and was now practicing over stacked straw bales. Prince spotted the activity in the meadow and halted abruptly when he saw Quarry circling the field at a brisk canter. Prince's ears were pricked forward and his eyes fixed on Quarry as the gray horse sailed over the jump.

"Think you'd like to try that some day?" Sarah asked, stroking his neck before she mounted from the block. Prince didn't move when Sarah nudged him forward, his attention still riveted on the horses in the meadow. "Come on," she said, using her legs firmly, and Prince finally walked forward while rubber-necking to watch Quarry. *Maybe the time will come when I'll be glad I have the crop,* she thought. *A little tap might help when he's distracted like this.*

When they entered the sand ring, Prince's attention was still focused on the horses in the field, but she put him into a brisk trot. Schooling figures required him to pay attention to what she was asking, so she rode countless circles, changes of direction, and walk-trot transitions. She felt Prince gradually relax and listen more attentively to her. When he seemed less distracted by the horses in the field, she sat the trot and asked for a right lead canter. Jack had explained that every horse had a stronger side and a lead he preferred—and Prince's was his right. Prince made a smooth transition and cantered a large circle of half the ring with good rhythm and cadence. Sarah had just brought him back to trot when she saw Jack and the Young Riders walking from the meadow toward the barn. *Time to scoot over to the indoor,* she thought.

The main entrance to the indoor arena was open, so Sarah could ride her horse inside without having to dismount to open the gate. The four other horses and their riders were warming up, mainly trotting on the track going large. The oversized arena provided ample space for all of them to work independently without getting in each other's way. Sarah scanned the group of adults sitting on the bleachers, noticing some people she'd never seen before.

Sarah had no sooner begun walking Prince on the track when Jack appeared through the side entrance. As in all his classes, he began by welcoming the riders and introducing her, the new addition. The lesson got no further before two women strode across the arena toward the instructor. One of the women had super-short brunette hair and large dangling earrings. Sarah thought she was Mrs. Hoffman, Kelly's mother, and although she couldn't be sure, it occurred to her the overweight second woman might be Nicole Jordan's mother. Immediately Sarah stiffened, fearing the worst.

When the two women got close to Jack, Mrs. Hoffman spoke loud enough for all of the riders and onlookers to hear. "What is *that* girl doing in this class?" she demanded, turning to point at Sarah. "I thought I made it perfectly clear that I didn't want that dangerous animal in a class with Kelly and Midnight Jet. I have too much invested in my daughter's horse to take a chance of him being kicked again, and I want Kelly to feel safe riding here."

It was the first time Sarah ever remembered seeing Jack at a momentary loss for words. He appeared totally unprepared for

Mrs. Hoffman's rude interruption and accusations, but he recovered quickly and responded in a pleasant, professional manner.

"I'm happy that Jet came out of the incident you described without a mark. I've yet to see him act sore or take a bad step. In fact, 'tis questionable that Crown Prince really kicked him. There's a difference between kicking out and actually kicking another horse."

Mrs. Hoffman inhaled a deep breath, rising to her full height. "It sounds like you don't believe what I told you. You're basically accusing me of lying, and I'm highly insulted!"

By now, all the riders in the class had halted their horses, and Sarah saw many eyes from the bleachers staring at her. If only she and Prince could gallop from this place, leaving all the ridiculous conflict behind! To hear her horse falsely accused of kicking Midnight Jet made her angry, and it was especially frustrating to know that it was all based on Kelly's lies. It was Kelly's word against hers. Perhaps other people couldn't be sure what to believe, but Jack had examined Midnight Jet, so at least *he* knew the truth. She glanced over at Kelly and saw the girl was sneering, thoroughly enjoying her mother's performance.

The overweight woman now stepped closer to take her turn addressing Jack. "I totally agree. I'm afraid that if Nicole rides in a class with that ill-mannered horse, it will be dangerous for Jubilee. You know how long it has taken for her to recover and become sound again. We can't take any chances Jubilee or Nicole might get kicked."

"Ladies," Jack said, his face grim and drawn, "my responsibility at Brookmeade Farm is to provide a quality equestrian program for *all* our riders. That includes excellent instruction in a safe, supportive environment. I would never place a horse I consider dangerous in a class where it might harm another horse or student. 'Tis my judgment that in this large indoor arena, Crown Prince does not put Jubilee and Midnight Jet or your daughters at risk."

Mrs. Hoffman's face was red and her fists were clenched. Not only had Jack ignored her directive, but now he was defending Sarah's horse, and this obviously intensified her anger. Her voice was even louder than before when she said, "Do you know how much money the Jordans and I spend at this farm every month?"

Jack looked at Sarah, who was feeling increasingly embarrassed. For a moment he appeared to consider how to respond to the situation. Then he turned from the two women and walked over to Crown Prince. Looking up at Sarah, he spoke in a hushed tone. "I'm sorry for all this, Sarah," he said. "What would you think of going back into your previous class, the Young Riders? You'd not have to deal with such hostile behavior."

To Sarah, Jack's words brought a giant swell of relief, as if she'd been plucked from the grip of a tidal wave. She could go back into her old class with Kayla where she wouldn't have to deal with Kelly and Nicole! Somehow Prince would catch up with the more advanced horses. Her delighted smile told Jack everything he needed to know.

"Why don't you walk Prince out of the arena and take him for a short hack," Jack said. "We'll talk more about this later." As Sarah headed for the out-gate, Jack walked back to Mrs. Hoffman and Mrs. Jordan. "We have a solution to what you insist is a problem," he said in a restrained, soothing voice. "Sarah is willing to ride Crown Prince in my Young Riders class, so you and your daughters won't be in the same arena with Crown Prince, and therefore under no threat." Then, more gruffly: "Now let's get on with this lesson. Too much time has been wasted!"

Just before Sarah reached the out gate, she glanced back at

Kelly. The smirk on the girl's face had been replaced with smoldering fury. *I guess she's not happy that Prince and I will be moving back into the Young Riders class* she thought, a little gleefully. *Serves those jerks right!*

Once outside, Sarah guided Crown Prince toward the old orchard trailhead, which brought her close to Kayla's horse trailer. Fanny had been loaded and was pulling hay from the net while Mrs. Romano put the tack away. Kayla walked toward Sarah, taking big bites out of an apple. She looked puzzled. "What's up?" she asked. "Why are you finishing so soon? Something wrong?"

"I'll say," Sarah answered, shaking her head. "Kelly's mother made a big stink in front of everyone, complaining to Jack that Prince shouldn't be in that class because he's a kicker and dangerous. Mrs. Jordan protested, too. Then Jack asked me if I'd like to ride in your class again, and of course I said yes. So Prince and I will be with you next week. Is that awesome or what!"

"Slow down," Kayla said, frowning. She paused, chewing more on her apple. "Because of Kelly's lie about Prince kicking Midnight Jet, your horse gets knocked out of the class? That doesn't sound fair. Doesn't Jack know what really happened?"

"He does, Kayla, but I don't care. I'm totally thrilled! I'll be riding with you guys again. It doesn't matter if I was thrown under the bus."

Rita walked over to join them. "How come your class was so short?" she asked Sarah. "Is your horse off?"

"Sarah's going to start riding with our class again," Kayla said. "Jack says Prince is a better fit with us than the four o'clock class."

Rita didn't appear happy when she looked up at Sarah. "You mean your green Thoroughbred that came off the track three months ago is moving up to our advanced Young Riders class this soon? Isn't that quite a leap? How can he possibly keep up with the stuff we're doing?"

Sarah closed her eyes and shook her head. Just when things were looking up, now she had to deal with Rita again. Kayla came to her rescue. "Look, Rita, after the training Crown Prince has gotten the last few months, he's at least on the level of Lady Tate and Gray Fox. Sarah used to do just fine in our class on those school horses. Don't make a big deal out of this."

"I can just see Jack having to take time to lower the fences when it's Prince's turn to jump," Rita complained. "Why should the rest of us have to wait around while he changes things for a green horse? I don't think my dad will be thrilled when he hears about this!"

Rita turned and started back to the Pyramid van. After taking a few steps, she turned back to them. "Do you always need to butt in, Kayla? Can't you let Sarah speak for herself for once?" Rita marched off and hopped in her van's cab with Judson."

"Terrific," Sarah said, as they pulled away, traveling slowly as the van labored up the hill. "Rita will go home and freak out to her father about this. I'll have another angry parent on my case!"

Kayla shook her head. "Just tell Rita you're in our class to stay and she better get used to it!"

Sarah waved to Kayla as her friend started toward her mom's truck. She turned Prince toward the trailhead and soon he was on the trail, stepping lightly on the pine needles. He seemed glad to be in the woods and looked ahead eagerly, perhaps remembering their recent ride up the ridge. The air felt fresh and cool, full of the aroma of the pine trees. Prince's ears flicked back and forth, listening to Sarah's aids while he worked the bit in his mouth. Sarah reached down to stroke his neck.

As Prince continued briskly on the trail, Sarah couldn't help thinking about the events of the afternoon. With no special accomplishments on their part, she and Prince had graduated into the Young Riders' advanced class. She would show her appreciation to Jack by following his instructions to the letter from now on. He'd suggested a short hack in the woods today, and that's what they'd do, regardless of how much Prince might want to go farther. She pushed all the unpleasantness out of her mind and let herself love the moment.

CHAPTER 10
The Meadow Trail

BACK AT THE FARM after their short hack on the trail, Sarah dismounted by the side door and led her horse to his stall. Prince's first group lesson had never gotten off the ground, thanks to Kelly and Nicole's mothers, but that hadn't stopped Prince and her from having a great trail ride. Sarah removed his tack, and after giving Prince a once-over with a soft brush, led him into his stall. He lowered his head so she could gently stroke his face and lightly tug on his ears, his eyes softening and wrinkling at the corners as they had the day they met.

Sarah was in Prince's stall when Derek returned with Bismarck after schooling in the outdoor ring. Sarah knew he would be full of questions, and she hoped he wouldn't notice her. She was tired of thinking about all the barn drama. But on his way back from the tack room, Derek noticed Sarah's slim figure standing beside her horse. He approached the stall, looking in.

"Everything okay?" he asked.

Sarah turned away from Prince and slipped out of the stall. When she said nothing, Derek studied her face, puzzled. She looked into his eyes for a moment and then hung her head wearily. "It's complicated," she said. "I really can't talk about what happened this afternoon, except to tell you I'm not going to be riding with Kelly and Nicole. I'll be in the Young Riders class."

"Didn't you ride with that class once before?"

"Yes, before I got Crown Prince. It seems so long ago," Sarah said. She felt strangely unenthusiastic.

Derek shook his head. "I get the feeling there's a lot of stuff going on under the radar here. Wanna fill me in?"

"Maybe sometime, but not right now. I've got to go feed the horses." Sarah turned away, heading to the feed room. She removed the key from around her neck and unlocked the massive door. A chorus of neighs rang out in the barn when she pushed the grain cart through the door. She went from stall to stall, dishing out dinner.

Derek was gone when Sarah returned to Prince's stall. For once, she was relieved he wasn't around. The events of the day had left her emotionally drained, and all she wanted was to go home. She stood back to take one final look at her horse. She had bedded his stall with fresh shavings, and now he was cleaning up the last of the grain in his feed tub. His water bucket was full, and two flakes of hay were stacked in the corner. Knowing he was well taken care of gave her a good feeling. No matter how many problems she encountered with the boarders at Brookmeade Farm, Crown Prince was worth it!

When she got home, Sarah sat on the bench in the mudroom removing her paddock boots. Her mother had heard the screen door shut and called out to her, "Hi, honey." When there was no response, she came to the doorway.

Sarah looked up. "Oh, hi, Mom."

Her mother frowned. She could tell from Sarah's expression that something was wrong. "After you've washed up, come on in and tell me what's going on." She retreated to the kitchen and the tossed salad she was making.

Here we go again, Sarah thought. She washed her hands and began to set the table while her mother sliced tomatoes and cucumbers.

"Weren't you planning to ride Crown Prince in a group lesson for the first time today? How'd it go?" Mrs. Wagner asked.

Sarah didn't feel like going through the whole thing again, and she hadn't even told her parents about the kicking incident. She was afraid the story would only give them more ammunition for labeling Prince a rogue, so she took her time responding to her mother's question. "Dad and Abby will probably want to hear about it, too. Can I tell you at dinner time?" Her mother cast her a sideways glance, but let it pass.

"Call me when dinner's ready," Sarah said after she finished filling the water glasses. Slowly she climbed the stairs and went to her room. She sat on the edge of her bed and buried her face in her hands. What was wrong with her? She should be ecstatic about moving back into the Young Riders class, so why did she feel so down? Was the burden of having enemies at the barn taking its toll? She looked at the tote bag she'd left in a chair earlier. The thought of the couple hours of homework she'd have after dinner actually sounded appealing. At least that would get her mind off her problems at Brookmeade Farm.

A short time later, snatches of muffled conversation drifting upstairs meant Abby and her father were home. When her mother called her for dinner, Sarah went down to join the family at the table. Spaghetti and meatballs was a favorite for all of them, and as they dug in, Abby was full of talk about school. But Sarah knew her turn was coming.

Finally her mother said, "Sarah's promised to tell us about her first group lesson with Crown Prince."

Sarah swallowed hard. She really didn't want to tell them the story about the kick, but she also didn't want to slip into telling any outright lies. "There's not much to tell, actually," she began. "Jack decided we should ride with the Young Riders, my old class, so I didn't have a lesson today after all."

"Well, well, you're moving up," her father said, smiling. "That sounds like good news to me."

Her mother looked at her intently. "Considering the good news, you looked kind of glum when you got home," her mother said. "Any special reason?"

"I'm just really tired, I guess. I've been working hard at the barn." That was absolutely true, and Sarah breathed a sigh of relief when her response seemed to satisfy everyone. The conversation shifted to Abby's chatter about a new bulletin board her class was working on.

"It's about good manners, being nice to people," Abby said. "It's supposed to stop bullying in our school.

I'd sure like to see a few good manners at Brookmeade Farm! Sarah thought.

* * * * *

Pedaling her bike to the farm after school the next day, Sarah tried to think positive thoughts. No more worrying about Kelly and Nicole. She wouldn't let Rita get under her skin, either. The crisp fall air felt cool on her face. It was a perfect day for a hack, and she was psyched! There would be time to practice flatwork in the ring another day.

Paige and Tim had gotten to the farm ahead of her, and their horses were already tacked up. They were in the courtyard when she arrived, getting ready to mount and take off. "Where are you going?" Sarah asked, slowing her bicycle.

"After the tough lesson yesterday, we're going to do an easy hack," Tim said. "We've got to get going, but maybe next time you can go with us."

"Hey, congrats on being moved up to the Young Riders," Paige said.

"Thanks, Paige" Sarah said, waving. "Have a great ride. I'd love to go with you some time."

With her horse turned out in a paddock, Sarah decided to do his stall right away. She finished by adding fresh bedding and then went out to retrieve her horse, hoping he'd not be a mud ball again today. Prince was no longer restricted to the smallest paddock, as he had been when he first came to Brookmeade Farm, so now he could pick up a little more speed if he felt like running.

Sarah spotted Prince in the far end of a paddock. He raised his head from the grass when she whistled softly and immediately left his grazing, coming to her through shadows cast by the afternoon sun. He nuzzled her sweatshirt. "Hey, buddy," she said, stroking his neck. She attached the lead shank to his halter and led him back to the barn, where Derek was now grooming Bismarck on the cross-ties.

"What's up for today?" he asked her, as she clipped another set of the cross-ties to Prince's halter.

"It's a perfect day for a hack," Sarah replied.

Dirt and dust flew out of his curry comb when Derek knocked it against his dandy brush. As he resumed currying Bismarck's hindquarters, he said, "Sure is. I want to find the meadow trail Mrs. DeWitt told me about. Want to come with me?"

Sarah's heart almost skipped a beat. This totally cool guy had just asked her to go for a ride with him!

"Ah, sure," she stammered awkwardly. "I'll try not to keep you waiting." She started for the tack room, and once around the corner and out of his sight, broke into a jog. But she had to move considerably slower on the return trip, carrying her tack, grooming equipment, helmet, and half-chaps all at once.

Sarah curried and brushed Prince in silence, quickly combing his mane and brushing the snarls out of his tail before saddling him. The cut on his leg had healed nicely and no longer required a polo wrap for protection, thank goodness. She didn't feel coordinated today! She glanced over to see that Bismarck was saddled and Derek was about to bridle him. Sarah quickly put on her half chaps and riding helmet. Now Derek was standing beside Bismarck, waiting for her to finish tacking up. She hurried as fast as she could, but seemed to be all thumbs. Her nervousness was making Prince tense, and he raised his head high in the air, making it impossible for Sarah to pull the bridle over his ears. She felt foolish and frustrated when she heard Derek trying to smother a laugh.

"Would you like a leg up to bridle your horse?" he asked, with a grin.

Sarah scowled, irritated, but when she looked up at Prince with his head in the clouds, she, too, couldn't resist a laugh. "He thinks he's part giraffe!" She put pressure on the reins around his neck and said with a tone of authority, "Down!" Once Prince had lowered his head, she quickly put on his bridle.

A few minutes later, Sarah and Derek led their horses out of the barn. Mrs. DeWitt was just arriving as they moved toward the mounting block in the courtyard.

"You've picked a glorious day for a ride," she said, smiling broadly.

"We're going to explore the meadow trail," Sarah said.

"Oh, I know you're going to like it. Have a wonderful time!" Sarah wasn't sure how to interpret the twinkle in Mrs. Dewitt's eyes. Was it because she and Derek were riding together?

Sarah mounted Prince from the block, but from the ground

Derek easily placed his foot in the stirrup and swung up into the saddle on Bismarck. Then they were on their way. The sun felt warm as they guided their horses to the farm's entry road and started climbing the hill to the O'Brien bungalow.

"Jack told me the trailhead is close to the carriage shed," Derek said. As they got closer to the building where the broodmares and Jack's horse were stabled, they spotted a worn area beside the road that led toward the nearby pasture's split-rail fencing. The path appeared to have been recently mowed, providing a four-foot-wide swath going away from the road. "This must be it," Derek said, as he steered his horse onto the path. It was new territory for both horses, and Prince seemed eager to follow Bismarck.

They hadn't traveled far along the path when a loud neigh pierced the quiet. A large liver chestnut horse suddenly burst from the far end of the pasture, charging toward them like an angry bull. His long mane billowed in the wind created by his speed. As the horse thundered toward them, Crown Prince became animated, sidestepping away from the fence and prancing with his tail plumed high. Bismarck stood his ground, his eyes riveted on the horse. As the chestnut got closer, he slowed dramatically, dancing as if on springs with his nostrils flaring. He'd never seen these horses before, and he snorted suspiciously.

"This is Jack's horse, Donegal Lad," Sarah said, while keeping a tight rein on Prince. "Maybe he likes to think the broodmares and their foals in the next pasture are his herd and he needs to protect them."

"What a beauty!" Derek replied. "He's good-sized and probably stronger than an armored tank. Look at those hindquarters! I'll bet he could easily handle a five-foot oxer."

"Jack rode him in the Olympics when he was on the Irish eventing team. I guess Lad was awesome going cross-country."

"Let's give him a little excitement," Derek said, as he asked Bismarck for an extended trot, continuing on the path that followed the fence line. Not to be left behind, Prince immediately took after him, and soon both horses were cantering briskly along the mowed path, with Donegal Lad galloping beside them on the other side of the fence. Both horses pulled against their reins to go faster, and Sarah and Derek found themselves laughing as they moved speedily across the field. Their horses were sleek, powerful machines, with their hoofbeats resounding like drumbeats.

While Bismarck and Crown Prince continued on the trail beyond the pasture fence, Donegal Lad was forced to come to a skidding halt at the corner of the fence line. His whinny of frustration pierced the air while the other two horses continued at a hand gallop, leaving him behind. When Prince lessened his pull on the bit, Sarah relaxed her hold. In response, Prince seemed to shift gears. He grabbed the bit in his teeth and exploded with a burst of speed that quickly put him far ahead of Bismarck. With every stride he distanced himself farther.

Looking ahead, Sarah saw the path would soon leave the field and enter a thickly wooded area. *Oops*, she thought, *this is getting out of hand!* Quickly she used the pulley rein technique that earlier in the summer had worked so effectively on the runaway, Gray Fox. She shortened her left rein while crossing the right rein slightly over Prince's neck and pulling it as hard as she could. Instantly, she felt his pace slacken, as he gave in to the pressure of the bit. Sarah pulled again, and this time her horse slowed noticeably. She was in control!

Prince had opened up a substantial lead over Derek's horse, but with Prince now back to canter, Bismarck galloped up beside him. "Wow!" Derek shouted to Sarah. "With speed like that, your horse should be at Churchill Downs."

"His former owner thought so, too," Sarah yelled back.

The horses came back to trot just as the trail led them into the darkened forest. It was probably an old logging road, wide enough for a vehicle, and the two horses were able to trot abreast. "That's something I'd like to know more about," Derek said. "Let's give the horses a break and walk for a while. You can tell me Crown Prince's story."

After slowing their horses, they made their way side-by-side deeper into the forest. Derek turned to Sarah, and his eyes met hers. "Why don't you start at the beginning?" he said. "We have plenty of time."

"You're asking for it," Sarah replied jokingly as she turned away. "I hope this trail will be long enough for me to cover everything." The story tumbled out, as Sarah told Derek about her mother's accident and her parents' inability to buy her a horse. She described how the DeWitts had arranged for her to choose a horse at the racetrack, and that she'd picked the one that was considered unridable, a rogue. And then a monster of a wolf tooth was discovered as the likely source of his bad behavior when bridled. She went on to tell Derek how she'd turned down a large sum of money, enough to put her through college—and a good one, at that—when Prince's former owner had tried to persuade her to give him back. She explained that in order to keep him, she still had to prove to her parents that Prince was safe to ride.

There was more Sarah could have told Derek, but she was reluctant to tell him about Rita. After all, as far as she knew, he hadn't even met Rita. She felt a twinge when she remembered his eagerness for an introduction.

Derek ducked under a low branch as Bismarck pushed forward on the trail. "When I rode with Kelly and Nicole last week," he said, "they were running on, telling me a million things about the farm and everyone who rides here. But I always felt they were skirting around some stuff."

"I can just imagine what they said about me," Sarah quipped, as she reached down to stroke Prince's neck.

"I got the impression they didn't want to talk about you. They had tons to tell me about Tim and Paige, though. Even Kayla. What's the deal?"

Sarah didn't want to sound like a gossip, and at first she hesitated. "I used to ride in Kelly and Nicole's class. Last year they both wanted to join the Young Riders, but Jack said they had to wait. It was before I got Crown Prince, and they were really ticked when I started riding in that class using schoolies. They've carried a grudge against me ever since." Then she told Derek about the kick. "Jack knows that Kelly lied to her mother and anyone else who would listen. He decided the best way to douse the flames would be to take me out of the four o'clock class. So that's why I'm back with the Young Riders, but I don't think Jack's plan thrilled those girls."

They rode in silence for a few minutes until Derek spoke. "This explains a lot."

Sarah shifted her eyes from the trail ahead to meet Derek's gaze. "There are some great people at Brookmeade Farm," she assured him. "You'll really like Tim, Paige, Kayla, and especially the DeWitts. The instructors are totally cool—I can't imagine there's a more awesome instructor than Jack. There are also a lot of boarders I don't know very well. And then there's Gus. He's on the grumpy side, but he takes great care of the horses." She shortened her right rein to keep Prince from grabbing leaves along the trail. "The farm's not perfect, sure, but you shouldn't feel bothered by my drama. I'm sorry if I unloaded some hostile stuff on you."

"I'm glad you did," Derek said. He grinned. "I seem to be seeing a lot of Kelly and Nicole these days."

Sarah shot him a grim smile. "According to Paige, Tim does, too, although perhaps less since you came to town."

They picked up trot on a straight section of the trail where the footing was good, with Derek and Bismarck in the lead. Sarah was relieved Prince didn't mind being in second place; he didn't pull on the reins or try to pass. Coming around a bend, they saw where the trail left the woods and entered a green field of waving grass. A mowed path ran along the edge of the field.

"Where are we?" Sarah called, bringing Prince back to walk. "I'm completely lost!"

Derek slowed his horse as well. "According to Mrs. DeWitt, we should be near the beginning of the entry road. The trail through the woods took us around the broodmares' pastures."

Looking over her shoulder, Sarah gazed at the open field of tall grass. At once she saw split-rail fencing and recognized the pastures she passed on every bike ride to the barn. Soon they were back on the farm road, heading home.

"I like trails that make a loop like this one," Derek said. "It's much better than retracing your steps."

After crossing the wooden bridge over the brook and climbing the hill to the O'Briens' bungalow, the full view of the barn and indoor arena was before them. Within minutes they were back in the courtyard.

Ouch! Sarah thought when she saw Nicole watching them from inside the main entrance. *When we get closer, I'm sure I'll see her eyes are green—green with envy, that is.*

CHAPTER 11

Young Riders

TWENTY MINUTES BEFORE HER LESSON was to start, Sarah led Crown Prince into the indoor arena and over to the mounting block in the corner. To be here this early, she'd set a record for how fast she got out of the house after the bus dropped her off, and her ride to the barn felt like she was on a rocket-propelled bicycle. Finally she and Prince would be in a group lesson, and the best part was she'd be with her friends in the Young Riders class.

The arena was deserted when Sarah arrived with Prince, but she knew the other four riders would be along soon. Paige and Tim were getting their horses ready in the barn, and both the Snyders' and Romanos' rigs were parked outside. She was glad the class would be inside today. Prince had spent a lot of time in the indoor, so he was usually relaxed there. A few barn swallows were flying in the upper regions of the arena, but Prince had seen them many times.

As Sarah settled into the saddle, Rita and Paige filed in with their horses. Rita gave no greeting and seemed to be entirely focused on Chancellor. Paige waved. "Great to have you back, Sarah!"

Sarah gave her a thumbs-up. "Thanks. It's awesome to be here!"

Sarah followed her usual warm-up routine with Prince. She started by asking him for an energetic trot on a long rein while going large in the arena to get her horse to reach forward and down with his head and neck. Jack called it riding "long and low." Then gradually she increased her leg pressure while shortening her reins, to put Prince in a frame between her hand and her leg. He seemed agreeable, trotting willingly and dropping his head down on the bit when she asked.

Sarah hoped Jack would be pleased with how Prince was going. They'd certainly put in a lot of hours over the summer practicing what he had taught her, and the fact Prince had such a willing attitude helped a lot. After going large for a while, she began trotting a circle, gradually spiraling it in and then reversing the process until the circle was its original size before letting Prince walk on a long rein. She reached down to stroke his neck. So far, he was being a good boy!

While she gave Prince a break, Sarah's gaze drifted to the bleachers near the front of the arena. As usual, there were quite a few people sitting there. Some were other boarders, but most were family or friends of the riders. The Dixons almost always came to watch Tim ride, and even if her parents were tied up at their restaurant, Paige's grandmother was usually there. Mr. DeWitt wasn't sitting on the bleachers, but Sarah saw him standing beside them, closely observing the riders as they warmed up.

As she looked closer, Sarah gulped in surprise when she saw *her mother* sitting in the third row. Wednesday was a day Mrs. Wagner usually went to the gift shop to do her bookkeeping, so having her show up for a lesson here at Brookmeade was a bolt from the blue. She must have made a special effort to get time off, but Sarah thought it strange she hadn't told her she was coming.

What was really strange was that her mother was sitting next to Richard Snyder, Rita's father. His business trips usually kept him away during the week, so he rarely, if ever, came to the farm to watch Rita's lessons. A slightly overweight man with thinning dark hair dressed in a business suit, he appeared deeply engrossed in conversation with Mrs. Wagner. Sarah also noticed Derek sitting in the top row with Nicole on one side and Kelly on the other. *Poor Derek*, she thought. *He's got those two leeches surrounding him, whether he likes it or not!* Just then Kelly's mother and Mrs. Romano walked into the arena together and found a place on the bleachers. *What's going on here?* she thought. *Since when are those two buddy-buddy?*

Sarah looked at the clock on the arena wall, wondering where Kayla was. It was unusual for her to be late. Tim had arrived right after Paige, and Jack would be showing up at any moment. The main entrance to the arena was still open, and a few minutes later Kayla trotted fast into the arena on Fanny. Kayla guided Fanny directly onto the track and continued trotting briskly, long and low. *I wonder why Kayla was late?*

Jack strode into the indoor. "Good day to all," he began. Even after living in the states a few years, Jack still spoke with a noticeable Irish accent. "After a cross-country school last week, today we'll be working to improve your horses' work on the flat." When he noticed Sarah, he added, "'Tis probably no surprise to you that Sarah Wagner has returned to this class with Crown Prince."

Jack walked to the center of the arena and began his instruction. "Drop your irons and knot your reins so you can proceed with your body stretching exercises." The group began by reaching down to touch their boots with the opposite hand, alternating from side to side. They had been doing this routine at the beginning of all their lessons since they'd started riding with Jack, and knew the exercises by heart.

The five horses were scattered about the arena, all walking on the track. After Sarah had knotted her reins to shorten them and taken her boots out of her stirrups, she felt Prince began to tense up. She'd never done exercises while on his back. *With my legs off his sides and no rein contact, he might feel abandoned,* she thought. *He's probably wondering what's going on!* A few times Sarah paused what she was doing long enough to stroke his neck. Finally Jack asked them to take back their irons and reins. Prince felt more comfortable when her legs were again in contact with his sides.

"Rather than spreading out to use the whole arena, I'd like you to form a line on the track behind Paige with one horse's length distance between you," Jack called out. "We're going to ride in a drill team formation today, which will require discipline and accurate control of your horses." He waited while some riders cut across the arena and others picked up trot to catch up to the line of horses. Sarah found herself right in the middle, behind Kayla and in front of Rita. Sarah slowed Prince's walk so he wouldn't get closer than one horse's length from Fanny, and then looked over her shoulder at Chancellor. Rita was being careful to maintain her distance, and Sarah noticed Rita's green eyes were glaring at her from under the brim of her expensive helmet.

Suddenly it dawned on her. Many of the observers sitting in the bleachers were there for one reason only. They were waiting, and in fact hoping, for her horse to make a mistake, preferably to kick out at another horse. No doubt Rita was telling anyone who would listen that Prince had nearly bowled Chancellor over on the trail, and of course Kelly was still broadcasting that Prince was a vicious kicker.

Sarah felt a knot growing in the pit of her stomach, and she struggled to turn her attention back to her horse. She breathed deeply to make herself relax. *I'm going to ride just as I did when I had private lessons with Jack,* she thought. *I'm not going to let them get to me!*

"Prepare to trot," Jack called out, and the five riders gathered their horses, getting ready for the transition. When Jack gave the signal, all five horses picked up trot on cue. Sarah was happy with Prince's reaction, moving forward willingly while no longer seeming tense. Being close to the other horses didn't seem to bother him. His ears frequently flicked back in her direction, a sign he was listening to her. At one point she caught their reflection in the mirror that ran the length of one side of the arena, and she was momentarily taken aback by what an eye-catching horse Prince was under saddle.

"Paige, lead the ride across the diagonal at F," Jack called out. Once they were all back on the track, he said, "Paige, circle back to take the rear of the ride." Now Kayla led the ride, and Jack asked every rider to make a fifteen-meter circle, returning to the track where they had left it, bringing them into line again. This required the horses to maintain the same trotting speed, and on the first attempt, Quarry got ahead of the others and Fanny needed to move with more impulsion. Sarah used her aids to ask Prince to bend his body to the shape of the circle, but with his naturally longer stride, she found it was challenging to keep him in sync with the others. She used frequent half-halts to check his gait.

When it was Sarah's turn to lead the ride, Jack asked them to turn across the centerline and to track in the opposite direction once they reached the other side of the arena. Traveling side by side, the riders could easily see the other horses' positions, and everyone arrived at the other side at the same time. "Excellent!" Jack said.

The lesson continued, with Jack asking the class to do various schooling figures while maintaining their positions. Finally he asked them to walk and let their horses go on a free rein. All five horses stretched their heads down, happy to have a break. Sarah was tempted to steer Prince closer to Fanny so she could ask Kayla why she was late, but Jack was talking to the class. She knew that idle conversation during the lesson would not be appreciated.

After a few minutes, Jack asked the riders to line up at the far end of the arena. Each of them would now be asked for individual work. He prescribed a simple equitation test of a figure eight at canter in the center of the arena with a simple change of lead at the center. *Now all my "fans" will be praying for me to totally blow it!* Sarah thought, with a touch of nervousness. In her lessons with Jack, they hadn't yet attempted this exercise. She'd seen this class do a similar exercise a few weeks before, and all of the Young Riders had aced it.

Kayla went first, and rode the whole test without any problems, getting praise from Jack. Fanny looked so pretty, her four white socks moving in rhythm. Tim went next, and Rhodes had amazing transitions in his figure eight. "Very good," Jack said, "although you need to avoid leaning to the inside on your circles, Tim." Paige's try was a little hurried, but for Quarry, it was acceptable. Jack praised them for a good effort.

Sarah was at the end of the line, and she expected Rita to go next, but Rita extended her arm as an invitation for Sarah to go before her. Sarah couldn't help be a little suspicious, but she willed any thoughts of Rita out of her mind. As she turned to the center of the arena to begin a figure eight, she suddenly felt unsure just how to proceed. Coming to the center, she sat the trot and asked Prince for his right lead. She was relieved when he picked it up and they began the loop.

Approaching the center once more, she thought, *I've got to be careful I don't canter beyond X!* She sat deeply in the saddle and asked her horse to come back to trot. Their transition was early, and they had several trot steps before she asked him for left lead canter. Perhaps she was a little frazzled, because Prince picked up the wrong lead. Sarah noticed it immediately and brought him back to trot. She had to make a circle to approach X again, and this time Prince correctly picked up the left lead. She finished the loop before trotting back to her place in the line. She felt self-conscious of her unpolished performance, and frustrated by her nervousness.

Sarah knew everyone had been watching them closely while she rode the short test, and that the spectators awaited Jack's reaction to her ride. "You need to work on this, Sarah," Jack said, "but for Prince's level of training, it wasn't too bad. You made the necessary corrections capably. I suggest you practice the exercise before the next lesson."

Rita smiled broadly as she now asked Chancellor to begin the test. The black Dutch Warmblood was not only correct in every aspect of the exercise, but his movement was beautiful to see. Jack had only flattering comments to make on her ride, and Rita was smirking when she returned to the line.

When the class came to an end, Jack had a few words for them before the group disbanded. "I suggest you all continue to work on your transitions, bending, and straight lines coming down the centerline. Next week I'd like to do more of the same work, and I may possibly be mounted so we can do drill team exercises with an even number of riders."

Kayla and Rita immediately rode their horses out of the arena to the parking area, followed by Kayla's mother, Rita's father, and Judson. Sarah was dying to talk to Kayla, but that would obviously have to wait. Instead, she rode Prince toward the bleachers where her mother was sitting. She halted Prince just as Mrs. Wagner was climbing slowly down from the bleachers. "Hi, Mom," she said. "This is a surprise! You got out of work early?"

Sarah thought her mother's speech and manner seemed reserved when she responded. "Actually, I had the day off. I'm glad I could see you ride. We have a few things to go over, though." She started for the exit. "We'll talk after you get home."

Sarah was dumbfounded. It wasn't like her mother to be short with her unless there was a major issue to be addressed. What was going on? Prince became restless and wanted to move forward. She was about to start for the gate when Derek walked up beside them. He reached up to stroke Prince's neck.

"Chill out, handsome one," he said to Prince, grinning up at her. "I can't imagine a more beneficial lesson for you guys."

Sarah was rattled, but Derek's presence seemed to calm her. For a moment she forgot her mother's coolness and could think only of the boy standing beside her. "Prince didn't totally ace the individual test. I guess we've got our work cut out for us."

"Sarah, he's only been off the track for four months. You've got to be realistic and not expect too much."

She took a deep breath before answering. "I don't think I rode him very well. He's only going to perform as well as I ride him, and when I misjudged the center at X, nothing went well after that."

"Take it easy on yourself," Derek said. "It was your first lesson in front of a lot of people in quite a while. Hey, I'm going to tack up Bismarck. Are you going back now? I'll walk with you."

"Sure," Sarah said, as she dropped her stirrups and slid down from her horse. After pulling the reins over Prince's head and running up her irons, she started for the outgate alongside Derek. They met Nicole and Kelly as they were leading their horses in for the four o'clock lesson.

"Hope you have a good class," Derek called cheerfully. The girls were too busy giving Sarah dirty looks to answer.

When they were out of earshot, Derek said, "Those girls certainly run hot and cold."

Sarah rolled her eyes. "With me, I'm afraid it's all cold."

Later, as Sarah did the night feeding, all she could think about was the conversation with her mother after her lesson. Something was going on. She knew it. She almost dreaded going home to find out.

But first to call Kayla. The Romanos should be home by now. Sarah was relieved when Kayla picked up right away. "What's up, kid?"

"What happened to make you late today? Was everything okay?"

Kayla laughed. "We've made the trip with Fanny over to Brookmeade so many times, you'd think we'd have the routine down like clockwork. Today I forgot my saddle pad. I'd given it to Mom to wash. Judson said Rita didn't have an extra one with her, so Mom ran to the barn to ask around. Mrs. Hoffman found an extra pad in Kelly's trunk."

So that explained Mrs. Hoffman and Mrs. Romano showing up together at the lesson. "Kayla, I think something's going on that I'll hear about when I get home." She swallowed hard before continuing. "Mom was sitting with Rita's father today. I don't know what he told her, but as she was leaving, she was acting funny and said there was something we need to talk about. I suspect she's heard Kelly's trumped-up story about the kick. Did you hear anything going around today?"

Kayla's voice got low. "I was going to call you later. Mrs. Hoffman told my mom she should be worried about Fanny because there was a horse in my class that is a dangerous kicker. Same old, same old. Mom didn't buy it and told her as much. Mom thinks that woman is a troublemaker." Kayla hesitated a moment. "But Sarah, there's something else you should know. After I got home, I got a group text message from Kelly that might have gone out to a whole lot of kids. It warned everyone to be careful around Crown

Prince because he's a dangerous kicker who injured her horse, and that you don't care."

Sarah felt as if *she* was the one who'd been kicked—right in the gut. At first she was speechless. When she was able to continue, she said, "So Kelly is texting all kinds of trash about me and my horse to who knows how many people?" She thought a minute. "Where could Kelly have gotten your cell number?"

Both girls instantly knew the answer and said in unison, "Rita!"

"There's more," Kayla continued. "After I read the text, I checked Kelly's Facebook page. The same lies are all over it." Kayla paused to draw in a deep breath. "I'm sorry to tell you about this, kid, but you need to know what's going on."

"Kayla, I really don't know what to do. I just hope people who hear this garbage will realize that's all it is."

"And here's a bit of news I learned from Rita," Kayla said. "I guess she's been calling Derek, probably so she could to make a move on him. He told her he has a girlfriend named Meredith in Chicago. He's going out to see her over Thanksgiving break. Bummer, huh?"

Sarah swallowed hard. She didn't want Kayla to know just how disappointing this news was to her. "Sure, Kayla. Thanks for being my eyes and ears on the ground."

After she put her phone away, Sarah didn't move for a few minutes. So Derek already had a girlfriend! She bit her lip and took a deep breath. Better not to fall for a guy who was already taken. She had enough problems on her plate without adding another one.

Sarah decided to see Prince one last time before she left for the day. She slid into the stall where he was eating his hay. "Good boy," she murmured, as she cradled his beautiful head and then hugged his neck for a moment. "I'm going to keep fighting to keep you, Prince."

CHAPTER 12

The Bullies

I'VE GOT TO FIND OUT what's going on with Mom, Sarah thought, as she pedaled her bike homeward. Sarah had left Brookmeade on time, so at least she wouldn't be holding up dinner. Braking to turn into their driveway, Sarah saw her father's Hyundai parked by the back steps. Her mother probably had told him about whatever was bothering her. *It looks like I'll have to face both of them,* she thought. Sarah removed her paddock boots in the mudroom and washed her hands before entering the kitchen. A quick glance at her mother confirmed that nothing had changed since the end of her lesson. Sarah had come to recognize that look—her mother was upset about something.

"What's going on, Mom?" Sarah asked, deciding to face the trouble, whatever it was, head on. Her mother glanced at the kitchen clock. Let's go in the den where your father is working. He'd like to be part of this."

As he often did when he first got home, Mr. Wagner was grading papers at his desk. He swiveled around in his chair when Sarah and her mother came into the room, and Abby looked up from a homework assignment she was reading. The air felt thick with tension as Sarah sat down in the wingback chair across from

Abby. After Mrs. Wagner got comfortable on the plaid loveseat, she looked at her husband. "Good time to talk?"

"Sure," Sarah's father said. "Let's get to the bottom of this."

Sarah's mother turned to her. "It appears there's been a lot going on at Brookmeade Farm we haven't been privy to, and I had to make a visit there today to learn the scoop." She was silent for a moment, looking intently at Sarah, waiting for her to volunteer information. When Sarah said nothing, her mother continued. "Rita's father filled me in on this business about Crown Prince kicking another horse. He told me Prince kicked Kelly Hoffman's horse, causing Kelly to fall off. Is this true?"

Sarah raised her hands and let them drop into her lap as she exhaled loudly. "It's a totally bogus story, Mom. You need to hear what *really* happened." Her parents listened closely as Sarah told them the details of that rainy afternoon, mentioning her suspicion that Kelly planned to upset Prince by intentionally coming too close to him. "I was looking back when Prince kicked out, and I *saw* that his leg didn't come anywhere near Midnight Jet. If Kelly had kept a reasonable distance when she came trotting fast behind Prince, it wouldn't have happened. Most horses would have done the same thing Prince did. When Mrs. Hoffman complained to Jack, he checked Jet all over and couldn't find any sign of a kick. The bottom line is, I know what really happened, because I saw the whole thing. Prince *didn't* kick Jet. I can promise you this is the truth."

"Why, Sarah, why?" her mother asked, a doubtful expression on her face. "Why would these two girls go out of their way to harass you?"

"I used to ride in their class. They wanted to go into the Young Riders class last spring, but Jack said they weren't ready. After that, Jack moved me up to that class, even though I was riding schoolies and they had their own horses. That totally frosted them, I guess. Maybe they get their kicks ganging up on someone. All I know is they've had it in for me ever since. Now they've told everyone in the barn to stay away from Prince because he's dangerous."

Mrs. Wagner frowned, obviously troubled. "Why didn't you feel you could talk to us about this, Sarah?"

"You've always said I couldn't keep Prince if he was dangerous. I was afraid you might make me send him back," she said, her voice beginning to tremble. She hung her head, struggling to regain her composure. "You saw how Prince acted in the lesson today. We were riding close to the other horses, and not once did he kick out. Mr. Snyder just told you what he heard from Rita, and it's all a pack of lies! Kelly's been spreading a lot of propaganda. Kayla got a text message from her this afternoon, and who knows how many others she sent it to. Nicole Jordan is gossiping too, and Kayla said they've got all kinds of garbage on Facebook about me and Prince. They're doing everything they can to hassle me." Sarah looked from one to the other, her eyes pleading for understanding.

Abby, who had stopped reading to listen closely, slammed her book shut and sat bolt upright. Her blue eyes grew large, as she jumped into the conversation. "This is what we've been talking about in school. Those girls are being bullies! They're trying to get everyone to gang up on you. They've been saying mean things about you behind your back." She looked to her parents for agreement.

Mr. Wagner scratched his chin, not wanting to jump to any conclusions. "You have a point, Abby," he said thoughtfully. His gaze shifted back to Sarah. "You say Mrs. Hoffman complained to Jack. I need to have a talk with him. It's my feeling those girls have taken this way too far."

"I'd very much like to be part of that conversation," Mrs. Wagner said. "The management at Brookmeade Farm needs to know what's been happening."

Sarah felt a weight lift from her shoulders. Her parents were on her side, and they were going to do something about it. They weren't blaming Prince for the trouble, either. She was filled with an enormous surge of relief!

"I'm going to call Jack to see if we might stop by to have a chat with him this evening," Mr. Wagner said. "I think we need to share some information."

* * * * *

"I hope this visit is convenient for the O'Briens," Sarah's mother said, as they drove the familiar road to Brookmeade Farm.

"Jack said eight worked well for them," Mr. Wagner replied.

Sarah sat in the back seat, her stomach once again in knots. She would give anything if she didn't have this problem to deal with. All she wanted was for Kelly and Nicole to leave her alone. Now she had to involve Jack.

Soon they were climbing the hill to the O'Briens' bungalow. As they topped the rise and prepared to turn into the driveway, Sarah immediately recognized Mr. DeWitt's Blazer parked to one side. *Oh, my God!* she thought. *The DeWitts are here, too.*

Her father parked beside the Blazer, and the three of them walked to the front door, hurrying in the chilly night air. Kathleen came to the door to welcome them. She ushered them into their living room, where a log glowed in the fireplace. Seated on a loveseat next to it, Chandler and Dorothy DeWitt greeted them, Chandler rising to shake their hands.

"Hello Martin, Alison, Sarah," Mrs. DeWitt said, smiling at Sarah. "When I called Kathleen to tell her about Pretty Penny's case of hives, she mentioned you folks were coming by tonight, as well as why you were coming. I asked if we could join the party. I hope you don't mind."

"Actually, I'm very happy you're all here," Sarah's father said, as they sat down on a sofa opposite Jack and Kathleen. "I assume you are all familiar with the 'kicking story.' There are also a few things I learned this evening I think you should be aware of."

"Yes," Jack said, "there have been goings-on I'm not happy about, and we need to discuss how best to handle them."

"First of all," Mr. Wagner said, "Sarah tells us that Kelly Hoffman rode her horse close to Crown Prince, and in response, Prince kicked out at the horse but didn't actually connect. I want to be sure we're all in agreement with this version of what happened."

Jack fielded the question without reservation, to Sarah's relief. "I believe that's a correct assessment based on more than just Sarah's account. I examined Midnight Jet immediately following Kelly's initial accusations and could find nothing to back up the charge that Prince had kicked him. Jet's body showed no signs of physical trauma. Also, I've never seen Prince show any inclination to kick out when he's in close company with other horses. If, as Sarah says, Midnight Jet ran close up on Prince's rear, that's a scenario when *most* horses would instinctively kick out to protect themselves."

After several of those gathered in the room nodded in agreement, Sarah's mother spoke. "Sarah seems to think the Hoffman girl and Nicole Jordan have been holding a grudge against her since she first moved into the Young Riders class. She feels Kelly has taken advantage of this kick business, fudging the facts a bit in order to make Crown Prince look bad."

When she paused, Mr. Wagner spoke up again. "What I find particularly disturbing is that it appears a campaign of sorts has been waged to spread the notion that Crown Prince is a dangerous horse, that he's a menace to other horses. Not only are the *girls* telling this to other riders, but their parents have joined in the crusade. Furthermore, it appears the gossip and falsehoods are being texted, e-mailed and even spread on Facebook. Unfortunately, this is not uncommon in this day and age, and it's called cyberbullying. In extreme cases this kind of relentless harassment has had deadly results, and the issue is being addressed in our schools here in Yardley."

Everyone in the room was quiet for a moment. Finally Jack broke the silence. "It's true that the parents are now involved. Mrs. Hoffman asked me to keep Sarah out of the class Kelly and Nicole ride in. She contends that Sarah shouldn't ride Crown Prince near other horses in any situation, saying the horse is a dangerous threat and a menace."

When Sarah opened her mouth to protest the claim, Jack raised a hand and continued. "Richard Snyder must have heard the rumors, because he called me last night. He was worried about Crown Prince being in Rita's class today. I assured him that Chancellor would not be at risk, but I don't think he believed me. I'm pretty sure he arranged to be in attendance so he could see for himself."

Kathleen rarely had much to say in group discussions such as this, but she spoke up now. "I'm not sure how the gossip about Crown Prince was spread, but I've spoken to three parents of riders who needed assurance their children would be safe in the same barn as Sarah's horse. Lindsay returned a few similar messages from our answering machine—people have the idea he is savage and out of control.

Chandler DeWitt had said nothing throughout the conversation, but now he stood up, his six-foot-plus frame towering over those seated, and walked to the fireplace. When he turned to face them, he was clearly angry. "This is a serious situation that demands intervention," he said. "Certainly Sarah should not have to deal with such unfair treatment. I will not allow bullying of any kind to take place at Brookmeade Farm, and I fully intend to take steps to stop those behind it."

Mrs. DeWitt's usually cheerful face was also clouded. She leaned over to speak directly to Sarah. "You're doing a wonderful job bringing Crown Prince along, Sarah. We certainly don't want this unpleasantness to slow your progress in any way."

"You've all been so kind to Sarah," Mrs. Wagner said, "and Martin and I greatly appreciate it. It's reassuring to hear that, after a few missteps, Prince is performing well." She glanced over in Jack's direction. "We trust he will continue to be a safe horse for Sarah to handle and ride."

Sarah's father looked at the clock on the mantle. "This is a school night," he reminded them, "so I think we'll be getting this student of ours back home." He and the others rose from their seats. "Thanks for your willingness to meet with us on short notice."

As Mr. DeWitt walked to the door with the Wagners, he pursed his lips and shook his head. "I'm not sure what I will do to address this nasty business, but, believe me, the harassment Sarah has experienced will not continue."

On the ride home, the Wagners rode in silence, each caught up in his or her own thoughts, wondering how the farm drama would play out. Sarah clasped her hands tightly, thinking about what Mr. DeWitt might do. Was there a chance Kelly and Nicole would be asked to leave Brookmeade Farm?

After a few minutes, Sarah's mother spoke up. "How do you feel about going back to the barn tomorrow, Sarah?"

"I'm not going to let those girls keep me from seeing my horse. It would be great if I didn't have to deal with them, but I don't expect that to happen any day soon. Mrs. Hoffman brings Kelly and Nicole to the barn almost every day."

"I'm sure you try to avoid them whenever possible," her father said, "and that's a good approach. We'll just have to see how Mr. DeWitt follows through on this."

* * * * *

Sarah followed her usual routine the next afternoon, leaving for the barn on her bike shortly after the school bus dropped her off at home. She noticed the leaves on many of the trees along the route had changed from forest green to shades of red and gold, and the air had a bit of a nippy chill. As always, she pedaled hard, eager to get to the farm and see her horse. As she coasted toward the parking area, she scanned the cars in the lot, looking for the Hoffmans' car. As expected, the green Volvo was parked at the end.

Prince was turned out in one of the paddocks, so she worked fast to clean his stall, using the manure fork to scoop soiled bedding and manure into the wheelbarrow. She was just about to wheel it to the manure pit, when Derek came around the corner leading Bismarck. "Hi, Sarah," he said. "I just saw Mr. DeWitt. He's looking for you."

Sarah froze. This undoubtedly had something to do with the bullies. "Thanks, Derek," she said, with a frown. "I'll try to catch him now."

After she'd emptied the wheelbarrow and put it away, Sarah started for the office. When she stepped inside, Jack was sitting at the desk talking to Kelly Hoffman's mother. "The girls are doing so well with their horses," Mrs. Hoffman was saying. "They do love riding them here, and they can hardly wait to go to horse shows. How soon do you think they'll be ready to compete?"

Jack was silent for a minute, looking thoughtful. "'Tis not possible to predict right now," he said. "We hope Jubilee won't have a recurrence of the tendon problem, and of course the more hours the girls spend in the saddle the better. They work hard in between their lessons, which will help them progress faster."

When Mrs. Hoffman noticed Sarah standing behind her, her eyes narrowed. "Well, I'll be on my way," she said. She laid a check on the desk blotter. "I added a little extra this time, to show how much we appreciate your excellent instruction."

Just as she started for the door, Mr. DeWitt stepped into the room. "Oh, hello, Mr. DeWitt," Mrs. Hoffman said, beaming. "I was just telling Jack how much the girls like riding here."

"Thank you, Mrs. Hoffman," Mr. DeWitt said. "I wonder if you and Kelly could come to my office for a moment. There's a matter I'd like to discuss with you. I assume Kelly is here with you?"

Mrs. Hoffman made a sour face, looking puzzled. "I'll have to go find her. She was grooming her horse a few minutes ago."

"If you would be so kind," Mr. DeWitt replied smoothly. "I'll meet you in my office. If Nicole and her mother are here, I'd like to speak with them as well."

Mrs. Hoffman shook her head. "I'm afraid Nicole had a dentist appointment this afternoon."

After Mrs. Hoffman went to find Kelly, Mr. DeWitt turned to Sarah. "I'm happy you're here, Sarah, because I'd like you to be present during the conversation I'm going to have with the Hoffmans. And you, too, Jack." He turned toward the door. "Shall we go?"

Sarah slowly followed Mr. DeWitt down the aisle toward his personal office, a hard lump in her throat. She dreaded this meeting, fearful of the expected showdown. She just knew Kelly and Nicole would label her as a snitch.

Mr. DeWitt opened the door to his office, which looked out on the turnout paddocks. It was decorated with the same hickory paneled walls and English foxhunting scenes as the lounge. He turned on the lights before seating himself at his oversized desk. He motioned for Jack and Sarah to sit in the two upholstered chairs to his right.

There was a knock on the door a few minutes later, and Mr. DeWitt got up to open it. "Please come in," he said to Mrs. Hoffman and Kelly. He motioned to the comfortable chairs to the left of his desk. Kelly and her mother both glanced at Jack and Sarah before sitting down stiffly.

The room was quiet until Mr. DeWitt spoke. "It has come to my attention that the practice of bullying, and in fact cyberbullying, has been taking place here at Brookmeade Farm. Bullying is something I do not condone and will not allow. I've asked you to meet with me today to make sure everyone here understands what has been happening and why it is absolutely not acceptable. If at any time you feel the facts are not being accurately stated, please speak up."

Mr. DeWitt leaned back in his chair and folded his fingers together before continuing. "Recently, when rain made it necessary to hold two lessons in our indoor arena simultaneously, a small area at the end was cordoned off for boarders. I understand that when Midnight Jet trotted very close to Crown Prince, Prince kicked out at him. I think we all can agree on that. But there are differing versions of whether or not Prince made contact with Jet. Kelly, what makes you believe that Prince actually kicked your horse?"

Kelly scowled as she stared angrily at Mr. DeWitt. "Because the kick made Jet jump sideways, and I fell off, that's why!"

Mr. DeWitt replied, "Can you acknowledge that Midnight Jet could have jumped sideways to *avoid* being struck by Crown

Prince?" Kelly sat sullenly, refusing to respond.

Mr. DeWitt continued. "Upon hearing about the incident from you, Mrs. Hoffman, Jack immediately examined Midnight Jet. Can you tell us what you found, Jack?"

"A veterinarian I'm not," Jack said, "but I've had enough experience looking for signs of injuries, such as heat and swelling. I found nothing on Midnight Jet to indicate he had been kicked, and the horse was never off."

"Sarah, will you tell us what *you* saw when your horse kicked out at Jet?" Mr. DeWitt said.

Sarah took a deep breath, and willed her voice not to waver. "When I looked behind me, I saw Midnight Jet trotting very fast toward Prince. I worried he might hit us. Prince also saw Jet coming, and just before it looked like they might collide, Prince kicked out with his left hind leg. Jet swerved sharply to his left to miss the kick, and Kelly fell off."

"I think we've gotten the facts as best we can know them," Mr. DeWitt said. "It's what happened next that is most troubling. I'm under the impression that you, Kelly, and your friend, Nicole, told a number of people—those who board their horses at the barn as well as students who take lessons here—that Crown Prince is dangerous and should not be allowed around other horses. Your rumor has been spread by word of mouth, texting, e-mail, and even on the internet. Is this true?"

Kelly's face flushed a deep red and she looked down, unable to meet Mr. DeWitt's gaze. Her mother looked at her shamefully. "Did you feed me lies, Kelly Hoffman?" she asked in a sharp voice. There was a long pause before Mrs. Hoffman turned back to Mr. DeWitt, shaking her head. "If what you say is true, my concerns for my daughter's welfare were all based on false information. I must apologize for that."

"Kelly," Mr. DeWitt said, "I hope you realize how serious your actions were. You've caused nothing but stress and pain for other people, not only for Sarah, but also those who worried their children might not be safe in the barns here, or riding in the arena with other horses. It showed Jack and Brookmeade Farm in a very bad light."

"In fairness to Kelly, there's something I'd like to add," Mrs. Hoffman said, looking at her daughter. "When my husband and I were divorced, it was hard on Kelly and her brother. I got her the horse to help her through a bad time, but she's still under a lot of stress. I hope you can give her another chance."

Mr. DeWitt sat quietly for a moment, deliberating. He looked directly at Kelly when he spoke. "Under most circumstances, I wouldn't hesitate to insist a bully move his or her horse from Brookmeade Farm," he said, "but I'm going to give us all the opportunity to put this behind us, Kelly. This goes for both you and Nicole, and I plan to speak to her as well. However, there's something you need to understand. If you get involved is another incident of bullying at Brookmeade Farm, you will no longer be welcome here."

Everyone in the room looked at Kelly, who seemed on the verge of tears. "Can you tell us it won't happen again?" her mother insisted.

Kelly nodded her head, as she covered her face with her hands. When she could speak, her voice trembled. "I love it here at Brookmeade Farm. Jet does too. I won't do it again. I promise."

Jack got up from his chair and pointed at both Sarah and Kelly. "'Tis time for *everyone* to be friends, to get along," he said. "'Tis time to enjoy riding together and to share your love of the horse. That's what Brookmeade Farm is all about."

CHAPTER 13

Autumn Days

DURING THE WEEKS THAT FOLLOWED, the days became shorter, the nights turned cooler, and the forests surrounding Brookmeade Farm became a flaming patchwork of red and gold leaves. The horses at the barn began growing winter coats to prepare them for the frigid temperatures to come. To discourage the long coats that would make cooling out difficult during the winter, Tim, Derek, and Paige were among the first riders at the barn to start blanketing their horses. As Sarah made the rounds feeding them, she noticed more and more winter blankets either on the horses or draped over a rack on the stall doors.

"I might want to do a few winter indoor shows that aren't too far away," Derek told Sarah, "and I can't have Bismarck sweating up when I'm jumping him. When I lived near Chicago, I found out firsthand with my other horse how hard it can be to get a horse's coat to dry out in the winter. After one show, my mother had to use her hair dryer on him!"

"I can just picture that," Sarah said, grinning.

When she was grooming Prince a few days later, Sarah noticed how much heavier his coat was getting. She pulled out her phone and punched Kayla's speed dial number. Her friend picked up right away.

"Hey, Kayla. A lot of people at Brookmeade are blanketing their horses. When do you start putting a winter blanket on Fanny?"

"I started last week. I've been blanketing Fanny early ever since I got her because of our lessons at Brookmeade over the winter. The blanket won't *totally* keep her from growing a winter coat, but it's not as long. What really keeps a horse's coat short but thick is plenty of groceries." She paused a moment. "What's up with you, kid?"

"I guess it's time for another trip to Atlantic Saddlery. I hope I've got enough money left on the gift card the DeWitts gave me to get Prince a blanket. Do you need anything? Wanna come along?"

Kayla paused a minute. "Actually we could use dewormers, and I'm getting low on the supplement I feed Fanny to toughen up her feet."

"I'll see when my mom can drop us off. Probably the next time she goes food shopping."

"Hey, would a trail ride Saturday morning work for you? Mom told me this afternoon she'd drop Fanny off at Brookmeade. I've been bugging her for a while."

Sarah was immediately excited. "We've been talking about doing that for ages! Sounds like a plan!"

"Okay. Mom said we'll aim to be there at nine. See ya!"

Sarah put her grooming equipment and tack away before going into Prince's stall to give him a final hug. He lifted his head from the pile of hay, surveying her with his large intelligent eyes while he chewed rhythmically. She wrapped her arms around his neck. "Good boy, Prince. You were super today." A few minutes later she left the barn.

On the way home, she thought about her ride on Prince that afternoon. She had been spending much of her riding time working on basic dressage exercises that Jack had mapped out for her, and Prince's progress was remarkable. Jack had said from the beginning that for a big horse, he was naturally well-balanced. With training, he was learning to carry a greater proportion of his weight with his hindquarters, making him lighter in the bridle. He was so different from the school horses she'd ridden that tended to be heavy on the forehand. Sarah was beginning to hope she and Prince might be able to compete in some small competitions in the year ahead.

Since Mr. DeWitt had stepped in to squelch Kelly and Nicole's bullying campaign, everyone seemed to have silently agreed to move on. Even Rita had been more relaxed when they rode in their lesson together. In the Young Riders class, Prince needed to jump bigger fences than he ever had in his early lessons, but so far he was holding his own. Even so, when the class was doing course work, Jack would sometimes give Prince easier fences than the other horses jumped. Jack told Sarah it was a good thing Prince always kept his cool when he was challenged, without getting rattled. He was willing to tackle the bigger fences without rushing or refusing. Sometimes he'd make a mistake and have a rail down, but he always did better on a second try. Not only was Crown Prince strikingly beautiful, but he was turning out to be a superior athlete with a wonderful temperament.

Sarah had a hard time falling asleep that night. She couldn't help thinking about how well things were going with her amazing horse. And, she was super excited that she and Kayla were finally going to take their horses on a trail ride together on Saturday. And perhaps Tim, Paige, and Derek would come along! Why hadn't she thought of that right away? Tim and Paige knew the trails on the other side of Ridge Road, and they could lead the way. With that happy thought, she finally drifted off to sleep.

* * * * *

The next day was Friday—almost the weekend. Sarah's mother was to pick up Sarah and Kayla at Yardley High after school and then drop them at Atlantic Saddlery while she did her food shopping. The girls were waiting when the SUV pulled up. Mrs. Wagner greeted them as they climbed in. "I hope you had a good day. How's school going for you, Kayla?"

"Okay," Kayla said. "It better. I have to get good grades or my riding privileges are taken away."

"I'll bet you do good work at school, Kayla," Mrs. Wagner said, "and I'm sure your parents are very proud of you." She paused a minute to glance at Sarah in the rearview mirror. "Do you know what kind of blanket you're going to get for Prince today, Sarah?"

"I looked online. I couldn't believe how expensive winter blankets are," Sarah said. "I hope I've got enough left on the gift card. If not, I'll have to dip into my birthday money."

When they arrived at Atlantic Saddlery, Mrs. Wagner stopped the car near the entrance to let the girls out. "I should be back in less than an hour. I'll take Kayla home first and then drop you at Brookmeade," she said. The girls quickly exited the car and hurried into the tack shop. It wasn't nearly as busy now as when it first opened several months before, and there were only a few other customers there.

"I think blankets are in the back," Kayla said.

"I'm going to have my gift card checked first," Sarah said, heading to the front of the shop. As she approached the cash register, she saw the shop's owner, who had helped her pick out her new saddle back in June. The woman must have recognized her, too.

"How's that saddle working out for you?" she asked, smiling at Sarah.

"It's great," Sarah said, handing her the card. "Now it's time to get a winter blanket, but I need to find out how much is left on my card."

The woman slipped the card through the register. "Oh, you've got a lot left," she said reassuringly. "You can get more than a winter blanket, even if you buy our best one."

"Cool," Sarah said.

"See, you worried for nothing," Kayla chided her. "Maybe you can get a sheet or a cooler, too."

On their way to the back of the shop, Kayla asked, "What color do you want? I don't remember that you picked out a color for Prince."

"Everything I got before was pretty generic, like black. I didn't even know what color my horse would be then." They stood before the big racks that had several styles of blankets bagged in plastic, with a few opened up and hanging on display. At the end of the rack was a bright red quilted winter blanket.

"I think red would go with a dark bay," Sarah said. "What do you think?"

Kayla scrunched up her eyebrows, thinking. "Actually almost any color would work for him. Red wouldn't look good on a chestnut like Fanny. That's why I went with green for her. Do you like the red one?"

"Totally. I guess there's no question what size Prince will need," Sarah said, laughing. She pulled out the blanket, a size LL, that took both of her arms to hold it, and checked the price tag. "That's settled. Want to look for your dewormer?"

They passed some beautiful high-quality halters as they walked down another aisle. "Look, Kayla," Sarah said, pointing to a fleece-padded leather halter on a model horse. "Prince would look so handsome in one of these."

"Yeah, I have fleece to put on Fanny's halter when we go to

shows," Kayla said. "I always get horse stuff at Christmas and for my birthday. Hey, if you've got money left on your card, why don't you get one of those?"

Sarah thought a moment. "Yeah, I could get the fleece and maybe a cheap leather halter for turnout. I hate it when Prince gets mud on his good one. I have to clean it and use neatsfoot oil on it, a real pain."

They walked further down the aisle until Kayla stopped before a bin. She scooped up a half dozen packages of dewormer of different kinds. "We have to stagger what we give the horses to hit different kinds of worms," she said. "With two horses in our barn, we go through these pretty fast." She looked at Sarah. "What about Prince?"

"Dr. Reynolds wormed him when he came to the barn last month. One of these days, I'll have to watch you give the meds to Fanny, so I can start doing it myself."

"Fanny hates the taste of it, so my mom holds her head up and then squirts it into her mouth while her nose is in the air. That way she can't spit it out."

Kayla walked further down that aisle. "And here's the Biotin supplement that I need. It's supposed to make horses grow a strong hoof wall."

After the girls paid for their purchases, they left the shop and stood near the entrance watching for Mrs. Wagner. "I hope she gets here pretty soon," Sarah said. "We've got better things to do than stand around waiting!" The afternoon was ticking away, and she still needed enough time to clean Prince's stall before she fed the horses. She wouldn't be able to ride, but with any luck, she might be able to longe Prince before her father picked her up.

"It must be good to have Kelly and Nicole off your back," Kayla said. "It took some nerve for them to send out all those text messages. You'd think they'd be smart enough to know they'd get caught." Kayla paused, and a lopsided smile crept onto her face. "Or maybe not!"

"Kelly still gives me dirty looks when I see her in the tack room or when I'm leading Prince to the indoor. She's kind of a ditz, if you ask me." Sarah looked up the street, watching for their SUV. "But I guess she's had a tough time with her parents' divorce."

"Oh," Sarah said, "I forgot to ask—how about Paige and Tim coming with us tomorrow? And maybe Derek?"

"Sure," Kayla said. "I think Tim knows those trails like the back of his hand, and we don't want to get lost out there. And who wouldn't like to go riding with a guy like Derek?" Kayla noticed Mrs. Wagner's SUV approaching. "I think this is your mother coming now."

When the SUV rolled to a stop, Sarah opened the hatch and put her new horse blanket in the back. Then she and Kayla hopped in. "It looks like you found one you like," Mrs. Wagner said.

"Yeah," Sarah replied, "I was just lucky there were quite a few bucks left on my card. I also got a cheap everyday halter for Prince, so he doesn't have to be turned out with his good one."

"You were lucky he came with an expensive halter with a name plate," Kayla said. "Horses always wear a halter when you buy them, but usually it's a tired nylon job."

"Let's face it, Kayla. I was lucky all the way around when I got Prince."

After dropping Kayla off, Mrs. Wagner turned off Ridge Road to take Sarah to Brookmeade Farm. "Your father will call you when he's leaving school, and he'd appreciate it if you could be ready when he arrives."

"Okay.... Bye, Mom," Sarah said as the SUV pulled to a stop near the barn's main entrance. "Thanks much!" She grabbed her purchases from the back of the vehicle, and with a wave, headed for the barn. After making her way up the cement steps and pushing in through the heavy entry door, she glanced into the office as she passed. Tim and Paige were talking to Jack. Sarah quickly put on the brakes and swung into the office. "I hope I'm not butting in," she said.

"Oh, no," Jack said, as he walked to the door. "It's time I got on French Twist, so I'll be off."

Paige noticed the red horse blanket Sarah was carrying. "I guess we'll see Prince coming from a mile off with that on," she said. "It's a good thing there aren't any bulls on this farm!"

Sarah grinned. "You're right. And for a big horse, it takes a big blanket." She paused, leaning her package on top of a chair. "Hey, Kayla's bringing Fanny over here tomorrow morning at nine to go for a trail ride with me. Any chance you guys are going to ride in the morning? Want to come with us to the trails across Ridge Road?

"Yeah, we're going to hack tomorrow," Tim said. He looked at Paige. "What do you think?"

"We haven't ever gone out on the trails with Kayla," Paige said. "She's a lot of fun. Sounds awesome."

"Okay," Sarah said. "See you about nine-fifteen. Now I'm going to Prince's stall while I can still carry this thing!"

Sarah was about halfway up the aisle when she saw Derek coming toward her. "I guess you won't have to worry about turning Prince out during hunting season with that," he said. When he got close to her, he reached out for the blanket. "Here, let me carry that for you."

"Oh, thanks," Sarah said, as he took the blanket. "You'd think pulling bales of hay around the loft would make me able to carry one horse blanket without any trouble, but that thing weighs a ton."

As they walked to Prince's stall, Sarah deliberated—should she ask Derek to come on the trail ride? She'd ridden with him a few times, but always at *his* invitation. She liked being with him, and their conversation came easy. She was always sorry when they got back to the barn. Now that she knew about his girl-friend in Chicago, she didn't want to give the impression she was making a move on him. *But this is a group ride,* she thought. *Oh, why not!*

"Are you riding in the morning?" she asked Derek, glad he wasn't looking into her reddening face when she said it. "Kayla Romano's mother is trucking Fanny over about nine, and Tim and Paige are riding with us. We're going across Ridge Road to the trails." She paused. *Here comes the hard part,* she thought. "Want to come?"

"Oh, wow," Derek said, immediately excited. "That would be awesome. I usually hack on Saturdays, when I have plenty of time. I've been hoping someone could show me those trails." He turned to look at her, and Sarah was reminded how intensely blue his eyes were. "Thanks for asking me."

* * * * *

On Saturday, Sarah pedaled her bike fast through the crisp fall air to be at the barn before seven. Once the horses had been fed, she grabbed a push broom and headed for the lounge to begin her sweeping chores. As she worked, she thought about how much fun the ride would be. She and Kayla had wanted to do this from the first day Crown Prince had come to Brookmeade, and *finally* it was going to happen. Tim and Paige were riding with them, and best of all, so was Derek.

After sweeping the lounge, feed room, and both tack rooms, she decided the two aisles would have to wait. She hurried back to Prince's stall. He had finished eating his hay and was watching Derek groom Bismarck.

"Hi, Sarah," he said. "Is Kayla here yet?"

"Not the last time I checked," Sarah said, going up to Bismarck and stroking his head. She loved his narrow blaze, and the horse enjoyed her attention. He pulled against the cross-ties to sniff her pockets. "I don't dare give you the carrot you smell," Sarah said to the horse. "Prince would call his lawyer."

"Don't feel sorry for Bismarck," Derek said, running a dandy brush over the horse's hindquarters. "He got his share of apples already."

It was only then that Sarah noticed Nicole Jordan leaning on Bismarck's stall on the other side of the horse. She decided it was a good time to head for the tack room to retrieve her grooming caddy and tack. When she returned, Nicole was gone. Sarah brought Prince out into the aisle and got busy with a curry comb.

When Derek had Bismarck tacked up, he said, "I'm going to school in the outside ring until everyone is ready." He started leading his horse away, but stopped after taking a few steps and looked back at her. His face sobered. "I'm not sure, but Nicole and Kelly might follow us. I didn't actually invite them—Nicole asked what I was doing today and then hightailed it out of here. Sorry," he said. He could see that Sarah wasn't thrilled.

After Sarah had finished grooming Prince, she went to a window to see if Kayla had arrived. Kayla was holding Fanny while her mother unhooked the trailer from their pickup. Sarah saw Paige down the aisle with Quarry on cross-ties, getting him ready, and guessed Tim was doing the same thing. Sarah rushed back to her horse and began to tack up. *I really hope I don't have to deal with Kelly and Nicole on this ride,* she thought.

When Sarah led Prince out to the courtyard to use the mounting block, Kayla was already on Fanny and talking to Derek. Paige led Quarry out of the barn, followed by Tim and Rhodes Scholar. Everyone was ready to go! Sarah was relieved that Prince seemed laid back and totally unfazed by the other horses milling around. After his weekly group lessons, this was no big deal.

Sarah rode Prince toward Kayla, giving her a thumbs-up. "How come your mother is leaving your trailer here?" she asked.

"Mom wants to do some errands without pulling the trailer around, and this way I can tie Fanny to it when we're through riding," Kayla said. She reached down and gave the mare a hearty pat on her neck. "We've been doing an awful lot of ringwork lately. Fanny is going to love getting out on the trails, especially some she's never been on before."

Tim and Paige joined them. "We'll follow the entry road to get to Ridge Road," Tim said. He turned Rhodes in that direction, with the others following. They had started walking up the hill away from the barn when Sarah turned in her saddle to speak to Kayla. Out of the corner of her eye she saw two other horses just starting up the roadway. She recognized them at once—Jubilee and Midnight Jet.

"Guess who's bringing up the rear," she said to Kayla, as she gestured over her shoulder with her thumb. Kayla looked around to see the two trailing horses and started laughing. "It looks like we're going to have a real big ride, almost like a foxhunt!"

Paige heard what Kayla said, and she looked back. "All we need now are the hounds!" she quipped. Derek and Tim were riding side by side in the lead, and hearing the laughter, they also turned to see what was up. Derek gave Sarah a knowing look. Those girls were totally predictable!

CHAPTER 14
Rock Walls

FROM THE SPRING IN HIS STEP, Sarah sensed Prince was happy going out with the other horses. He took the bit eagerly, and despite the distractions, he listened to her constant communications through the reins and her leg aids. Sarah reached down to pat his neck, thankful to have such a super horse. A cool breeze made her wish she'd worn a vest over her sweater, but she knew she wouldn't be chilly for long. The sun on this crisp, cloudless morning was taking the edge off the coolness and lighting up the fall foliage like a neon sign. *This is incredible!* Sarah thought. *I'll remember this day for the rest of my life.*

When the riders neared the O'Briens' bungalow, Kathleen was coming out of the carriage shed. Her auburn hair blended with the blazing backdrop of maple trees as she hurried out the driveway to wave to them. "'Tis a grand day!" she called." Have a wonderful ride."

Soon they had reached the foot of the small hill beyond the bungalow. "Let's trot!" Tim called to everyone. Rhodes and Bismarck picked up a lively trot. Sarah and Kayla rode side-by-side, their two horses trotting as a pair behind Paige. Because Prince's stride was longer than Fanny's, Sarah found herself frequently using half-halts to check his pace, and Kayla had to ask Fanny to extend her trot.

The group trotted along the gravel road and over the bridge, the horses' hooves drumming loudly on the planks. The turned-out broodmares, whose foals had by now been weaned and sent away, raised their heads from grazing in the fields to watch them go by. After a long trot, the riders got closer to Ridge Road and could see the trailhead directly across the way. Tim raised his right arm to signal a downward transition. After coming back to walk and halting to make sure there was no traffic coming, they walked their horses across the asphalt.

Sarah looked behind to see if the other two horses were still following, but there was no sign of them. "I guess Kelly and Nicole decided to go a different way," she said to Kayla.

Kayla also looked behind. "They could be hidden by that bend in the road, or they might have gone on the meadow trail. That would be just as well, don't you think?" Sarah raised an eyebrow as she nodded.

The trail began on what appeared to be an old farm lane, where a thick bed of crisp, fallen leaves rustled under the horses' feet, sending up their own pungent aroma. The narrow road eventually opened into a large field with a worn path around the perimeter. "There are a few trails that go off from this field," Tim said. "Do you want the one that climbs Sutters Hill? It's pretty steep in places, and can be rough and rocky. Good view from the top, though."

Paige offered a suggestion. "How about the rock wall trail? There's a great stretch where you can jump the stone walls or go around them. I think there are at least four walls not too far apart. It's good galloping ground, too. Tim and I use the trail to get our horses ready for events."

"Sounds awesome!" Kayla cried out.

Derek agreed with Kayla. "Cool. Maybe Bismarck will decide he wants to become an event horse."

Sarah nodded her head, too. She couldn't help being excited, even though she clearly remembered the first time she and Prince had jumped in a group, when Prince had plowed into Chancellor. She'd have to keep a tight hold on him today!

"Why don't Quarry and Rhodes go first?" Paige asked. "Our horses have done this before. What do you think, Sarah?"

"As long as I don't go last, I don't care. Remember the old orchard trail ride?" Sarah replied.

"Fanny won't mind being left behind for a little while," Kayla said. "I'll go last."

Derek was thoughtful. Finally he said, "I'll follow you, Sarah."

"Okay, you guys," Tim said. "Paige and I will meet you in a small meadow after the fourth rock wall. Give the rider ahead of you a few minutes before you start, just in case there's a problem." He guided Rhodes into the field and trotted a big circle before asking for canter and heading to the trail opening.

Tim had just gotten out of sight when Kayla spotted movement in the field behind them. Turning in her saddle, she saw Kelly and Nicole riding toward them. "Oh, boy," she said. "Look who is coming." The riders watched Kelly and Nicole pick up trot to close the gap between them. When they reached the group, both Midnight Jet and Jubilee were breathing heavily.

"Why didn't you guys wait for us?" Nicole said. "We've been trying to catch up with you from the beginning. It seemed like you trotted forever, and we couldn't keep up."

Kayla wasn't sympathetic. "We had no idea you were coming with us. Did you tell anyone?"

"Look, it's time for me to go," Paige said. "You guys figure out who's going when." With that she cantered Quarry in a circle in the field and then disappeared onto the rock wall trail.

Derek walked Bismarck toward Kelly and Nicole, clearly concerned with their presence. "We're going to do some serious jumping on this trail. Are you sure you girls are up to it?"

After scanning the riders in the group, Nicole spoke loud enough for everyone to hear. "If Sarah Wagner can do it on her green horse, than we can do it," she said. "Don't worry about us, Derek."

Derek caught Sarah's eye for a moment before turning back to Kelly and Nicole. "Are you really sure your horses are fit enough to canter for some distance, as well as jump four rock walls?

Both Kelly and Nicole nodded their heads resolutely.

"Well, if you're going to insist on doing this, I'll go last and follow you," Derek said with obvious frustration.

Prince stood like a statue with his head raised and his ears pricked forward, listening for the horses that had gone before him. Sarah reached down to run her hand along his arched neck. They'd be going next. She wouldn't mind putting some distance between herself and those girls. Maybe Kelly and Nicole had dropped the kick issue, but they had by no means buried the hatchet.

"Okay, guys. See you later," she said as she gathered her reins and asked Prince to move off the track and into the field. He willingly picked up trot and then canter on a circle, but he seemed a little unsure when Sarah guided him onto the rock wall trail. He didn't like leaving the other horses behind, but once he got into a cantering rhythm, she sensed he was focusing on the trail ahead. She had never ridden here, and was glad the path was wide with good footing.

After they'd cantered around a slight bend in the trail, Sarah saw the first rock wall ahead of them. It was good-sized. The trail went around the wall, so it was possible to skirt it. For a fleeting moment, she considered that option. Prince had never been on this trail before, and his only jumping experience going cross-country was the big log on the old orchard trail. *No,* she thought. *We're going to jump this!* Coming closer to the wall, she sat deeply and closed her legs to tell her horse they were committed. Prince responded with a surge of energy, and a few strides later they were in the air, soaring over the wall.

Prince landed smoothly and ran on, but now he increased his pace from a canter to a hand gallop. His fleet hooves seemed to eat up the ground, and soon a second rock wall loomed ahead of them. This time there was no hesitation, as he attacked the jump, leaped over it, and galloped on. *That was a little quick,* Sarah thought. *I can't let him rush the next one.* The trail wound around an old cabin before abruptly leaving the woods and entering a field. The worn path clearly went straight across the field to a third rock wall on the other side. This one had a telephone pole on top of it. As soon as Prince saw the wall, his ears pricked forward. Now he knew what this was all about, and he pressed forward, anxious to get to the jump. Sarah sat back and with the reins, played the bit in his mouth, asking him to stay soft in the bridle and not rush. Prince responded and kept a steady pace to the base of the wall before jumping it smoothly. *He really loves this!* she thought. *And so do I!*

They were back in the woods now, the trail made darker by thick evergreen trees on both sides. It seemed like they galloped on for a long time, with Sarah frequently checking her horse to keep his pace from getting too quick. Finally she saw a rock wall ahead. This would be the last one, and she could vaguely make out the images of Tim and Paige in the field beyond it. This time Prince approached the wall with a lot of confidence, and without increasing his speed, they sailed over it.

Tim and Paige were waiting in the middle of the meadow, and they both pumped a fist in the air and whooped when Sarah and Prince came cantering toward them. Sarah slowed her horse before reaching Rhodes and Quarry, and then circled around them. Prince had found the jumping exciting, and he pranced with his glossy black tail held high. Sarah was catching her breath, but laughing. "He loved it! That was so much fun."

Tim was walking Rhodes in a small circle. "If you liked jumping those walls, you're going to love eventing. How did Crown Prince do?"

"He started to get a little quick, so I had to keep half-halting to slow the pace," Sarah said. "But other than that, he was great—and I'm totally addicted to cross-country!"

"Listen!" Paige said, looking back toward the wall. "I think I hear hoofbeats."Sure enough, a few minutes later Fanny's bright chestnut face with the perfect diamond came into view as she and Kayla approached the last rock wall.

"Fanny's really booking!" Tim said. "I've never seen her move out like that."

Fanny's small ears were pricked forward as she and Kayla came over the wall in good form, and her audience cheered loudly. "Good ride, Kayla!" Tim called.

Kayla was also out of breath, but beaming, and her face was almost as red as her hair. She enthusiastically slapped Fanny's neck. "I can't wait to do it again!" she said.

Paige looked back to the rock wall. "So now we're waiting for Derek and those two girls," she said.

"Yeah," Kayla said, still breathing fast. "Derek tried to talk Kelly and Nicole out of jumping the walls, but they insisted that they could do anything Sarah's green horse could do." She rolled her eyes as she paused to take a deep breath before continuing. "Both

Midnight Jet and Jubilee were pretty winded when they caught up with us, and I think Derek doubts they're fit enough to do this. He said he'd go last, probably to make sure they get through okay."

Tim frowned. "I don't like the sound of this. If they don't come along pretty soon, maybe we should start back."

A few minutes later there was still no sign of either Kelly or Nicole. "I think we should see what's going on," Paige said.

The riders walked around the rock wall and then began trotting on the path in single file. Except for a bird's call of alarm at their presence, the woods were quiet. When they approached the next wall with the telephone pole, Prince began to pull on the reins. He wanted to jump it, and Sarah had to use a strong hand to keep him to the path that went beside it. The riders came to the next wall, with still no sign of anyone.

"I'm getting worried," Tim said. He pressed Rhodes forward into a faster trot, and the others followed. The horses moved along the woods trail until the first rock wall came into view. Kelly was standing in the clearing on the other side of the wall holding both Midnight Jet and Jubilee.

"Something must be wrong!" Paige cried. They guided their horses around the jump, coming to walk as they approached Kelly. She stood in the middle of the trail holding a horse's reins in each hand while tears streamed down her face. Then they saw Nicole! The girl was lying on her back next to the rock wall, with one arm over her forehead.

"Oh, my God!" Kayla said. Tim and Paige immediately jumped off their horses, and Tim took Quarry's reins while Paige rushed to Nicole's side.

"Derek called 911," Kelly said between sobs. "He's gone to meet them and show them the way. He told Nicole not to try to get up until someone comes."

Nicole was moaning incoherently when Paige reached her. "Help's coming, Nicole," Paige said. "Try to remain still. Are you in a lot of pain?" Nicole mumbled a response Sarah couldn't understand.

Kelly seemed to regain her composure, somewhat, and began to tell them what had happened. "Nicole went first, and Derek and I were talking while I waited to follow her. All of a sudden Jubilee came running back without Nicole! She came right up to Jet, so I jumped off and grabbed her. Derek took off on Bismarck, and he found Nicole like this. He called 911 right away. Then he came back and told me to walk the horses to Nicole and stay with her while he rode to meet the rescue people. He gunned it out of here on Bismarck."

The faint strains of an emergency vehicle could now be heard in the distance. "It won't be long now," Tim said. "Thank goodness the trail is wide enough for a vehicle."

"Let's hope Derek is at the trailhead so he can show them the way," Kayla said.

They heard the siren coming closer, and then a flashing blue light was visible. Moments later a white rescue vehicle, led by Derek trotting on Bismarck, came slowly along the path. It was a tight fit, with little clearance from the trees on each side and overhead. The riders made way for them, and the rescue unit pulled up near where Nicole lay at the base of the rock wall. Two emergency technicians leaped out and rushed to her. From where the riders held their horses at the edge of the clearing, they could see Nicole and the men examining her. Kelly stood closer to Nicole, still holding Midnight Jet and Jubilee.

After one ET asked Kelly a few questions, he returned to the vehicle, pulled both back doors open, and removed a backboard, which he placed on the ground beside Nicole. She moaned in pain as the two men carefully lifted her onto it and then carried her to the back of the vehicle.

"We're out of here," the driver said as he came out of the unit, shutting the doors behind him. "But before we go, young lady, can you call your friend's parents to let them know what's happened?" He looked closely at Kelly for confirmation she would do as he asked.

"Yes, I'll do it," Kelly said, pulling out her cell.

"Tell them she's being taken by rescue unit to the Winchester General Hospital," the ET said. A few moments later, with one man still in the back with Nicole, the vehicle backed up to reverse direction and pulled away. The riders looked blankly at one another. It was hard to reconcile what had just happened with the thrill of the beginning of their ride.

"Does anyone have any idea how badly Nicole is hurt?" Paige asked.

"Not a clue," Derek said, "but I suggest that after Kelly calls the Jordans, we get our horses back to the barn. While I was waiting by Ridge Road, I called Jack. He's bringing someone to ride Jubilee back."

Kelly had calmed down considerably, and she punched the Jordans' number in her contact list. "I just hope someone's at.... Oh, Mrs. Jordan?" Kelly looked relieved. "Nicole fell off Jubilee, and she's on her way to Winchester Hospital by ambulance. The ETs told me to call you." She paused for a few moments, listening. "I don't know anything else, Mrs. Jordan. I'm sorry." As she slowly lowered the phone and returned it to her pocket, more tears flowed. For a moment she was choked up. "The Jordans are heading for Winchester," she said haltingly.

Tim led Rhodes close to where Kelly was holding Jet and Jubilee. "Kelly, why don't you get back on your horse. I'll lead Rhodes and Jubilee behind you until we meet Jack." Kelly nodded and turned to mount Midnight Jet. The other riders got remounted and started walking their horses back along the trail, with Tim on foot behind them leading Rhodes and Jubilee.

Prince picked up on Sarah's tension, and nervously tossed his head. He wasn't content to walk quietly and jigged occasionally. Sarah used a tight rein and half-halts to insist that he walk. They had gone only a short distance when they saw the farm's pickup with Jack and Kathleen coming toward them. Jack stopped the truck as he approached and jumped out, looking anxious and worried. "Is the rescue unit on its way to the hospital?" When they all nodded, he asked, "Do you know what happened? Does anyone know the extent of Nicole's injuries?"

"I'm afraid not," Tim said. "They put her in the ambulance on a backboard."

"I tried to talk Nicole out of trying to jump the rock walls, but she was insistent Jubilee could do it," Derek told Jack.

"Most unfortunate. I'm going to turn around in the field up ahead and then go straight to the hospital. Kathleen can ride Jubilee to the farm with you."

Once Kathleen and Tim were mounted, the group continued on its way. The ride back to the barn was a somber one for the seven riders, each quiet and lost in his or her own thoughts. They had no way of knowing if Nicole was badly injured. Everyone was glad when they reached the top of the hill by the bungalow and could look down on the farm. Prince no longer tugged on the bit to go faster, and Sarah sensed that he, too, was tired by the events of the morning. His remarkable performance on the trail was marred by the accident, and Sarah could no longer take any joy from the beautiful day.

Mrs. Romano was waiting for Kayla and Fanny with the trailer hooked up. Kayla and Sarah parted company at the edge of the parking area. "Let's talk later," Kayla said, "as soon as either of us finds out anything."

The other riders dismounted in the courtyard and led their horses into the barn. "This was quite a workout for our horses" Sarah said to Derek, as they untacked on the cross-ties. "Prince seemed to be dragging a bit on the way home."

"Yeah," Derek said. "I think they'll both be glad to be back in their stalls with some hay to munch on."

"I'm sorry you didn't get to jump the rock walls. It was a blast," Sarah said. Then before she thought about what she was saying, it slipped out. "Maybe we can go back there sometime." She felt her cheeks warming and quickly turned away from Derek so he couldn't see her blush.

"I'd like that," he said. "Bismarck deserves a chance to try some cross-country." He slapped his horse on his neck affection- ately. "Right, old buddy?"

They were brushing their horses when Mrs. DeWitt came around the corner. She wasn't dressed in jodhpurs as usual when at the barn, and her face was serious. "I've just come from the hos- pital," Mrs. DeWitt said in a quiet voice. "Nicole has two broken ribs from the fall she took today. Evidently she was thrown into the rock wall when her horse refused. Thank goodness she was wearing her riding helmet, because there was a large dent in it. Without its protection, she could have suffered a skull injury—and that could have been fatal."

"She's going to be all right, isn't she?" Sarah asked.

"Oh, yes. According to Mrs. Jordan, Nicole was given medica- tion for pain. She's young and in good health, so she should be good as new before long."

"I just wish she had listened to me," Derek said, frowning. "I had my doubts Nicole and Kelly's horses were experienced or fit enough to try that cross-country run. But they were determined to do it." He looked down and shook his head. "Maybe I should have argued the point more forcefully."

"What's done is done," Mrs. DeWitt said. "You shouldn't bear any guilt over this, Derek. You weren't put in charge of them. Some people in this world are headstrong and get themselves into trouble." She turned to head back down the aisle. "There are others waiting to hear how Nicole's doing, so I'll be going. But I also want to thank you for all you did in response to the accident, Derek. I hear you were the hero of the day, calling 911, telling Nicole not to move, and then leading the ET's to the site of her fall. You handled it all in an impressive, mature manner."

After her horse was resting comfortably in his stall and belatedly eating his noon hay ration, Sarah swept both long aisles in the barn. She felt incredibly tired and wanted to go home. When she finally pedaled down Ridge Road, she mulled over the best way to share the day's events with her parents. Hearing about this accident was bound to put them on edge, worrying about *her* safety. But not to tell them about it… well, she'd been down that road, and by now she knew the best policy was to be open and honest.

CHAPTER 15

First Snow

SUNLIGHT SPLASHING ACROSS her face woke Sarah from a restless sleep. Raising her head to look at her clock radio, she sat up abruptly. She had overslept! She must have forgotten to set her alarm. It was Saturday, and she needed to get to the barn to feed the horses. When she looked out the window, Sarah couldn't believe her eyes. With Christmas only a week away, a surprise storm during the night had dropped a goodly amount of snow on the ground, the first of the season. The weather front must have been fast-moving, for now morning sunshine reflected brightly on the crystal white surface.

No time for breakfast, she thought, as she hastily splashed some cold water on her face, brushed her hair into a ponytail, and grabbed some clothes from her bureau. Jeans, any old jeans, and a sweatshirt would do. She reached for the feed room key on the wall hook and slipped its chain over her head. She'd hate to face Gus at the barn if she left home without it.

Sarah hurried downstairs, where her father was in the kitchen drinking coffee and reading the newspaper. She went to a living room window to check on the condition of Ridge Road. It appeared to be plowed, but looked too slippery for bike travel.

"Dad," she said, rushing back into the kitchen, "could you possibly take me to the barn? I don't think I can bike it today. And I need to be there ASAP!"

"What about breakfast?" he asked, frowning. "You've got a long day ahead of you."

"No time for that right now," Sarah said, dashing to the mud-room closet to find her winter boots. She pulled out her heavy jacket, a ski hat, and some warm gloves. After stuffing her pad-dock boots and a pair of barn sneakers into a plastic bag, she went back to the kitchen for Prince's carrots and the sandwich she had made the night before.

Her father handed her two granola bars and an orange. "Put these in your bag. You're going to need more nourishment today. And don't forget your water bottle."

In a matter of minutes, they were headed to Brookmeade Farm in her father's Hyundai. The trees along the way were made beau-tiful by snow clinging to their branches, and the wreath with a large red bow Mrs. DeWitt had hung on the farm sign was frosted in white. Soon they were traveling along the farm road, the sun's rays glistening on the snow in the fields. There was no sign of the broodmares, and Sarah could imagine them enjoying their hay in the comfort of their warm stalls this morning.

"Gus must have been out first thing to plow this road," Sarah commented.

"He's probably an early riser," Mr. Wagner said, as he pulled up in front of the barn's main entrance. "Call me or your mother when you need a ride home. I'll be around most of the day."

Sarah gathered her things and pushed the car door open. A blast of frigid air smacked her in the face as she made her way to the barn's main entrance. She was glad she had worn winter boots and wouldn't have to be outside in the bone-numbing cold long. The steps and walkway hadn't been shoveled, but she broke a path through the new snow and pushed the door, with its own festive wreath, open. The barn was quiet, the stillness interrupted only by the occasional sound of a horse moving in a stall.

The horses were eager to be fed, but Sarah couldn't resist going to Crown Prince's stall first, as always. He didn't sound his usual welcoming nicker in response to her soft whistle, and instead of moving to his stall door as she approached, Prince remained at the back of the stall looking out the window. She slid his stall door along its track and went into the stall. She was puzzled when he didn't turn to her, even to look for carrots. He stayed by the window.

Then it dawned on her. Prince had probably always been at Hank Bolton's farm in Florida during the winter months. He might never have seen snow before! Sarah smiled. No wonder he was fascinated by the view. He finally took the carrot she offered, but then turned back to the window.

Leaving the stall, Sarah went to the tack room to leave her bag on her trunk before hurrying to the feed room. On the way, she saw Gus coming in her direction carrying a shovel and a broom. "Good morning," she called as they passed. Gus only grunted an acknowledgment, his eyes staring straight ahead. Oh, well. Gus loved all the horses at Brookmeade and had enough good qualities to make up for being a complete grouch.

After the horses had been fed their morning grain rations and she'd knocked hay down into their stalls, Sarah returned to Crown Prince. She was relieved to see he could tear himself away from his window long enough to clean up his grain and eat his hay. Turning him out after he'd finished eating would be fun. She was dying to see how he would react to the snow!

Paige was stamping snow from her boots when Sarah stopped by Quarry's stall on her way to begin sweeping. "It sure looks like Christmas out there," Paige said. "We'll definitely be riding inside this morning."

"Prince was all bug-eyed looking at the snow from his window," Sarah said. "I think he may never have seen it before. I'm going to turn him out later so he can play in it for a while."

"Did you hear that Nicole Jordan might be able to ride again in a month or so?" Paige asked. "Kelly told me yesterday. Nicole was lucky, you know. She had two broken ribs, but it could have been worse. If she wasn't wearing a helmet, who knows what might have happened.

Paige grabbed Quarry's halter and lead shank before opening his stall door. "Don't let Prince make any snowmen in his paddock," she said, with a twinkle. Sarah walked away, smiling. She picked up a push broom and went to sweep the lounge, thinking about Nicole's accident. Sarah had been relieved that her parents didn't freak out and become paranoid about *her* safety when they heard about it.

After sweeping the lounge and two tack rooms, she checked her watch. Prince should have cleaned up his hay by now, and hopefully it had warmed up some outdoors. She was glad that with all the horses' body heat, the barn stayed warmer than it was outside. Prince had finished eating and was looking out his window again when she got back to his stall. "Okay, big boy, it's time for an adventure," she said, going to him with his halter and lead. She picked out his feet and removed his winter blanket. He would be outside only a short time, and could play in the snow better without it. Grooming him could come later. After putting on her parka, hat, and gloves, she led her horse to the exit leading to the paddocks.

When Sarah slid the barn door open, Prince's head came up and he snorted loudly. Squinting in the bright sunshine, he held back when she stepped out into the snow. "Come on, don't be a sissy," she said, as she put more pressure on the shank. With more urging, he reluctantly stepped off the cement. When his feet sank into the snow, he began prancing, lifting his feet high. Sarah couldn't help laughing. His walk became more normal as they got closer to the paddock and he became more confident in the snow.

No other horses had been turned out yet, so Sarah could choose any paddock except the one reserved for the school horses. The snow crunched under her boots and she hunched against the cold as she led Prince into the largest one on the end, a paddock that was usually taken. He'd have plenty of room to frolic in the snow there. She unsnapped his lead shank and slipped back through the gate. At first Prince stood like a statue, surveying the snow-covered landscape. The only movement she could see was the intermittent streams of vapor his breath shot out into the cold air.

Suddenly Prince half-reared, and when he came down, he bolted for the far end of the paddock, his movement beautiful to watch. He had no difficulty getting traction in the snow, and as he neared the end of the turnout, he made a large loop, which brought him back toward Sarah. "He likes the snow! she thought. Without slowing his pace, Prince continued circling the paddock. At one point, he cut to the center and came to a skidding halt. After pawing the snow a few times, he slowly lowered his large body into it and rolled onto his back. With his legs waving above him, he swung his back from side to side. Then he was up and off again, going even faster.

After Prince had circled a few more times, Sarah began to worry. At this rate, he would probably get sweated up, if he wasn't already, and it was too cold for that! She let herself back into the paddock and started walking toward the center, whistling softly. She fished down into her coat pocket for her last carrot, hoping that would bring him to her. Prince slowed as he went by her, and when he saw Sarah's outstretched hand with the carrot, he turned and came trotting back. He quickly scooped up the carrot. Without touching him, Sarah could see that his neck and chest were wet with sweat.

"You had quite a run for yourself," Sarah said, as she clipped the lead shank to his halter and led him through the gate toward the barn. She usually cleaned his stall while he was turned out, but that plan had backfired. She headed to the indoor, where she could walk her horse until he was cool. Derek was riding Bismarck there when they arrived, and he walked his horse over to them.

"Looks like he did some running in the paddock," Derek said, his eyes running over Prince. "He's pretty steamy."

"Yeah, I put him in the big paddock, and he made it into a mini-racetrack. He acted like he'd never seen snow before. He ran for quite a while before I could nab him." She reached up to run her hand along Prince's neck. "I'm afraid he got pretty sweated up."

"Do you have a cooler?" Derek asked.

"That's on my Christmas list, along with some galloping boots," Sarah replied. "It's too bad Santa can't deliver them this morning."

Derek remained serious. "I think he needs a cooler right now, Sarah. It's pretty cold, and you don't want him to get sick. I've got one in my tack trunk." Derek dismounted from Bismarck, tossed his irons over the saddle, and handed the reins to Sarah. "Hold him while I go grab it for you."

While Sarah stood holding both horses, Prince kept reaching out to playfully nip at Bismarck, who shook his head, pulling back.

She was glad when Derek returned a few minutes later. He tossed a maroon wool cooler over Prince's back and drew it high up on his neck, securing it in front. "You want to put this on him instead of his winter blanket, because the wetness from his body will wick up through the wool. Once he's cool and dry, you can put his winter blanket back on."

Sarah felt embarrassed. She guessed she'd been pretty stupid to turn Prince out in the large paddock, knowing he would run. "Thanks, Derek," she said. "I guess I totally blew this one, putting him in the large paddock. No way will I be riding him today."

While Sarah walked Prince slowly around the indoor, she had a chance to watch some of the other Brookmeade horses being ridden there. Lindsay's class would begin soon, and cavalletti would divide the arena into two work areas. The new boarders, Jan and Brian Smith, who had moved their two Appaloosas to Brookmeade in early December, were doing some basic flatwork. Paige must have finished schooling Quarry, but Kelly was riding Midnight Jet and Tim was on Rhodes practicing some of the movements Jack had introduced in the last lesson. Sarah was relieved that Kelly appeared to be keeping her distance from Crown Prince.

When Prince felt dry beneath Derek's cooler, Sarah headed to the gate and led him back to his stall. She let him have a small drink from his bucket before putting on his winter blanket. She neatly folded Derek's cooler and was placing it with his things when Derek returned with Bismarck.

"Are you going to be here for a while?" he asked. "I can't hang around today, but I'd like to turn Bismarck out for a bit. Would you be willing to bring him in for me?"

"Sure," Sarah said, secretly pleased to have the chance to help Derek. "No problem. That's the least I can do after you saved Prince from maybe getting sick."

Derek untacked his horse and led him out to a paddock while Sarah finished her horse's stall. Then she swept the aisles in the barn. She was famished by the time she finished and took her lunch to the lounge. After she'd polished off her sandwich, she decided it was time to bring Bismarck back to his stall.

Stepping out into the path of packed snow, Sarah breathed in the cold fresh air. She looked for Bismarck and saw that Derek had also chosen the farthest paddock. Bismarck stood at the far end, intently watching something by the woods, his breaths coming in visible puffs. As she got closer, she could see that his body was rigid and his head high as he sniffed the wind. He moved closer to the fence, his nostrils quivering. Sarah was immediately curious. What was grabbing his attention? She slipped through the white rails and walked toward the horse.

Getting closer, she saw what Bismarck found so interesting – something she had never seen before. Coyotes were standing at the edge of the woods surveying the paddocks and stable area. Sarah immediately knew what they were from a newspaper article her father had pointed out not long ago. It had said Yardley's police chief was concerned about the growing number of sightings of coyotes in town, and the newspaper included a picture of two coyotes feeding on an animal they had killed. Mr. Wagner read aloud from the article that two dogs and a number of cats were reported missing, and that everyone, especially farmers in the north end of town, should remain vigilant. A young sheep had been killed on a Yardley farm, and the chief surmised that the wild deer herd might be severely cut back.

Sarah stopped in her tracks and watched the coyotes closely. After a few minutes, she walked slowly toward Derek's horse and stood beside him. The large bay was engrossed with the coyotes, and he didn't acknowledge her presence when she leaned against him and stroked his neck. The coyotes were so close Sarah could have hit one with a stone. She counted seven in the pack, a few much bigger than the others. The largest coyote stood in front, showing no fear as he stared directly into her eyes. His coat was a grayish-yellow with reddish fringe around his ears. Finally the coyote's gaze turned away as he surveyed the farm and other horses in paddocks near them, his head turning slowly to take in a wide span of the acreage.

Sarah gripped the lead shank tighter, anxiety coursing through her. There were so many of them! What if they rushed at her and Bismarck? She needed to get Derek's horse back to the safety of the barn and away from them. Quickly running her shank over the horse's nose and attaching it to his halter, Sarah pulled him around and started for the paddock gate. "Come on, Bis, let's get out of here," she said. Bismarck resisted, not wanting to let the coyotes out of his sight, but Sarah pulled harder. He pranced beside her until they were out of the paddock and heading for the barn.

Tim was leading Rhodes to his stall when they got back to the barn. Sarah called out to him. "Tim! You'll never guess what I just saw! There's a pack of coyotes near the edge of the woods by the paddocks, at least six or seven of them. It was like they were staking out the place."

"Really?" Tim replied in surprise. "I didn't know there were coyotes around here. I know in California, where my cousins live, coyotes are everywhere, even in the suburbs. In some places they've crossed with wolves. They're called coy wolves and can grow almost as big as timber wolves."

Sarah shuddered. "I suppose they wouldn't mind having a horse on the menu once in a while."

Tim shook his head. "I think our horses might be too big for them to handle, but they could make a meal of one of the foals, if they were still around."

"I think Gus and Jack need to know about this," Sarah said. She led Bismarck back to his stall and picked the packed snow out of his hooves. She rubbed her hands together to warm them before leaving to find the two men. As she rounded the corner, Gus's red baseball hat came into view. He was pushing a wheelbarrow toward the school horses' section of the barn, and Sarah hurried after him. As she got closer, she scuffed her feet on the cement so she wouldn't startle him. "Excuse me, Gus."

The burly man swung around. "What do you want?" he said, scowling.

"I saw a pack of coyotes near one of the paddocks when I brought Bismarck in a little while ago. I thought you'd like to know."

Gus's face softened a tad, and he stepped closer. "Did you happen to notice how many of 'em there were?"

"I think there were seven, and a few of them were pretty big. One especially. They were on the edge of the woods, and close to the far paddock. It seemed like they were checking things out, looking all around."

"I heard 'em howling last night," Gus said. "Sounded like they were up on the ridge."

"Do you think they would ever go after one of the horses?" Sarah asked.

"Well, it wouldn't be the first time. A coyote can move pretty fast, and if a pack of 'em had a horse cornered in a paddock, they could do some damage. As long as the horse isn't too big, a couple of 'em will try to hamstring him from behind while the others go for the jugular. I've seen it happen. Just like wolves."

The more Sarah heard, the more she feared for Crown Prince

and all the other horses. Those coyotes were so close to Bismarck today, and they seemed to have no fear.

"Do you think it's safe to put the horses out in the paddocks?" Sarah asked. "What if the whole pack of coyotes ganged up on one of the horses?" This scenario filled her with terror. "I'm going to tell Jack about this," Sarah said to Gus, as she hurried to the office, hoping Jack would be there. She hadn't seen him around the barn all day, which was rare.

Sarah was surprised to find both Mr. and Mrs. DeWitt in the office talking to Lindsay. They turned to greet Sarah when she entered the room. Spin and Cameo rushed to jump up on her, and she gave them each a quick pat.

"My, but you look serious, Sarah," Mrs. DeWitt said. "Is something wrong?"

"I hope not," Sarah replied. She went on to tell them about the coyotes, adding what she could remember from the newspaper article. "Do you think the horses are in any danger?"

"I saw that article, too," Mr. DeWitt said, frowning, "and I've been hoping the coyotes wouldn't make it to our farm." His gaze shifted to Lindsay. "Do you know if there have been any other sightings here?"

"None that I know of," Lindsay replied. "I think Jack would have mentioned it to us."

Mr. DeWitt quickly looked up a number in the directory and then reached for the office phone. Once someone picked up, he asked a few questions and then listened intently. He turned to them after he hung up, his face creased with worry lines. "The officer I just spoke to said that while there are quite a few coyotes on the rural side of town, there hasn't been an incident of them attacking anything larger than a young sheep. But he feels that while they wouldn't bother adult horses, we shouldn't turn out anything smaller." He turned to Mrs. DeWitt. "Dogs and cats are particularly vulnerable, so we'll have to keep our terriers in unless we're with them. I also think we should keep the ponies inside too, at least for a while."

Mrs. DeWitt bent over to hug Cameo. "We certainly can't take any chances," she said.

Despite the reassurance Mr. DeWitt had gotten from the policeman, Sarah felt a gnawing concern. Was Prince at risk turned out in the paddocks? She excused herself and left the office.

CHAPTER 16
An Announcement

MORE SNOW FELL during the weeks that followed, and as to be expected during the month of January, the thermometer frequently plunged, often dipping to near zero. After the coldest nights, there would be a coating of ice on the horses' water buckets in the morning, and until the snow got packed down after a snowstorm, it was a challenge leading the horses to the turnout paddocks. As he did every winter, Gus had outfitted the farm pickup with a plow, and he faithfully kept the farm road open. He also sanded the road when it got icy.

Everyone had been asked to report further sightings of coyotes on the farm, but none were noticed after the first snow. Sarah was worried for a while, but eventually she began to relax when her horse was turned out. After a week without any unsupervised turnout, Pretty Penny and Snippet went back into their paddock, but Mrs. DeWitt continued to watch the terriers closely.

Sarah wasn't happy she'd have to suspend riding her bike to the farm, since that meant she'd depend on her parents for transportation. She looked forward to the time she'd once again have the flexibility of pedaling herself to and from the farm.

Chores on the weekend took longer in cold weather. Sarah had to deal with frozen buckets on some Sunday mornings, and her sweeping often involved cleaning up snow the horses tracked into the barn. Almost all the boarders wanted their horses turned out wearing blankets. Crown Prince had come to accept the snow as no big deal, and he stopped galloping in the paddock. His short but thick winter coat was darker than his summer coat, and even more beautiful. To keep him from slipping on ice, the farrier had shod him with winter shoes tipped with borium.

Kayla's mother still trucked Fanny to Brookmeade for her weekly lessons, and the Snyders' van also made the trip, although sometimes it was touch-and-go climbing the long hill out of the parking area on the way home. Four-wheel-drive certainly helped. "You're lucky you have an indoor to ride in," Kayla complained to Sarah, as they rode home from school on a lesson day. "With all the snow we've had this winter, there's no way I can ride in the ring at home. Sometimes it's even too icy to hack. Rita's got it made—her indoor arena was finished before cold weather set in."

"Fanny's been doing great in the lessons, though," Sarah replied, grabbing the seat when the bus wrenched to the side to avoid a deep rut.

"That's probably because we've been doing a lot of jumping, and Fanny likes that. The fences are getting up there, don't you think?"

"Yeah. I'm relieved Prince can keep up with you guys," Sarah replied. "Maybe there'll be a January thaw one of these days. I wish the snow would settle enough so we could do a little hacking. I worry Prince will get bored with all the ringwork." She swung her knees to the side so Kayla could get by her as the bus slowed by the Romanos' driveway. "See you at the barn!"

Later that afternoon, the Young Riders class was warming up for their lesson when Jack arrived a few minutes early. He wore a heavy parka, thick gloves, and winter boots. A few spectators preferred to watch the lesson from the heated lounge, but those who wanted to hear Jack's comments braved the cold on the bleachers. It was surprising how many people turned out to watch the class when the temperature hovered near the freezing mark. The DeWitts were almost always there, with Spin and Cameo on leashes and wearing their Baker dog blankets. Sarah's mother usually begged off when it was this cold, but Derek always came to watch the lesson. Today was no exception.

"Would you please line your horses up in the center?" Jack called out. The riders looked puzzled as they brought their horses to walk and came to face him in the middle of the arena. This was not the way Jack usually began his lessons. "I have something to share with all of you before we begin today," he said, as he removed a glove and pulled a piece of paper from his pocket. "I received some information today about an upcoming competition."

The riders looked at one another. Rita rolled her eyes. "Oh, I know," Jack continued, "you're not looking for shows or events to compete in right now. This competition won't take place until early summer, but it's an exciting team event that will take some preparation and give us something to be working toward."

After drawing his reading glasses from his jacket pocket and putting them on, Jack scanned the paper before continuing. "I'm not sure how many of you have heard of Wexford Hall. It's an equestrian center a few hours' drive from here that holds two major recognized events each year. They offer Intermediate and Advanced divisions in the fall, which not many competitions do, so a number of riders long-listed for the Olympic team usually compete there."

Jack adjusted his glasses before continuing. "The announcement notified me of a special competition for junior riders, The

Wexford Cup, which will be held for the first time this year in mid-June. They want to prepare more young riders to represent the United States in future international equestrian competitions. Using a more traditional event format, over three days competitors ride a dressage test, a cross-country course, and a round of show jumping, with cumulative scores."

Jack looked up from the paper to speak to his students. "'Tis exciting, I think, because 'twill follow the Olympic format and have riders competing in teams of four. One additional team member will serve as a stable manager, to help the riders and keep the team organized. The team with the highest total score for all four riders will take home the Wexford Cup." The class exchanged looks, each rider obviously enthusiastic about the prospect of riding in the competition.

"I know this event is several months away," Jack continued, "but it's something we'll have to train for, if indeed you're interested in participating." Tim, who tended to be competitive, was smiling broadly. Sarah looked at Kayla, who replied with a thumbs-up. Sarah wasn't sure what to think, except she had a pretty good idea who the stable manager would be—the rider in the class whose horse had the least experience!

"This sounds like a grand competition," Jack continued. "I expect a large number of teams from near and far will be entered, which will give all of you an opportunity to meet other young talented riders and see their horses in action. It will be a beneficial experience, to be sure."

Rita raised her hand. "If this is held over three days, where will the riders stay?"

Jack looked down at his notes. "There's a private school nearby, The Belmont School, which is making a dorm available for lodging."

"Does it say which dressage test will be used and how high the fences will be?" Tim asked.

"I'll post the details on the bulletin board by the office. Anyone who rides at Brookmeade is eligible to try out for the team, and I'll announce the competition in other classes, as well. And I should mention that because the team will be representing Brookmeade Farm, the DeWitts have agreed to cover related entry fees." He removed his glasses and put them away. "If any of you aspire to make the Brookmeade Farm team and do well at Wexford Hall, you must be prepared to work hard and spend a lot of time conditioning your horses. Now let's get to work, beginning with your exercises."

As the lesson progressed, Sarah's mind kept coming back to the news of the team competition. Wouldn't it be wonderful if Jack's team brought the Wexford Cup back to Brookmeade Farm! He certainly was an outstanding instructor—and deserved a winning team!

After the class had finished with the flatwork portion of the lesson, Jack suggested they let the horses walk on a long rein. The dressage exercises required hard work and concentration, asking the horses to stretch and use muscles in challenging ways. Sarah knew that Prince always tried his best for her, and she reached down to run her hand along his neck. "Good boy," she said softly.

While the horses and riders took a short break, Jack made some adjustments on a gymnastic line of jumps he had set up earlier. Jump standards were in place for what would be a jumping line, but to start, only a few of the poles had been placed in the cups. Jack placed one pole on the ground a stride in front of the first jump to serve as a ground line. It would place the horses in the right spot to easily jump the first fence, a cross-rail. Next in line was a vertical jump. It looked pretty simple, except for one thing. The cross-rail was quite close to the next fence, a vertical.

Jack pointed to the jump. "You can see the distance from the cross-rail to the vertical is short. This kind of a combination is called a bounce, which means your horses will land after the cross-rail, and without taking a stride, should immediately jump the vertical." Sarah was immediately anxious. With Prince's long stride, would he land too close to the next fence to be able to jump it? And while the rails were low to start out, she knew that once the horses got the hang of it, the rails would go nowhere but up.

Jack called out to the class when it was time to resume work. "I'd like you to gather your horses and spread out in the arena tracking right." He watched, pleased that the horses were well spaced along the track using the whole arena. "Now pick up canter from walk, and with Rita as your lead rider, come through the combination. Keep a good distance between horses, and don't let them be strung out or quick. The ground rail should set them up perfectly for the bounce."

The riders picked up canter as Jack had asked, although Prince took a few trot steps before breaking into canter. Rita, the lead rider, shifted her focus to the jump line as she came off the track, setting up Chancellor to come in straight to the cross-rail at an ideal speed. He cantered over the ground rail, jumped the cross-rail, and without taking another stride, easily jumped the low vertical. "Good job, Rita," Jack called.

Sarah was passing the bleachers just as the group of spectators sitting there clapped loudly for Rita, causing Prince to shy sideways and speed away from them. *Darn!* Sarah thought. *The timing couldn't have been worse!* She brought Prince back to the track and slowed down his canter. But he was rattled, and she knew it would take a few minutes for him to regain his concentration. Jack had noticed what happened, and he held his arm toward the bleachers, signaling the onlookers to hold future applause.

Kayla was next in line, and she turned Fanny toward the jumps to get a straight approach. Fanny's ears were straight forward as she eyed the combination, sizing up the challenge. Kayla sat tall in the saddle and waited for the mare, who jumped everything in good form. "Excellent, Kayla," Jack shouted as they cantered away. Paige also did a great job on Quarry, keeping him from being too quick without putting him in a strangle hold. Jack praised her for her finesse in the approach. Tim and Rhodes were next. The strong bay horse went through as if he'd done it a thousand times, earning good compliments from Jack.

Now that it was Sarah's turn, her heart was in her throat. Prince had never done a bounce before. She needed to keep him in a frame so he wouldn't go too fast or get strung out. Coming toward the jumps, Sarah could feel that Prince was committed. He was such an honest horse! But he was green, and she needed to use her aids correctly to help him figure it out. The ground pole put Prince in a good position to jump the cross-rail, and on landing he immediately jumped the vertical. But in jumping out, he misjudged the height of the rail and scraped his rear feet against it.

"Come around and try that again, Sarah," Jack called. The practice helped Prince, for this time he went through the combination cleanly. Jack had them trot momentarily while he raised the height of the cross-rail and the vertical jump.

"Come through again, beginning with Rita," Jack called. This time all the horses handled the bounce with no problem, prompting Jack to again raise the height of the vertical. Now jumping it would require a substantial push from behind. When once more the horses met the challenge, Jack asked the riders to walk while he dragged standards and another rail into place to change the vertical into a square oxer. Now the jump out of the bounce had changed from a single rail to a substantial spread fence, requiring even more effort from the horses.

"You'll continue to have the advantage of the ground rail and crossbar to place your horses perfectly for the last jump," Jack said. "But to jump it cleanly, they will need to push harder with their hindquarters and tuck their knees up in front, a good training exercise."

When the riders picked up canter once more, Sarah couldn't help feeling somewhat intimidated. This would be the most difficult challenge Prince had ever faced in a lesson. The oxer looked so big! Maybe she should just close her eyes and let Prince figure it out. *No!* she reminded herself. *If Prince needs my help, I must be there for him. We're a team!*

Rita looked confident and relaxed as she approached the fences, and Chancellor calmly went down the line, demonstrating a perfect jump over the oxer. Kayla was next, and from the way she was gripping the reins, Sarah could tell her friend was nervous. But Kayla was determined to do it and she rode the combination with a strong leg. When Fanny sailed over the oxer with room to spare, Kayla was delighted. "Good girl!" she called out, slapping Fanny's neck.

"Were your spurs meeting in the middle, Kayla?" Jack teased.

Jack called to Paige as Quarry turned from the track to approach the combination. "Remember that speed won't help him over this, Paige. It will only make his jump flat. Keep your legs on while you control the pace." Quarry leaped over the cross-rail and immediately pushed off with a round jump over the oxer. Paige was beaming as she rode her horse back to the track. Tim went next. Rhodes didn't seem to notice that the jump was more challenging, as he cleared it in good form before returning to the track.

Here we go, Prince, Sarah thought. She took a deep breath and began her approach. Prince had gained confidence from going through the bounce a few times, and now he showed no hesitation. Even as he jumped the crossrail, he understood a bigger effort was needed for the oxer, and his powerful hindquarters pushed him and Sarah over it easily. As they cantered away, out of the corner of her eye, Sarah saw someone in the bleachers stand up and pump his fist. It was Derek, and in spite of herself, she felt her heart leap. If only her parents could have been here too! Kayla shot her a thumbs-up as Sarah passed her on her way back to the track.

"Let's close up behind Rita one horse's length distance, and then come back to walk," Jack called out. When the riders were together, Jack walked beside them while they kept their horses moving. The horses were warm from the long period of canter and needed to walk on a long rein. Glad to have a break, they all stretched their heads and necks down.

Fanny was the only horse that seemed slightly stressed. She had perspired a lot, and she was breathing rapidly. "It looks like your mare has lost some condition," Jack said, his face showing concern. "With the winter weather, have you not been able to get her out?" Kayla nodded. "Even if you can't ride in your ring, I suggest you hack her along the road every chance you get, except when it's icy. The Yardley town crews plow the snow back to give you a generous shoulder to ride on, so you and Fanny should be safe from traffic. Of course Fanny will need winter shoes with borium to do this, and remember to always ride with traffic on the right hand side of the road."

Sarah felt Prince's neck. It was warm, but he hadn't broken into a sweat. *He must be getting fit,* Sarah thought. *All the riding I've been doing has paid off.*

"You all did very well today," Jack said to the group. "Exercises such as the bounce are an excellent way to strengthen your horses and prepare them for jumping higher fences." He paused a moment to watch the horses as they walked by. When he was satisfied none were taking any lame steps after the workout, he continued. "We'll be doing more gymnastic work as we prepare for the Wexford Hall event, although you'll profit from it no matter what discipline you choose—hunters, jumpers, equitation, eventing, or dressage. As the weeks progress, we'll be adding additional elements to the jumping line, which will be even more challenging. We'll be riding courses too, and, of course, we'll continue to work on your dressage."

Sarah's fingers tightened on the reins. Were she and Prince ready for all this? He was trying hard, and so far he had handled every challenge sent his way. But was he being rushed? Could Jack be pushing him too fast? She'd read about horses whose training was moved along too quickly. Somewhere along the line they'd lost confidence, something that couldn't always be regained. She certainly didn't want that to happen to her horse!

After the riders were excused, Derek walked back to Prince's stall with Sarah. "Considering how long he's been in training, you've got a star here," he said. "I wish you could see how good he looks going over a fence."

Sarah couldn't help smiling. Anything Derek said was exciting to her, and he had certainly given her some wonderful compliments. She became more serious. "Is it possible Jack is pushing Crown Prince too fast, just so we can keep up with the Young Riders class? I don't want my horse to hit a brick wall one of these days, if he can't deal with what's being asked of him." She watched Derek's face closely, waiting for his answer.

"I ride with Jack, too," Derek replied. "I never get the sense that Bismarck is being overly challenged. In fact, as Jack did in your lesson today, he always presents things in such a measured way that we work up to the big challenges gradually. Jack's approach makes things seem easy."

"But you're having private lessons," Sarah reminded him. "In my case, Prince has to do what is best for the rest of the class. I just hope Jack doesn't ask for more than Prince is ready to do."

As Sarah earnestly confided her concerns to Derek, he looked into her dark eyes with their long lashes. From the minute he'd met Sarah, on the day Bismarck arrived at Brookmeade Farm, Derek had felt an attraction to this girl. There was something special, something different about her that appealed to him. Perhaps it was her unassuming personality and dedication to her horse. She was so different from the girls who routinely had it on their agendas to snag him. But while she had always been friendly and fun to be with, there was a certain aloofness about her that gave the impression she wouldn't want to be more than just his friend. Perhaps he was imagining this. It was time to find out.

There was a pause in the conversation as Derek looked intently at Sarah, hesitating. Finally it slipped out. "There's going to be a winter carnival at my school this weekend. They've got a lot of cool things planned. Would you like to check it out with me Saturday afternoon?" Now he studied her face, holding his breath, waiting for a reply.

For a minute, Sarah wondered if she had heard Derek right. Had he actually asked her for a date? Ever since she'd learned about that girl named Meredith, Derek's girlfriend in Chicago, Sarah hadn't allowed herself to think of Derek as anything more than a friend who shared her love of horses and riding. But now this! Did she want to be a convenient second-best girlfriend because number one was a long way off? She was a little tempted, but more irritated and offended.

Sarah met Derek's gaze for a moment before she turned away, shaking her head. "I don't think so, Derek. I've got way too much going on, what with school, my job here at the barn, and my horse. Let's just be riding friends, okay?"

CHAPTER 17

The Quarrel

FOR THE REST OF JANUARY and through the end of February, frequent snowstorms kept Sarah and Crown Prince off the hacking trails, and with a lot of ice everywhere, it wasn't safe to even take the horses for walks on the farm road. They had no choice but to ride in the indoor and practice the regimen Jack prescribed.

The lessons with the Young Riders were always challenging, and Sarah and Prince managed to keep up with the more experienced riders. The flatwork in the classes was as demanding as the jumping, as more difficult dressage movements were gradually introduced. Jack frequently reminded them that before moving up in dressage, a horse must have a strong foundation of the basics. Along with exercises such as leg-yielding, shoulder-in, and counter-canter, Jack taught the class how to lengthen and shorten their horses' strides. With his long, elastic movement, Prince excelled at this. Mrs. DeWitt came up to Sarah after one class to tell her how impressed she had been watching Crown Prince lengthen across the diagonal of the arena. "He's such a good mover!" she gushed. "Chandler and I are so happy to see you two blossom."

The better Prince performed in their lessons, the more aloof Rita became. She clearly resented another horse begin to approach Chancellor's brilliance. Her earlier argument that Prince would hold the Young Riders class back hadn't materialized—Prince and Sarah had shown dramatic improvement and clearly deserved to be there.

As winter slid into spring, Sarah was happy to have a Thursday afternoon off from school because of teachers' conferences. For once she could be at Brookmeade in time to watch Derek's two o'clock private lesson with Jack. Sarah was cleaning her horse's stall when Derek finished tacking up Bismarck. Derek rode in an all-purpose saddle for hacking, but today he was using his jumping saddle. With its extreme forward flaps, it worked well with the shorter stirrups he'd need for jumping high fences. His bridle had a Dr. Bristol bit and a figure-eight noseband.

"I finally get to see one of your lessons," Sarah said. "It's about time!"

"You mean I'll be observed by the critical eye today?" Derek said, grinning. "Now's your chance to get revenge for all the horrific things I've said about you and Prince." They both knew that the opposite was true. Derek was constantly reassuring her on days Sarah felt she hadn't ridden well. His words had gone a long way toward boosting her self-confidence and helping her believe she was capable of riding with the more experienced riders.

Sarah tossed a final forkful of soiled bedding into the wheelbarrow and pushed it to the manure bin. After spreading a load of fresh shavings in Prince's stall, she made a beeline for the indoor. Derek was warming Bismarck up when she got there. Jack hadn't arrived yet, and there were no other spectators as Sarah climbed to the third row on the bleachers. When Bismarck trotted by, Derek called out, "Have mercy!" Sarah only smiled.

A few minutes later Derek's parents strode into the arena. As they climbed up the bleachers to sit beside her, Mrs. Alexander beamed at Sarah. "It's a nice surprise to see you on a day that finally feels like spring," she said. "You're not usually here when Derek rides."

"We had a half day of school today," Sarah replied. She considered how good-looking Mrs. Alexander was, with expensive clothes, attractive makeup, and her hair stylishly coiffed.

"Derek's fortunate that Winchester Academy allows his riding activities to substitute for phys ed, so he can leave school early on Thursdays," Mrs. Alexander said. "We make a point of being here to watch his lessons with Jack whenever we can."

"We've been hearing good things from Derek about Bismarck's neighbor, Crown Prince," Mr. Alexander said. "He tells us your horse has a world of potential."

Sarah wasn't sure what to say. She always felt embarrassed when showered with compliments. After pausing a moment, she said, "We owe everything to Jack and his awesome instruction. Prince and I have learned so much from him."

Jack arrived at the same time Kelly and Nicole came into the arena and climbed up on the bleachers. Without saying a word, the girls went to the top row and slid to the far end away from Sarah.

Various jumps had been set up to make a course in the arena—spread fences, verticals, and combinations. Sarah was shocked by the size of the jumps. They were far bigger than anything her class had been asked to tackle. She was surprised when Jack began the lesson exactly as he did for the Young Riders, with exercises and flat work. After Derek trotted Bismarck in a long-and-low frame, he gradually gathered him between hand and leg and started bending and counter-bending exercises. These were followed by leg-yielding and counter-canter, frequent transitions and changes of direction. Lastly Derek worked on flying changes of lead, which Sarah knew were important on a jumping course.

When Jack felt Bismarck was sufficiently supple, he asked

Derek to come back to walk and shorten his stirrups before starting work over fences. Finally Derek had the handsome bay Holsteiner trot on a circle at one end of the arena before approaching the in-and-out. It had a moderate cross-rail as the first element, making it simple and inviting. *This is very much like what we do in my class,* Sarah thought, *except the jumps are higher and we've not gotten to flying changes of lead.*

There was no ground line in front of the in-and-out, but Bismarck trotted smartly to the cross-rail and jumped it easily. After taking one stride upon landing, he lifted off for the second element, a vertical, jumping it well. Jack quickly put the rail in a higher set of cups, and Derek came through again. "Don't get ahead of him," Jack called out, as he again raised the rail. The size of the vertical had risen dramatically, but it didn't seem to faze Bismarck or his rider. Jack raised the top rail one more time, and after Bismarck jumped it without difficulty, Jack asked Derek to continue on to a large oxer he had set up earlier.

Bismarck cantered confidently down the arena toward the jump. "Keep that pace," Jack called out, "and after the oxer, change direction and come to the red-and-white vertical. I hope to see a clean flying change four or five strides after the oxer." Bismarck pulled against the bit, anticipating the jump as he got closer, but Derek prevented him from going faster. They met the jump in just the right spot and sailed over in good form. "Well done!" Jack said.

Bismarck cantered away, and a few strides after the jump, Derek asked him to change from his left lead to his right in preparation for turning into the next jump. But Bismarck changed only with his front legs, and not behind, leaving his canter awkward and unbalanced. After a few strides, the horse corrected himself, but Jack called out, "Skip the red-and-white, and repeat the oxer. This time sit up and have your horse strongly between hand and leg before you ask for the lead change." On the next attempt, Bismarck again jumped the fence athletically, and following it, Derek got a clean change of lead without being temporarily disunited. "Bravo!" Jack called out. "Now continue to the red-and-white. Following it, repeat the two fences again."

At one point Derek's mother leaned over to Sarah and whispered, "What do you think?"

"Compared to what my horse jumps, these fences are like skyscrapers!" Sarah replied.

After a short break, Derek and Bismarck finished by jumping a full course that included all the fences. It was an excellent performance, and Sarah was definitely impressed.

When Derek had halted his horse in the center, Jack walked over to speak with him a few minutes. Kelly and Nicole scampered down from the bleachers, and when Jack turned and left the arena, they ran over to Derek, walking beside him as he rode his horse toward his parents on the bleachers.

"You were amazing!" Nicole said, reaching up to pat Bismarck's shoulder.

Kelly beamed up at Derek. "You and Bismarck are awesome!" she said.

"Thanks," Derek said, looking ahead to his parents and Sarah. When he came to a halt in front of them, Kelly and Nicole continued to stroke Bismarck, standing in front of him. They peppered Derek with questions and compliments. In the face of Kelly and Nicole's exhibition, Sarah hung back. Finally Derek said, "Excuse me, girls," as he vaulted off his horse. They continued to stand between him and his parents as he ran up his irons.

Mrs. Alexander was frowning and seemed taken aback by the girls' aggressive behavior. She cleared her throat and said in an authoritative tone, "Excuse me, girls. If I may, I'd like to speak to my son." Kelly and Nicole looked surprised as they swung around to face her, mumbling, "See ya, Derek," before walking away.

Mrs. Alexander raised her eyebrows. "You are certainly being hounded by those two," she said.

"Oh, they're harmless," Derek replied, watching them go.

"Well, you and Bismarck performed incredibly well," Mr. Alexander said. "I think Jack O'Brien is bringing out the best in both of you."

"Thanks, Dad. I need to get Bismarck moving. He worked pretty hard. I'm going to walk him in the indoor after I put his cooler on." As he started to turn his horse away from them, his gaze landed on Sarah, standing shyly in the background. He stopped. "I hope we weren't too bad, coach," he said, grinning.

Sarah couldn't resist a smile. "Not *too* bad." Turning to leave, she waved to Derek and his parents. "I need to bring Prince in."

On her way to the paddocks, Sarah passed Quarry's stall. The door was shut, but Sarah stopped in her tracks when she heard a sob come from inside. She didn't move, listening. Yes, someone was in there with Quarry. Turning back to look more closely, she saw Paige standing on the far side of her horse, her face buried in the gray gelding's mane.

"Are you okay, Paige?" she said softly. There was no response for several moments, but then Paige came toward the door and slid it open enough for Sarah to squeeze in. Paige was obviously distraught, her face wet with tears, her eyes red and puffy. Sarah instinctively gave her a hug.

Other boarders might be within hearing distance, so Sarah's voice was low, almost a whisper when she said, "Is there anything I can do?"

Paige leaned back on the stall wall and covered her face with her hands, sobbing. Finally she pulled them away and met Sarah's gaze. "Tim and I had an awful fight," she murmured. "It's the first one we ever had, but it was serious. It might be a deal-breaker." Her head dropped, and she began to cry again.

Sarah was silent, wishing there was something she could say or do to comfort her friend.

When Paige could speak, she went on. "There's a girl that lives near Tim, and he's been giving her rides to school. Do you know Amy Campbell?"

Sarah nodded. "Not very well. You guys are a year ahead of me, but I know who she is."

"Well, I saw them in the cafeteria together, and they were definitely flirting. Tim says it's nothing. He says I've got a rich imagination, and that if I can't trust him on this one…. Her voice broke off, and more sobs followed. She reached into her pocket for a tissue and blew her nose loudly.

Sarah wished she knew the right thing to say. Paige had been her friend since she started riding at Brookmeade. "Would it help if you talk to Tim some more about this?" she said. "Maybe he's had a chance to think about it. Maybe he's sorry."

Paige shook her head. "He walked away from me. I'm not going to go crawling to him!" Quarry seemed to sense something was wrong and reached around to nuzzle Paige's hair. She gently pushed his gray muzzle away and reached out to stroke him. "I think I'm going to take off," Paige said. "I can't ride today. Quarry was turned out this morning, so he'll be okay."

"Are you sure there isn't anything I can do to help?" Sarah asked again.

Paige shook her head. She hugged Sarah and then her horse one last time. "Bye, Quarry," she said as the two girls left the stall. Paige slid the door shut and hurried down the aisle.

Sarah wondered if Tim was at the barn, but she saw no sign

of him as she walked down the aisle on her way to the paddock to bring her horse in. Paige was such a knockout! How could Tim even think about another girl? Sarah wondered if his interest in Amy Campbell was for real.

When Sarah neared his paddock, she saw Prince on the far side, grubbing for bits of grass where the snow had melted thin. This was the first day in a long time he hadn't worn a blanket when turned out. When she whistled softly, his ears shot forward and he raised his beautiful head to look her way, his large eyes watching her inquisitively. Against the backdrop of snow, he was like a noble statue.

Sarah slipped through the gate and went to her horse. He stretched his neck to lift the piece of carrot she held in her hand, chewing it as she attached the lead shank to his halter. His eyes were soft and wrinkled in the corners, showing he was glad to see her. "C'mon, buddy," she said, and they started back to the barn.

Derek was on his way to the side door as Sarah led Prince into the barn. She halted her horse in the aisle and called to Derek, speaking as he walked back to her. "I'm glad I caught you before you left. You and Bismarck were amazing today!" she said. "I can't imagine *ever* jumping fences that tall and wide."

Derek grinned. "But that's all we do," he said. "Bismarck doesn't have to do dressage tests or cross-country." He thought a minute. "He's a specialist."

"I don't know about that," Sarah said. "You were doing as many dressage movements in your warm-up with Jack as we do in our lessons. With all the flatwork training he's getting, Bismarck could be a fantastic event horse." She steadied Prince, who was tugging on the shank to get closer to Wichita in his stall. "Bismarck is a wonderful horse, Derek. I'm sure your parents think so, too."

"Yeah," he said. "They're looking forward to when we can start showing again. As for our flatwork, doing all the dressage stuff is entirely new to us. My instructor in Chicago didn't bother with anything except some generic walk, trot, and canter before we started jumping. Bismarck is going so much better with Jack's approach." He stepped back to leave. "Thanks for coming to my lesson."

Once Prince was on the cross-ties, Sarah got busy with her curry comb and brushes. He'd come to enjoy being groomed and was completely relaxed. His head drooped as she curried his rump in a strong, circular motion. While she was tacking him up, Sarah began to have second thoughts about what she and her horse would do that day. It was so warm and spring-like outside. Maybe she'd ditch her plan to work in the indoor and just hack Prince on the farm road instead. Yesterday's lesson had been like all of Jack's lessons—challenging—and perhaps Prince could use an easy routine today. The higher temps as of late had melted all the ice on the entry road, leaving the gravel surface soft and forgiving.

After putting on her helmet and grabbing her crop, Sarah led Prince from the barn to the mounting block in the courtyard. The afternoon sun was warmer than it had been for some time, promising spring and green grass around the corner. As they started up the entry road hill, she unzipped her jacket part way, soaking up the sun. At that moment she wished Derek was riding with her. They could talk about so many things, and after watching his lesson, she had a lot of questions.

Prince seemed content to walk without pulling to go faster, which was a blessing. She wasn't in a mood to contend with a feisty horse, and was glad he was walking quietly on a longish rein. After rounding the top of the hill by the O'Briens' bungalow, Sarah saw a car coming toward them, making its way along the road and over the bridge. It was Tim's black Jeep. Fortunately Gus plowed the road wide enough so Tim would have plenty of room to pass her, in spite of the remaining snow banks. When he got closer, the Jeep slowed and stopped right beside her.

Sarah halted her horse as Tim rolled down his window, wearing his typical grin. "Has a little spring fever driven you outside?" he asked?"

He's such a neat guy, Sarah thought. *It's no surprise lots of girls would put him in their sights.*

"I guess you could say that," she said. "After the winter we've had, the sun sure is nice. What are you doing today?"

"I'm not sure." He paused a moment. "Do you know if Paige is riding Quarry?"

Before she could bite her tongue, Sarah blurted out the words. "She left for home a little while ago. She seemed pretty upset." Sarah studied Tim's face, waiting for a response.

Tim shook his head and then looked up at Sarah. "Look, she's got this crazy idea that Amy Campbell and I've got something going. Amy lives a couple houses down from us. You know her, right?" When Sarah nodded, he went on. "Just because I give her a ride to school, Paige thinks I'm hitting on her."

Sarah thought a moment. "Why can't Amy take the bus like most of us do?" she asked. "Wouldn't that solve the problem?"

"The problem is that Paige doesn't trust me!" Tim said heatedly. He jerked his Jeep into gear and gunned off, spraying gravel back at them.

Prince shied at the car's sudden takeoff and pranced as Sarah turned him in a small circle. She sighed when he resumed walking quietly. Had she put her foot into her mouth big time? Maybe Paige wouldn't be thrilled she'd gotten involved. The last thing she needed was more drama at Brookmeade Farm! And this new development certainly didn't boost their chances of sending a winning team to Wexford Hall in June.

CHAPTER 18

Spring at Last

THE COMING OF SPRING brought expected changes to Brookmeade Farm. The outdoor sand ring went back into use, and riders could once again hack on the trails connected to the farm. The horses rolled in the paddocks regularly as they shed their winter coats, and winter blankets were laundered and stored away. As Sarah rode her bike to the barn once again, she reveled in the smells of thawing ground and budding trees. It was great that she didn't have to depend on anyone for a ride, and she could get to the barn on her own schedule.

The school break in April meant Sarah had a week of almost unlimited time with her horse. On their lesson day, she biked to the farm several hours in advance, thinking how nice it was not to be rushed. Prince would be turned out now, so after parking her bike by the side door of the barn, she first went to see if Paige was around. Quarry was on the cross-ties while Paige brushed his luxurious silver tail with a hairbrush just like the one Sarah had at home. Sarah grinned and shook her head as she pointed to it.

"It works better than anything I could get at a tack shop," Paige said. "It's gentle and doesn't pull out a lot of hair." She laughed. "Quarry's getting ready for his first movie, you know." Sarah was glad to hear Paige laugh again, something that had been rare lately.

Just then the Brookmeade Jack Russells came barreling down the aisle to play with Sarah. Spin and Cameo raced around her while she clapped her hands and spun in circles. She stopped and petted them as Mrs. DeWitt came closer.

"I have some news, girls," she said. "Athena has finally had her foal, a filly. I'm heading up there to see her. Would you like to come along?"

"Of course!" Paige said. "I'll put Quarry back in his stall." Sarah was equally excited. The other two mares had foaled over a month before, and everyone had been wondering why Athena was so late. They piled into Mrs. DeWitt's Mercedes for the ride to the carriage shed.

"Jack had a feeling last night would be the night," Mrs. DeWitt said, as she drove up the hill. "Athena was waxing, which is a good sign foaling is about to happen soon. Jack has a surveillance system set up so from the bungalow he can see and hear anything going on in the foaling stall. That, plus making regular checks, allows him to keep on top of things."

"What's waxing?" Sarah asked, leaning forward to hear her better.

"That's when the mare begins secreting milk from her udder," Mrs. DeWitt said, "usually just before foaling." When they pulled into the driveway, Jack stepped out of the bungalow on his way to the carriage shed. He waved.

"Aren't we lucky! Jack can tell us all about it," Mrs. DeWitt said.

The girls and Mrs. DeWitt found Jack looking into the roomy foaling stall at Athena and her filly. The chestnut filly with a large white star looked at them curiously, but Athena's ears were pinned back. She was by nature very protective, and quickly moved between the visitors and her baby.

"The foal's legs are so long!" Paige exclaimed. They watched as the filly took a few steps before reaching under her dam to nurse.

"It's nature's way of helping her flee from any predators," Mrs. DeWitt said. "Flight is a horse's primary defense against them, and a foal can run with its dam when just a few hours old." She looked to Jack. "I heard from Kathleen that you both were here for the birth."

"Yes. Fortunately there weren't any complications, and Athena would have preferred we mind our own business. About three this morning, I heard the sound of the mare moving in the straw on the intercom. I immediately checked the surveillance monitor and saw she was walking in the stall. When I came out, Athena was down, and the filly was born within minutes. Both mare and foal were on their feet not long afterward. At first the filly walked with little wobbly steps, but a few minutes later she could have been running, if need be. We're lucky everything went so smoothly. It was warm enough that we didn't need to use the infrared heat lamp."

"Things haven't always gone so well," Mrs. DeWitt said. "We lost both a foal and the mare in a difficult foaling a few years ago. It was a breech birth, when the foal wasn't positioned properly, and the mare had gone into an early labor unnoticed in the field. Dr. Reynolds came as fast as he could, but he wasn't in time."

"Fortunately, most foalings go smoothly," Jack said. "I love to hear the mare nicker to the little one shortly after birth, as Athena did." He pushed his tweed cap higher off his forehead. "My father was an excellent foaling man. He could help a mare that was in trouble better than many a veterinarian."

At that moment, the filly turned from her dam and with awkward steps began making her way toward the visitors standing close to the bars. Athena quickly interceded, rushing to get between her foal and the people looking in at them.

"Athena is a sweet and friendly mare, except when she has a new foal by her side," Jack warned. "Then 'tis best to keep your distance."

A short time later Mrs. DeWitt drove the girls back to the barn so they could get their horses ready for their lesson. With school vacation, Tim was at the barn earlier than usual, and Rita and Kayla also showed up well ahead of schedule. Derek was tacking up Bismarck when the girls came to Prince's stall.

Rita walked around Derek's horse, studying his conformation. "How did you find your horse in Germany?" she asked.

"Actually my Chicago trainer tracked him down," Derek said as he continued putting the saddle on his horse. "Bismarck had a show record, so we were pretty sure of what we were getting. Of course we had a vet go over him with a fine-tooth comb over there."

From Rita's face, Sarah could tell she wasn't happy to see a horse at the farm that might challenge Chancellor's status in her mind as the most superior horse. Even though they probably wouldn't face each other in horse shows, since Derek competed only in the jumpers, Rita really didn't like *any* horse that could conceivably beat hers in competition. A few minutes later, Rita left them, mentioning she was going to check in with Tim. Kayla stayed a few more minutes before going back to get Fanny ready.

The Young Riders lesson that day included jumping a course of fences Jack had set up in the indoor, and when they were finished, he had the class come to the center. "The fields and woods have thoroughly dried out," he said, "so we can use them for schooling without chopping the ground up unnecessarily. I plan for us to work on cross-country obstacles next week, weather permitting, so you should have your horses' legs wrapped with polos or protected with galloping boots, both in front and behind. The Wexford

Hall event isn't that far away, so we'll be doing a goodly amount of cross-country schooling between now and then."

Sarah had received mostly horse equipment from her parents at Christmas, and now she had a nice set of galloping boots and new polo wraps in her tack trunk. The cooler she had hoped for had also been under the tree.

Rita spoke up. "What about saddles? Should I use my all-purpose or my jumping saddle?"

"For cross-country, I suggest you use your jumping saddle," Jack replied.

Sarah noticed Kayla's raised eyebrow. Both knew what the other was thinking. *Rita is the only one in the class with more than one saddle. She couldn't resist reminding us of that.*

"And one last thing," Jack continued. "You've all worked hard over the winter to make your horses better jumpers, doing gymnastics and jumping courses here in the indoor. Consequently, you should all see marked improvement in their cross-country jumping, as well. I will also remind you that none of the cross-country obstacles are to be used for schooling unless it's under my supervision."

Sarah gave Prince a pat on his neck. He'd done very well in the lesson, and she was so proud of him. She followed the other riders out of the arena.

Jack walked with them as they filed out. "The old orchard trail is dry enough for riding," he said, "in case you want to cool out your horses that way."

"Anyone want to hack to the old orchard?" Tim asked. This would be the first time anyone in the class had hacked there since the snow came.

"I wish I could," Kayla said, "but Mom will want to truck Fanny home. Maybe we can bring her over one of these Saturdays, and ride to the beach. It won't be all that long before the tourists come back."

Sarah wondered what Paige would say about going to the old orchard. It had now been a few months since she and Tim had parted ways, and while they were supposedly still friends, they didn't hang out as they had before. Paige never made any negative comments about Tim, but she spent more time with Sarah at the barn these days. Kayla told Sarah confidentially that she thought they would both like to get back together, but were too stubborn to make the first move.

"Are you up for a trail ride, Sarah?" Paige asked.

Sarah had cleaned Prince's stall before the class, thinking they might go for a hack afterward. "Sure," she said. "You, too?" Paige nodded.

"How about you, Rita?" Tim asked.

Rita looked at her watch and then smiled broadly at Tim. "Of course!" She was elated to get what she perceived to be an invitation to ride with him.

Sarah was sorry Derek hadn't been around for her lesson that day. She knew he had to take his mother for an eye appointment right after he rode Bismarck, but she found herself wishing he was there. Riding was so much more fun when Derek was along. At the same time, she didn't harbor any hope their relationship would ever extend beyond seeing him at the barn or going for an occasional ride. His girlfriend, Meredith, was always in the background, and Derek's invitation to his school's winter carnival months ago—that Sarah had, of course, turned down—was his last overture.

The four horses made their way across the parking lot and disappeared into the forest on the old orchard trail. Tim led the ride, with Sarah following and Rita next in line. Sarah noticed that Paige purposely held Quarry back so she would be at the rear of the ride.

Parts of the trail looked bare without any leaves on the trees, although the pines and other conifers provided their year-round greenness. Buds on the other trees promised leaves before long. The horses seemed happy to be back on the trail after so many months being ridden inside, but they had to step carefully over downed limbs and other windfall that lay on the path. Prince had been on a number of group trail rides last fall, and now he was behaving like a seasoned campaigner, with no jigging or pulling to go faster.

"I hope this isn't a time for moose to be out and about," Sarah said. "Or wild turkeys, for that matter."

Tim turned his head and raised his voice. "Last spring, a group of us from the barn went out with Gus and Lucas to rake up all this mess on the trails. I guess it's time to do it again."

"With all the money you pay out to Brookmeade Farm every month, you shouldn't have to do that," Rita said. "Let the hired people do that work. That's what they get paid for."

Paige raised her voice from the back of the line. "Actually, it was fun, Rita. The DeWitts had us all up to their house for lunch afterward. And after that the trail was super to ride on. Quarry feels so springy when he's walking on this thick bed of pine needles."

They were almost to the fallen log jump when Rita asked, "Who do you guys think will be on the Wexford Hall team? Jack said at the beginning that any Brookmeade junior rider is eligible."

Paige volunteered an opinion. "I think the riders in the Young Riders group have got an edge. Derek has a pretty nice horse, but he only does jumpers. He wouldn't be up to snuff on dressage. The Wexford Cup is restricted to junior riders, so none of the adults who ride here are eligible."

"I think Kelly would like to try out," Rita said. "Nicole and Jubilee lost a lot of time after she broke some ribs, but Kelly stayed on with her lessons in Jack's class. She should have a chance."

Sarah wanted to keep her thoughts on the matter to herself, so she refrained from commenting, but Tim spoke up. "Listen, Rita, do you really think Kelly has any business doing an event?" he said. "Nicole was lucky she just broke a couple ribs when she went crashing into that rock wall last fall. This event is probably going to be tougher than most. I don't think Kelly is that far ahead of Nicole, and I don't think you should encourage her to try out for the team."

Rita was quick to reply. "But there's no reason she couldn't be the stable manager. I think she'd be super in that job. She takes great care of Midnight Jet."

The log came into view, ending the discussion. Tim trotted Rhodes to its base, and they cantered off down the trail after jumping it effortlessly. Compared to the fences they'd been jumping in the indoor over the winter, the log now looked small to Sarah. She gathered Prince, asked him to trot, and then followed Tim over the log, happy that her horse calmly followed Rhodes down the trail. Chancellor and Quarry also sailed over it and followed the others.

"I need to be heading back," Paige said, as the horses caught up to Tim. Sarah decided to follow Paige, since she had things to do at the barn before going home.

"Nobody's coming to the top with me?" Tim asked, sounding disappointed. Paige shook her head, but Rita spurred Chancellor to catch up with Tim.

"I'd love to ride up there with you, Tim!" she said excitedly. Paige and Sarah looked at each other before turning their horses in the opposite direction and making their way back to the barn.

After Sarah put her horse away and cleaned her tack, she

headed for the feed room. She wanted to finish soon and leave for home on time. Approaching the large door, she reached for the chain she always wore around her neck that carried the feed room key. When she didn't immediately feel the key or the chain, she came to a halt and groped for the key with both hands. But there was no chain around her neck. *Oh, my God!* she thought.

Just the possibility of losing the feed room key had always filled Sarah with horror. To face Gus with the news that she'd lost it sent a chill up her spine. After looking through all her pockets, she ran back to Prince's stall to search the cement area in front of it. No luck. Could the chain have broken while they were on the old orchard trail or during the lesson? She distinctly remembered slipping the chain around her neck when she'd changed her clothes after school. How could the chain have broken and the key slipped away?

Some of the horses were getting restless in their stalls, and a glance at her watch told Sarah the horses needed to be fed. She'd have to find Gus. She had never been to his apartment over the barn, but she knew how to get there. With more than a little dread, she stepped outside the barn and made her way up the wooden stairway. A light was on inside, but there was no response to her knock on the door. She rapped again, louder this time.

When Gus pulled the door open, Sarah was taken aback to see the craggy faced man without his red baseball cap. He looked so different, his longish gray hair slicked back. The smell of something cooking filled his living space, and a glance beyond his figure in the doorway showed he was preparing his evening meal. Gus's unshaven face, bristling with stiff gray hair, registered his surprise at seeing her at his door. "The horses all right?" he demanded.

Sarah wasn't sure how to break the news. She took a deep breath before blurting it out. "Yes, but I have a problem. I've lost the key to the feed room, and the horses need to be fed."

Gus's hawkish eyes narrowed. "That key should have been kept safe day and night!" he said between clenched teeth. Don't you know what could happen if someone left the feed room open? A horse could get in there and eat so much grain he'd probably die of colic. Don't you care?" The more Gus raised his voice, the angrier he got, his face crimson, his fists shaking.

Sarah was terrified and didn't know what to say. Nothing she could think of would calm the man's rage. She felt like running back down the stairs to get as far away from Gus as she could.

Gus continued his rant. "I knew it was a mistake to hire a girl! I'd rather have six boys to manage than one of your kind."

"I've looked everywhere," Sarah pleaded. "Maybe it's at home. But right now the horses need to be fed."

Gus turned on his heel and took giant steps to a shelf in his kitchen. Grabbing a set of keys, he stormed by her, muttering as he heading down the stairs. Sarah reluctantly followed him to the feed room where he unlocked the door.

"I'll lock it up later," Gus said. "But you better find that key!" With that he stalked off.

Sarah couldn't hold the tears back as she went into the feed room. No one had ever spoken to her like that. She'd always tried to keep the key safe, and now it seemed to have vanished into thin air. How could she have lost it? For several minutes she leaned against the feed cart until she could regain her composure. Finally she straightened and wiped her face before pushing the cart into the aisle. She could just imagine what she looked like! It was late, and hopefully all the other boarders had left for the night.

Sarah had nearly completed her rounds with the grain cart when she approached Medina's stall. Her heart sank when Spin and Cameo ran to see her just as Mrs. DeWitt exited the stall. There was no way she could avoid talking to her.

"Hi, Sarah," Mrs. DeWitt said cheerfully. But then her face clouded when she saw Sarah's puffy eyes and her face streaked with tears. "What's wrong, my dear?" Mrs. DeWitt asked with alarm. "I hope it isn't anything serious."

"I've done something stupid. I lost the key to the feed room."

Mrs. DeWitt came to her and put an arm around Sarah's shoulders. "That can't be the end of the world. It will probably show up, and we can always have another one made. Gus must have the original."

Sarah hung her head. "Gus isn't very happy with me right now," she said.

Mrs. DeWitt immediately sized up the situation. "So Gus opened up the feed room for you?"

Sarah nodded.

"I expect he had a few choice remarks to make, now didn't he?" When Sarah only hung her head, Mrs. DeWitt said, "Excuse me, Sarah. Just go about your feed detail." She turned abruptly and marched toward the side door, her dogs following behind.

Sarah fed Medina before returning to the feed room to dish up the morning grain rations. Had Mrs. DeWitt gone to confront Gus? Mrs. DeWitt knew the curmudgeonly barn manager all too well, and no doubt had witnessed his tirades before. What would she say to him? *If Mrs. DeWitt calls him up on his rude behavior, then Gus will really have it out for me,* Sarah thought.

Sarah had nearly finished dishing up the grain when Gus suddenly appeared. Sarah stepped back, anticipating more of his poisonous tongue. But Gus just held out his hand. "Here's another key," he said evenly. "Be careful with it." With that he retreated out of the feed room and was gone.

Sarah sighed, relieved that she had a key back in her possession and Gus had his temper under control. Mrs. DeWitt had come to her rescue once more. But that didn't change the fact that the lost key was still out there somewhere, and how she wished she could find it—the key on the buffalo head key ring. Sarah checked the feed cart to be sure every horse's pail contained its morning grain before leaving the feed room and locking the door. With the hay detail still to do, she called her mother to let her know she was running late.

Sarah had just gotten home when her phone rang. She sat down on the mudroom bench to answer it. "What's up, kid?" Kayla said. "How was the ride to the old orchard?"

"Fine. I wish you could have come. Rita started talking about the Wexford Hall event. You know who she thinks would be the perfect stable manager?" Without waiting for Kayla to answer, Sarah said, "Kelly. I think Rita's going to urge her to try for it."

"You've got to be kidding!" Kayla said. "Kelly pretends to be all-knowing, but it wasn't that long ago she didn't know a halter from a bridle."

"This means she'll probably be competing with me to be stable manager. I'm the newest rider in the Young Riders class, and Prince is the greenest horse, so it's a total no-brainer who the four riders on the team will be."

"I don't think there will be an actual tryout, so it will all depend on who Jack picks. You never know, kid. Prince has been going super."

Just then Mrs. Wagner poked her head around the corner. "Dinner's almost ready," she said. "We could use a hand setting the table."

"Sure, just a sec," Sarah answered. Then into the phone she said, "Listen, Kayla, dinner's ready. I'll call you later." Her mother had cut the conversation short, so there was no time to tell Kayla about the lost key. It would have to wait.

As soon as Sarah had removed her paddock boots and washed her hands, she rushed to her room, taking the stairs two at a time. She looked to the wall hook where she always hung the key chain when she wasn't wearing it. The hook held nothing. After checking the top of her bureau, Sarah hurried down the stairs to help Abby set the table.

When the family had gathered around the table and started eating dinner, Abby couldn't wait to talk about her softball team. "Coach made the cuts today. I'm pretty sure I've got second base locked up. We play Winchester a week from Friday."

Next Sarah told them how well Prince had performed in the lesson and on the old orchard trail. The days of her worrying that her parents might consider him too dangerous for her to ride had slowly slipped into the past, and now she enjoyed bragging what a wonderful horse he was. As for the lost key, she didn't want to talk about it.

"What about that competition you told us about?" her father asked. "Has Jack decided who will be on the team?"

Sarah held up a hand while she finished chewing. "No, but we're going to start schooling on the cross-country course next week," she said. "The ground is finally dry enough. I can hardly wait!"

Her father wanted to know more. "What kinds of jumps will there be on the cross-country course at that event?"

"Jack told us that Wexford Hall has everything you could imagine. That means water obstacles, ditches, banks, and drops. They probably have a table jump, a coop, and who knows what else."

Her mother was frowning. "Jack wouldn't expect Prince to be part of that, would he?"

Sarah wanted to reassure her mother. "No, Prince is the new kid on the block. I'm sure Jack will pick Rita, Tim, Paige, and Kayla." She reached for the mustard to go with her ham. "But maybe I'll get to be the stable manager."

Her mother thought about that for a moment. "That would be fun for you. Prince couldn't possibly be ready to take part in something as challenging as the Wexford Hall event."

CHAPTER 19
Cross-Country School

WHEN THE YOUNG RIDERS CLASS arrived in the indoor arena for their lesson the following week, they were surprised to see Jack mounted on French Twist. They'd known they would be doing a cross country school that day, but they weren't aware Jack would be on horseback.

French Twist, a lanky chestnut Thoroughbred, was a resale prospect that had come to the farm off the racetrack almost a year earlier along with a second Thoroughbred, Hedgerow. Jack had retrained them to be sport horses, and at the end of the summer, both had been put on the market with high price tags. Hedgerow, a superior mover, was sold soon after the horses were advertised, going to a woman looking for a show hunter. There was also interest in French Twist, but for two different buyers he failed to pass the pre-purchase exam. In both cases he appeared to be slightly off, and although the vets couldn't put a finger on what was wrong, neither buyer wanted to take a chance on him. Jack felt confident French Twist was a sound horse that just needed more time after his racing career was over.

Jack had the riders do their usual flatwork warm-up, and once the horses were supple and moving freely, he called the riders into the center. "We're going out to school on some cross-country fences now," he said. He reviewed some of the things he wanted them to remember about jumping cross-country obstacles. "We'll begin with two you're already familiar with in the meadow near the barn," he continued. "After that we'll take the trail that will bring us to the brook, where we can school in water."

The riders filed out of the indoor behind Jack and made their way to the meadow. Closest to the barn was a jump made out of yellow straw bales, recent replacements for the soggy, tired bales that had been exposed to the weather for a year. On the other side of the meadow, a telephone pole-to-a-bank combination awaited them. The spectators who'd been watching the lesson from the bleachers followed the horses outside and stood near the driveway at the edge of the meadow.

"We're going to start with the straightforward straw bales jump," Jack told the riders, as they walked their horses toward the meadow. "'Twill will be a good warm-up. 'Tis uncomplicated, so you can go behind one another as long as you spread out a good distance between horses. Follow me." Jack asked French Twist to canter on a large circle in the field, and soon the riders in the class were following him over the jump.

Sarah went last, and although Crown Prince hadn't jumped in the meadow before, he showed no hesitation and followed Fanny over the bales. "Good boy!" Sarah stroked his neck to let him know she was pleased with him. After the riders had jumped the straw bales three times, Jack asked them to come over to the bank combination and halt by the edge of the woods.

When Sarah looked the obstacle over, she began to feel nervous. Prince had never jumped anything like this, and it looked intimidating. The telephone pole element was a solid jump, not something designed to fall down if a horse hit it or landed on top of it. If a horse had a problem there, he could conceivably get hung up. The bank, an earthen mound several feet high and reinforced with railroad timbers, would be scary to a horse that had never jumped up on one before. The class had schooled over these two obstacles shortly before she joined it, so she was at a real disadvantage. Sarah definitely wanted to go last, and she halted Prince at the end of the line.

Jack called on Paige to start, and Quarry jumped the combination without hesitation. Kayla and Fanny did equally well, and both Tim and Rita's horses showed excellent form going through it. All at once it was Sarah's turn, and every face was looking at her, waiting.

Jack was well aware this was Prince's first time to be faced with jumping up onto a bank. "Sarah, I want you to do the bank without the vertical first, coming in from the side. Ride it as you would any other fence, having solid contact with his mouth while your legs ask him to go forward. After he lands on the bank, continue the one stride across the top of and jump off the opposite side."

Sarah swallowed hard and took a deep breath to calm herself as she asked Prince to pick up trot and circle toward the bank. Before they straightened to approach it, she asked him for canter and then focused on getting a forward and straight line into the obstacle. She felt her horse hesitate when he became aware of what was ahead, but with her legs pressing hard against his sides, she sent him on. With a huge jump, Prince took off well in front of the bank, landing beyond its center. Sarah again asked him to continue going forward and jump down off the bank, but he was at an awkward distance and instantly skidded to a halt, coming to a standstill on top of the mound.

"'Tis all right, Sarah," Jack called. "We must remember he's green. Just keep your legs on him and let him take a look."

Prince had his front legs braced, unwilling to go forward.

Sarah felt extreme tension in his body as he contemplated jumping down. She reached to stroke his neck, to reassure him. A few moments later she used her legs to vigorously kick him forward, and this time he cautiously lowered himself off the bank, almost in slow motion, and cantered off. Sarah was relieved she hadn't needed to use her crop.

"Do it again!" Jack called, as he continued walking French Twist in a circle. On the second try, Prince jumped up on the bank, landed in a better place, and continued across it, jumping down on the other side.

"Again!" Jack shouted. Once more Prince jumped on and off the bank, this time without any hesitation.

Jack called out, "This time circle into the telephone pole and jump this obstacle as a combination."

Sarah felt a stab of fear, knowing this would be challenging for her horse. She forced the thought out of her mind. If Jack asked them to do it, he knew they could do it. She must believe in her instructor and believe in Crown Prince. As they got closer to the telephone pole, Sarah called on all the drills and practice over fences they had done in the indoor over the winter, and with her legs sent him forward to the combination. Prince responded with a somewhat awkward jump, but he was over it, and after one stride he pushed up onto the bank and then off it. "Good boy!" Sarah shouted. She stroked her horse as he cantered away.

The spectators and all the riders except Rita clapped their hands and cheered. "Why do we have to waste so much time with a green horse in our class?" she said out loud. Jack glared at her but did not favor her with a reply.

After they had gone through the combination two more times, Jack asked Sarah to let Prince walk and take her place in the line. Kayla gave her a thumbs-up as she passed. As Sarah halted her horse, Rita spoke under her breath, so no one else could hear. "Do you know Jack spent longer getting your horse through the combination than it took the rest of us combined? I have better ways to spend my time than wasting it waiting for you!" Sarah said nothing. She had become accustomed to Rita's sarcastic comments and had learned it was better to ignore them.

"All right, then," Jack said, "Let's make our way to the brook." He pointed French Twist in the direction of a woods trail off the far corner of the meadow. Sarah turned her horse away from Chancellor so she could ride beside Kayla.

The path was wide enough for two horses to go abreast, and except for occasional windfall on the trail, the packed gravel footing was smooth and suitable for any gait. Rhodes and Quarry had undoubtedly been over it many times last year when Jack took them to school in the brook before their eventing competitions. It was unlikely Chancellor or Fanny had been on the trail, and Sarah knew it was a first-time experience for Crown Prince.

The horses were excited to be on the trail. Fanny carried her pretty head high, looking everywhere and moving with a slight prance in her step. Quarry's silver tail was raised, and he occasionally jigged forward. Rhodes and Chancellor showed their customary poise, but they were more animated than usual. Even though he was minding his manners and not pulling on the reins, Sarah could feel an eagerness running through Crown Prince.

"Fanny is loving this!" Kayla called out.

"Quarry too!" Paige said.

"We can trot once we're in single file," Jack called out. A few minutes later he glanced back, and when satisfied, asked French Twist to move out. The others trotted behind him until Jack saw the stream ahead of them. He raised his arm, signaling the group behind him to walk.

As always in springtime, the water level in the brook was higher than it had been in the fall. Instead of a lazy waterway slowly meandering toward the ocean, it had a stronger current sending the water from spring rains and melting snow downstream. Sarah wondered how deep the water was. They'd be able to tell once French Twist stepped into the brook. With a gradual gravel path both entering and exiting, it was an ideal place to cross.

As they got closer, the riders saw a white painted coop in the field just beyond the stream. *Will we be jumping that today?* Sarah thought.

When the riders had closed up behind him, Jack gave them instructions. "We're going to walk across the stream and halt in the field on the other side. Even if your horses are comfortable going into water, we're first going to walk them across the brook. They haven't been through water for several months, and our objective is to reassure them that they have nothing to fear. If we have an argument with them, their fear will be confirmed. Now, let's close up to one horse's length distance, so every horse but mine will have another horse leading the way. Having a lead gives a horse confidence."

Jack rode French Twist boldly into the brook and marched across it, walking up the path on the other side. Sarah noticed the water came almost to French Twist's knees. *That brook isn't shallow!* Sarah thought. *Prince has probably never been through water before.* She worried how he would react when asked to go through it.

Rita pushed Chancellor to the front, and her horse walked obediently into the brook. Without hesitation, Rhodes followed, with Fanny right behind him. "Fanny's gone through lots of water riding through the game preserve at home," Kayla said. Quarry remembered the brook from last year, and he willingly followed Fanny across.

That left Prince bringing up the rear. When he first noticed the brook, his eager walk slowed dramatically, and Sarah could feel his body stiffen. When he got to the edge of the water, Prince put on the brakes, even as Quarry moved away from him. Watching from the other side sitting on French Twist, Jack called to her. "Stay calm, Sarah, and let him look at the water. Give him a minute. Then look up to the other side and firmly ask him to move forward."

Rita looked back as she halted Chancellor. "Oh, no," she said. "Here we go again." Jack swung his head in her direction, looking at her sharply, but then turned his attention back to Sarah.

"He's probably never walked through water before," Jack said, "and he's forgiven a stop to check it out. 'Tis just like the first time he loaded onto the horse trailer."

Sarah took a few deep breaths. They were all waiting for her. But she needed to stay calm. Keeping a good contact on the reins, she pressed her legs firmly on Prince's sides and spoke out firmly, "Walk!" From his experience being longed, Crown Prince knew the word. Her voice in addition to her other aids must have made a difference, because Prince tentatively placed first one foot and then another into the water. Slowly at first and then quickly he moved across the brook. Sarah felt like leaning down to hug his neck! He trusted her! Even though he was fearful, he had done what she asked.

"Good job, kid!" Kayla called out.

After Prince was up the bank, Jack rode French Twist into the water and halted him in the middle. "Bring your horse back in, Sarah," he said. This time, Prince walked into the brook without hesitation. Sarah praised him as she stroked his neck.

Jack then had the class go up the trail a short way, turn, and trot their horses back through the brook. When it was Sarah's turn, Prince came back to walk before stepping into the water, but then he picked up trot when Sarah asked and trotted across the brook. On the return trip, he trotted willingly into the water. For the last part of the exercise, Jack had them trot through the water, proceed up the bank, and jump the white coop. They were exuberant when all the horses did it perfectly the first time, and Jack had them celebrate by cantering across the field to the farm road.

Paige was laughing when Quarry came roaring past Prince, who pulled to join in the race. Sarah held him firm, not daring to test whose speed was greater. All the horses came back to walk when they reached the road. Paige purposely kept Quarry a distance from Tim, but Rita was more than happy to ride beside him, and she chattered to him all the way back to the barn.

As they approached the courtyard, Jack spoke to the riders. "I have a few things I want to say to you, so please gather in the courtyard before dismounting." After they halted their horses near the mounting block, Jack turned French Twist to face them.

"We're only a month away from the Wexford Hall Cup," he said, "and I know many of you are wondering who will be riding on the Brookmeade Farm team. After I've done a last check with the DeWitts tonight, that list will be posted tomorrow on the bulletin board by the office. I think people who are going to compete need to know so they can plan accordingly. We will have to consider transportation to the event and inquire about stabling arrangements. As you know, lodging and meals for the members of the team will be at the Belmont School, and the organizers will take care of that. But many of your parents will want to stay nearby, and I plan on looking into various lodging options."

The riders grinned at each other, excited in anticipation of seeing the list. They'd soon know if they'd made the team. Most were optimistic.

But Jack hadn't finished. "There's something else I want to

impress on you. For people who will be competing at Wexford Hall, 'tis important your horses be fit enough to handle the cross-country phase. 'Tis going to be fairly long, and the terrain in that area will allow the course designer to include any number of hills. Galloping the course while at the same time jumping obstacles and climbing hills will require stamina. So you must be conditioning your horses for what lies ahead. This means riding them almost every day, with lots of hacking on trails. Hill work will help make them fit. If you'd like some help with an exercise plan, just let me know."

Kathleen came out of the barn and walked over to them. "Your four o'clock class is waiting," she said to Jack. After he had dismounted from French Twist and run up his irons, he handed her the reins. The other riders also got off their horses. They'd cooled out on the walk back to the barn and could go directly to their stalls.

Bismarck wasn't in the barn when Sarah brought Prince back. She put her horse on the cross-ties, untacked him, and cleaned his stall. She had finished and was picking out Prince's feet when Kathleen came around the corner. She smiled at Sarah. "Jack asked me to give you a message," she said. "He'd like you to come to the office after his class has finished."

Sarah didn't know what to think. "Oh, okay," she said. After Kathleen left, she went back to work with her hoof pick. While removing the packed earth from Prince's hooves, her mind raced. *What is this about?* Her watch told her that the lesson would be over soon. She picked up a soft brush from her grooming caddy and went over her horse, brushing away some of the last traces of winter coat he was still shedding. After Prince was relaxed and eating hay in his stall, Sarah headed toward the office.

Paige was getting ready to leave the barn when Sarah stopped at Quarry's stall. "Quarry was a star today," Sarah said. "All the experience he got eventing last year really shows."

Paige paused to face Sarah. "Thanks! For a first-timer, your horse was totally awesome. It won't be long before you two will be out on the campaign trail."

"Not for a while. I'm sure he'll be holding down the fort here at Brookmeade when you guys compete at Wexford Hall. Maybe I'll be lucky enough to be your stable manager."

"I really hope so. But Prince's time will come."

Looking into the office, Sarah saw that Jack wasn't there. She stopped to look at the bulletin board outside the door. There were only a few items posted—classified ads announcing horses for sale and a notice asking riders to stay off the hunt course. But tomorrow they would all know who had made the team. *Not that there will be any surprises,* she thought. *Today showed how far ahead of me the other kids are.*

Sarah heard the distinctive sound of Jack's boots clicking on the cement as he approached. "I'm glad you got my message," he said, as they both entered the office. When Jack shut the office door, Sarah thought, *This must be serious.* He went around the desk to sit down while motioning her to take one of the office chairs.

"You know the team for Wexford Hall will be posted tomorrow," Jack began, his voice measured. "I'm glad I have a chance to talk to you before it becomes public." He paused to stroke his chin thoughtfully. "Since you may be disappointed, I want to give you advance notice that you won't be named stable manager for the team."

Sarah took in a big breath and let it out. She hadn't realized how much she was counting on the chance to be part of the competition with her friends. She'd really wanted to part of the team.

Jack could see that Sarah was disappointed, but he continued.

"We're going to name Kelly Hoffman to be the stable manager. Kelly works very hard in her lessons and is diligent in caring for Midnight Jet. She's owned her own horse much longer than you've had Prince. She and Jet aren't anywhere near competing, but the DeWitts and I think she would be greatly encouraged by being the team's stable manager. There were extenuating circumstances when she and her friend caused you so much unpleasantness several months ago. But we feel she has turned a corner, and should be given this opportunity to be part of the team."

Jack's words didn't make Sarah feel any better. It would be so exciting to be part of the Wexford Hall event—to stay in the Belmont School dorm with Kayla, Paige, and Rita, and to help the team in their quest for the cup. Now Kelly Hoffman would be given that job. Sarah wondered if Rita's father had made a phone call to advance Kelly's chances.

Jack sat back, giving Sarah a chance to speak. She realized that it wouldn't do any good to grouse to Jack. The decision had been made.

Sarah frowned. "I'd be lying if I said I wasn't hoping to be the stable manager. But I know Kelly has been disappointed in the past. Maybe this will make it up to her. Maybe this will help build some bridges."

Jack smiled. "I had a feeling you'd handle your disappointment with a lot of maturity," he said. "You'll have your chance. You and your horse are exceptionally talented, and if you continue to work hard, there's no doubt in my mind you'll be rewarded someday. You and Prince have a bright future ahead."

Sarah rose from her chair, preparing to leave, but Jack stopped her before she got to the door. "One last thing, Sarah. I've told you this information in confidence. I wanted to break it to you before you see the list that will be posted tomorrow. But please don't share this information with anyone. Will you promise to keep it confidential?"

Sarah turned back. "Yes, Jack, I will," she said, and then left the office. It was almost time to feed the horses, but first she needed to see Crown Prince. He raised his head from his water bucket when she entered the stall, and then stood quietly as she wrapped her arms around his neck and pressed her head against his mane. Just feeling his warmth lifted her spirits. As disappointed as she was, she was fully aware that having a horse as grand as Crown Prince was a million times better than being on the Brookmeade team. She'd be staying in Yardley when the team went to Wexford Hall, but Prince would be here, too.

While Sarah stood with her horse, Derek returned from schooling Bismarck in the outside ring. He noticed her right away and halted his horse in front of Prince's stall. "I've got some good news," he said, smiling.

Sarah moved away from Prince and came out of the stall, sliding the door shut behind her. "Some good news would be great right now," she said.

"Gus and Lucas just moved four stadium jumps into the outside ring," he said. "Now I won't have to reserve schooling over fences to the indoor or hunt course." Derek paused as he looked at her more closely. "You look like you just lost your best friend. What's going on? Are those bullies at it again?"

Sarah hung her head and then returned his gaze. "I wish I could tell you, Derek, but I can't. Not until tomorrow. And I've got to feed the horses now." Frowning, he watched her walk away.

CHAPTER 20
Wild Ride

SARAH HADN'T BEEN HOME five minutes when her cell phone rang. It was Kayla. "I'll be down in a minute," Sarah called to her mother, as she hurried up the stairs to the privacy of her room. Once she was seated on the side of her bed, she spoke to Kayla. "What's up?"

"You know what Jack said about conditioning, getting the horses fit for the event?" Kayla began. "Paige and I want to ride to the beach on Saturday. Paige says there's an awesome trail that goes around the Quimby farm and comes out near the cottages on Dune Grass Lane. If we go at low tide, maybe we can let the horses run a bit on the beach! Anyway, want to come?"

"Oh, wow," Sarah said. "That's a no-brainer! Just let me know what time." She shifted to get comfortable on her bed. "You know, it's a shame Tim and Paige broke up. Riding in the same class makes things totally weird for everybody. Except Rita. She practically throws herself at him, even with Paige right there. But Tim doesn't seem to take the bait."

"Tim knows Rita too well. I noticed he had a long face when he was looking at Paige this afternoon. Do you know if he still hangs out with Amy Campbell?" Kayla asked.

"I haven't a clue," Sarah replied. "But I could ask around. I just wish Tim and Paige would stop being so stubborn. It's easy to see they'd like to get back together."

"So who do you think will be on the list Jack's going to post? All the Young Riders? Rita and I haven't evented before, but Jack will have us whipped into shape by the middle of June. And you're a sure bet to be the stable manager."

There was silence as Kayla waited for a response. Sarah hated to be less than honest with her friend, but no way could she tell Kayla who the stable manager would be. She'd made the promise of secrecy to Jack. "I guess we'll just have to wait and see," she said.

Another long pause, until Kayla said, "Is something going on? You don't sound yourself."

Sarah took a deep breath, determined to sound upbeat. "Hey, wasn't Fanny awesome today! She's going to be great in that event."

Kayla wasn't buying it. "I think you know something you're not telling me, Sarah Wagner." There was an awkward silence. "And I'll bet it came from Jack." Sarah said nothing, confirming Kayla's suspicion. "Well, kid, I can understand you don't want to get into any trouble."

"Everyone will see the list tomorrow," Sarah said. "I've got to help Mom in the kitchen. See ya!" Sarah closed her phone. Kayla was pretty sharp. But she'd just have to wait to learn that Kelly Hoffman would be part of the Brookmeade Farm team.

* * * * *

The next afternoon Sarah was riding her bicycle on the farm road heading to the barn when she met Rita leaving the farm in her convertible. The car braked to a stop beside Sarah, and Rita ran down her window. "I had to come over to see the list," Rita said. "No surprises, but do you want to know who's on the team?" she teased. After a long hesitation, she said, "I am, along with Tim, Kayla, and Paige." And then with a vicious smile, she added, "Kelly Hoffman will be the stable manager."

When Sarah didn't appear the least bit surprised or disappointed, Rita seemed annoyed. It wasn't what she'd expected, and she decided to go nasty. "I hope you can get a car one of these days. It must be a total drag riding that bicycle all the time." Now she paused to smirk. "Well, I've gotta get home to ride Chancellor in my new indoor arena."

As Rita drove away, Sarah remembered Rita's confession last summer. Rita had admitted she was jealous of Sarah, but not just because of Sarah's spectacular horse. While Sarah's mother had survived a terrible car accident, Rita's mother had died when she was born. Rita was carrying a heavy burden of loss. No, Sarah wasn't going to let Rita get under her skin. Rita was to be pitied. *She puts on a pretty good act that she's the happiest person on earth because of all the things her father's money can buy,* Sarah thought, *but she's not.*

Sarah continued biking along the roadway. There were three young foals with their dams in the broodmares' pastures to her left, all healthy and growing fast. The O'Briens' bungalow came into view, and once she'd topped the rise, she coasted the rest of the way to the parking area. She hurried into the barn, planning to clean Prince's stall while he was turned out, but she couldn't resist swinging by the office to see the notice posted on the bulletin board.

The list was exactly as Rita had described, although there was one additional detail Sarah hadn't considered. Each team would be allowed a coach, and of course Jack would be the coach for the Brookmeade Farm team. And as Sarah had known in advance,

Kelly Hoffman was named the team's stable manager.

Sarah headed for the shavings shed to pick up a wheelbarrow and manure fork. While she was working in the stall, Derek arrived back with Bismarck. He'd had his weekly lesson with Jack earlier in the afternoon and then taken his horse for a short hack. As soon as Bismarck was on the cross-ties, Derek came over to Prince's stall.

"Hi," Derek said. Sarah stopped what she was doing and came to the stall's doorway. "I saw Kelly was named stable manager," he said. He studied Sarah's face for signs of disappointment, but instead she smiled.

"I'm not surprised, actually," Sarah said. "Kelly has had her own horse longer than I have, and she probably knows a lot more about taking care of horses. The team deserves the most experienced person."

"Are you okay with this? Everyone thought you'd get it."

Sarah picked up the manure fork, and after tossing more soiled bedding into the wheelbarrow, she turned back to Derek. "I don't have time to waste feeling jealous of Kelly Hoffman. Besides, going with the team to Wexford Hall would keep me away from Prince too long. I'm thinking about taking him to the Meadow Mist Farm show in Winchester in July. Kayla wants to show Fanny there, and she said her mother could truck Prince, too. We need to work hard to be ready." She reached toward Prince's water bucket to skim off some hay floating on top before turning back to Derek. "How was your lesson today?"

"The fences are getting pretty high, but Bismarck's holding his own. I'm looking for some shows, too. I wonder if they have a jumper division at that Winchester show."

"I'll ask Kayla," Sarah said, just as she remembered the trail ride on Saturday. It would be so much fun to have Derek come with them. "And by the way, Kayla and Paige asked me to come with them Saturday when they're going to ride to the beach. Would that work for you?"

"This Saturday?" Derek asked. When Sarah nodded, he shook his head. "That sucks! My dad wants to take me to look at a few colleges on Saturday, and there's no way I can get out of it. I'd love to go with you sometime."

Just then Kelly burst around the corner, heading straight to Derek. "Guess what!" she exclaimed. "I'm going to be the Brookmeade Farm team's stable manager at Wexford Hall. Isn't that awesome?" Kelly turned and gave Sarah a smug smile, before turning back to Derek. "Jack must think I know more about taking care of horses than anyone else in this barn." She looked at Sarah again, smirking.

"That's great," Sarah said, hoping she didn't sound obviously insincere. *Kelly must have gone totally bananas when she saw her name on the list,* Sarah thought. *I hope she feels she's evened the score and will take me off her most-hated list.*

"Congrats," Derek said. "I'm glad you're so happy. I hope it won't be a lot of totally grungy work."

But nothing was going to bring Kelly down from the cloud nine she was soaring on. She danced away to get Midnight Jet ready to ride.

* * * * *

The sun was barely up Saturday morning when Sarah's clock radio came on, awakening her from a deep sleep. She lay there a few minutes until she remembered why she'd set the alarm so early. Today they were going to ride the horses to the beach! She needed to get to the barn extra early to make a dent in her barn chores before Kayla and Paige were ready to go. She gulped down a light breakfast before retrieving her lunch and several carrots from the refrigerator. She got on her bike and headed to Brook-meade Farm.

It was one of the few times Sarah had been the first person to arrive at the barn, beating out the early birds who liked to ride when the day was coolest. She first went to her horse and hugged his dark bay head before giving him his mandatory carrot. Prince had a coating of shavings on his left side where he'd lain down in the night.

Stepping out of the stall, Sarah noticed the sounds of horses anxious to receive their morning hay and grain. It was still early to feed, but the horses knew she was there. Many of them were circling their stalls, expressing their impatience with soft nickers and occasional deep throated neighs. But Gus would have to give his approval for her to change the feeding time, and she certainly didn't want to cross him! Sarah hoped he had finally gotten over being mad that she'd lost the feed room key. It had never shown up, leading Sarah to believe the chain had broken when she was riding on the trail that afternoon. Its replacement was on a new, sturdier chain around her neck.

There was no sign of Gus when Sarah looked down the front aisle, and he wasn't in the back of the barn either. It was hard to believe Gus wasn't already filling water buckets. Sarah decided to start with her sweeping chores, but she had just begun with the push broom when Gus appeared, red baseball cap and all. He must have noticed her bicycle parked outside the doorway, because he showed no surprise when he saw her. Sarah leaned her broom against the wall and walked up to him. "Is it too early to feed the horses?" she asked.

Gus looked at his watch. "Won't do any harm," he said before turning abruptly to retrieve the long hose.

Great! Sarah thought. *Prince will have plenty of time to polish off his hay before we leave.* She went to the feed room to get the grain push cart. When she arrived at Prince's stall, he stood near his feed tub tossing his head and then dove into the grain after she poured it into his tub. Bismarck nickered softly as she approached with his ration.

Later in the morning, after both aisles, the lounge, and the two tack rooms had been swept, Sarah went outside to see if Kayla had arrived. Mrs. Romano and Kayla were just pulling into the parking area in their pickup with the trailer in tow. Sarah waved to Kayla and went back into the barn, where Paige was grooming Quarry in the aisle. "Be ready in a few minutes!" Sarah called to her.

She couldn't help being excited. She'd always dreamed of someday riding a horse on the beach, cantering along a huge expanse of packed sand close to the ocean waves. She could almost smell the salt air and hear the sound of the white-capped surf. And now it was going to happen. They'd soon be on their way!

Sarah hurried back to Prince's stall and put him on the crossties. She had groomed him earlier, so it was just a matter of tacking up and getting herself ready. Once Prince was saddled and bridled, she put on her half chaps and helmet and led her horse to the courtyard. Paige was already outside on Quarry, and Kayla was approaching the barn riding Fanny. Sarah led Prince to the mounting block and moments later she was astride her horse.

"Hey, kid," Kayla greeted her as she rode Fanny into the courtyard. Sarah could tell Kayla was keyed up too. "In all the time I've had a horse, I've never ridden on the beach before," Kayla said.

"How about you, Paige?" Sarah asked, as Fanny and Crown Prince came alongside Quarry. "Didn't you and Tim ride to the beach last year?"

For a brief moment, a pained look spread across Paige's face at the mention of Tim. Then she recovered. "Yeah, but lots of summer people were still in the cottages, and horses weren't allowed on the beach. So we just rode to the end of Dune Grass Lane. There's a fantastic view of the beach from there. It was high tide, with big waves, and Quarry was totally turned on, prancing with his tail up! I don't think he had ever seen the ocean before." She reached down to stroke Quarry's neck. "Well, today he's going to gallop close to it and maybe walk in the waves!"

Sarah laughed. "The pulley rein may come in handy."

"Fanny will leave your two Thoroughbreds in the dust," Kayla said, "at least for the first quarter of a mile. That's why they're called Quarter Horses."

The three girls rode their horses to the end of the farm road, crossed Ridge Road, and with Paige in the lead, started on the trail to the beach. Prince had gone on several group trail rides last fall, and now he was relaxed going out with other horses. They wove their way in back of the Quimby Farm, where gentle meadows flowed into a wooded countryside. This was a working farm that was home to a large dairy herd, and at one point the trail ran parallel to a pasture where cows were grazing. Prince snorted when two of the cows approached the fence to get a better look at the horses.

Paige looked back at Sarah and laughed. "If Prince is going to live in the country, he'd better learn not to be afraid of cows!"

It's great to hear a joke from Paige, Sarah thought. *She's so darned serious these days.*

"Do you think Rita would have wanted to ride with us today?" Kayla asked.

Paige twisted around in her saddle to answer. "After what happened to Taco last summer, Rita was easier to deal with and more civilized. But it didn't last. Now she's back to her old ways, and lately she's been totally obnoxious. I, for one, am glad she's not here."

"Rita is funny," Kayla said. "Sometimes she's really nice, but if things don't go her way, she can turn on you real fast."

After they'd ridden past the farm, the trail broadened into what had been an old logging road. "Let's trot," Paige called back. The horses picked up the faster gait, and ten minutes later they arrived at a main road leading to Yardley village. Once it was clear of traffic, they crossed the road and turned onto Dune Grass Lane, heading directly to the beach. Paige swung Quarry to the right. "We're supposed to always ride on the right side of the road, with traffic," Paige said. "I guess that's so horses won't be frightened by cars coming directly at them."

The cottages lining the road appeared to be unoccupied, but with Memorial Day right around the corner, this whole area would soon be bustling with activity. The sound of the ocean surf in the distance became increasingly louder as the horses walked briskly along the road. "It won't be long now," Sarah said. Prince was moving with his head high, looking ahead with his ears pricked.

As they approached the last cottage on the dead end road, two small children came running out of the yard to get a closer look at the horses. A woman on the cottage's porch warned the kids to keep their distance. The family waved to the riders as they passed. "Your horses are beautiful!" the woman called out as they went by.

The girls waved back, and Paige asked, "Doesn't the path to the beach start along here somewhere?"

"The opening is on the other side of that big maple tree," the woman said, pointing. "Have a good ride!"

As Prince followed Quarry onto the sandy beach path, Sarah could feel him becoming increasingly anxious. His walk was animated and he continually chomped on the bit. When they came over the top of a large sand dune, a spectacular panorama of sand and ocean stretched before them. Prince stood like a statue, frozen in place, as he stared incredulously at the waves and the gulls swooping onto the sandy beach. Quarry and Fanny were equally transfixed. The ocean breeze whipped their manes in all directions as the horses took in the beach scene.

"These horses have been stuck on the farm too long," Paige said. "I hope we can get them closer to the waves, where the sand is packed the hardest." When she used her legs and tapped her crop on Quarry's neck, the gray horse moved forward, at first tentatively. Prince slowly followed Quarry after Sarah kicked him forward and sharply said, "Walk!" Fanny was the least affected by the strange sights and smells of the ocean, and she willingly followed the other two horses. They all gradually relaxed as they walked on the beach sand, occasionally stepping through pools of water left by the tide. The long line of cottages at the beach's edge were silent, all of them waiting for their families to return for the summer.

"Are we ready to trot?" Paige called out over the wind.

"Of course!" Kayla shouted. "Let's go!"

The three horses began trotting smartly down the beach, making good traction on the hard-packed sand as they pulled on the reins to go faster. First one and then another broke into canter, until the three horses were running slowly abreast, heading toward the far end of the beach a few miles away. Sarah had a tight hold on Prince, who tried to grab the bit and was fighting for his head. He wanted to gallop, really gallop, but Sarah didn't dare let him go faster. She wasn't sure she could pull him up in this setting, even with a pulley rein. He was psyched, and it was all she could do to hold him.

Sarah looked over at Kayla. She was smiling broadly and her face was flushed with pleasure as she rode in a two-point position in the saddle to let Fanny canter faster. Fanny's shorter legs were moving like pistons as she motored down the beach, easily keeping up with the larger horses.

Paige had a firm hold on Quarry. The former racehorse pulled hard on the bit, trying to level out and lengthen his stride. In his former life, he, too, had been trained to run fast over long distances on the track, but Paige's intermittent use of the pulley rein kept him under control.

The horses cantered down the beach, their hoofs sending the beach sand flying behind them. As they approached a flock of seagulls spread over the sand, the gulls suddenly took flight with a great flapping of wings. The three horses slowed to trot, allowing their riders to shorten their reins and slow their pace even more.

"I think we'd better walk for a while," Kayla shouted. "Fanny's getting tired."

"Good idea," Sarah called back.

Soon all three horses were walking side by side, their nostrils flaring as they took quick breaths. They were exhilarated, moving with springy steps and loving the first run they'd had for a long time. Soon they neared the end of the beach, where large ledge outcroppings extended into the water.

"Look!" Paige said. "I think there's a path beside the rocks. Let's see where it goes." With the others following, she steered Quarry away from the water and toward a worn opening that ran between the tall marsh grass and the ledge. Quarry stepped boldly onto the trail, followed by Kayla and Fanny, with Sarah and Crown Prince bringing up the rear.

"This trail's getting narrow and overgrown," Kayla said. "Do you think it actually goes anywhere?"

"Let's see what's around this bend," Paige replied.

After she'd negotiated the turn, Paige called back to the others. "The trail ends here with someone's compost pile. I guess it's a dead end. Time to do a one-eighty."

"Okay," Kayla answered. "Back to the beach."

They had nearly turned their horses around on the narrow path when Sarah and Kayla suddenly heard Paige scream. Looking back, they saw Quarry had stepped into the marshy area beside the path and quickly sunk to such a depth that his knees and hocks were out of sight! In a panicked attempt to get out of the quagmire, Quarry began to thrash wildly, but rather than free himself from the mucky bog, his crazed movement was making him sink deeper.

"Get off him Paige!" Kayla yelled. "He's sinking!"

Paige made a tremendous lunge from the saddle toward the path, landing with her upper body on solid ground but with her legs trailing into the bog. She clawed the earth, crawling forward, until she was able to right herself on the path. Quarry continued his frenzied thrashing.

"I'm calling 911!" Sarah cried out, as she whipped out her cell. After she stabbed in the numbers, seconds seemed like hours as she waited. When nothing happened, she looked down at her phone. Her heart sank when she saw that it remained completely dark. She should have remembered. The high ridges in back of the village cut off any cell tower transmission! Quarry continued to flounder, struggling desperately to free himself. His eyes were glazed, and his frenzied fear sent white flecks of foam spewed from his mouth.

"I'm going for help!" Sarah cried. "But in the meantime, you've got to keep him from struggling. It's just making him sink deeper. Can you get the reins?"

"I'll try!" Paige said, choking back a sob. She got down on her knees and leaned out to grab Quarry's reins. When she was able to pull them over his head, she made contact with his mouth to try to keep him still and calm him. "I've got him," Paige called. "Go for help!"

Sarah swung Crown Prince sharply toward the open beach. Her mind locked onto the cottage they'd passed on Dune Grass Lane where the woman with the children would surely have a phone to call a rescue service! Sarah immediately leaned forward and extended her arms, giving Prince his head, as she kicked her heels hard against his sides. "Run, Prince," she cried. "Run! Run!"

As if he understood the urgency of the situation, her horse bolted forward. In a matter of seconds, he was in a full gallop, his giant strides swallowing up the beach. Long and low he moved, going faster and faster. As his strides lengthened, his action was breathtakingly smooth and fast. He ran as he had been bred to run! The blood of generations of champion Thoroughbreds coursed through his veins, and now he displayed the same brilliant speed they had shown on the race course. But instead of running for glory and a pot of gold, Crown Prince ran to save Quarry's life!

Sarah had never imagined a horse could run this fast. She lay low over his neck, clinging desperately to his mane as Prince flew down the two-mile beach. The wind whipping against her face made tears stream down her cheeks while Prince ran with free rein, sprinting as he pleased. After he had been running at top speed for what seemed an eternity, Sarah lifted her head, trying to see ahead. Prince would have to slow down if they were going to negotiate the beach path that would take them to Dune Grass Road. She squinted her eyes to focus. *Oh, my God!* The end of the beach was only a hundred yards ahead. She had to stop him!

CHAPTER 21

The Team

AS CROWN PRINCE THUNDERED down the beach toward the steep dune banks, Sarah sat up in the saddle and shortened her reins. "Whoa, Prince!" she cried. She positioned the reins to use as a pulley and then pulled with all her strength on the right rein. A great wave of relief washed over her when she felt her horse slow slightly. She pulled again, and he slowed his pace even more. Soon Prince was under her control, coming back to trot and then walk just as they reached the sand dunes. She rode him up the sandy path toward Dune Grass Lane.

Once on the road, she stroked his neck, now wet with sweat from his bullet run down the beach, as she guided him up the driveway of the last cottage. There was no one in sight, and Sarah called out loudly. "Help! Can someone please help?" The front door burst open and the woman they'd seen earlier strode out onto the porch.

"My friend's horse has gotten mired in the marsh at the other end of the beach!" Sarah cried, riding Prince closer. "Do you have a phone to call the Yardley Rescue?"

"Of course! But they'll need to know just where the horse is— can you tell me?" the woman asked.

"All I know is he's at the end of the beach where the ledge extends into the water. He's down pretty deep."

The woman hurried inside and, with the door still open, Sarah could hear her phone conversation with a dispatcher. "A horse is mired in the marsh at the far end of the beach in Yardley! He's down pretty deep close to where the ledge goes out into the water. The horse's owner is there with him. Please hurry!"

When the woman reappeared, Sarah thanked her and made another request. "I also need to call Brookmeade Farm to let them know what's happened. Could you please make another call in Yardley?"

The woman thought a minute. "You know, if you can get off your horse and lead him closer to this doorway, I think my phone cord will extend so you can make the call yourself."

"Awesome," Sarah said, dismounting from Crown Prince. "I know the number."

After she'd run up her irons, Sarah led Prince to the doorway and accepted the phone the woman handed her. *Please let someone be in the office!* Sarah thought. She was thankful when the phone rang only once before Kathleen picked up.

"Oh, Kathleen," Sarah said, her voice shaky. "Something awful happened to Quarry! He's mired in a boggy part of the marsh at the end of the beach, and someone just called 911 to have him rescued."

Kathleen was immediately alarmed. "Where are you?" she asked. "And I need the phone number there so Jack can call you right back. He's teaching now, but I'll run and get him."

Sarah handed the phone back to the woman and asked her to give Kathleen the number. As she hung up, the woman said, "By the way, I'm Anne Winfield. You have a magnificent horse!"

"Thank you, Mrs. Winfield. I'm Sarah Wagner, and this is

Crown Prince. He just gave me the ride of my life. I can't believe how fast he ran down the beach!"

Prince's nostrils were still dilated, his breathing rapid, and his coat lathered with sweat. Sarah knew she had to get him moving. She quickly removed his saddle and circled her horse in the short driveway while she waited for Jack's call. The two children Sarah had seen earlier appeared from the house, and she was relieved when their mother gave them firm orders not to get close to the horse.

It seemed like an eternity before Jack called back, and Mrs. Winfield again handed the receiver to Sarah. "I want you to stay where you are, Sarah," Jack said firmly. "I've checked with the dispatcher, and they've already sent a fire department team to rescue Quarry. I just called Dr. Reynolds office, and Dr. Jenson from the vet clinic is rushing over there. Mrs. Romano is coming with her trailer to pick up Fanny and Crown Prince, even though you're in different locations. I'm bringing the Brookmeade trailer for Quarry. We know where you are—just stay put."

Sarah again walked her horse up and down the Winfield's driveway, and gradually his breathing came back to normal and his coat became cool to the touch. Mrs. Winfield brought some water in a pail so Prince could drink a few swallows at a time. She continued walking Prince, all the while worrying about Quarry. Would the fire department get there in time?

The minutes dragged on until finally Sarah heard a pickup and trailer rumbling down the road toward them. Mrs. Romano pulled beyond the Winfield's driveway and then backed the trailer into it. Kayla flew out of the truck's passenger side, rushing to Sarah. "They got him out! Quarry's okay," she cried. "The fire department came right after the call came in. They knew just where to come, and they brought special equipment."

Mrs. Romano came up behind Kayla. After Sarah introduced her to Mrs. Winfield, Mrs. Romano said, "Quarry was already out of the bog when I arrived with the horse trailer, but Kayla can tell you more about it."

"They put these wide straps around Quarry," Kayla said. "There was just enough space between his belly and the muck for them to push the straps under him. Then they used a winch to lift him out of the bog. Luckily, Quarry stopped struggling during the rescue. He was exhausted, and it almost seemed like he knew the men were there to help him."

"Dr. Jenson got there right after they lifted Quarry out," Mrs. Romano said. "She thought he was walking okay, but gave him some IV fluids. She's going to come by the barn later to check him again."

"How is Paige?" Sarah asked.

"She's still pretty shaken up," Mrs. Romano said, "but greatly relieved Quarry is okay." She looked directly at Sarah. "It's thanks to your quick thinking and action that he made it, Sarah."

"Yeah," Kayla chipped in. "I watched you and Prince fly down the beach. I've never seen a horse run so fast!"

Sarah looked up at her horse. "You were a star, Prince," she said, as she hugged his head. Turning back, she spoke to Mrs. Winfield. "I don't know what we would have done if you hadn't had a landline phone."

"Yes, we owe you a debt of thanks," Mrs. Romano said to Mrs. Winfield. "Now let's load this guy and get the horses home. I hope the halter I brought for him is big enough."

Quarry was already at the farm when the Romanos' trailer got there. After Prince was unloaded, Sarah walked him to the barn, with Kayla following carrying Prince's tack. Once he was in his stall, the girls rushed to the wash stall where a crowd of onlookers, including Mrs. Romano and Jack, were watching Paige bathe Quarry.

Much of the muck and bog mud had already been hosed off the gray gelding, and Quarry stood quietly with his head lowered as Paige sponged warm soapy water on his head and neck. After going over his upper body, she applied the sponge along his underbelly, sheath, and high up between his hind legs. She sponged his legs and feet, and lastly dunked his tail in the soapy bucket. Quarry almost closed his eyes when Paige applied warm water from the hose to rinse all the soap and grime from his body. After she removed as much water as she could with a sweat scraper, Paige led him slowly back to his welcoming stall, where fresh bedding, hay, and water awaited him.

"Good job, Paige," Jack said. "Dr. Jenson will be coming soon to look him over carefully, and once she gives the okay, we'll apply some liniment on his legs and wrap them with support bandages."

As soon as the others left and Quarry was in his stall, Sarah and Kayla together hugged Paige, tears running down their faces. So much pent-up emotion flowed freely, with images of the struggling horse mired in the quagmire still fresh in their minds. "Thank you, Sarah," Paige murmured. "You and Prince saved my horse. The rescue people said they got him out just in time, that he was close to going into shock."

Kayla and her mother left a few minutes later, and Sarah went back to her own horse. It was Prince's turn to be bathed and cared for.

* * * * *

Paige was at the barn when Sarah arrived the next morning. She had removed Quarry's bandages and was walking him slowly in the courtyard. "How's he doing?" Sarah asked.

"Dr. Jenson said it could have been a lot worse, but Quarry severely stressed his tendons, especially in his hind legs. Even with Bute meds and the support bandages I put on him last night, his legs are swollen this morning." Sarah nodded her head after she bent down to look at Quarry's legs more closely. "Dr. Jenson said he's going to need some time off," Paige continued, "with stall rest and just hand-walking for a while."

Sarah knew immediately what this meant for Paige. Her plan to compete Quarry at Wexford Hall had vanished. In fact, unless the horse made a quick recovery, their whole competition season was in jeopardy. Sarah felt badly for the girl who worked so hard to bring out the best in herself and her horse.

A few minutes later Sarah went to check on Crown Prince. After giving him his daily carrots, she put him on the cross-ties and quickly removed his bandages. At Jack's suggestion, she had applied liniment to his legs before wrapping them for the night. Prince had run extremely fast for two miles on hard-packed sand, something he wasn't conditioned for. She sighed in relief when she could find no sign of heat or inflammation.

Sarah was about to put Prince back in his stall and feed the horses when Jack appeared. Worry lines creased his forehead. He checked her horse's legs, running his hand down the tendons, and looked relieved as he straightened. "Except for being a bit tucked up, your horse seems none the worse for his run on the beach yesterday," Jack said. He looked intently at Sarah. "You've talked with Paige?" When she nodded, he said, "Then you must know there's no chance Quarry can be part of the Wexford Cup team." Jack paused. "It looks like Crown Prince will have the chance to take his place." Sarah abruptly jerked her head in Jack's direction, her eyes opened wide. "Would you and Prince feel up to the challenge?" he asked.

Sarah's head was spinning. In all the excitement, that thought hadn't crossed her mind. She had been so preoccupied with Quarry and her own horse that the implications of Quarry's injuries hadn't occurred to her. Now Jack was suggesting that Crown Prince could take Quarry's place on the team.

"But Jack," Sarah said, "he's just learning to do cross-country obstacles! How can he possibly do the Wexford Hall course?"

"We have a month," Jack said. "Based on how quickly he caught on when we worked on cross-country last Wednesday, I think we can have him ready. The class will be doing a fair amount of cross-country schooling in the next few weeks, and I'm willing to give you and Prince as much additional training as it will take to prepare him for the competition. Is this something you'd like to do? Maybe you need to think about it, and certainly talk to your parents."

"Yes, I need a little time," Sarah said. "A little time." Jack turned and headed back to the office.

Sarah couldn't stop thinking about being part of the team as she made the rounds feeding the horses. If Jack thought Prince could be ready for the event, then maybe she should have faith in his judgment. But would it be fair to her horse to expect so much of him? Would her parents be shocked at such a proposal and forbid her to even consider it? Would she be letting the team down if she didn't at least try? They needed a fourth member. Tim, Kayla, and Rita would be so disappointed if they had to miss the event.

When she'd finished refilling the ration pails, Sarah decided the lounge would be a place she could think while Prince finished eating his hay. Turning him out could wait. Scouring and refilling the water buckets could also wait. She made herself comfortable on the sofa and looked into the indoor arena, empty and quiet at this hour. She continued to deliberate on the proposition Jack had thrown out to her. So many questions with no clear-cut answers.

And then suddenly Sarah knew what she needed to do. Mrs. DeWitt could help her sort through the pros and cons. The lounge clock showed it was almost half past eight. She was pretty sure the DeWitts would be up and about, but it would be best to call them first.

Mr. DeWitt picked up on the second ring. "Good morning, Mr. DeWitt," she said. "It's Sarah. I hope I'm not calling too early. By any chance is Mrs. DeWitt there?"

Mrs. DeWitt must have been close by, because she came on the line right away, and when Sarah asked if she might come to talk with her, Mrs. DeWitt urged her to come at once.

"A mug of hot chocolate or coffee awaits you," she said. "Spin and Cameo are already excited!"

It took Sarah only a few minutes to walk the hilly driveway to the DeWitts' farmhouse, and soon she was seated in their breakfast nook with the Jack Russell terriers on either side. After initially greeting her, Mr. DeWitt excused himself to retire to his office.

"We have been so worried about Quarry," Mrs. DeWitt said. "I'm relieved that he just needs some time off. What a terrible ordeal for Paige and her horse to go through!"

Sarah took a sip of her coffee. "Paige said he was stiff when she walked him this morning, and there's swelling in his legs. A sad part of this is that Quarry can't possibly compete in the Wexford Hall event. No one works any harder with her horse than Paige. She doesn't deserve this."

"Jack tells me that you played a big part in Quarry's rescue," Mrs. DeWitt said. "Did Crown Prince have a pleasant gallop down the beach?"

Sarah smiled. "It was a wild ride. I've never dreamed a horse could run that fast! I know his sire won the Kentucky Derby, and I'll bet Prince was running just as fast as his dad did. He seemed to know we needed to get help." She set down her coffee mug and looked directly at Mrs. DeWitt. "But all this brings up a question." Mrs. DeWitt sat back, waiting.

"Jack suggested that Prince should take Quarry's place on the team." Sarah paused a moment, letting her words sink in. "He says that we have a month to do more work on cross-country obstacles, and he believes we can have Prince ready for the event."

Mrs. DeWitt mulled this over before speaking. "What do you think about this, my dear?" she said softly.

"I'm worried we could be rushing Prince. Maybe asking him to tackle a championship course with so little training under his belt would be a mistake. I've heard about riders who rush their horses and ruin them by overfacing them before they're ready. I'd never forgive myself if I did that to Prince!"

Sarah took another sip of coffee before continuing. "Since we started riding with the Young Riders, there have been many times when the jumps were really big for a horse that had just started jumping. Sometimes, coming into a fence, I could feel he was unsure, but when I pressed my legs harder to tell him he could do it, he trusted me. He went over the jump every time! But I'm afraid if I ask him to tackle things that are way beyond him, maybe he'll lose that trust." She looked into Mrs. DeWitt's clear blue eyes for guidance.

"If you feel this way, then why are you in a dilemma?" Mrs. DeWitt asked. "Why is it a hard decision to make?"

Sarah thought a minute. "I'd hate to let the other kids down. There's really no one else to be the fourth rider on the team. Derek told me Bismarck isn't a candidate because he hasn't done any dressage or cross-country."

"Sarah," Mrs. DeWitt began, "do you know the reputation Jack has in the eventing community all around the world? He's watched you and your horse improve every step of the way. He's seen the amazing progress you've made. Do you think he would encourage you to take on this challenge if he wasn't sure you and Prince could succeed?"

Sarah hung her head. "I guess you think I should have more faith in my riding instructor."

Mrs. DeWitt reached out to put her hand on Sarah's arm. "Yes, dear, I do."

"I know this," Sarah said. "Jack has never let me down."

"You also need to look deep inside yourself. You have a brilliant, athletic horse. You must have confidence in him. And faith in yourself."

As Sarah walked back to the barn, she thought about what Mrs. DeWitt had said. Now she could look at the situation clearly, and she knew how she would respond to Jack's invitation to join the team. Based on his skill as an instructor and Prince's athletic talent, she *did* believe she and Prince could do it. But there was one more wrinkle—her parents! She would have to convince them Prince was ready to meet the challenge, and that she as his rider wouldn't be at risk.

When she'd finished her Sunday chores, Sarah turned Prince out into one of the unoccupied turn-outs. The spring grass had come in thick and rich, and he buried his nose in the grass without his usual canter around the paddock with a few bucks thrown in. He was tired today, and for good reason. Yesterday's wild ride on the beach had left him drained.

Sarah brought out her lunch and settled into a comfortable spot beside the paddock where she could lean her back against a maple tree. It felt so good to soak up the mid-May sunshine and watch her horse graze. As she ate a turkey sandwich, her eyes feasted on her handsome horse. It was almost a year ago that he had come to

Brookmeade Farm, and the regular exercise and training he'd been getting had changed the way he looked. Most noticeable were his heavily muscled hindquarters, and moving forward on the bit in his dressage work had produced stronger muscling in his crest. He'd added weight, which had filled out his frame, and his coat had a healthy bloom. Sarah felt proud. She knew how much time and hard work had gone into making these changes in her horse's appearance. With his dark bay coat shimmering in the sunshine, he was more beautiful than ever!

Prince continued to move slowly in his paddock, searching out the best morsels of grass. As Sarah watched, he stopped grazing and pawed the earth with a front leg. He paused momentarily and then lowered himself to the ground. Instead of rolling to scratch his back as he usually did, he stretched out on his side and lay still.

It looks like he's going to take a nap, Sarah thought. *The sun probably feels as good to him as it does to me.* She watched her horse for several minutes before quietly slipping through the paddock fence and going to him. He lifted his head as she came closer, but made no move to rise. When she was close enough, she sat down in the grass beside him, gently stroking his neck and speaking to him softly. "Good Prince, good boy," she repeated. Prince partially closed his eyes, loving her voice and touch.

Sarah wasn't sure how long she had been sitting on the grass beside her horse when a voice behind her broke the quiet. "I wish I had my camera." It was Derek, grinning at her.

Sarah smiled back. "Have I died and gone to heaven?" she asked. "The sun feels so warm. Prince and I are both loving it."

But Derek's presence had caught Prince's attention. Sarah moved quickly out of the way as he scrambled to his feet. Shaking his head, he ambled to a clump of thick grass and resumed grazing. Sarah went to where Derek was leaning on the fence. "I suppose you've heard about what happened to Quarry yesterday," she said.

"Yeah, it's all over the barn. Paige is walking him in the courtyard now. Tough luck."

Sarah bent down to pull up a long shaft of Timothy from the taller grass. She leaned against a fence post and chewed the stem. "What will happen to the team?" Derek asked.

"Jack wants Prince and me to fill Quarry's slot." Sarah looked thoughtfully at Derek, as he considered what she had told him.

"Are you going to do it?" he asked.

"Jack says he will help us prepare. We have only a month before the event, but he thinks we can do it. I was undecided until I talked to Mrs. DeWitt. She said I must have faith in Jack and confidence in Prince. We're going to compete."

Derek smiled broadly. "Awesome! Your horse is going super, and Jack is a fantastic instructor. You guys will kick butt!"

As Sarah biked home that afternoon, she considered how she would break the news to her parents. She had related yesterday's events to them in great detail, and she knew her mother felt uneasy about Prince's fast gallop on the beach. How would they react to having her ride in the Wexford Hall competition? Sarah decided to wait until after dinner to bring it up.

After the table had been cleared and the dishes placed in the dishwasher, Sarah checked the kitchen wall clock. She had fifteen minutes before one of her parents' favorite programs, *60 Minutes*, would begin. Her father was already in the den when she approached her mother in the kitchen. "There's something I want to talk to you and Dad about. Can we do it now?" Her mother frowned, sensing something serious, as she followed Sarah.

Once they were all seated, Sarah spoke. "After his injury, there's no way Quarry can be part of the Brookmeade Farm team

242

that's going to compete at Wexford Hall," she began. "Jack spoke to me today. He thinks Prince and I can do it, and he wants us to take Quarry's place."

Her mother drew in her breath sharply before looking at her husband and then back at Sarah. "Is this the competition you told us about, where the horses have to jump all kinds of solid jumps on a cross-country course?" her mother asked.

Sarah nodded her head. "There are also dressage and show jumping phases. Except for the cross-country part, it's all the things my Young Riders class has been working on all year. Everyone says Prince is awesome. Sometimes he does better than the horses that have been in that group for a long time."

Sarah knew she had some convincing to do. "The event lasts three days, and we'll be staying in a dorm at the Belmont School. Jack's going to coach the team. There have to be four riders on a team, so Kayla, Rita, and Tim really need me. Jack says Prince will be ready."

"But you need our permission," her father reminded her.

"Of course, Dad," Sarah replied. "But this is so exciting! I'll get to take Prince to Wexford Hall and ride on those beautiful grounds. Because we're representing Brookmeade Farm, the DeWitts are paying our entry fees. I'll stay in a dorm with the other kids. It will be a blast! I've been riding Prince for almost a year, and with Jack's help we've learned so much. We've worked hard, and now here's a chance for Prince to show everyone what he can do and what an amazing horse he is."

Sarah's eyes sparkled as she talked, and when she had made her case, she sat quietly, gripping the arms of her chair, waiting to hear her parents' reaction. They looked at one another, and then back at Sarah.

Finally her father spoke. "We seem to have had conversations like this in the past, Sarah, always wondering if something you're doing with that horse might be too dangerous. We've worried you could be at risk. For a long time all has gone well, but now you're proposing to ride him in a competition over a demanding cross-country course, where you could be in harm's way."

"This isn't an easy question," Sarah's mother said. "You say Kayla and your other friends will be riding in this event." There was a long pause as she and her husband exchanged glances.

"Give us a minute." Mr. Wagner said. Sarah's parents got up and walked to the kitchen. From where she sat, she could hear a hushed conversation. Sarah found herself holding her breath. Were they arguing? Were they trying to figure out how to say no? She braced herself for what might be bad news.

After the Wagners came back into the den and sat down, her mother spoke. "When we've had to make similar decisions this past year, your dad and I talked about the fact that you are growing up. In a few years, you'll be on your own, making all your own decisions. We'll have to let go someday, and maybe this is the time. So as much as we'll worry about your safety, we must have faith in Jack's judgment. If you feel confident in your riding skill and your horse's ability, we won't hold you back from riding at Wexford Hall."

Sarah looked at first one parent and then the other, smiling with tears in her eyes. "No kid could ever have parents as great as you guys are," she said. "I will always remember this."

CHAPTER 22

Ditched

A FEW YEARS BEFORE Sarah rode at Brookmeade, when the DeWitts knew Jack O'Brien was coming from Ireland to take over the training duties at the farm, they had begun construction of a cross-country course on the property. With Jack at the helm, they envisioned Brookmeade Farm becoming an equestrian center where training sessions, clinics, and eventually competitions could be held. In addition to building a few jumps in the meadow close to the barn, others were placed on the network of trails around the farm, often taking advantage of existing resources such as stone walls, a gate, hedges, and logs. Other obstacles had required an investment in materials. Eventually more obstacles would have to be built if competitions were to be held at the farm, but for now, there were plenty to help the Brookmeade team prepare for the Wexford Cup.

The next Young Riders lesson was devoted entirely to cross-country riding, with Jack mounted on the chestnut Thoroughbred, French Twist. While Quarry was out of action, Paige would be riding school horses, and today she was on McDuff, the bay Morgan gelding. Even though she wouldn't be on the team, Paige still wanted to train with the class and keep riding fit.

Jack gathered the riders in the indoor to speak to them before they headed out. "Having a season's eventing experience under his belt, Tim has a definite advantage when it comes to cross-country riding. But the rest of you have a solid foundation of dressage and jumping in the indoor arena and on the hunt course, which should help immensely. I think with the work we'll be doing in the coming weeks, you'll be well prepared for the competition." French Twist was getting antsy, anxious to be on his way, and Jack circled him before continuing.

"Brookmeade Farm doesn't come even close to having all the kinds of obstacles you'll be facing at Wexford Hall, but we have enough to cover the basics. We'll use the brook for training in water, and we've already schooled on the bank with a drop in the meadow next to the barn. We're lucky that stone walls abound here. Ditches appear on most cross-country courses, and sometimes people make the mistake of underestimating the challenge they pose. Today we're going to ride toward the north field so we can school over a white gate, a cordwood pile, a coop, and a table. Coming back on the loop, we'll jump a stone wall and a ditch."

The six horses and riders filed out of the arena, with Jack leading the way toward the hayfield trail. Crown Prince was relaxed, happy to be with the horses he'd gone on hacks with many times. McDuff was almost always used in lessons in the outdoor ring or indoor arena, so he was excited to be going out on a trail for a change. Paige had to ask him to slow his pace several times, but she was used to riding a quick horse. "Do you have any idea what the Wexford Hall course is like?" Tim asked Jack, as they walked along the trail. "It was a little farther away than my dad wanted to travel to an event, so I didn't ride there last year."

Jack twisted in the saddle to reply to Tim. "I've not been there either, but I'm told the terrain has some steep hills. That's why 'tis so important for our horses to be well-conditioned. It takes a fit horse to gallop on hills." Jack slowed French Twist and then turned back to Tim. "As for the kinds of obstacles, I suspect they'll have the typical things like water, banks, drops, and ditches in various forms. We'll get a look at everything when we walk the course before the competition.

Kayla was close enough to overhear the conversation. "The horses don't get to see the obstacles ahead of time, right?"

"Correct, so it requires a real partnership, with horse and rider trusting each other," Jack replied. "But *you* can walk the course as many times as you'd like. I recommend walking it several times, once to get an overview, and then at least once more so you can analyze each obstacle. As your coach, I plan on walking the course with you."

After they'd ridden a few minutes longer, Jack halted French Twist and pointed to a good-sized obstacle of neatly stacked cordwood in the distance. "We're going to jump the cordwood you can see down there. I'll go ahead and will be waiting on the other side so I can watch you." He paused to scan the five riders in front of him. "Let's go in this order: Tim, Kayla, Rita, Sarah, and Paige. I checked this trail yesterday and removed a little windfall on the ground, so the footing should be good."

Soon Jack and French Twist were cantering toward the cordwood, jumping it easily. The riders could see where Jack had halted in a small clearing on the side of the trail. One by one they followed Jack's example. When it was Sarah's turn, Prince approached the obstacle with a lot of confidence, jumping it easily. She pulled him up before they reached the other horses and listened to Jack's critique of her ride. "Good pace coming into the obstacle, and Prince jumped it in good form. Excellent." Paige followed her on McDuff, who also jumped it well.

The group continued walking along the trail until Jack stopped them again. "The white gate that's at the entrance to the north hay field is farther along the trail. Let's proceed as we did for the cordwood. I'll be waiting in the field. Your horses may be eager to get to the open field, but don't let them rush coming into the gate." After Jack had left them to jump the gate into the field, all five horses followed him in order and all five jumped the white gate in good form. They gathered with Jack in the field where he critiqued each ride.

Sarah was so proud of Prince! He had never seen any of the obstacles they had jumped that day, and yet he was fearless and forward! Afterward they checked out a table jump and a large gray coop that awaited them on opposite sides of the field. While the jumps were good-sized and the table had width to contend with, they were in open, inviting locations with straightforward approaches.

Jack addressed the group before they went any farther. "Don't forget you'll receive penalties at Wexford Hall if you don't complete the course in the time allowed. Your horses will have to move consistently at a hand gallop, and you will have to know how to rate them along the way. So let's jump these two obstacles while circling the field at a good clip."

There were no problems until Paige approached the table on her horse. McDuff was used to jumping much smaller fences in the riding school's program, and he was intimidated by this obstacle. When Paige sensed his hesitation, she sat deeply, using her seat and legs to urge him forward. It wasn't enough, and McDuff came to an abrupt stop in front of the table.

Jack immediately trotted French Twist closer. "Please come away from the table and out into the field," he said to Paige. "I want you to trot a figure-eight, making sure your horse bends properly and moves forward with impulsion. He needs to be listening to you." Paige followed Jack's directive, and once McDuff was moving correctly, Jack spoke again. "Now I want you to pick up left lead canter and come off the circle straight toward the table. The instant you feel McDuff hesitate, use your crop behind your leg and continue strongly to the table. If he loses impulsion a second time, use your crop again."

Paige asked McDuff for canter and came in a straight line toward the obstacle. As soon as McDuff knew they were heading for the table, he attempted to slow his pace. Paige reacted immediately by sitting deeply and reaching back to smack him behind her leg with her crop. McDuff leaped forward. With no more hesitation, he approached the table and jumped it with plenty of room to spare. He continued cantering and easily jumped the gray coop ahead of them before turning back to the class. The riders clapped and cheered.

"Next we're going to jump out of the field over that stone wall," Jack said, "and as you continue along the trail, jump the ditch across the path. It's flagged, so you'll have no trouble spotting it. Be sure to keep your eyes up. If you look down into the ditch, your horse will feel your head drop and sense that you're worried. I'll be waiting for you." French Twist didn't hesitate when Jack rode him toward the stone wall, and soon his hoofbeats sounded faintly in the distance. The other riders followed in order.

Prince had some experience jumping stone walls, and even though this one was good-sized, he approached it boldly. After landing lightly, he cantered along the trail until Sarah could see the markers on each side of the ditch. She was concentrating on looking ahead, loving the feel of her powerful horse propelling them forward, when suddenly she felt Prince lose impulsion. Coming into the ditch, he slowed dramatically. Sarah followed her instinct to look down at what had caught her horse's attention, realizing too late what she had done. Even though she sat deeply to urge him forward with her seat and reached back with her crop the way she'd seen Paige do it and smacked her horse's side, it made no difference. Crown Prince slid to a stop in front of the ditch and snorted as he stood looking down into its cavernous bottom.

Prince had stopped! It was the first time he had ever refused a jump, and Sarah was mortified. She sat quietly for a moment, letting him look down inside the deep opening with its sides revetted by telephone poles. Prince snorted again, backing away from the ditch as Jack rode back to them.

"Paige will be coming." Jack said. "Let's get the horses off the trail until she goes by." Soon after they turned their horses into the woods, Paige and McDuff approached. As if he had learned his lesson, the bay Morgan sailed over the ditch and went to wait with the other horses.

Jack looked at his watch. "I'm afraid we don't have time to address this situation right now," he said to Sarah. "'Twouldn't be fair to hold the others up, so I suggest we bring Prince back tomorrow afternoon." As they walked their horses around the ditch, Prince shied away from it and snorted again. Sarah noticed that Rita's eyebrows were arched and a faint smile was on her lips when they joined the group.

Riding back to the barn, most of the riders talked in glowing terms about their cross-country ride, but Sarah was quiet. She was in shock that Prince had for the first time refused to jump when she asked him. When they reached the parking area and Kayla waved goodbye to the class, Sarah continued beside her toward the Romanos' trailer. "Tough break," Kayla said.

Sarah knew just what she was talking about. "Maybe I made a mistake deciding to let Prince do the Wexford Hall event," she said. "Maybe I'm rushing him. Maybe he hasn't had enough time on woods trails, and he showed it by having the heebie-jeebies when he saw that ditch. I'm glad Fanny's going so well, but maybe I'm expecting too much of Prince."

"Look, Sarah," Kayla began. "Prince just needs to learn there's no boogie man that's going to pop out of that ditch and grab him. It's a horse's nature to fear a hole in the ground, going back to when they had predators lurking in dark places. Fanny wouldn't have gone over that ditch so willingly if she hadn't jumped lots of them in the game preserve near my house."

Sarah hung her head as she reached down to stroke her horse's neck. "That's it, totally—Prince's lack of experience. Maybe I should tell Jack to take me off the team."

Kayla was taken aback "How can you think of giving up so soon? Jack's going to work with you and Prince tomorrow. Don't you think you should at least give it a try? Come on—buck up, kid."

When Sarah got home that afternoon, she tried to act as if nothing had happened. She knew how her parents would react if they heard this latest development. They could always backtrack on their decision to let her compete at Wexford Hall if they were convinced Prince wasn't ready to compete. She'd be off the team in a heartbeat. During dinner, Sarah pretended it had been just another day at the farm. She was relieved when Abby's excited talk about a school project demanded their attention.

As Sarah rode her bike to the barn the next day, she considered what she could do to help her horse get over his fear of the ditch. One thing she would *not* do is look down as they approached it. It was possible Prince's problem was entirely her fault. She must have let him down.

Jack suggested she have Prince ready to ride at four o'clock, when he had no lesson scheduled. That gave her plenty of time to do Prince's stall and warm up in the outside ring. She had just finished trotting some schooling figures when she saw Jack come out of the barn on foot followed by Kathleen on Wichita. As Sarah walked Prince out of the ring to meet them, Kathleen offered her an encouraging smile.

"Good old Wichita will provide Prince with a lead today," Jack said. "It should bolster his confidence." He started toward the trail that led to the ditch, with the two horses falling in beside him. "The challenge we have with your horse is not a problem of a fence being too high or too wide; his dilemma is in his head, the hardest of all problems to address. He fears the unknown. He's afraid of what might be in the ditch that he can't see as he approaches it."

Sarah half-halted Prince, who, with his long stride, was getting ahead of Jack and Wichita. "How can we make him know there's nothing to be afraid of?" she asked.

"You'll see," Jack replied. They entered the trail, with Prince and Wichita walking ahead of Jack and occasionally stopping to wait for him. As they neared the ditch, Sarah could feel tension rising in her horse, and he nervously chomped on the bit. "Halt for a minute," Jack called out, catching up with the horses. He walked ahead to inspect the ditch carefully. "Lucky for us, this ditch is fairly wide, at least three feet, making it more visible to him," Jack said. "With mainly sand on its bottom, he'll see there are no snakes or wild tigers hiding in there." He beckoned for them to join him.

Kathleen halted Wichita as they approached the ditch, leaving Sarah to walk her horse forward for a closer look. Prince reluctantly took a few steps before putting on the brakes, looking warily at the ditch in front of him. "One thing we must avoid is beating him across the ditch," Jack said. "A quick smack with your crop can be helpful when a horse hesitates, but if you beat a horse over something, he will always be afraid of it."

Jack walked to Prince's head, rubbing him gently and talking reassuringly to him. After taking hold of the reins, he clucked to the horse, asking him to move forward. Sarah also used her aids, and Prince walked closer and closer to the ditch. Finally he was looking down into it, his wide eyes showing white around the edges. Jack dropped the reins, and after slowly lowering himself into the ditch, he began walking from one end to the other, trying to appear as relaxed as possible and whistling softly. Prince watched him intently, his tense body poised to jump back. After a few minutes, Jack climbed out and led Prince around the ditch to the other side. The same exercise was repeated.

"He's looked into the ditch from both directions and he's seen that I wasn't swallowed up," Jack said. "Now Wichita can help us." He beckoned to Kathleen to join them. "Sarah, 'tis important you remain calm at all times. He needs to sense you're not afraid, that you're in command, and that he can rely on you."

Kathleen brought Wichita to Crown Prince's side, and they listened to Jack's directions. "I want both of you to trot to the stone wall, turn, and with Wichita in the lead, approach the ditch at a trot. It should be less challenging for Prince to jump the ditch heading for home with Wichita going in front of him. Stay firm yet relaxed, Sarah, and keep looking ahead."

Sarah gulped and took a deep breath as she asked Prince to trot down the trail following Wichita. When they reached the stone wall, Kathleen smiled. "I've seen many horses with this same problem. Jack always turns them around." Sarah took a deep breath. Kathleen's encouragement made her feel so much better.

They turned their horses, and once Wichita was trotting away, Sarah asked Prince to follow him several horses' lengths behind.

She applied pressure against his sides with her legs while keeping a firm contact with the reins. Prince knew what was coming—his head was up with his ears pricked forward. Wichita soon reached the ditch, and after willingly jumping over it, cantered easily down the trail away from them.

At that moment, Sarah felt Prince hesitate, and she responded by sitting deeply in the saddle and urging him on with her legs and seat. *Go, Prince, go!* her heart cried out to her horse. Suddenly, a stride before the ditch, Prince gathered himself, and with a tremendous leap, launched them extremely high in the air and over the ditch. Sarah found herself laughing as he landed and took off down the trail, soon catching up to Wichita. Both riders pulled their horses up and rode back to Jack. He clapped his hands and shouted, "Excellent! Now come back, and we'll do it again from the opposite direction."

The horses jumped the ditch several more times, until Prince no longer over-jumped it or showed any hesitation in his approach. And he no longer needed Wichita's lead. Finally, Jack asked Sarah to jump Prince over the ditch heading for home and continue cantering to the barn. As Prince ran down the path after jumping the ditch, Sarah was beaming. She slowed her horse to walk when they got to the farm's gravel roadway and threw her arms around his neck. "You wonderful horse!" Sarah cried out. She was proud and elated.

* * * * *

Over the next few weeks, Sarah followed an intense training program with Crown Prince that Jack mapped out for them. When she arrived at the farm after school, she and her horse first worked on dressage movements in the outdoor sand ring, and when Jack was free, he helped her train over one or more of the cross-country obstacles on the property. Sometimes Kathleen or Lindsay would take one of Jack's lessons to free him up to work with Sarah. Often Jack would be mounted on French Twist, so he could provide a lead horse, if needed.

During a long stretch of outstanding May weather, Sarah and Prince made significant progress. The telephone-pole-to-bank combination in the meadow near the barn became old hat to them. "He's learned to do a bank and a drop in one obstacle," Jack pointed out.

One afternoon, Jack had them approach the white gate from the north hay field, and after jumping it, continue at canter toward the ditch. Although Prince shortened his stride coming into it, he jumped the ditch without hesitation. After spending several days splashing through the brook, a small coop was placed at the edge of the water. Sarah was thrilled when Prince jumped the coop and landed directly in the brook the first time he was asked. He seemed to find jumping into water exciting, and after landing, he splashed through the brook and up the bank on the other side.

Jack considered one obstacle, a huge stone wall that separated two fields, too big for Sarah's horse. Other obstacles asked technical questions, and Jack felt they were also too challenging for them. *Prince's time will come,* Sarah thought. *One of these days he'll soar over everything as if he has wings!*

CHAPTER 23

Making Plans

AS THE WEXFORD HALL EVENT got closer, Jack called a Saturday afternoon meeting of the team members and their parents. It was time to go over their plans for the competition. Gus had brought extra chairs into the lounge so everyone could be seated comfortably. Anticipating the meeting might be crowded, Mrs. DeWitt had left her terriers at home. Tim's mother surprised everyone with chocolate chip cookies that were eagerly sampled by the group. Sarah was surprised when Derek and his parents showed up. "Derek wants to volunteer to be water boy for the team," Mrs. Alexander said jokingly, "and we just want to cheer for the team."

Jack stood on the fireplace hearth so everyone could see and hear him easily. "Thanks for coming," he began. "The Wexford Hall event will be here before we know it, and we need to discuss what you can expect. This should be an exciting competition for our riders and the stable manager. Tim, Rita, Kayla, and Sarah will be able to show how well trained their horses are and how well they can ride. In addition to taking care of her own horse, Kelly's been studying a few books on horse care and eventing so she can offer support to the riders."

I just hope Kelly won't have a chip on her shoulder, Sarah worried. *It would be nice if everyone on this team could get along and work together.*

"We'll be travelling to Wexford Hall on Thursday, the fifteenth of June," Jack continued, "and we're grateful Richard Snyder has offered us the use of his four-horse gooseneck trailer and the new truck that pulls it. His employee, Judson, will be driving the horses to Belmont. Between the Brookmeade Farm pickup and the Snyder's truck, we'll be able to provide transportation for the five team members. Tack will go in the trailer's dressing room, with tack trunks in the truck."

Sarah thought of her father's old-fashioned steamer trunk that doubled for her tack trunk. It would stand out like a sore thumb compared to the gorgeous modern tack trunks the others had, but her trunk served its purpose.

"The horses will be put up in temporary stabling under a large tent," Jack continued, "and our team will have one additional stall for storing our feed, shavings, and tack. This will be the stable manager's headquarters, and I'll be going over Kelly's job with her separately. I plan on bringing hay and bagged shavings in the Brookmeade truck, along with feed tubs and water buckets. For Fanny and Chancellor, we ask you to bring your own grain, so they're fed what they're used to getting at home. Please have individual meals divided into small paper bags with labels, which will be a huge help to Kelly when she's feeding the horses. Your individual paper bags should be stored in a small plastic barrel with a top that has your name on it."

Jack paused when Rita's hand shot up. "Will there be any limits on what we can bring for our horses?" she asked.

Sarah and Kayla exchanged knowing smiles as Jack answered her question. "With only so much space in the trucks, we ask that you bring only the essentials you'll need to take care of your horses and yourselves—and one of each, please." There were a few snickers from those who remembered the Brookmeade tack room when Rita had moved Chancellor there for a week's training. "With the exception of your saddle, all your horse equipment must be stored in your tack trunk."

When there were no further questions, Jack continued. "I spoke with the event organizer yesterday. They received our entry on time, along with those for seven other teams. As you know, the team will be staying in a co-ed dorm at the Belmont School, with a shuttle bus making regular trips back and forth to the event grounds. Eventing rules will prevail, and I'll be giving the riders information on these. Each rider will receive a packet of information when we arrive, which will include the times they will ride for dressage and cross-country on Friday and Saturday. Show jumping on Sunday will be in reverse order of standings."

Kayla raised her hand. "What should we bring for clothes? Will we be getting a list on that, too?" "You'll need to bring competition clothing for each of the three phases, as well as casual attire for the other social activities that are planned. I understand there will be a barbeque on one of the evenings, as well as an equestrian quiz game at some point, just for fun. As soon as I get more specific information, I'll let you know."

Now Jack turned to another subject, lodging for the family members. "There are two motels, plus the Juniper Bed-and-Breakfast Inn in Belmont, and we have a handout with information on those places for any of you parents who plan to stay over. How many of you are planning to come?"

Tim's father spoke first. "Carol and I went to all of Tim's events last year, and we certainly wouldn't miss this one." Mr. Snyder indicated he planned to be there over the weekend, and Kayla's mother said she wanted to be around all three days. Mrs. Hoffman would be having house guests, and she might be driving them up to watch for one day. The Alexanders' plans were up in the air, and Sarah wasn't sure about her parents—it depended on her dad's work schedule at The Creamery, which had opened for the season.

Jack appeared to have finished his remarks, so Chandler DeWitt took the opportunity to say a few words. "Dorothy and I are proud to sponsor this Brookmeade Farm team that's riding in the first Wexford Hall competition for junior riders. The material Jack will give you describes the rules that the organizers will have in place." He paused for a moment, as if trying to think of the next words. "I don't anticipate any problems, but please be reminded that any use of alcohol or drugs will be cause for dismissal from the competition, and smoking anywhere near stabling or at the Belmont School is not allowed. It's important to remember that you're representing this farm, and good sportsmanship and courteous behavior must be shown at all times."

Mrs. DeWitt also wanted to address the team and their families, and she stood up to face them. "We've decided that with his eventing experience, Tim is the logical captain of the team, which means that any communication from the organizers to the team will go through him." She held up a large shopping bag. "And I hope you're as excited about this as I am. In keeping with our farm colors of red and white, Chandler and I got each of our team members a red-and-white striped rugby shirt to wear on cross-country, as well as matching helmet covers."

"Cool!" Kayla said, as the shirts and hat covers were handed out. "They've got the Brookmeade Farm jumping horse logo."

Mrs. DeWitt reached into a separate bag and withdrew a red body-protecting vest. "In keeping with the new requirement that all eventing competitors wear adequate body protection when they're jumping their horses, we're also providing team members with one of these vests. Thankfully the incidences of riders coming off their horses during a competition are rare, but should something go wrong, we want our team to be ready."

Mrs. DeWitt thanked the riders and Kelly for their hard work, praised the horses on the team, and thanked the parents for supporting the riders. "And there's one thing more. The Wexford Cup is actually a large silver bowl. It will be a challenge trophy, so the name of the winning team will be engraved on it, and it will go home with that team until next year's event. Who knows, maybe it will come to Brookmeade Farm. We wish all of you good luck!"

As they left the lounge, Sarah invited her parents to come see Crown Prince. Neither one had visited the farm in some time. Sarah had groomed him earlier, since she had another cross-country school with Jack scheduled for later that afternoon. When they turned the corner to approach his stall, Prince raised his head from eating hay and nickered softly when he saw Sarah. "He must be very fond of you, Sarah," her father observed.

Sarah picked up her lead shank and went into the stall to bring her horse out for her parents to see up close. Her mother quickly stepped back when Prince came out of his stall. "He seems even bigger than I remember!" she said.

Sarah laughed. "He's a big pussycat, Mom. He wouldn't hurt anyone." She hugged Prince's head as she did so often, and the horse half closed his eyes, enjoying her attention.

That evening, Sarah called Kayla. "Are you totally psyched?" she asked when Kayla picked up. "I can't believe we head out in two weeks! I'm really glad you talked me out of quitting the team. Prince has been awesome jumping the cross-country fences, including the ditch, although he still hesitates for a moment when we get close to it. I wish there was another place we could school over other ditches."

Kayla thought a minute. "I think our dressage could be tighter. Fanny doesn't have a very good extended trot, and if there are many spectators, she's bound to be distracted."

"Oh, my God, I hadn't thought of that," Sarah said. "With eight teams, there will be lots of spectators, even on cross-country. I can't afford to have Prince looking anywhere except where he's going."

"Fanny's jumping well these days, and I'm pretty sure she's fit enough. I've been taking her to the preserve at least three times a week and doing some galloping in a big field. There are a few hills, and we've been doing those too. How about you?"

"With all the cross-country schooling we've been doing the last month and our rides to the old orchard, Prince must be fit."

"I do wish Paige was on the team with us," Kayla said. "I'll miss her! But listen, I've gotta go."

For their lesson later that week, Jack had the class work on the dressage test they'd be riding at Wexford Hall. They all seemed to handle the movements well enough, but Jack caught many accuracy problems. "If your test calls for a transition at E, then it means at E, not a stride after or a stride before," he said more than once.

Training for show jumping was also a high priority, and their last lesson was devoted to work on the hunt course. The jumps were set high and wide, and Jack had designed a course with sharp turns and changes of direction. "'Tis quick thinking you'll be needing to get around this course clear," he said. "You must always be planning for the next fence."

CHAPTER 24

Wexford Hall

AFTER DOING HER MORNING CHORES at the barn, Sarah sped back home on her bike. Today was the day she and her teammates had been waiting for! The Snyder's four-horse trailer would be arriving at Brookmeade Farm at eleven o'clock to pick up the horses going to the Wexford Hall event. Her suitcase was packed, her tack oiled, her tall black boots polished, and a brand new black show coat was ready to go. Later in the morning her mother would be taking her and her things back to the farm.

Mrs. Wagner greeted her when she came into the house. "Is there anything I can do to help you, Sarah?"

"Thanks, but no, Mom. I'm going to take a quick shower and change. My tack trunk is packed, and I groomed Prince, so all I'll have to do when I get back to the barn is put on his shipping boots." *He hasn't worn them since he went to the vet clinic to have his wolf tooth removed,* she thought. It seemed a long time ago, and so much had happened since then. Training had transformed Crown Prince from a green Thoroughbred off the track to an event horse ready to compete in dressage, cross-country, and show jumping.

"I hope Gus will be able to do all your work while you're

away." her mother said. "When I saw him last week, he looked awfully tired. And a lot older."

"Mrs. DeWitt told me they'll have Lucas work some extra hours. Gus knows I won't be here for a few days, and he'll make sure the horses are taken care of. This morning I did the sweeping that I usually do on Saturday. That should help a little."

After Sarah had showered and changed into some fresh jeans and a T-shirt , she and her mother packed her things into the SUV. "Are you sure you have everything?" her mother asked.

"I checked the list Jack gave us," Sarah replied, hopping into the front seat. "Except for my helmet, everything's in my suitcase, even my body vest. My helmet is in my tack trunk, along with my boots. Let's go!"

As they drove toward the parking area at the farm, Sarah was surprised to see the Snyder's new gooseneck trailer already pulled up near the barn. It was sparkling white with green Pyramid Farm lettering, and matched the new white truck that pulled it. They were early, which meant Chancellor would have a longer time to stand in the trailer before they left the farm. Jack and Judson stood near the Brookmeade pickup that had several bags of shavings stacked in its bed, and Gus was tossing hay bales in beside them.

"I think we can put my things in the trailer's dressing room," Sarah said. When she stepped inside with her suitcase, she noticed her saddle and a few others were already on the racks. *One less thing to bring out from the barn,* she thought. Her mother handed her the plastic garment bag that protected her show coat and her boot bags. After they had made the transfer, Sarah gave her mother a hug. "I hope I'll see you on Saturday," Sarah said. "I'll call you with my cross-country time as soon as I find out."

"You be careful, Sarah," her mother said, frowning. "And good luck." Sarah waved and watched her mother pull out of the lot.

As the SUV started out the farm road, the Romanos' silver trailer was coming down the hill. Sarah started for the barn to get Prince wrapped. When she stepped inside, she saw Tim had Rhodes on cross-ties in the aisle near where his tack trunk, a suitcase, and other things were piled. Sarah scooted over to touch base with him. "It looks like you're ready to go," she said, noticing Rhodes was already wearing his shipping boots. "Rhodes looks like a seasoned traveler, and a handsome one at that."

"Now that you're here, I guess we're just waiting for Kayla," Tim replied.

"Kayla's trailer is pulling in right now. All I have to do is move my tack trunk to the truck and put Prince's shipping boots on." Sarah thought a minute. "Where's Rita? I didn't see her outside."

"She was in the feed room with Kelly dishing up the rations for Prince and Rhodes," Tim replied.

"I'd better get Prince ready to load," Sarah said, turning away from Tim. As she started along the aisle, out of the corner of her eye she saw Paige by Quarry's stall. She hurried over to her.

Paige was looking in on her horse, but turned as Sarah got closer. "I wanted to see you before we left," Sarah said. "You deserve to be going to Wexford Hall, not me. I wish things had turned out differently."

Paige came over to Sarah and gave her a hug. "You're so sweet," Paige said. Her pretty face was sad, with no trace of her usual smile or laughter. "Some things just weren't meant to be, I guess. But Quarry's legs are getting better. We'll have our chance another time."

"Do you think you'll get over to the event?" Sarah asked.

Paige thought a minute. "I don't have to work on Sunday. Maybe I'll drive over to watch the show jumping."

Just then Sarah heard Jack calling her name. She rushed to the doorway and waved to him. "We're going to be ready to load your horse in ten minutes," he said. "We put your tack trunk in the truck and your saddle in the dressing room."

Sarah turned and bolted for Prince's stall. The hay she had left for him earlier was completely cleaned up, and he stood quietly in his stall. His shipping boots were where she had nested them by the door. Picking up his lead shank and good halter with the sheepskin liners, she slid into the stall. Prince was so beautiful! When she had groomed him earlier, the last step was to go over him with a soft cloth, and now his dark bay coat shined like cut glass. He looked at her closely. Could he sense something unusual was going on?

Sarah had oiled his fancy halter with the nameplate so it looked brand new. Once he had it on, she brought him out of his stall and snapped him on the cross-ties. She quickly put on his shipping boots, making sure they were tight enough not to slip down. With a last glance around to make sure she wasn't forgetting anything, she unclipped the ties and led Prince out of the barn, walking to where Kayla and Tim stood with their horses near the rear of the big trailer. Fanny also wore shipping boots, and her chestnut coat shone brightly. "What a gorgeous young lady!" Sarah said.

"Me or Fanny?" Kayla asked.

From that angle, they could see Chancellor in one of the stalls, his black coat gleaming in the sunlight that streamed in one of the large windows. Jack signaled for Tim to bring Rhodes Scholar on. After his partition was secured, it was Sarah's turn to load her horse. This large rig may have resembled the vans that had shipped Prince to the racetrack, because he walked on with no hesitation. *I hope you'll be as agreeable about everything else this weekend,* Sarah thought.

"Your mare will stand on the outside," Jack said, as he

motioned for Kayla to bring Fanny on. Fanny pulled back only slightly before following Kayla up the ramp. The big gooseneck was far different from her Quarter Horse trailer. Before the ramp was closed, Sarah could see that Prince and the other three horses were relaxed in the familiar company and pulling hay from the nets hung in each compartment.

Jack motioned for the team members to come closer. "Rita and Kelly are going to ride with Judson," he said. "Kayla, Tim, and Sarah—you'll come with me in the pickup. I think everything's been loaded, so we'll be on our way. I'll follow Judson, just in case there's a problem on the road."

While everyone was getting into the vehicles, Mrs. DeWitt came hurrying out of the barn carrying two picnic hampers. "We don't want our team to get hungry on the road, so I've packed some chicken salad sandwiches, chips, and water bottles for all of you." She brought one of the hampers to Judson's truck and one to the riders in the Brookmeade truck. Mrs. DeWitt shushed the chorus of thank yous. "I want everyone to have a wonderful time," she said. "Chandler and I will be there cheering for you!" Sarah saw Spin making a beeline toward her and shut the truck door quickly. *He'd love to jump right in with us!* she thought.

Soon the Pyramid truck with its powerful diesel engine was effortlessly pulling the large trailer up the hill away from the barn, with Jack's pickup following behind. When they reached the interstate, Judson began picking up speed until his rig was moving with the flow of traffic. Sarah wished she could see her horse inside, but the back doors completely obstructed her view. *He has horses he knows on either side,* she reassured herself. *He'll be okay.*

The three riders and Jack soon became engrossed in conversation, and the time flew by. They exited the interstate a few hours later, and after a short drive, approached the estate in Belmont. A large gilded sign by an entrance road welcomed them to Wexford Hall. "I wonder where the mansion is," Kayla said, looking out her window. A turn-off arrow on the stabling sign directed them down a gravel road toward an enormous blue and white striped tent packed with portable stalls.

A man in overalls waved them to a place where the horses could be unloaded. Jack slowed to inquire about the Brookmeade Farm stabling assignment. "Brookmeade Farm," the man said, looking down his list. "Let's see, your stalls are on the back side, numbers 21 through 25. They're already bedded with shavings, so your horses can go right into the stalls. Any additional bedding you must provide yourselves, and the stalls must be stripped before you leave, or you forfeit the stabling deposit. Don't forget that horses must wear a halter or a bridle at all times, and make sure your riders don't tie a horse to the stall partitions—they're not that sturdy."

Kelly and Judson already had the ramp down on the trailer, and one by one they unloaded the horses and led them to their stalls. A number of horses were just arriving, and with all the activity in and outside the tent, it was noisy as riders got their stalls organized and talked excitedly. "This stall is pretty rickety," Rita said, after she'd brought her horse into stall 22. "I hope it will hold Chancellor." Sarah led Prince into stall 25, an end stall, which put him next to Fanny in stall 24.

Sarah was happy with Prince. He hadn't sweated up on the trip, and he seemed relaxed. *This probably seems a lot like the racetrack to him,* she thought. Fanny seemed a little nervous, moving around in her stall and watching the activity around her closely. Kayla went into the stall to stroke Fanny and talk to her softly.

Jack approached them pushing a Brookmeade wheelbarrow which, after the riders' trunks had been loaded in the Synders' truck, they'd barely managed to squeeze in. He lifted out two plastic barrels holding the grain bags and motioned to Kelly. "These will go in our tack stall for you to organize." The group made several more trips to unload their supplies, and Tim and Judson carried in the riders' tack trunks to place in front of their stalls. Finally the trailer and truck were completely unloaded, and Judson left to park the gooseneck trailer in a nearby field.

"We need to be efficient with our space," Jack called out. "The watering hose is outside the tent, and you can fill your water buckets and put them in the stalls." He gave each rider a horse information form to fill out and tack on the stall door. "If anything goes wrong, the attendants will know who to contact and how to reach you by cell."

"May I have an extra bag of shavings?" Rita asked. Somehow her question had the tone of a command. "This stall isn't bedded anywhere near enough for Chancellor. As I've said before, he's used to straw bedding, not these cheap shavings."

Jack was frowning when he responded. "We've brought two extra bags for each horse, one to add tomorrow and one to add Saturday. If you use one of yours now, you'll have only one left. I'll let you make that choice."

Rita and Kelly immediately went into the tack room to get a shavings bag for Chancellor's stall. No one else made a move to get more shavings, and Sarah caught Kayla's raised eyebrow.

After the horses had hay and water in their stalls, Jack gathered the riders around him. He had picked up the team's packets from a woman seated at a table near the tent, and now he handed them out. "I may not have mentioned an event rule that insists you wear a helmet anytime you are on a horse. Be sure you're not eliminated for that infraction." He stepped back out of the way of a horse being led by them. "If you want, you can hand-graze your horses, perhaps near where the trailers are parked. When you use the wheelbarrow in the tack stall, empty it in the manure bin after each use. Kelly will be topping off the water buckets occasionally, and she'll be feeding the horses their hay and grain."

Jack looked at his watch. "It's almost time to feed. Then we'll head for the Belmont School. We'll come back later this evening to check on the horses. We can pick out stalls, top off water buckets, and feed hay for the night. There should be a shuttle bus running by then."

Soon, along with their suitcases, show coats, and boot bags, the team was back in the two vehicles heading for the Belmont School. "Where are you staying, Jack?" Tim asked.

"The DeWitts have been kind enough to reserve a room at the Juniper B-and-B Inn for Kathleen and me. After her last lesson tomorrow, she's coming up with Kayla's mother. Judson is needed to care for the Snyders' horses, so he'll be leaving soon to drive the truck back to Yardley. But he'll be back here on Sunday to truck the horses back to the farm."

Passing by The Belmont School sign and up the tree-lined driveway, they admired the Georgian-style brick buildings and the sweeping lawns on the campus. The dorm was easy to find, and after getting room assignments, they carried their suitcases and event packets to their rooms. Sarah was glad she could room with Kayla. Kelly and Rita were continuing the friendship they had struck up the summer before and seemed happy to room together. Tim was assigned to a room on the second floor with a boy from another team.

Sarah and Kayla opened their event packets as soon as they got to their room. The first thing that fell out of Sarah's was the paper pinny she'd wear on cross-country. "I'm Number 21," Sarah said. "I guess Prince and I will go after 20 other riders. What's your number?"

Kayla unfolded her pinny. "I'm Number 14," she said, "so Fanny will go before Prince. I wonder where Tim and Rita will be in the order. There are 32 horses on the eight teams."

The packets also contained corresponding bridle numbers, a map of the competition grounds and one of the cross-country course, and a beautiful full-color program, which listed the riders and horses on the teams. Kayla sat cross-legged on her bed looking through the program. "I see the DeWitts put an ad for Brookmeade Farm in here." She turned a few pages. "Holy cow, there's one team that came all the way from Riverton."

After she'd unpacked her suitcase, Sarah turned to face Kayla. "What do you think so far?"

"This is a great experience for Fanny. She hasn't spent a night away from home since I got her." Kayla paused in thought. "I just hope everyone stays friendly once the competition starts tomorrow."

"Yeah, but I won't be surprised by anything Rita does," Sarah said. "I know her too well. I just hope putting Rita and Kelly together in one room doesn't add up to trouble with a capital T."

"You're usually their favorite target, but if Fanny is Supermare in the competition, I'll have to watch my back, too."

Later, as the competitors were eating dinner in the cafeteria, the event organizer, Matthew Campbell, welcomed the riders. "We're happy to have eight teams competing for the Wexford Cup, with several driving a long distance to get here. I want to remind you to read the material in your event packets carefully. For things to run smoothly, every competitor needs to observe the rules, demonstrate good sportsmanship, and show up on time."

He took a few swallows from his water glass before continuing. "You're all aware that the prize going to the team with the highest cumulative score is the Wexford Cup, but there will also be ribbons through sixth place presented to the top-scoring individual riders. There will be a simple breakfast available here in the cafeteria from six to nine every morning, and the shuttle bus runs every half-hour from six in the morning to nine at night. Tomorrow night, after competition ends for the day, we're holding the Equus Quiz, with every question related to horses or equestrian activities. We have prizes donated by the Wellington Tack Shop for members of the winning team, so be sure to come. And don't forget that dinner on Saturday evening will be a barbeque on the South Lawn. There's a ticket for that in your packet. Now I wish all of you the best of luck, and may the best team win!"

Shortly after the Brookmeade team had finished eating, they met Jack at the entrance to the cafeteria. "We can get a ride on the shuttle bus that leaves in about ten minutes," Jack said. "Your horses weren't walked after the ride here, so I suggest you take them out of their stalls for ten minutes or so. 'Twill give you a chance to see a little of the grounds. We're lucky to have the June days stay light so late."

Sarah was glad they were going back to the stable. She was anxious about Prince in this different environment. The stalls weren't very substantial, and they were small for a horse his size. The riders hurried to their horses after the shuttle let them off near the big tent. Prince nickered softly when he saw Sarah approaching. She quickly unlocked her tack trunk and grabbed one of the carrots from the three-day supply she'd stashed there. Prince was quick to take it when she entered the stall and stroked him. He had eaten much of his hay, and his grain bucket was empty.

"Want to walk the horses?" she called to Kayla.

"Sure. Right after I finish picking out Fanny's feet." In a few minutes Sarah and Kayla were leading their horses out of the tent and around the event grounds. Swatting at mosquitoes as they walked, they followed a gravel road beside a field where a few cross-country obstacles had been built. One was constructed of giant spools, and another appeared to be a facsimile of a doll-house. "I hope Fanny will be bold and not look twice at these strange jumps," Kayla said.

"I want to get through dressage tomorrow before I even start thinking about the cross-country," Sarah replied. It was starting to get dark, so they decided to head back to the stable area. Once Prince was back in his stall, Sarah hurried to get the wheelbar-row so she could pick out any droppings before leaving. When it wasn't there, she looked in Chancellor's stall. Kelly was bent over, tossing soiled bedding into the wheelbarrow with a manure fork while she chatted with Rita, who held Chancellor. Sarah poked her head into the stall. "I'd be happy to empty that for you when you're finished," she said. "I need to pick out Prince's stall."

Rita stared at Sarah. "Since when are you so nicey-nice? We'll take care of the wheelbarrow, thank you." Kelly looked down, not trying very hard to smother a laugh.

Sarah just walked away. Tim, whose horse was in the next stall to Rita's, had overheard the exchange and rolled his eyes at Sarah as she walked by. She went to Prince and stood stroking and talk-ing to him until Kelly returned from the manure bin and let the wheelbarrow fall with a loud thud in front of Prince's stall. As Kelly walked away, Sarah thought, *Here we go again*. She shook her head as she picked up the manure fork and began to work on the stall.

When the horses had been taken care of for the night, Jack called a meeting of the team. He sat on Tim's trunk, holding open an event program while he went over their dressage rides the next day. "Tim, you're the early bird: your ride time is 8:56 tomor-row morning. I'll be at the warm-up ring twenty minutes before you ride your test to coach you. You can make the call as to how much time over and above that Rhodes needs to be ridden to be at his best."

Jack looked around at the others. "The same goes for the rest of you. Your times are listed in the program. You'll have your horse tacked up appropriately for dressage, and you'll be dressed as I described on the sheet I gave you. Any questions?" Jack asked.

"Yes," Rita said. "With cross-county on Saturday, can you walk the course with us sometime tomorrow?"

"Of course, Rita. Let's all meet here at the tent at half past three, after your dressage rides. If anyone brought rubber boots, you might want to wear them. We may have to cross water the old-fashioned way, before bridges were invented. You'll probably have time to walk it a second time later on. Depending on when you ride on Saturday, you may be able to walk the cross-country again Saturday morning."

Jack stood up when they heard the shuttle bus approaching. "A word of caution," he said. "Even though the stable is lighted at night and there's a night watchman on duty, lock your tack trunks." Sarah fingered the substantial chain her key was on around her neck. But Jack hadn't finished. "Remember that Kelly is coming here about seven tomorrow morning to feed your horses. We want them to have plenty of time to digest their breakfast."

Back at the dorm, Sarah called her mother to give her an update and the time for her cross-country ride on Saturday. Kayla talked to her mother as well.

When their phone conversations were finished, Sarah and Kayla batted around Rita's earlier unpleasantness. "Just as I suspected," Sarah said. "Rita and Kelly are difficult enough to deal with one-on-one, but together they're even worse. Those two are a bad combination." She yawned. "I need to think about the

274

dressage test now, and not Rita and Kelly."

"Yeah," Kayla replied. "The less we deal with them the better."

"I don't ride until after noon," Sarah said to Kayla as they both got ready for bed. "Maybe I can help you with Fanny in the morning."

"Cool," Kayla said. "But now I think we should hit the hay." She grinned. "No pun intended."

Both she and Kayla wanted to get to the barn early the next morning, so Sarah set her cell for a six-thirty wakeup. As she waited to fall sleep, she began running through the dressage test she'd memorized. She was asleep before she got halfway through it.

CHAPTER 25

The Test

BOTH KAYLA AND SARAH were awake before their alarm went off the next morning. After showering, they dressed in their show shirts and buff breeches. "I'm glad Jack said we can use a stock pin on a collar, and not wear a stock tie," Kayla said. "I haven't the slightest idea how to tie one."

"Me either," Sarah said, as she slipped a pair of jeans over her buff breeches and pulled on a lightweight polo to protect her show shirt. "I guess this will keep my duds clean until it's time to get on Prince." She tied the laces on her barn sneakers.

The girls ate a bagel with orange juice and coffee before grabbing their tall boots, show coats, and packets and heading for the shuttle bus stop. Before long, they were on their way to the event grounds. A lot of other competitors also wanted to get back to their horses early, and the bus was almost full. Rita had probably come on an earlier shuttle with Kelly, and with an early test, Tim should already be there. Sarah couldn't help worrying about her horse. "I hope Prince didn't get cast in that small stall," she said.

"You'd have heard from someone if he did," Kayla replied. "Chill."

When the bus stopped by the tent, the riders swarmed off. The girls found Kelly holding Rhodes in his stall while Tim groomed him. Sarah rushed to Prince's stall. Her horse was standing in a relaxed position, with one hind leg drawn under him, pulling mouthfuls of hay from his hay net. He left his hay when she came into the stall, expecting a carrot.

"How's Fanny?" Sarah called over the stall wall.

"She might have been a little uptight last night, because she didn't eat much of her hay. She'll probably be her old self after I get her outside. She'll think it's just another horse show."

"I'm going to pick out Prince's stall," Sarah said, "and then I'll do Fanny's." She was happy to find the wheelbarrow in the tack stall. As she walked by Rhodes's stall this time, she saw Kelly on a stool braiding Rhodes's mane while Tim held his horse. Rita was working on Rhodes' tail. *I guess Rita is trying to collect brownie points with Tim,* she thought.

Sarah cleaned Prince's stall, working around her horse as he ate his hay. When she finished, she wheeled the wheelbarrow to Fanny's stall. "Why don't you take her outside for a little grass while I do her stall?" Sarah suggested. Kayla eagerly agreed. After cleaning the stall and returning the wheelbarrow, Sarah took Prince out to join Kayla and Fanny. Her horse would love some green grass.

Kayla and Fanny were in the field where the trailers were parked, some of which were huge custom rigs. Kayla had picked a place where the grass was tall and succulent, and Prince tore into it. After ten minutes, Kayla said, "I think Fanny's had enough. Let's put them away and go down to watch Tim's test. I called Mom while Fanny was grazing, and she won't be here until just before I ride."

When they got back, Tim and Rhodes had left for the warm-up ring, and there was no sign of Rita and Kelly. *Rita must love being so cozy with Tim without Paige around,* Sarah thought. She studied the event map from her packet, making a mental note of various locations. "Tim's going to ride pretty soon. I think we need to book to the dressage arena," Sarah said.

On their way, the girls saw the Wexford Hall mansion across a field in the distance. "Wow!" Kayla exclaimed. "It looks like a palace. I wonder how many people actually live there."

"I wouldn't be surprised if there are twice as many staff as residents," Sarah said. "I hope the people who live here ride, so they can use these beautiful grounds."

Tim wasn't in sight when they arrived at the dressage arena. A large set of bleachers, which was filling up fast, ran the long way of the arena, and Tim's parents were sitting in the middle section with the DeWitts. Mrs. DeWitt waved enthusiastically, and the girls climbed up the bleachers to join them. Mrs. DeWitt spoke in a hushed tone, asking how the horses were doing and all the details of their stay so far.

Everyone turned when Mr. Dixon said, "There's Jack!" He paused. "Number 6 is in the arena now, so Tim should be here any minute." Jack walked briskly toward the bleachers, followed by Rita and Kelly. They climbed up to join them. "How's Rhodes going?" Mr. Dixon asked Jack.

"He warmed up well. Rhodes is always so poised. Never gets rattled, even with all the horses in the warm-up and the crowds milling around."

What will Prince be like? Sarah worried. *How will he handle all the hubbub?*

A few minutes later, the next horse entered the arena and put in a respectable test, not flashy, but accurate. After the applause quieted down, the announcer spoke into the loud speaker: "Next is Number 8, from the Brookmeade Farm team, Tim Dixon riding Rhodes Scholar." The Brookmeade fans watched anxiously, some with their fingers crossed, as Tim entered the arena on his handsome bay horse and began his test. Rhodes was relaxed yet moving with good impulsion, and Jack pumped his fist when Rhodes extended beautifully across the diagonal. "Brilliant!" he said under his breath. After Tim saluted the judge and walked Rhodes from the arena on a long rein, Jack commented, "Very solid! He should get high marks for that test."

Kayla and Sarah hurried back to the tent to groom Fanny and braid her mane. "I've never braided before," Sarah said. "But Jack said I should try."

"Not to worry," Kayla said. "I should have time to help you with Prince. I braid Fanny for all our shows, so it won't take me long."

The girls worked on the mare until her copper coat shone brightly and her four white stockings gleamed. "You can hold her while I braid," Kayla said. "I hope Rita won't mind if I borrow her stool." As Kayla braided, she looked down at her watch. "I think we're okay on time. Fanny doesn't need much warm-up."

Rita and Kelly returned as Kayla worked. Right away, Rita noticed Kayla standing on her stool and she scowled, shaking her head. "Do you always help yourself to other people's property?" she asked Kayla.

"I knew you wouldn't mind, generous person that you are," Kayla chirped. She didn't look up, but continued braiding. Sarah was at Fanny's head, trying to hide her smile by keeping her head down. Kayla had a great way of putting Rita down while not getting riled by her caustic remarks. "And I know you won't mind if I use it later to braid Crown Prince," Kayla said.

At that moment, Tim approached his stall leading Rhodes. With his helmet under his arm, Tim was especially good-looking in his black show coat and stock tie.

"Awesome test, Tim," Rita said. The others also complimented him on his ride.

"I'm glad to have that behind us," he said, flashing a smile. "Now on to cross-country,"

As soon as Fanny was braided and tacked up, Sarah took the reins. "I'll hold her. Get yourself ready." She reached into Kayla's packet and withdrew the number 14 that would attach on Fanny's browband on her near side.

Kayla looked sharp when she came back from the tack stall wearing her black show jacket, white breeches, and helmet. Her tall boots were polished to a high sheen. Snapping the helmet's clasp, she said, "Thanks for remembering the bridle number." She tightened her girth and then led Fanny from the tent to a mounting block outside. Before she rode off in the direction of the warm-up area, Kayla commented, "I hope my mom makes it."

"She'll be here. And good luck! I'll be rooting for you," Sarah called after her.

Sarah saw from her watch that Kayla wouldn't have much time to warm-up. She decided to touch base with the others before leaving for the dressage arena. After removing his tack, Kelly and Rita had taken Rhodes outside to sponge him down. Rhodes drank deeply from his water bucket once he was back in his stall. When Tim came back, he had changed into more comfortable clothing. "Do you guys want to go up to watch Kayla's test?" Sarah asked.

Rita and Kelly looked at each other, as if they weren't sure how to respond, but Tim said, "Of course. I'm ready. Rhodes deserves some rest time and a chance to eat his hay."

The four of them left the tent and went to sit with the Brookmeade contingent in the bleachers. Mrs. Romano had arrived just in time to see her daughter's test. She spoke to Sarah. "I knew Kayla wouldn't be in the stable area, so I came directly here."

While everyone was talking about Tim's super test and how that would help the team, Sarah was thinking about Kayla. She wondered how her warm-up was going. Jack soon joined them in the bleachers, and a few minutes later the announcer introduced Kayla: "Number 14, from the Brookmeade Farm team, Kayla Romano riding Fanfare."

Kayla began her test with a straight line to the judge. Fanny looked spectacular, the beautiful chestnut with four white stockings and a diamond on her forehead stepping forward smartly. The mare bent correctly into the corners and continued doing well on the parts of her test until she was to pick up right lead canter at A. Some of the spectators gasped when they saw Fanny cantering on her left lead! *Fanny must have thought she was supposed to counter-canter!* Sarah thought. Kayla quickly recognized the error. She brought Fanny back to trot and picked up canter on the correct lead, but the damage was done. Points would be deducted for the error, and Kayla seemed to come unhinged by her mistake. Fanny lost impulsion, as if Kayla wasn't riding as deliberately. She managed to finish the test, but when Kayla left the arena, she knew she'd not ridden her best.

Sarah left the bleachers and ran to find Kayla. Her friend had dismounted from Fanny near the warm-up ring and stood with her head hung low. When Sarah caught up with her, there were tears on Kayla's cheeks. She unbuckled her helmet, yanked it off, and ran a hand through her carrot-colored curls.

Sarah slipped an arm around her best friend's shoulders. "It's okay, Kayla," she said. "It was just one mistake, and plenty of kids will do worse."

"I doubt it," Kayla said. She handed her helmet to Sarah, ran up her irons, and loosened the girth. Fanny stood quietly, watching the horses warming up in the ring. Turning back to Sarah,

Kayla said, "I've let Jack and the team down."

"Knock it off!" Sarah said. "Dressage is only one part of this event. Let's take Fanny to her stall."

Back at the tent, Sarah and Kayla sponged Fanny outside before the mare's braids were removed. The chestnut Quarter Horse seemed glad to go back in her stall with a new ration of hay. While Kayla changed out of her competition clothes, Sarah looked in on her own horse. Prince was resting quietly in the back of his stall.

Their time had come, she thought. After almost a year's hard work, today she and Prince would have their chance to show what they could do in a dressage test. She opened her tack trunk to retrieve her grooming caddy and set it inside the stall. Grabbing her lead shank, she went to her horse and leaned to press her cheek on his muzzle. "We'll try our hardest," she whispered.

Kayla came back looking more comfortable in jeans and a T-shirt. "After my totally blown test, it's all the more important for you and Rita to ride well. Let's get started on Prince."

Kayla was holding Prince while Sarah curried him when Kayla's mother came into the tent. She walked up to Kayla and gave her a hug. "I blew it, Mom," Kayla said, hanging her head. "I'm sorry."

Mrs. Romano stepped back and put her hands on her hips. "What do you mean, blew it! That's absurd. Fanny's wrong lead was only one small part of the whole test." She moved closer to Kayla and reached out to lift up her chin. "I can tell you one thing. You won't be helping your team by moaning and groaning about your test. You've got two more phases to go!"

Kayla glanced over at Sarah and then back at her mother. "Mom, if you'll hold Prince, Sarah and I can work together." Mrs. Romano took the shank, and Sarah resumed grooming Prince while Kayla brushed out his tail. When Kayla tried to comb his mane, she looked up at Prince's neck and started laughing. "No way can I braid this horse unless I have a tall stool!" She left to grab Rita's stool from the tack stall.

After Prince was braided and tacked up, Sarah stood back to survey her handsome horse. This was the first time his mane had ever been braided, and the effect accentuated the pleasing arch of his long neck. "I'll be right back," she said, leaving Kayla holding Prince while she went to the tack stall to get herself ready. A few minutes later she returned wearing her gleaming tall boots and show coat. Once she'd put on her helmet and riding gloves, it was time to go. But before she took the reins, she gave Kayla a hug. "Thanks for your help, pal."

There were many good-looking horses at the Wexford Hall event, but when Sarah rode Crown Prince into the warm-up ring, heads turned their way. The ring was busy, with lots of horses going in different directions. Prince's head was up and his ears flicked in all directions. *He's uptight!* Sarah thought. She was unsure how to start their warm-up, so she walked him around the large ring, giving him a chance to see everything. It was a relief when she saw her instructor coming their way. Jack stopped by the rail, and when she got close, he said, "Sarah, you should be warming Prince up the same way you do at the beginning of all your lessons."

Duh! she thought. Of course. It was the routine Prince knew. Once she'd trotted him long and low going large in the ring, she gradually increased her leg pressure while shortening her reins to put him in a frame between her hand and leg. She could feel his back come up and his hind legs reach further underneath him. They dodged a few horses as she guided Prince off the track to ride a large circle, shrinking its size and then leg-yielding to make it large again. Coming back to walk, she practiced over-bending and counter-bending until Prince felt supple and forward.

Jack beckoned her to come closer, and Sarah listened intently to his instructions. "I want you to sit the trot, pick up canter at C, and ride a serpentine of three loops, doing a simple change of lead on the center line each time you cross it." She had only done that exercise twice when Jack called to her again and pointed at his watch. It was time to report to the dressage arena steward. Sarah gripped the reins tighter as she felt a knot beginning to form in her stomach. The first test of how well she had schooled Prince under Jack's guidance for the last year would soon begin. She knew her horse was capable of doing well, if only she could give him the ride he deserved.

With Jack walking beside them, Sarah rode Prince out of the warm-up ring toward a steward standing near the dressage arena entrance with a clipboard. The man smiled and patted Prince on his neck before he checked to make sure his bit was legal. There was no problem with the mild, fat snaffle, and after checking Sarah off on his list, the steward pointed to the arena. "As soon as number 20 leaves, you may ride on the outside of the arena until the judge signals you with the bell to start your test."

Sarah thanked the steward and walked her horse in a small circle while keeping her eyes on the chestnut horse finishing his test. Prince had gotten over his initial nervousness in the warm-up ring, but now he eyed the large crowd on the bleachers, his head high. *He's used to the bleachers at Brookmeade, but there are so many more people here!* Sarah thought.

Jack must have read her mind. "'Tis important not to telegraph your nerves to your horse, so breathe deeply. It will help him to know you're calm and confident." When the chestnut horse left the arena, Prince reacted to applause from the spectators by jumping to the side and pranced a few steps. "Breathe deeply!" Jack reminded her as he walked away, "and good luck."

Sarah shortened her reins and turned Prince toward the dressage arena, asking him to walk energetically around the twelve-inch-high crisp white boards with letters posted on them. "One of the best ways to get your horse's attention is to ask him to do something," Jack had said more than once. Directly behind C, the judge and her scribe sat in a booth filling in scores and comments from the last ride. From her vantage point, the judge would see if their entrance down the centerline was straight and if, at the end of the test, their halt at X was square. Prince scrutinized the two women as Sarah rode him past the booth. *Thank goodness he has a chance to see them up close before we begin*, she thought.

After circling the arena once at walk, Sarah asked Prince to trot and go on the bit. He had lost his fascination for the bleachers and was listening to her, his ears flicking back in her direction as she communicated to him with her aids. They had just passed the judge's booth a second time when she heard the high-pitched ring of the judge's bell—the signal to begin. The announcer spoke into the microphone: "Number 21 is from the Brookmeade Farm team, Sarah Wagner riding Crown Prince." Sarah shortened her reins again and tried to clear her head of everything except the dressage test she had committed to memory. At the arena's entrance, she turned down the centerline, her eyes glued to the letter C, her target for a straight line.

Later Sarah wouldn't remember riding all the parts of her test, but she did recall that her transition from canter to working trot at A was slightly late. She remembered his last trot extension vividly. When she asked Prince to extend his trot across the diagonal, he responded with a wonderful burst of energy, his stride long and elastic. Finally she sat the trot as they turned up the centerline and halted at X in the center of the arena. Sarah dropped her left hand

and nodded her head to salute the judge, who, in keeping with protocol, returned the salute. Sarah noticed that the judge was smiling at her, probably a good sign. She let Prince's reins slide through her fingers as she rode him out of the arena.

The test was over, and she felt an amazing relief, as if a hundred-pound boulder had slid from her back. She laughed when Prince jumped sideways in response to loud clapping from the crowd. They'd liked what they saw! Kayla and Tim came down from the bleachers and ran to them. "You aced it!" Kayla squealed.

"Oh, no," Sarah protested. "There were a few stumbles, but we got through it. Prince was listening to me the whole time!" Sarah suddenly felt very tired, and she fell forward to hug her horse's neck.

When she sat up, Tim gave her a thumbs-up. "Unbelievable!" he said. "For a horse just a year off the track, he was fantastic."

Sarah slipped from the saddle and ran up her irons. "Let's go back to the big top. Now it's Rita's turn. Maybe we can help her get ready."

Kelly was holding Chancellor as Rita stood on her stool braiding him when they got back to the tent. Chancellor's black coat glistened like ebony. He tossed his head repeatedly while Rita worked on him, prompting her to snap at him in frustration. "Jerk horse!" she complained.

Sarah led Prince into his stall. The day had turned hot, and she couldn't wait to shed her show coat. Kayla held him while she hung the coat in the tack stall, slipped into her jeans, and exchanged her tall boots for barn sneakers. When she returned, Kayla had removed Prince's tack, and they took him outside for sponging. When Prince was back in his stall, they went to check with Rita.

"Anything we can do to help?" Kayla asked. Kelly gave Kayla

one of her signature dirty looks, but waited for Rita to respond.

"Naw, you'd just be in the way," Rita said. Kayla and Sarah looked at each other, shaking their heads. Rita turned to them from her braiding. "Remember that Jack wants the team to meet back here at three-thirty. He might want to critique our tests before we walk the cross-country course." Sarah swallowed hard at mention of cross-country. She had been so focused on her dressage test that she hadn't been thinking about cross-country. *Time to switch gears,* she thought.

Kayla motioned to Sarah. "We're not needed here," she said. "Let's split for the snack bar." The air was filled with the aroma of hamburgers and onions on the grill when they reached the food booth staffed by volunteers from a local church. After waiting only a few minutes, the girls got wraps and water. They carried their lunches to the dressage arena bleachers, where Sarah heard some nice comments on her dressage ride from everyone. She wasn't surprised when Mrs. DeWitt gushed over her test, but Mr. DeWitt, usually quiet and reserved, praised her. "I can't wait to tell Hank Bolton what a wonderful job you've done training his horse," he said. "Oops! *Your* horse," he added, chuckling.

It was almost time for Rita to ride, and the rest of her team waited for what they expected would be one of the best tests all day among the thirty-two riders. When Number 28 exited the arena, the announcer introduced Rita: "The last rider from the Brookmeade Farm team is Number 29, Rita Snyder riding Chancellor." Rita began her walk around the arena, Chancellor looking proud and majestic, each of his steps strong and deliberate. His jet black coat shimmered in the sunlight, and Rita was well turned out with the best attire and tack money could buy.

Chancellor entered the arena shortly after the judge's bell rang, beginning an impressive ride. With every transition precise and his movement lovely to behold, Rita accurately rode her horse through the various movements, culminating with a spectacular extension of his trot. Although the crowd had been urged to withhold applause until a horse had exited the arena, the spectators roared their approval with loud clapping.

Kayla's brows were knitted into a frown when she spoke to Tim. "Have they posted any of the scores yet?" she asked.

Tim shook his head. "I think Jack is going to get the final results before coming back to the tent to meet with us. The organizers know that everyone is eager to see them, so I bet they won't waste any time posting them. And not just individuals—they'll probably list the current team rankings."

Later, with their horses resting in their stalls, the team members sat on the grass outside the tent while they waited for Jack. He hurried over when he spotted them. Jack sat down, and after he pulled a pad of paper from his pocket, it became very quiet. He fished out his glasses and put them on. "Here's the scoop," he began. "Rita has made us all proud by earning the highest score of the day. You're in first place, Rita," Jack said, smiling as the other clapped their hands." Rita smiled smugly, also clapping.

Jack paused to look at his pad again. "Tim is also to be congratulated for being in fourth place out of 32 tests. Rhodes was marvelous today! You beat out some exceptional rides, Tim." Again clapping.

"And now Sarah…." Jack said, scanning his pad. "This is remarkable," he said, looking up. "In his first time to compete since he arrived at the farm from the track a year ago, Prince and Sarah put in a ride that puts them in ninth place." Sarah covered her face with her hands as the others clapped for her. *Oh, my God!* she thought. She'd expected to be happy with her score, but not to beat out so many other riders! She could hardly wait to call her parents! And she wanted Derek to know, too. She'd hoped the Alexanders would show up, but so far, no sign of them.

It became quiet as the group waited to hear Kayla's score. "Kayla and Fanny had a few slips in their test today. I know they'll shine tomorrow, though. Currently they're in twenty-fifth place." Kayla hung her head. She had been expecting a low score, but not this bad. "There's something to be learned from what happened to Kayla today," Jack continued. "She was riding quite well until Fanny misread her cue and picked up a wrong lead. Unfortunately, Kayla appeared to give up, as if her entire test was ruined by one mistake. Actually, the way dressage tests are scored, *only* that one movement would have received a low score. If Kayla had put that mistake behind her and focused on the remainder of the test, she would have done a lot better."

Jack paused to let this sink in before continuing. "And 'tis important to apply this lesson to your remaining jumping phases. If you have a rail down in show jumping, put that behind you and ride the rest of the course as if you have a clean round. The same goes for cross-country."

"What about the team standings?" Tim asked.

"I can't imagine you'd be interested in that," Jack said, grinning as he paused. "The good news is that Brookmeade Farm is in third place!" Everyone cheered as Jack stood up and pocketed his glasses. "Grab your course map out of your packets, and let's go walk the course."

CHAPTER 26

On Course

JACK AND THE FOUR RIDERS strode across the field, their cross-country course maps in hand. The grass had been mowed short to provide good footing for the horses that would be galloping over it the next day, and two jumps had been set up in a warm-up area. When they reached the three-sided starting box made of white pipe, they stopped to look toward the first obstacle, an inviting brush jump.

"When it's time for you to begin," Jack said, "the starter will count down the seconds from ten. So your horse doesn't get antsy standing in the box, wait until the count is down to five before you slide inside. When the starter says go, you'll be off." Just hearing Jack say this sent chills down Sarah's spine.

They looked down at their maps. "Wow!" Tim said. "There are twenty-one obstacles on this course, and it's a lot longer than anything Paige and I rode last year."

"'Tis a bit on the long side," Jack said. He looked off in the distance. "This valley is surrounded by mountains. If there are several hilly stretches on the course, the top placing riders may be those who brought fit horses. To avoid time penalties, you'll have to move at a good clip. I hope all of you have been conditioning your horses as I suggested." His eyes scanned over them.

As the group marched toward the brush, Jack made some comments. "This jump is straightforward, as the first obstacle should be. You'll have plenty of time to get your horse moving in a balanced hand gallop before you reach it, just as we've done when schooling at the farm."

Following the course mapped out for them, they continued across the field toward the second obstacle, a log pile, followed a short distance later by a woods trail. Along the path they met a slatted coop, a stone wall, and a large log. "Your horses will probably be a bit strong at this point, fresh out of the box, but don't let them gallop on so fast you'll have trouble getting them balanced and off their forehands before the jumps," Jack said. "You'll also need to save something for the hills."

They came to a point where the trail turned sharply right, taking them out of the woods and toward a sizable bank that was followed a few strides later by a telephone pole jump. Across the field they could see the next obstacle, a pig pen—a square made out of fencing they would have to jump into, and without taking another stride, immediately jump out of. "This is like the bounce we did in class," Kayla remarked.

From here, the map took them up a long, steep hill in the field, which had the riders short of breath when they reached the top. "I'm glad Chance is in better shape than I am!" Rita joked.

"Where do we go from here?" Sarah asked, looking around. She was anxious to see the ditch that was listed on the map. Prince had overcome his fear of the ditch at the farm, but how would he react to a different one? She swallowed hard as she searched the trail ahead.

"This way," Jack said, pointing to some whiskey barrels at the treeline. "This will be challenging to your horses because you're jumping from light to dark, and horses can't quickly see what's ahead of them. Their eyes must adapt, and they'll have to trust you. Ride strong into this fence, to be sure."

A short way after the whiskey barrels a park bench was waiting for them. The trees grew closely together here, making the trail dark and shadowy. *I hope the ditch isn't on this trail,* Sarah thought. *Who knows what monsters Prince might imagine are in a ditch in the woods!*

Sarah was glad when they came into another field. There was a vegetable stand loaded with all kinds of fresh veggies, plus farther along, a Chinese puzzle and a double-drop heading down a hill. At the foot of the hill, a brook had been dammed up to make a water obstacle. They would have to jump a big log into water, gallop through the water, and jump a narrow vertical two strides out of the water. "You'll have to ride accurately to avoid missing the vertical," Jack warned them.

After they consulted their maps once more, the riders looked at each other in disbelief. Their route followed a path up another hill, although this one wasn't as long or steep as the one before. Obstacle 14, a wagon loaded with bales of hay, was in their path once the terrain leveled off, and a large rolltop was in the distance. Kayla took a deep breath. "We must be near the end," she said.

"I'm afraid not," Jack replied, shaking his head. "There are quite a few obstacles ahead of us." He pointed off in the distance to a rustic table perched near the treeline. After the table, they jumped a cordwood pile that brought them into the woods again. As they continued down the trail, Sarah saw flags on either side, but nothing solid between them. This must be it!

The ditch was a lot like the one at Brookmeade—wide, with its walls revetted with telephone poles, except this one had leaves and sections of tree branches scattered along its bottom. She caught Jack's eye after they'd looked into it. "You'll ride it just like the one on the farm," he said. "Keep your eyes up, and with your aids, tell him 'tis a go." The other riders didn't give the ditch much thought, but Sarah couldn't get it out of her mind. She'd dream about it that night for sure.

A coop bringing them out of the woods was closely followed by a sharp right-angle turn into a narrow post-and-rail fence. "You must ride the turn accurately, or you'll miss the second fence." Jack said. They continued by a copse of trees and into the field where Sarah and Kayla had seen the giant spools and the dollhouse. Another hill followed, and Sarah stopped and pointed. "Look what's on the top!" she said. It was the finish flags, and tomorrow a timer would record their times when they went through them.

Jack looked up the last hill. "'Tis here you'll know if your horses have heart, that quality that makes them strive on even when they're spent."

This hill was not as long as the others, nor as steep. But except for Rita, the riders were all thinking how demanding the course would be for their horses. "Chancellor is so strong behind," Rita said. "He won't have any trouble pushing up these hills. He zooms up the hill we have in back of my barn."

Tim looked at her quizzically. "There's a difference between running up one hill and doing three all at once on a long course with twenty-one obstacles along the way."

"I'm not worried," Rita sniffed. "As a matter of fact, anything but first place isn't on my radar screen."

Later that afternoon, once they'd returned to the dorm, Sarah and Kayla took their second shower of the day and changed for dinner. They met Tim, Rita, and Kelly in the dining room. "I hope we've all gotten rid of the cobwebs on our brains and can ace the Equus Quiz questions tonight," Tim said, grinning.

Sarah frowned. She'd forgotten about the quiz and had planned to go back to the event grounds after dinner. She wanted to walk Prince and let him have some grass. But it was a team activity, and she didn't have much choice.

"It's too bad we don't have Paige here," Kayla said. "She reads horse stuff all the time. She'd probably know all the answers." Sarah noticed Tim frowning when he heard Kayla mention Paige.

After they'd eaten the buffet dinner, which featured strawberry shortcake for dessert, the teams moved to a large meeting room. Everyone seemed to have fun playing the game, and the Brookmeade team members didn't disgrace themselves. On Sarah's first question, she was asked the name of the Native Americans who first bred Appaloosas. She was happy she remembered it was the Nez Perce tribe. The team that drove such a long distance, the Riverton Riders, must have been studying during their long trip, because they finished in first place. For a prize, each member got a leather lead shank.

It was almost half-past nine when the quiz ended, too late to return to the event grounds. Sarah and Kayla went back to their room and pulled their cross-country maps out to look at the course one more time. "What do you think?" Sarah asked Kayla.

"I'm afraid Fanny might spook at some of the strange-looking obstacles, like the dollhouse. There's a lot out there our horses have never seen before." She stretched out on her bed to study the course map more closely.

"I just hope Prince won't freak out at the ditch," Sarah said. "And those hills are going to slow everybody down. Thank goodness for the old orchard trail!" She'd been making it her conditioning ride at least three times a week, and sometimes they'd galloped up the ridge to the top.

Kayla put her map down to look at Sarah. "There are some

hills in the preserve where I ride, but they're not nearly as steep as the ones on the course." Her eyebrows scrunched up with concern. "I guess I just won't push Fanny tomorrow. I want to go clear, and I'm not going to worry about time penalties."

"Yeah," Sarah said. "This is our first event. I'm more interested in not stressing my horse than bringing home the Wexford Cup."

Kayla banged a fist on her bed. "The team is in third place. I wonder where we'd be if I hadn't blown the test!"

"Forget about today," Sarah said. "We need to think about tomorrow. Let's go over early enough so we can walk the course again."

* * * * *

The next day dawned bright and clear—so far, their luck was holding on the weather. When Sarah and Kayla arrived at the event grounds, Tim and Kelly were already there, but there was no sign of Rita. Tim was changing his shoes, getting ready to walk the course. Kelly had fed the horses, and when Sarah went to check on Prince, he was cleaning up the last of his grain. He was quick to leave the bucket to come to her for the carrot she offered. After she hugged him and stroked his face, Sarah went back to Tim.

"Kayla and I want to walk the course again. Mind if we come with you?" Sarah asked.

"No problem," Tim said. "Is Kayla ready?"

"Ready!" Kayla called out, as she came out of Fanny's stall. "Fanny has settled in, and last night she cleaned up all of her hay. Let's roll 'em."

As they got closer to the starter's box, they saw quite a few other riders walking the course. Directly in front of them was a rider from the Castleton Stable team. Colin Dahlberg, a thin blond boy, was in second place behind Rita in dressage, and his team was in first place. He had paused at the brush fence, carefully inspecting the footing on the approach, when the Brookmeade riders caught up with him.

"What do you think of the course?" Tim asked him.

Colin shook his head. "I'm actually surprised the technical delegate let them include so many hills. The terrain makes this course really challenging. I've been working on conditioning for some time, but I still wonder if my horse will handle it okay."

"I guess I'll take it slow and easy," Kayla said.

"Yeah," Tim said, "one competition isn't worth ruining your horse."

Especially if it's your horse's first event, Sarah thought.

Colin joined them as they walked, often making interesting comments. Sarah had a pretty good memory of the course from yesterday's walk, but of course there was one obstacle she especially wanted to inspect a second time. As they approached the ditch, she tried to decide what she would focus on so she wouldn't look down. *I hope Prince won't think those thin branches on the bottom are creepy-crawling things!* she thought.

The team had visitors when they arrived back at the tent. Jack, the Dixons, and the DeWitts had arrived at Wexford Hall after a bountiful breakfast at their B-and-B, and the Alexanders and Richard Snyder had driven to Wexford Hall from home that morning. Sarah was disappointed her parents and Abby weren't there yet, but she was glad to see Derek.

The area around their stalls was crowded, and Kelly was trying to answer their questions as best she could. Sarah went to say hello to the DeWitts. "We can see it's busy here," Mrs. DeWitt said. "Chandler and I are going to head out onto the course with our folding chairs and picnic lunch to find a pleasant spot to watch the horses come through. The Alexanders also brought chairs, and they're coming with us." She paused to give Sarah a quick hug.

"Good luck to you and Crown Prince. Throw your heart over the jumps, and your horse will follow!"

Jack was relieved to see Tim return. "Will you be getting Rhodes ready now?" he asked. "Your start time is not far off. Kelly has brushed Rhodes and picked out his feet." Tim went to the team stall to get his tack. His parents stood outside Rhodes's stall as Tim tacked him up.

Mr. Snyder walked up to Jack. "Do you have any idea where Rita is?" he asked. "She should be here!"

Kelly overheard the question and piped up, "She doesn't ride until this afternoon. I think she's sleeping in."

Mr. Snyder appeared disgruntled as he turned away from them, yanking his phone from his pocket.

Mrs. Romano and Kayla had disappeared into Fanny's stall, while Derek stood looking at Crown Prince. Sarah was attempting to pick out his feet, but Prince was nervous with all the commotion and kept moving in his stall. "Whoa!" Sarah said, beginning to get exasperated. Derek slid through the door and went to Prince's head to hold on to his halter.

Derek had heard about the dressage rides from the DeWitts. "I've been telling you Prince is a world-beater," he said, grinning. "Seriously, you should be proud of yourself—and your horse."

Sarah turned her head to smile up at him, as she released Prince's near hind leg. "Thanks. But I can't dwell on yesterday. The course is going to be tough, with lots of steep hills. I just hope Prince is fit enough."

"I haven't seen any of the course, but with all the hills around here, I can just imagine," Derek replied. "Will you take me out to watch some of Tim's ride?"

Sarah was taken aback, as she always was when Derek suggested doing something with her. This was a guy who was supposed to already have a girlfriend. She looked at her watch. "Tim will be heading for the warm-up any minute. After I pick out Prince's stall, we can find a place to watch, if you'd like." She reached in her jeans pocket for the course map and handed it to Derek. "Here, while I get the wheelbarrow, maybe you can figure out the best place to see the most obstacles."

Tim had a crop in his hand and was wearing his helmet and tall boots with spurs when he led Rhodes from his stall. Tim's red and white hat cover matched his rugby shirt and red body vest, compliments of the DeWitts. He mounted Rhodes, and to a chorus of good luck calls, headed to the warm-up area. Jack and Tim's parents followed close behind.

Sarah quickly picked out Prince's stall, working around her horse as he pulled hay from his net. After she had emptied the wheelbarrow and returned it, she looked in on Kayla and her mother. "Will you have time to watch any of Tim's ride?" she asked.

"I don't think so," Kayla said. "I don't want to be rushed getting Fanny ready. I've got Mom to help me, so you go along. Tim's going to tell me how the course rode once he's back."

Derek poked his head into the stall. "Good luck, Kayla. We'll be watching," he said.

As they walked away from the tent, Sarah asked, "Did you decide on the best place to watch?"

"Well, the best vantage point is probably on one of the hills," he said. "Duh!"

Sarah laughed. "How about the last hill that's near the finish? I think we could see some of the last obstacles on the course, like the dollhouse, and watch Tim finish."

"Sounds like a plan," Derek said. "Lead the way."

Derek and Sarah found a spot with a good view near the finish line, and they sat down in the grass. The scene had changed dramatically since Sarah had walked the course earlier. From their vantage point, they saw fence judges with clipboards sitting on folding chairs near every obstacle, and there was a lot of activity near the finish flags. Sarah noticed the ominous presence of an ambulance parked nearby, always at the ready if disaster should strike. Part way down the field, a photographer was poised to snap pictures of the horses as they came over the giant spools. With the sun bringing out the deep green of the fields, it was a perfect day to photograph horses in action, and many of the spectators carried cameras.

Loudspeakers in various locations helped fence judges and spectators know when horses were on course. Sarah closed her fists tightly when they heard the announcement, "Number 8, Tim Dixon riding Rhodes Scholar, is now on course."

As Derek and Sarah watched a few riders ahead of Tim come galloping up the hill, they noticed that all the horses were blowing hard as they came through the finish flags. Sarah's eyes were glued to the woods where Rhodes would first appear. Suddenly the red-and-white Brookmeade colors came over the coop. Tim turned Rhodes sharply to jump the post-and-rail fence that followed it, and then galloped strongly away. He jumped the giant spools and the dollhouse boldly, and as he started up the last hill, Tim leaned low in the saddle, asking Rhodes for all he had left as he ran toward the finish.

Derek and Sarah cheered and jumped up and down when Tim and his horse flew through the flags. They ran to where Tim had halted Rhodes. The horse's flanks heaved as he gasped for breath, his nostrils flaring, as Tim jumped off and ran up his irons. "We went clear!" he said, trying to catch his breath. After Tim loosened Rhodes's girth, the three of them walked the horse back to the tent. Everyone, especially Tim's parents and Jack, were elated to learn he'd gotten around the course so well.

Once Rhodes had been cared for, Tim described his course ride to Jack, Kayla, and Sarah. "There were no surprises," he said. "The footing was awesome. One thing, though. The coop followed by a narrow post-and-rail is really tight. Be prepared to turn almost in the air to make the turn." Later, they were happy when the scoreboard showed Tim had no cross-country jumping or time faults, so his dressage score would remain unchanged.

A little over an hour later, Sarah, Derek, and Tim returned to the same spot to wait for Kayla to come through. Sarah was so nervous for her friend! After watching several more horses gallop up the last hill, finally Number 21, Fanfare, emerged out of the woods and over the coop. Fanny wasn't running quite as fast as Rhodes had, but she was certainly trying her best. She jumped all the obstacles in her path until she was galloping up the last hill and through the flags. They ran to her, cheering.

Like Rhodes, Fanny was literally exhausted, her breaths coming fast, her flanks heaving. Kayla was also trying to catch her breath as she quickly dismounted, her face flushed and a shock of moist red curls sticking out from beneath her helmet. Mrs. Romano came running up to Kayla. "How did it go?"

Kayla was hugging Fanny when she cried out to them, "She went clear! I'm so proud of her!" Sarah gave Kayla's mother a high-five. When they got back to the tent, Fanny's tack was removed and she was allowed to plunge her muzzle into her water bucket for a few swallows. Kelly was waiting with a bucket of sudsy bathwater that had been warming in the sun, and Fanny received a much deserved bath and some carrot treats.

"She was really tired," Kayla said. "I probably got some time penalties because Fanny just couldn't go very fast up the hills. But I don't care. She was wonderful, giving me her all. She jumped everything beautifully, and I think she was having a great time roaring around that course."

Sarah looked in at Prince. He had finished his hay and was resting in the far corner of his stall, his eyes half closed. She chose to leave him alone. He needed all the rest time he could get. It wouldn't be long before it would be their turn.

"Has Rita shown up yet?" Derek asked Kelly.

"She and her father are out walking the cross-country," Kelly replied. "Tim and his parents just went down to the snack bar."

Kayla, Mrs. Romano, Derek, and Kelly decided to also head out for some lunch, but Sarah had no appetite. She would stay with her horse. Going back to his stall, she sat on her tack trunk and studied the cross-country map one more time. It felt like cramming for a geography test. She closed her eyes to recite the course from memory and then checked the time once more. Her parents and Abby were scheduled to be there, and she was surprised they hadn't arrived. She pulled out her cell and dialed her mother's number. When there was no answer, she called her father, but his phone was also unavailable. *What's going on?* she thought.

The minutes ticked by until it was time to get Prince ready. Now it was their turn. When Kayla and Derek returned, they helped with Prince's grooming and getting him tacked up. Derek insisted on putting on Prince's galloping boots, to be sure they were positioned correctly—tight, but not too tight. Prince seemed to sense the tension in the air, and he chomped on his bit nervously.

Sarah slipped away to remove the jeans covering her riding breeches and pull on her tall black boots. After buckling her spurs and putting on the red body-protecting vest the DeWitts had given the team, she slipped into her number 21 pinny. Once her helmet was on, she grabbed her crop and took Prince's reins.

With more bravado than she truly felt, she said, "Thanks, guys. See you at the finish."

CHAPTER 27

Prince's Challenge

SARAH HAD SHORTENED HER STIRRUPS for jumping before she mounted Crown Prince and headed for the cross-country course. At Jack's suggestion, she was also wearing lightweight riding gloves. No way did she want the reins to slip through her fingers! On the way to the warm-up, Sarah took long, deep breaths. It was important not to telegraph her nervousness to Prince. But she couldn't fool him. Her horse was too attuned to what she was feeling, and he could sense she was uptight. His head was up, and he chomped on the bit occasionally as they walked down the gravel path to the starting box.

Jack was waiting for them near the warm-up, where several riders were taking their horses over the practice jumps set up there, a vertical and an oxer. He eyed her horse. "Prince appears a little anxious." He checked the time. "Let's get him moving. Do some trot and canter work, following your usual routine. Once he's relaxed and supple, you'll put him over a few fences. But not many. He should be saving his energy for the course ahead." After trotting long and low for a while, Sarah gradually shortened her reins and increased her leg pressure to put Prince in a frame. Canter work and suppling exercises followed, until Jack beckoned to her. "Trot to the low vertical fence a few times, and then canter to both jumps."

They had gone over the oxer twice when Jack motioned to Sarah again, this time pointing to his watch. She walked Prince toward the box, where the starter checked her against the list on his clipboard. "You'll be next, after Number 20," he said, pointing to a gray horse waiting to go. The gray's tense body looked like a coiled spring about to be released. He knew what was coming! Moments later the horse was rocket propelled out of the box to begin the course.

Sarah swallowed hard, her heart beating a mile a minute. They were next! Prince crabstepped nervously, sensing something was about to happen. When she felt the dark bay body beneath her quiver and then shift uneasily, she reached down to stroke his neck. A few minutes later, the starter began counting backward from ten. Sarah gathered her horse and guided him into the box. "... three, two, one, go." Their time had come!

Sarah pressed her legs hard against Prince's sides, and he moved quickly out of the starting box and onto the course. In seconds they were galloping toward the brush box, Prince's ears flicking back to her, not quite sure what this was all about. *We're going to jump it, Prince,* Sarah said with her aids. Her horse responded by pulling against the bit and quickening his pace. Soon they were soaring over the brush and heading for the log pile. Prince jumped it easily, landing lightly on the other side. He was immediately in full stride, starting up the woods trail.

As always, whenever Sarah rode her horse cross-country, she could tell Prince loved it. He eagerly galloped up the trail, flying over the slatted coop and the large log, and she thrilled to the power of the horse beneath her. The stone wall loomed in front of them, massive and solid, but Prince didn't hesitate, jumping it with room to spare. She checked his speed before they turned off the trail to jump up the bank obstacle, and two strides later Prince lifted over the telephone pole jump that followed it. Coming out of the trees, they were in a field with the pigpen ahead of them. As they got closer, Prince slowed slightly, not sure what this square obstacle was all about. *We can do it, Prince,* she communicated with her aids. Prince responded by nimbly jumping inside, and without another stride, immediately jumping out of the pigpen. They had done the bounce!

When Sarah turned Prince toward the first long hill on the course, he grabbed the bit, wanting to extend his stride and race up the hill. Sarah decided that fighting her horse would drain more of his energy than letting him run, so she settled for checking his speed only slightly. Prince's powerful hindquarters thrust them up the steep incline, much as he had done many times on their runs to the old orchard trail. Sarah was relieved when the course leveled off.

Next they galloped around a small knot of trees, bringing the whiskey barrels into view. Sarah noticed how much darker it was in the woods on the other side. She remembered Jack's warning about the challenge of jumping from light to darkness, and she pressed her legs harder on her horse's sides. Hesitating slightly, Prince jumped the barrels and then resumed his speed as he headed down the trail to the park bench. After sailing over it, he continued out of the woods toward the vegetable stand. When her horse first focused on it, his head came up and Sarah could feel his stride shorten. *He's not sure about this,* she thought. *All those veggies must look weird!* She pressed her legs firmly on Prince's sides as they got closer, and was relieved when he jumped it cleanly. *He trusts me!* she thought, elated.

They were going slightly downhill as they got nearer to the

Chinese puzzle combination. Again Prince seemed unsure, but Sarah was there with her aids to reassure him, and her horse jumped through it, carefully tucking up his knees. She kept his pace slower for the double drop ahead. Prince jumped down the first drop, and a few strides later, the second one. Then it was on to the water obstacle. A lot of riders anticipated problems here, and there was a crowd of spectators gathered near it. Prince had done so well on the water jump at the farm that Sarah was confident he would jump this one willingly. But she remembered Jack's warning. "Don't be complacent about any obstacle, because that's when your horse will refuse. Don't be asleep at the switch."

Prince was taken aback by all the people near the water, and he slowed unexpectedly. Sarah immediately sat deep in the saddle and kicked him on. *Go, Prince, go!* she thought. She looked beyond the log between the flags and rode him strongly forward. Once Prince got closer to the water, he shifted his focus from the spectators and rewarded Sarah with a nice jump over the log. They landed in the water with a noisy splatter and then Prince was splashing through it, as he loved to do in the Brookmeade brook. Just in time Sarah remembered the narrow vertical two strides out of the water and she steered Prince to it. As he landed after the jump, Sarah happened to notice some people close to the jump cheering. It was her family, and Abby was bouncing up and down!

They started up the second hill, and while it wasn't as long as the first one, the hay wagon obstacle was immediately at the top where the terrain leveled off. Prince didn't seem fatigued when he reached the top, and he had no fear of the hay wagon or the roll-top that followed it. All the cross-country schooling Jack had put them through on the farm was paying off! Prince seemed to understand what galloping this course was all about, and now he was eager, always looking for the next obstacle. Sarah turned him toward the rustic table near the treeline, and once it was in his sights, he attacked it, jumping it boldly. Next they jumped the cordwood pile that took them into the woods again.

Oh, my God! Sarah thought. *The ditch is next!* But this was no time to be nervous. She must be strong. And calm. They galloped along the trail until Sarah saw the flags for the ditch and the fence judge sitting in the woods near it. Prince had become accustomed to seeing these people at the previous obstacles, and he thundered forward until he was close enough to see the ditch. As he had done at the veggie stand, he slowed down, but this time he didn't respond to her aids and resume his pace as before.

Eyes up, eyes up! Sarah thought. She sat deeply and pressed her legs hard on Prince's sides, but he continued slowing down, eyeing the ditch. Sarah was desperate! She feared a refusal was coming. Keeping her eyes up, Sarah pleaded with her horse. She used her seat to urge him forward and kicked him on harder than she ever had before. "Go, Prince!" she shouted out loud. Suddenly, from over a stride in front of the ditch, Prince leaped high into the air, almost unseating her. He landed far beyond the ditch and continued galloping down the trail.

Sarah's heart sang! The dreaded ditch was behind them, and now Prince was running full out, his long strides devouring the trail. The coop with the sharp turn to a post-and-rail wasn't far ahead, and Sarah knew she'd have to slow him down. "Whoa, Prince, Whoa," she called out, as she pulled back with her reins. She was relieved when her horse slackened his stride and came back to her! They were almost to the coop when she asked for an even shorter stride. As they were in the air over the coop, Sarah twisted to look at the fence on their right and turned Prince's head in that direction. He landed on his right lead and easily jumped the post-and-rail.

Now it was on to the last two obstacles. They galloped through the field toward the giant spools, and with no hesitation, Prince jumped them cleanly. One obstacle to go—the dollhouse. A number of horses had found it spooky, and Sarah wasn't taking any chances. She used her seat and legs to urge Prince forward, and with no hesitation, he was over it.

The last hill and the finish flags were before them, and Sarah leaned forward, extending her arms to give Prince his head. "Run, Prince!" she called to him, and although he was tired, Prince accelerated, giving her all the energy and stamina he had left. His powerful haunches propelled them up the hill and through the finish flags, to the cheers of the Brookmeade fans waiting for them.

Sarah slumped limply in the saddle, holding on to Prince's mane while calling for him to stop. "Whoa, boy. It's over," she gasped. Prince seemed to understand, and without any rein aids, he came back to walk and then halted. Sarah sat for a minute, trying to catch her breath, before she slid off his back. As she ran up her irons and loosened the girth, Derek and Kayla hurried over to her. Before they reached Sarah, they stopped to admire Crown Prince, the picture of an arrogant and noble war horse. With his head raised high, he looked back down the hill from where they had come. His breaths from dilated nostrils came fast, as he claimed victory over the challenging course they had run.

Jack hurried up to them, wanting to know how it had gone. Kayla and Derek pumped their fists into the air when Sarah could finally tell them she and Prince had gone clear. "We almost had a stop at the ditch," she said between fast breaths, "and he was distracted by the people at the water." She stopped a moment to try to catch her breath. "We finished the course because he trusted me," she said. "He was unsure about a lot of obstacles, like the veggie stand, but he listened to me. He went when I asked him."

Prince turned his head toward her, and Sarah hugged him. After a few moments she tugged on the reins. "Come on, Prince. It's back to the tent and some carrots."

"Well-deserved carrots," Kayla said. "I know how tough that course was. I'm proud of you, kid."

The stabling tent was quiet when they returned, with many people out on the course to cheer for their teams. Rita and Kelly were among those getting a horse ready for the cross-country run. Mr. Snyder was observing the girls at work, but he turned to watch Prince as Sarah led him into his stall. Kayla and Derek were right behind her, and after they took Prince's bridle off, he was allowed to have a short drink from his water bucket. Then the three of them began removing his saddle and galloping boots.

"How did it go, Sarah?" Rita called to her.

"She went clear," Derek answered, "and from the way Prince was booking, she probably doesn't have any time penalties."

Rita came out of the stall and walked up to them. "That makes three clear rounds, and after I go, it will be four." She thought a minute, pursing her thin lips. "You know, Kayla, if you hadn't screwed up on your dressage test, I'll bet we'd be in first place." As Rita went back to Chancellor's stall, Sarah and Derek looked quickly at Kayla. She had been leaning over, unbuckling one of Prince's galloping boots. When she stood up, the blood had drained from her face as if someone had punched her in the stomach.

Sarah wasn't at all surprised by Rita's thoughtless remark. Rita was being Rita! But Sarah was amazed that Rita's father, who undoubtedly had overheard the conversation, didn't respond in any way. *But then, Rita acts like this all the time,* she thought. *It's her normal behavior. He probably never reprimands her about anything.*

Sarah went to Kayla and hugged her, while Derek looked in the direction of Chancellor's stall, shaking his head. Finally Kayla stepped back. "Rita calls 'em like she sees 'em, I guess," she said, picking up the other dirt-covered galloping boot. "But your horse needs a bath. And so do these."

After Sarah had removed her tall boots and pulled her jeans on over her breeches, she led her horse outside the tent where a bucket of water had been warming in the sun. With Kayla holding Prince, Sarah went over him with a soapy sponge, rinsed him with the hose, and then removed a lot of the water from his coat with a sweat scraper. Sarah took the shank from Kayla and looked up at her wet horse. "Let's go for a walk, old buddy."

Sarah was bringing Prince back after walking him dry when she saw her parents and Abby approaching the tent. Abby came running up to her. "How'd you do?" she asked. Sarah gave them a big smile. She was so happy she could announce to her family that she and Prince had gone clear.

"Fantastic!" her father said, coming to give her a hug. "We saw you jump the log into the water and the skinny fence after it. Prince was really going fast when he took off across the field!"

"Did you have any trouble?" her mother asked, her face still creased with worry. Sarah knew her mom was secretly relieved Sarah's ride was over but determined not to dampen anyone's spirits. She could just imagine how her mother's heart had been in her throat when she saw Crown Prince galloping by on that course.

"Prince was a star today, Mom," Sarah said. "He went over everything." She decided not to describe the close call when Prince almost stopped at the ditch.

When Kayla and Derek came out of the tent, Sarah waved them over. "Derek, I don't think you've met my parents," Sarah said before introducing them.

"I'm happy to meet you, Derek," Mr. Wagner said. "Sarah has told us about the insanely high jumps your horse goes over."

Derek extended his arm to shake hands with them. "Yes, as a matter of fact, Bismarck and I have a show tomorrow, the first one of the summer."

Sarah's head snapped in his direction. "Really?" she said.

"There's a show in Granger with a jumper division. I just heard about it this week," Derek said. "So I won't be here tomorrow."

"I think the competition has stopped for a lunch break," Mrs. Wagner said. "We're going to get some burgers at the snack bar before we have to head home. We'd love to have all of you come with us."

"Derek and I had lunch earlier," Kayla said. She pointed at Sarah. "But your daughter must be famished. She didn't want to eat before she rode."

The mention of lunch reminded Sarah how ravenously hungry she was. "Yeah, Dad," she said. "After I put Prince in his stall, let's get some grub." A few minutes later, they started for the snack bar, with Abby asking Sarah a million questions.

Later, after Sarah had wolfed down a grilled cheese sandwich with chips, she hurried back to the tent. The competition was about to resume, and Rita was nearly ready to go to the warm-up with Chancellor. He looked spectacular, his black coat shining like polished ebony. Along with the expensive saddle and bridle, he wore a white quilted saddle pad that had the Pyramid Farm logo stitched in one corner. Rita was turned out equally well. In addition to the team's red-and-white hat cover over her helmet and the Brookmeade rugby shirt, she had on highly polished custom boots and the same protective body vest the other riders wore.

"Kelly, I want you to have a bucket of water ready for Chancellor near the finish flags," Rita called out, as she rode her horse toward the cross-country warm-up area. Her father picked up his folding chair and walked stiffly behind her.

Kelly took Chancellor's water bucket outside to rinse with the hose and fill with fresh water. "Would you like me to carry that for you?" Derek offered. "We're going back to see some of the other rides and watch Rita finish."

Kelly looked darkly at Sarah and Kayla before turning back to Derek. "Okay, I guess," she said. They hurried back to the cross-country finish and sat in the same spot they'd shared earlier. A few minutes later, Tim and his parents joined them. "What's happening?" Tim asked.

"Number 27 just came through," Kayla said. "You remember Colin Dahlberg, the guy we walked the course with?" When Tim nodded, Kayla said, "He's Number 28, riding Senator, so he should be next."

Their eyes turned to the coop obstacle just in time to see a chestnut horse come over it and then turn adroitly to jump the post-and-rail at right angles to it. Senator moved speedily through the field to the giant spools and continued to the dollhouse, jumping both boldly. Then they were galloping up the hill and through the finish flags. Colin had a lot of supporters cheering for him as he brought his big chestnut to a halt.

"What a gorgeous horse!" Kayla said.

Kelly sat stony-faced beside the full water bucket they'd brought for Chancellor. It was obvious she was uncomfortable being around Sarah and Kayla, and could hardly wait for Rita to return.

While they waited for the next horse to finish, Derek mentioned a conversation he'd had with another spectator. "He said a lot of riders have had problems on the course, and several were eliminated. One girl fell off in the water. Her horse quit dirty in front of the log, and the girl went right over his head. Several more have had time penalties."

Now that Number 28 had come through the flags, they all closely watched the coop in the distance. It seemed like a long wait until suddenly Tim said, "There she is!" Chancellor had jumped the coop and was turning to the post-and-rail. *Something doesn't look right,* Sarah thought. Once over the fence, Rita turned her horse in the direction of the giant spools. But compared to how the previous horses had been moving across the field, Chancellor was crawling at a snail's pace. He appeared to move sluggishly, no longer demonstrating his usual dynamic movement and power. In fact, as he moved toward the giant spools, Chancellor was actually losing speed.

Sensing her horse was slowing down, Rita raised her crop high over her head and forcefully struck Chancellor on his side several times. He responded by increasing his speed slightly, and with what looked like a humungous effort, he jumped the giant spools. Rita steered him toward the dollhouse, but now he slowed dramatically, and despite the many blows she wielded on his side with her crop, Chancellor came to a stop before he reached the last jump. Sarah winced to see the magnificent horse treated so brutally. The Brookmeade riders gasped in shock! This was Chancellor, the perfect horse who never made a mistake? He had refused a jump!

Just then the technical delegate came running down the hill toward Rita. "I'll bet he's going to pull her!" Tim said. "I'm surprised it didn't happen earlier on the course. That horse is totally used up."

"Yeah," Kayla said, "and don't they penalize a rider for excessive use of a crop? I think I read that in the rulebook."

By this time, Rita had dismounted, run up her irons, and with the technical delegate at her side, was leading Chancellor out of the path of oncoming horses. The black Warmblood walked slowly with his head low. His breathing through red dilated nostrils was rapid, and his body was lathered with sweat.

Kelly picked up the water bucket and hurried down the hill to the exhausted horse and his rider. Chancellor was allowed to drink a few swallows, and he eagerly plunged his muzzle, bit and all, into the bucket. Meanwhile, the veterinarian on duty arrived to check the horse. After he took Chancellor's temperature and listened to his heart, Rita was told to walk her horse back to the tent to cool him out properly. Kelly went with her, carrying the water bucket. The Brookmeade group followed them back to the tent, but afraid they'd be the brunt of Rita's anger over what had happened, they were reluctant to approach her.

As they got closer to the stable area, Jack appeared on the gravel roadway, and he walked hurried toward Rita. Word must have traveled fast, because Jack was obviously aware of everything that had happened. From his reddened face and heated manner, he was obviously angry. Despite his measured voice, everyone listening knew he was livid. "How dare you bring an improperly conditioned horse to this competition! You could have killed him! You ignored my repeated instructions to condition your horse so he'd be to fit enough to compete here."

Rita appeared dazed, and she said nothing while Jack continued on his tirade. "You were not only eliminated from the competition because your horse failed to finish the course, but you were disqualified for continuing to press an exhausted horse and excessive use of the whip. The technical delegate made this ruling against you!" Jack's fists were clenched as he continued. "Your performance here today is shocking. I'm embarrassed to be the coach of someone who behaves as badly as you have. Now take care of your horse!"

Without a reply, Rita hung her head and turned Chancellor toward his stall. Her father had arrived at the tent and had heard every word Jack said. Mr. Snyder followed them inside and stood in the stall's doorway, waiting for Rita to enter and turn the horse in his stall. Once she was facing him, he glowered at her, his mouth tightened into a thin line. "Rita, I'm extremely disappointed in you. Take care of this poor horse and then get your things together. You're going home!" He turned abruptly and walked away. With an arm over her forehead, Rita slumped against the stall wall, her shoulders shaking as she sobbed.

CHAPTER 28

Show Jumping

THAT EVENING, the remaining members of the Brookmeade Farm team attended the festive barbeque put on by the Belmont School. The DeWitts had purchased tickets for the team and the other adults staying at the Juniper Inn—the Dixons, the O'Briens, and Kayla's mother. Along with the other competitors and supporters, they gathered on the lawn outside the residence hall. A tantalizing aroma wafted from the oversize grills the caterers had set up near a large tent filled with tables and folding chairs.

Conspicuously absent were Rita and her father. Mr. Snyder had phoned Judson and instructed him to bring their smaller horse van to Wexford Hall immediately. Chancellor was to be shipped back to Pyramid Farm that afternoon, although Mr. Snyder assured Jack that Judson would be bringing the other three horses back to Brookmeade in the larger rig following show jumping on Sunday.

The group wasn't in a mood to celebrate. With Rita's disqualification for abuse of her horse, the Brookmeade Farm team was eliminated from the competition, along with two other teams that had also dropped out of contention. All four riders from one team were woefully underprepared and failed to finish the cross-country course. Only five out of the original eight teams were still in the running for the Wexford Cup.

But there was some hope on the individual placings, since Tim, Kayla, and Sarah had gone clear in the cross-country phase with no time penalties. Kayla had refused to press Fanny on the hilly course, but she and her chestnut mare had still squeaked in under the time limit. The grueling course had caused ten entries to have time penalties added to their scores. In a competition based on penalty points, where the lowest score wins, the addition of time and jumping faults changed the scoreboard considerably.

With Rita removed from the competition, Colin Dahlberg and Senator were now in first place, and Tim and Rhodes Scholar had moved from fourth place up to second. Sarah and Prince had improved from being in ninth place after dressage to fifth place in the standings, but Kayla and Fanfare had jumped the farthest, from twenty-sixth up to fourteenth place. With one phase yet to go, everyone was hoping to avoid penalty points by having a clear jumping round with no rails down. The competitors would ride in reverse order of the standings, so the winning team and the winning individual rider wouldn't be known until the last horse had finished the show jumping course.

Mrs. DeWitt was trying hard to cheer everyone up. She made a point to congratulate the three remaining riders on their great cross-country rides. "We had a wonderful spot near the hay wagon on one of the hills," she said. "We arranged our folding chairs and picnic hamper so we could see all of you go through the water obstacle and much more. You and your horses looked incredible!"

Jack hadn't had a chance to review their trips with the individual riders, so he took advantage of this opportunity. He spoke with Tim first. "From what I saw of you and Rhodes, your horse was moving forward with good energy and was jumping boldly.

How did he feel to you?"

Tim grinned. "It might have looked smooth, but there were several obstacles Rhodes didn't like the looks of. I didn't expect him to be spooky at the Chinese puzzle, but he was. I had to ride him really strong there."

"Fanny was totally amazing," Kayla said. "There wasn't anything that really fried her mind, although she wasn't sure about the pigpen. Once she was committed to jump it, though, she went through like a gazelle."

Jack looked at Sarah. "So Prince was anxious at the ditch?"

"It was close," Sarah said. "We almost had a stop there. I could tell he was about to freak out. I never hit him with my crop, but I sat deep, and kicked him on as hard as I could. I think I was talking to him, too. More like pleading! And I did keep my eyes up. I was looking at a hawk's nest in a tree up ahead. Prince took off about a stride early."

"Yes," Jack said, smiling. "Those hawks' nests come in handy sometimes. There's something else I don't think you're aware of, Sarah." He paused as she waited expectantly. "When I studied the cross-country scoreboard carefully, I saw that you and Crown Prince had the fastest time of the day."

Sarah stared at him, wide-eyed and speechless. She had known for a long time that Crown Prince was fast, but this news was overwhelming. Kayla jumped up to give her a high-five.

Jack smiled broadly. "This is one reason why 'tis a great advantage to have a horse with a long stride like Crown Prince does. He can cover more ground in a shorter time. You should be very proud of him."

"Oh, I am," Sarah said. "I certainly am. And now, prouder than ever!"

Mr. DeWitt had been chatting with Kayla's mother, but now he motioned to them. "The line is forming for ribs," he called. "Come and get it!"

Jack gathered the riders for a brief meeting after the barbeque. "I'll be at your tent so we can walk the course at nine tomorrow. The show jumping will be on the large lawn behind the manor house. Don't forget to bring your show jackets, and your horses will have to be turned out as for dressage—well-groomed and braided—but have your stirrups short enough for jumping." As he turned to go, he frowned and added as an afterthought, "Bring your rain gear, because the forecast is for showers tomorrow. With eventing, the competition doesn't shut down for a few raindrops."

* * *.* *

The show jumping phase wouldn't start until half past ten on Sunday morning, so everyone but Kelly could come to the event grounds a little later than usual as long as they were on time for the course walk with Jack. As Tim, Kayla, and Sarah rode over on the shuttle bus, the sky was gray and rain pelted the windows. Sarah was glad she had packed her poncho, her old faithful for commuting to the barn on her bike in the rain, but she worried what the footing would be like for jumping.

Kayla looked out the window as the school bus bumped along, and then turned to Sarah, scowling. "Some of the other riders have studs to put on their horses' shoes," she said. "I hope Fanny won't slip on the grass." This made Sarah worry even more.

The riders went straight to their horses after they got off the bus. They saw that Rita had neglected to strip Chancellor's stall of bedding before she left, which meant that chore would have to be done by the other team members. Kelly seemed like a lost soul without Rita around. She had never warmed up to Sarah and Kayla during the whole competition, so she hung around Tim's stall, offering to help with Rhodes. "Could you hold him while I groom?" Tim asked. "Maybe later you could help strip Rita's stall."

The steady rain drummed on the tent roof as they prepared to clean stalls and groom their horses. Sarah found Prince relaxed and eating hay, but he expected carrots and quickly came to her. As he chewed them, his eyes softened and wrinkled in the corners. He was probably still tired after yesterday's cross-county ride, so he wouldn't need much warm-up today. Just a lot of suppling exercises, in case he was stiff. Sarah lifted the grooming caddy out of her tack trunk and got busy. She had nearly finished grooming Prince when Jack and Kathleen arrived at the barn.

"The rain has let up a little," Jack said, "so we should walk the course now. Later on it may begin to rain harder again."

The riders were prepared for foul weather as they followed Jack to the show jumping area. Kayla had an umbrella, and Sarah and Tim wore ponchos. Jack's waterproof Irish coat and a tweed cap would keep him dry. When they turned a corner on the gravel road, the Wexford Hall mansion came into view, towering over the expanse of green manicured lawns where the jumping course had been set up. There were already many spectators with brightly colored umbrellas sitting in the bleachers. *I wonder what Prince will think of those umbrellas,* Sarah worried.

They went first to the judge's stand, where a diagram of the show jumping course was posted. The riders studied it for several minutes until Jack motioned for them to follow him. "This is not a simple course," he said. "There are several changes of direction and some tight turns, which might be tricky on grass in this weather. But I believe all of you can do it." He looked intently at Sarah when he said it. "The important thing to remember is that you need to stay calm. And don't lean in—sit up tall. You need to help your horses stay balanced."

Sarah looked at the maze made by the assortment of standards and striped rails. The jumps were as high as anything she and Prince had ever encountered in their lessons. To make matters worse, the tightly cropped grass seemed saturated with rain and squished as they walked. Would it stay firm when Prince cantered around the course and pushed hard against it to jump? Sarah swallowed hard in response to the lump that was forming in her throat.

Jack led them around the course. "The brush box is an inviting first fence," he said, as they approached it. Once on the other side, Jack began pacing the strides to the second fence. "This should ride well," he said. "'Tis a good distance to give you four strides. Just maintain a good tempo and don't get ahead of your horse."

Jack and the three riders continued around the jumping course, walking from one clearly numbered fence to another. The course consisted of a dozen jumps and had two combinations. Number Four was an in-and-out, and late on the course a triple-element contained two vertical jumps and an oxer. "At least there's nothing tricky about the striding here," Jack said. "You won't have to lengthen or shorten strides in the combinations unless your horse gets into the first fence poorly."

As they approached a post-and-rail jump with a tray of water underneath it, Jack said, "I see they've got a Liverpool on the course." He paused to study the fence and then look back at the preceding jump. "This Liverpool has a long approach, so your horses will have ample opportunity to be well aware of it." He walked closer to the jump. "Keep your eyes up and ride it like any other fence."

Sarah knew Jack didn't want to frighten her by suggesting that Prince might react the same way to the Liverpool as he did to ditches, but she knew that was just what he was thinking. It was another case of something on the ground looking scary. And she had thought the ditch issue was behind them! As they started back to the tent, Jack had one final bit of advice. "Think of this course as a dressage test with bumps. Be exact and disciplined as you ride it."

When the riders and Jack got back to the tent, the Dixons and Mrs. Romano had arrived. "Would you like me to hold Fanny while you braid?" Kayla's mother asked her. Tim's mother was also willing to help by holding Rhodes. Without Rita's stool, they had to settle for turned-over buckets to stand on. "I'll try to finish with Fanny in time to braid Prince for you," Kayla called over to Sarah as she worked.

Kathleen overheard the remark and came to Prince's stall where Sarah was brushing him. "May I braid his mane for you?" she asked. "I haven't done it in a while, and the practice would do me good."

"Oh, cool," Sarah said. "I was thinking I should try it, and for my first time braiding a mane, Prince would probably look weird."

"'Twould take more than a poor braiding job to make this horse anything but beautiful," Kathleen quipped, smiling, as she left to empty the water bucket outside. In a few minutes she was standing on the bucket braiding Prince's mane while Sarah held him. Kelly kept busy carrying wheelbarrow loads of bedding out of Rita's stall to the disposal area.

When they had finished, Jack called the riders together. "With six horses eliminated and ten others with time penalties, there have been many changes on the scoreboard," he said.

"How will we know when we ride?" Kayla asked.

"You'll need to know where you are in the order, which is posted on the scoreboard, and be ready to ride in that order. I'll be there to help you with that."

Tim spoke up. "I think we already know that Kayla is in fourteenth place, Sarah is in fifth, and I'm in second."

"Yes," Jack said, "and because there are a number of horses scheduled to go before you, there's no need to have your horses tacked up and ready to go at the start time. We don't want them standing in the rain unnecessarily. I suggest you leave them in their stalls and go watch some of the rounds. 'Twill give you an idea of how the course is riding."

Sarah decided she had time to go over her tack with saddle soap. It would offer a bit more protection for the leather if the rain started up again. She knew this was a job Kelly was supposed to help with, but she didn't want to ask her. As Sarah worked, in her mind she went over the course she and Prince would be jumping soon. An occasional announcement from the loudspeaker penetrated the stable area, reminding competitors to be on time for the show jumping phase.

When the first entry was announced, the Brookmeade riders made their way back to the show jumping area, where the bleachers had quickly filled. Sarah saw where the DeWitts, the Dixons, and yes, her parents and Abby, were sitting. They had returned home to Yardley the day before, and made the drive to Belmont again today. Sarah waved to them just before the riders slipped through the crowd to find a good place to watch the first round. Moments later, the horse in last place in the standings was trotting off the course, leaving two dropped rails behind him. A bay mare was the next to go. The rider halted to salute the judge, and after the whistle blew, she asked her horse for canter and circled for the first fence.

"Notice how that girl is sitting tall between fences, helping her horse stay balanced," Jack said just loud enough for his students to hear him. Sarah watched closely to see how the horse traveled on the soggy surface. She noticed chunks of grass go flying when the horse pushed off to jump the fences. *By the time Prince and I go, the ground in front of the jumps will be totally chewed up!* she thought.

After watching a few more rounds, the riders left to get their mounts tacked up. "I'll meet you in the warm-up," Jack said. With Sarah and Kathleen helping Kayla, Fanny was ready to go in no time. As she had for her dressage test, Kayla looked impressive in her black show coat and white breeches. Even her Prince of Wales spurs gleamed from a recent polish. After Kayla had mounted Fanny, her mother took a few pictures and then Kayla was off for the warm-up ring, Mrs. Romano following behind. "Kick butt!" Tim called after them.

Sarah wished she could watch Kayla's round, but there just wasn't time. She had to get her own horse ready. Kathleen helped her tack up Prince, and after his galloping boots were buckled in place, Kathleen held Prince so Sarah could get herself ready. She had kept her buff breeches, the only nice ones she owned, reasonably clean by wearing jeans over them when she wasn't riding. She had just attached Prince's number to his bridle when they heard the announcement of Kayla's round. "In fourteenth place is Kayla Romano riding Fanfare." Sarah and Kathleen stood still, waiting, waiting. Finally the loudspeaker crackled again and a voice came through. "Kayla Romano has four faults for one rail down." Sarah stamped her foot. She'd wished a clear round for her friend.

In a few minutes, Sarah was ready to ride. She wondered if she could avoid telegraphing her tension to her horse. Prince seemed to sense something exciting was going to happen, but only his large dark eyes betrayed his excitement. When they arrived at the warm-up, Kayla was outside the ring talking to Jack. She turned to Sarah as Prince drew closer. "We had one rail down," Kayla said. "It's slippery out there. Be careful on the far end, where it's really soggy in places. Fanny's not usually spooky about fences, but she wasn't crazy about the Liverpool. Ride it hard!" Sarah took a deep breath. It wasn't what she wanted to hear!

"Let's get him moving," Jack said, motioning Sarah into the warm-up ring. "Do your regular warm-up, but be sure to do plenty of bending. I expect he's a little stiff after his run yesterday."

Prince's head was up, and he snorted when he saw the brightly decorated show jumping course. *I've got to stay calm.* Sarah told herself. *It won't help Prince if I'm freaking out!* She took several long, deep breaths and then guided her horse toward the warm-up ring. At the walk, she did some over-bending by pulled his head toward her knee, first in one direction and then the other. He still felt stiff when she asked him to trot long and low, but after moving forward on small circles with several changes of direction, his movement became freer. After a little canter work on both leads, she took him over the two practice fences set up in the ring.

Sarah left the warm-up ring when she saw Jack motion to her. As she walked Prince to the entry point with him, the rider in seventh place was about to start her ride. Waiting on deck was a pretty girl on a chestnut Thoroughbred who was in sixth place, which meant Sarah would go after her. Prince wasn't as hyper as he'd been when they first arrived to warm-up, but his ears flicked in all directions as he looked at the course. He also checked out the bleachers mobbed with spectators and umbrellas. Her parents were there, watching her with worried eyes. To keep Prince's attention, Jack had her walk her horse in a small circle while they waited.

I hope I'm not overfacing Prince! Sarah thought, as she looked out at the sea of jumps positioned on the rain-sodden grass. *Is it fair to ask him to do this?* She had a moment of doubt.

The girl in front of her rode to the judge's stand, and after saluting, began her round. Minutes later, her horse came off the course with three rails down. Sarah gathered her reins, waiting for the announcement. As they stood motionless, she felt the raindrops begin to fall, softly at first, and then progressively harder until there was a steady, soaking rain coming down. Prince shook his head, annoyed by the rain, and stepped sideways. Sarah reached down to stroke his neck.

"In fifth place is Sarah Wagner riding Crown Prince," the announcer's voice droned, as if he hadn't noticed the heavens had opened up and it was raining hard. The show would go on. Sarah pressed her legs on Prince's sides and asked him to trot to the judge's stand. Once he had halted, she curtly saluted the judge and then turned her horse to face the course. The whistle blew, and they were off.

After picking up canter, Sarah focused on the brush box so she could bring Prince into it straight. She felt hesitation and uncertainty in his gait. Her legs pressed hard on his sides while her reins channeled him toward the jump. *Yes, Prince, we can do it,* she spoke with her aids. Then they were in the air, landing, and heading for the second fence. Now he knew what they were here for. Prince took the bit, moving strongly toward the jump. All thoughts about the rain were gone.

The route after the second fence doubled back toward the start, and as Sarah turned her horse in that direction, she felt him stiffen, his strides slowing and becoming more deliberate. The ground was giving way under his feet as he turned, and Prince was working hard to keep his balance. This was the area of the course Kayla had warned her about! Finally the line straightened to an oxer, and once over it, the in-and-out combination loomed ahead. Sarah looked beyond the two fences, as she asked Prince to keep his pace coming into them. He jumped the first element easily, and after one stride, pushed off cleanly over the second.

So far so good. Now they were turning again, this time toward a jump in the middle of the diagonal. The footing on this end wasn't nearly as soggy, and with Sarah being careful to sit tall, Prince negotiated the turn without a problem. He jumped the next fence well and continued over the triple bar that followed it. But again they were heading into the soggy section, and Prince moved cautiously along the course. He was aware how slippery the going had become, and as they approached the wettest section, instead of the smooth, green lawn it had once been, the takeoff area in front of the next jump was black churned-up earth. When Sarah felt her horse begin to lose forward impulsion, she sat deeply to urge him forward and pressed her legs hard on his sides. *You can do it!* her heart cried out to her horse, and he responded with a powerful thrust through the mud and into the air. As they descended, Sarah heard a dull thud from behind them. Had Prince knocked down a rail with a hind leg? But she mustn't think about that now!

Somehow they made it to better footing, but ahead Sarah could see the fence she dreaded most! The Liverpool was next, and the steady rain made the countless ripples in the water tray ping-pong up and down. On this jump she couldn't wait! While they were still some distance from the Liverpool, Sarah sat deeply and with her legs asked Prince to attack this jump with all his strength and resolve. Together they could do it! As they got closer, she felt a gathering of powerful muscles and then her upper body was moving forward with her horse in the air over the jump.

After making it successfully over the next two jumps, Sarah knew another huge challenge was ahead. They were turning, with deliberate, cautious strides, into the triple combination, the three separate fences in a row that were only a few strides apart. She remembered Jack's words. He had said them so many times. "Sit up and wait for your horse." With Prince firmly between her hand

and her leg, Sarah rode him toward the triple. Prince got into the first element well, which set him up for the second element and then the third. Sarah felt like hugging her horse!

Now the final jump was ahead of them, the last jump on the course, and Sarah was apprehensive. She remembered what Jack had told the class: "'Tis easy to think 'tis almost over. Riders relax too much, and their horses often have a rail down on the last fence." Sarah aimed her horse squarely for the vertical jump with standards designed to look like lighthouses and pressed her legs against his sides. She felt his muscles gather as he took off perfectly and soared over the jump. In spite of the rain and the soggy going, they had finished the course! But had they jumped clear? Did they have a rail down?

Sarah brought Prince back to trot and headed for the exit. He was prancing and pulling a little when the announcer's voice boomed out. "Number 21, Sarah Wagner riding Crown Prince, has no jumping or time faults." Despite the rain that was coming down harder by the minute, the stands erupted in applause. Sarah's eyes were shining and her face radiant as she looked for her parents in the crowd. When she spotted them, they were waving wildly. She waved back. *Now they've got to truly believe in my horse,* she thought.

CHAPTER 29

Tough Luck

THE RAIN HADN'T LET UP as Sarah guided her prancing horse to where Jack was talking to Tim on Rhodes. The rider in fourth place was starting now, so it wouldn't be long before Tim would ride. Tim gave her a thumbs-up as she got closer.

"Brilliant ride!" Jack said, his face dominated by a big smile. "One rail rattled in its cups, but it didn't come down. Do you have any thoughts on the course that would be useful to Tim?"

"Just what Kayla told me. The back section is, like, totally soggy, very slippery. On the turns, Prince was working hard just to stay upright." She reached down to pat his neck. "The approach to one fence in that area is really chewed up."

They were interrupted by the loudspeaker. "Number 24, Emily Barrett riding Make It Snappy has four jumping faults and no time faults."

Tim's eyes widened and Jack smiled again. "You've moved up to fourth place, Sarah," Tim said. "She must have had a rail down."

Jack accompanied Rhodes and Tim to the start. They would go next. As he had suggested to Sarah, Jack had Tim walk Rhodes in a small circle while they waited. Sarah could see the jumping course perfectly, sitting astride Prince as she walked him in a circle. It seemed as if the horse ahead of Tim had barely gotten started on jumping the course when they heard groans coming from the bleachers. The horse had slid to a stop in front of Fence Four, his hind legs leaving huge gouges in the grass. A refusal! The rider turned her horse away from the jump, picked up canter, and approached the jump again, this time pushing hard with her seat and giving her horse a smack on his side with her crop. No amount of hard riding worked, and the horse refused the fence a second time. Immediately the judge's whistle sounded. The rider knew what that meant, and she trotted her horse off the course. "Number 18, Brittany Sanchez riding Lord Bellamy, has been eliminated," boomed the loudspeaker. *Oh, my God!* Sarah thought. *That means I'm in third place now.* She looked back at Tim. *If only the rain would let up for him,* she thought.

"Take it slow," Jack said, as Tim gathered his reins to begin the course. "Help your horse stay balanced. Sit tall."

Tim trotted Rhodes to the judge's stand, and after saluting, began his course. He cantered a straight line to the brush box and Rhodes jumped it well, moving eagerly to the second fence. He jumped this fence in good form also, his knees up and even, and his back rounding over the fence. They were heading into the rain-sodden section, but Rhodes didn't seem to mind the mushy going, moving forward at a fairly rapid pace. *It looks like he's handling the footing,* Sarah thought. Tim guided his horse around the 180-degree turn, his eyes focused on the third jump.

Then it happened. As Rhodes turned on the half-circle to head in the opposite direction, suddenly his hind legs seemed to slip out from under him. His hindquarters slid down first, followed by the rest of his body, and in a split second he was flat on the ground. Tim flew from his horse, landing in a crumpled heap not far from where Rhodes lay on his side.

Tim didn't move, but Rhodes quickly scrambled to his feet. He stood for a moment, looking disoriented, and then took off at a gallop, his reins dragging and stirrups flying. The crowd immediately parted to make way as he headed for the gravel roadway leading to the stabling tent.

All eyes were now on Tim, who lay motionless on the rain-soaked grass. Before the ETs from the ambulance could swing into action, a slight figure darted from the grandstand and ran across the wet grass to his side. It was Paige, and Sarah could see she was crying as she knelt beside Tim. The spectators were hushed, every eye glued to the downed rider.

Just as the two ETs reached Tim, he sat up, shaking his head. "Don't move," an ET said. "Do you feel any pain anywhere?"

Tim looked at them blankly for a moment and then moved his arms and legs. "I'm okay," he said. "I guess I got the wind knocked out of me." He looked at Paige, who was holding his hand. "Where's Rhodes?" he asked.

"He took off," Paige said, pointing to the road Rhodes had followed.

"Let's make sure you're all right before we worry about the horse," one of the young men said. "The way that horse was running when he left here, I doubt there's anything wrong with him."

Jack and Tim's father arrived at that moment, alarm written all over their faces. "I'm okay, Dad," Tim said. "I'd like to get up to show all of you I'm fine." He smiled up at Paige. "I hope this girl will give me a hand." A few minutes later Tim and Paige, arm in arm, were making their way off the show jumping course ahead of the others.

Sarah rode Prince to meet them. Paige usually wore her hair in a ponytail around the barn, so it seemed different to see her beautiful blonde hair down and loose over her shoulders.

"Tough luck," Sarah said to Tim. "You're okay?"

Tim looked at Paige and then back at Sarah. "Honestly? I haven't felt this good in a long time," he said, grinning.

Kayla came running up to them, gasping for breath. "Rhodes is okay, Tim," she said. "He went back to the tent. Kathleen and Kelly are with him right now."

"Hey, Sarah," Tim said. "After Rhodes and I bombed out, you and Prince are in second place. You better watch this round."

Just then the announcer's voice came over the loudspeakers. "Our last entry, currently in first place, is Colin Dahlberg riding Senator." All eyes turned to watch Colin, sitting alert and confident on his big chestnut horse.

After saluting the judge, he sent Senator toward the brush box, riding conservatively at a fairly slow pace. The horse jumped the brush boldly and moved steadily to the second jump. Once over it, Colin steered his horse in a large arc to follow the course, sitting tall and moving cautiously over the rain-sodden grass. With one careful turn after another, he maneuvered his horse to all the jumps on the course, not missing a beat at the Liverpool or the two combinations. When Colin and Senator sailed clear over the last fence, the Castleton Stable spectators in the bleachers and along the sides of the rope barrier went wild, giving each other high fives as they danced up and down.

As the cheering subsided, it suddenly hit Sarah. Out of thirty-two competitors, she and Prince were in second place! They had finished with their dressage score. She would take a red ribbon home with her. Of course, as proud as she was of her horse and his spectacular performance, she couldn't help feeling bad for the other riders on her team who would go home empty-handed. But there was something else to celebrate—it looked like Tim and Paige had patched things up.

The announcer spoke again over the loudspeakers to announce the final placings. Colin's team, the Castleton Stable team, had finished in first place and would take the Wexford Cup home with them. In addition, Colin received a large blue ribbon for being the individual winner. And Sarah rode Crown Prince to the judge's stand to receive the biggest, most beautiful red ribbon she'd ever seen.

Before going back to the tent, Sarah rode Prince to where Colin's friends were swamping him with handshakes and slaps on the back. Colin waved to her when she got closer. "Congrats to you and Senator. Way to go!" Sarah called over the celebration. "Thanks, and right back at ya!" Colin shouted back.

The Brookmeade fans had climbed down from the bleachers, and they rushed over to congratulate Sarah. Mrs. DeWitt could hardly contain her excitement. "I wish I could pull you off that wonderful horse to give you a hug!" she called out. Abby was bouncing up and down as she and the Wagners came toward them, looking proud and happy. Mrs. Romano, following behind, blew her a kiss.

Mr. DeWitt cupped his hands around his mouth so Sarah could hear him. "Was everything you went through to keep Crown Prince and train him to be an event horse worth it?"

Sarah's big smile said it all. She gave him a thumbs up. "Absolutely," she called back. "Not a doubt in my mind!" The rain had finally stopped, and as Sarah slowly walked her horse back to the stabling area, a sliver of sun poked its way through the clouds.

* * * * *

It was a tired and damp team that prepared to leave Wexford Hall that afternoon. The riders had packed their bags in the morning before leaving the Belmont School, and Jack had made a stop to pick them up. The adults had long since departed for Yardley, leaving the team to attend to their horses. After stripping the stalls and loading all their equipment and supplies in the trucks, they were ready to head back to Brookmeade Farm.

As promised, Judson had shown up with the Snyders' big rig, and with their legs properly wrapped, the three horses were soon eating hay from nets inside it. Tim told the others he was riding home with Paige and would be waiting for them at the farm.

When Judson fired up the diesel engine of his truck, Kelly gave Sarah a dirty look and then ran to jump in the cab. *I guess she wants to steer clear of Kayla and me,* Sarah thought. Kathleen motioned to them, and she and Kayla climbed into the Brookmeade pickup's back seat.

Before long they were on the highway, the pickup again traveling a short distance behind the large gooseneck trailer. Jack seemed rather preoccupied as he drove, without much to say, and Sarah noticed how gloomy and tired he looked. She knew he was upset over Rita's performance in yesterday's cross-country ride, and he undoubtedly felt badly about Rhodes Scholar's fall. She was glad when Kathleen tried to cheer him up. "'Twas lucky that neither Rhodes Scholar nor Tim were injured in the fall," she said.

Jack nodded. "Yes, I suppose there's a silver lining in the events of the last few days." He looked into the back seat through his rear view mirror. "All the hard work you've put in with Crown Prince paid off, did it not, Sarah?"

Sarah had hardly let the red second-place ribbon she and Prince had been awarded out of her sight, and now she held it up to answer Jack's question. "I'm totally thrilled with Prince. I'm the luckiest person in the world."

Jack's eyes shifted to Kayla. "You rode extremely well, Kayla. I think you learned a valuable lesson from your dressage test. And to go clear cross-country and have only one rail down in that quagmire they called a show jumping course is surely something to be proud of."

"Yeah," Kayla said, "and I think I like eventing as much as showing. I'd like to try this again."

Sarah looked at Kayla. "Fanny was awesome. This was her first time to go cross-country, and she aced it."

Kayla grinned back at her. "I know another horse that did the same thing."

When they pulled into the parking area at the farm, Mrs. Romano was waiting with their horse trailer. After Fanny and Kayla's things were transferred into their truck, Kayla gave Sarah a big hug. "Thanks for all your help, kid," she said. "You did super."

Sarah stepped back to give her a high-five. "I couldn't have done it without you."

Paige and Tim came out of the barn to unload Rhodes. Paige was all smiles and laughter—her old self. "I hope Rhodes decided to stay on four legs during the ride home," she said. *Paige is back!* Sarah thought happily. Her laugh sounded so good!

Before taking Prince off the trailer, Sarah ran to his stall with the red ribbon and attached it prominently to his stall door. She could hardly wait to show it to Derek.

Prince tugged on his shank as Sarah led him into the barn, eager to get back to his stall. "I guess you've missed this place," Sarah said. "It's really home to you now." Once Prince was in his stall, she grabbed his water bucket and scoured it clean before filling it with fresh water.

Sarah looked at her watch. On the ride home, she'd called her father, and he would be there soon to pick her up. She gave Prince a kiss on his velvet-soft nose and then slid his stall door shut. "I'll be back later to feed you," she said, before making her way to the parking area with her suitcase. She also planned to take her saddle and bridle home with her. After getting soaked that morning, they needed a good soaping.

Sarah's father and Abby arrived a few minutes later. Sarah was tired and eager to get home, so she was even a little irritated when Abby insisted on visiting Prince in his stall to present him with an apple. Prince took a big bite and chomped on it, the juice running from his mouth. His eyes wrinkled in the corners when Abby stroked his neck and told him what a star he had been at Wexford Hall.

When she got home, Sarah decided there was time to oil her tack before she had to return to the farm to dole out the evening hay and grain. After taking her bridle apart and removing the stirrup leathers from her saddle, she applied neatsfoot oil with a soft cloth until the leather was soft and pliable again. The saddle soap she worked into her saddle and the girth would also preserve it. Her father walked by as she worked. "Good job," he said. "Water is leather's worst enemy." He paused and looked back. "I'll take your tack back to the farm when I go that way tomorrow."

Once she had put her bridle together, Sarah went upstairs to get the feed room key before heading back to the farm on her bike. It had been several days since she'd done the evening feeding, and it actually felt good to be getting back to the old routine. A chorus of neighs greeted her when she walked up the aisle toward the feed room. The horses recognized Sarah and knew what was coming.

After the feed detail, Sarah went to Crown Prince. Derek hadn't gotten back from his show with Bismarck, and except for the sounds of horses eating, the barn was quiet. She slid through Prince's stall door and went to her horse, encircling his neck to hold him tightly while he ate his grain. He had exceeded her wildest expectations, giving her his best in all three phases of the event. His famous Thoroughbred ancestors would be proud! He had demonstrated the class that had come down through many generations. She couldn't love him more than she did at that moment.

To celebrate her performance at Wexford Hall, her mother had prepared her favorite dinner—fried chicken with cranberry sauce and mashed potatoes. Sarah had so much to tell them as they gathered around the table, and Abby pestered her with question after question. "You find this stuff interesting," Sarah said, grinning at her. "Are you ready to start taking riding lessons?"

Mrs. Wagner immediately interceded. "I think Abby should stick to softball and soccer," she said. "I'm not sure my blood pressure could take having two riders in the family."

Sarah went to bed early that night, and even though she was exhausted, she tossed and turned. The events of the last three days whirled through her mind. Finally she drifted off into a deep sleep. She didn't hear her cell phone or the house phone ring a few hours later, but she was awakened by her father's raised voice. He had flicked on the light in her room and was standing by her bed in his pajamas.

"Sarah, wake up! Derek just called. He said you should get to the barn right away. Prince is in trouble!"

CHAPTER 30

To the Rescue

SARAH ROLLED OVER IN HER BED, opening her eyes in response to her father's urgent voice. As her head cleared, she sat upright. Was this a dream? Had her father just told her Prince was in trouble?

"Get dressed! I'll meet you downstairs," her father said, as he hurried from her room. Sarah jumped out of bed and quickly pulled on her jeans and a T-shirt. After slipping into a pair of sneakers, she rushed down the stairs. Her mother was in her bathrobe, waiting to see them off. "Call me," she said, as Sarah and her father went out the back door.

Sarah had never known her father to drive as fast as he did on their way to the farm. It was late, and there was no other traffic on the road. With no moon or stars showing on an overcast night, the sky was pitch black as they turned into the farm road. *What could possibly be wrong?* Sarah thought. Prince had been perfectly fine when she left him. It had been like any other night when she'd fed the horses and then headed home.

As they gathered speed going down the last hill, it looked like every light in the barn was on, and the parking area was brightly illuminated. Derek's pickup and trailer with its ramp down were parked near the barn. Sarah jumped from the car when it came to a stop and sprinted toward the barn's side door. She dashed down the aisle, noticing as she passed the feed room that the door was wide open and the floor was littered with grain and feed pails from the cart. She kept running.

When Sarah turned the corner close to Prince's stall, she screeched to a halt, her hand flying to her mouth as it opened in shock. Derek was looking into Prince's stall where Gus stood at Prince's head, holding his halter tightly to keep him from moving. Prince's moist body was covered with bedding, and his white-rimmed eyes mirrored fear and pain as he attempted to pull back from Gus's strong hold.

Sarah ran to the stall. "What's wrong with Prince?" she demanded.

Derek's brow was creased with worry lines. "When I got back from the show with Bismarck, Prince's stall door was wide open, and he was down and thrashing," he said. "I ran to get Gus. You probably saw the feed room when you came in."

"Is it colic?" Sarah asked, as her father came up behind them.

"Of course it's colic!" Gus barked at her from inside the stall. He glared at her sullenly. "You must have left the feed room doors open when you fed tonight."

Stunned and speechless, Sarah swung around to Derek.

"Gus gave me Dr. Reynolds's number," Derek said. "His answering service got in touch with the vet, and he called about ten minutes ago. He should be here any minute."

With tears streaming down her face, Sarah went to her horse. She pressed her face to his warm, moist neck, and ignoring Gus's glare, she spoke to him through her sobs. "Prince, Prince," she said over and over again, as she tried to suppress a rising panic.

"Leave this stall," Gus growled. "This horse may have a

twisted intestine, and he wants to go down." His face was twisted in anger when she didn't respond, and he raised his voice. "Get out!"

Sarah retreated in the face of Gus's angry words just as Dr. Reynolds came hurrying toward them with a stethoscope in his hand. He had also noticed the wide-open feed room. "I assume this is a grain-induced colic," he said as he entered the stall. Gus nodded.

From outside, clutching the bars, Sarah felt as if a vice gripped her chest, making it hard to breath. She found herself shaking uncontrollably.

The veterinarian listened to Prince's pulse and then checked his respiration—both were elevated. After placing the stethoscope on the horse's side and listening for a few moments, he looked relieved when he stepped back. "There's plenty of activity in the gut, which is usually a good sign," he said. "If we're lucky, he won't require surgery." He went back to his truck.

Sarah took a deep breath and closed her eyes, sensing immense relief at Dr. Reynolds's words. A few minutes later the veterinarian entered the stall to administer a pain reliever and muscle relaxant to her horse. When he'd finished, Dr. Reynolds said, "I'm going to insert a tube into his stomach. We need to relieve him of gas in the digestive tract and at the same time add mineral oil to help him pass all that grain." He left the stall for a few minutes before returning with the tube and oil in a bucket along with a pump. "He's not going to like this," Dr. Reynolds said to Gus. "Take a good hold of his halter."

Seeing her horse in extreme pain and having a plastic tube run through his nose to his stomach, Sarah was emotionally distraught. Tears ran down her face as she watched Dr. Reynolds insert the tube and then administer the mineral oil. Sarah was only vaguely aware of Derek putting his arm around her shoulders to comfort her.

A voice sounded behind them. It was Mr. DeWitt. "What's going on here?" he said, as he strode closer, his thick white hair tousled and his eyes puffy behind his steel-gray glasses. "I saw all the lights on down here."

"It's colic, Chandler," Dr. Reynolds said in a measured tone, as he slowly withdrew the stomach tube. "I just hope we got it in time."

"Oh, no," DeWitt said, shaking his head sadly. "I assume he got into the feed room." His gaze turned to Sarah.

Sarah pulled away from Derek to face Mr. DeWitt. "I locked that room after I finished feeding," she said firmly, looking him in the eye. "I know I did, and I took the key home with me." She paused to wipe her eyes. "I came to see Prince just before I left. He was fine, and I'm sure I locked his stall door."

Mr. DeWitt looked back at Crown Prince. "Right now the important thing is to save this horse. Colic is the leading cause of death in horses, and he may be fighting for his life."

Dr. Reynolds stepped out of the stall. "That pain med I gave him is fast-acting, and I suggest you hand-walk him for twenty minutes. That will help get things moving. Then it'll be best to rest him for half an hour before walking him again. Let's hope he starts passing manure soon."

Dr. Reynolds gathered up his things. "I have a second emergency call, so I'll be off. Please report any passing of manure, which will mean things are moving, and of course I want to know if he takes a turn for the worse. If he recovers enough to show any interest in eating, start him off with a warm mash." The vet started to leave, but turned back. He paused, his face somber. "It's fortunate someone discovered him. By morning, it might have been too late."

"Thanks for coming at this late hour," Mr. Wagner said.

Dr. Reynolds just nodded, looked back at Crown Prince, and then hurried out of the barn.

After the veterinarian left, Sarah picked up the shank and went to her horse, who already appeared more comfortable. She ran her hands over his face as her tears started again, and when he lowered his head, she hugged him close. Finally she stepped back to attach the shank to his halter.

"I'm going to clean up the mess," Gus said, heading for the feed room.

The indoor arena was quiet and dark when Sarah arrived there with her horse. After Derek turned on the overhead lights, she led Prince through the gate and started walking him in a large circle. Derek, Mr. DeWitt, and her father watched from the sidelines as Prince followed her slowly, his head low. Sarah needed to urge him forward when he occasionally halted.

"I see you have your pickup and trailer outside," Mr. DeWitt said to Derek.

"Yes," Derek replied. "It was late when I got back here from the show. That's when I discovered Prince."

Sarah kept checking her watch, and when twenty minutes had passed, she turned him back toward the gate. They had almost reached it when Prince came to a halt, and with a slight groan, passed a large pile of manure.

"Yea!" Derek called out. "This is the first time in my life I've been excited to see this." Sarah was still too tense to laugh with the others.

"I suspect things are looking brighter," her father said, "so I'm going home to get some shuteye. Do you want to come with me, Sarah?" She shook her head. "I think you'll have a long night here, but call when you need a ride."

There was no sign of Gus when Sarah walked Prince back to his stall, but the grain had been cleaned up and the door to the feed room was shut with its padlock in place. Once Prince was in his stall, Mr. DeWitt said, "I'm glad Dorothy didn't wake up when I left. She would have been terribly upset to see this horse in distress." He turned to Sarah. "At some point, we'll need to find out how this happened. You're positive you didn't leave either of the doors open, Sarah? Is there any other explanation?"

Sarah looked directly into Mr. DeWitt gray eyes. "I would *never* leave Prince's stall door open. As for the feed room, my key is at home, and I remember locking the feed room before I left. Someone else must have a key." Mr. DeWitt's brow furrowed into a scowl, but Sarah continued. "My first key came up missing about a month ago. The chain I always kept the key on must have broken, because it wasn't there when I was ready to feed. Gus flipped out when I told him I'd lost it, but he gave me another key. Since then I've looked everywhere, and I finally decided the chain with the key must have broken when I was riding Prince. Now I wonder if someone else found it."

Mr. DeWitt and Derek stood quietly, pondering what Sarah had said. Finally Mr. DeWitt spoke. "If someone plotted to do this, their specific objective would have been to harm your horse, Sarah."

An eerie, dark feeling swept over Sarah. After a moment, she said, "You already know I'm not the most popular person in this barn, Mr. DeWitt. There are a few people who've been jealous of me." She looked up at the red ribbon hanging on Prince's stall door.

Derek shook his head. "It's hard to believe anyone would stoop so low as to intentionally harm a defenseless horse," he said. Sarah covered her face as the tears started again.

Mr. DeWitt pulled out his phone and dialed Gus's number, asking the barn manager to come back down. Almost before DeWitt could put his phone away, Gus emerged around the corner, looking disheveled and exhausted.

"Gus," Mr. DeWitt began, "Sarah is convinced she left the feed room locked. She tells me her key came up missing about a month ago, and you supplied her with a replacement. Her original key was never found." Mr. DeWitt paused to look in on the horse, who was looking depressed with his head hanging low. DeWitt turned back to Gus. "I'd like to know if you observed anyone else coming to the barn tonight."

Gus scratched his head for a moment before responding. "I was expecting Derek to bring his horse back tonight," he said, "so I wouldn't have thought twice about the sound of vehicles coming and going." Gus paused, looking ashamed. "To tell you the truth, I fell asleep watching my Sunday night program, and I didn't even hear Derek come in with Bismarck."

Mr. DeWitt shifted uneasily on his feet, frowning. "Thanks for coming down, Gus. You can try to get some sleep now. I'm sorry your night was disturbed."

After Gus had gone back to his apartment, they were all relieved to see Crown Prince pass more manure in his stall. "It looks like your horse will be okay," Mr. DeWitt said. "I think if he's resting comfortably for the next hour, you can probably leave him and go home. I'm going back to the house now, but don't hesitate to call me if he takes a turn for the worse."

"Good night, Mr. DeWitt," Sarah said. "Thanks for all your help. But you should know—I'm not leaving my horse until I'm sure he's okay."

Mr. DeWitt smiled. "I'm not surprised." But then he turned serious. "I also want to assure you I won't rest until I find out who is behind this."

Derek walked out of the barn with Mr. DeWitt to unhook his horse trailer, and he went around shutting off many of the lights that illuminated the parking area. While he was outside, Sarah got a dandy brush from her grooming caddy and began removing the shavings that clung to Prince's coat. Her horse had cooled down, but he continued to stand quietly with his head lowered. Bismarck moved restlessly, stopping frequently to watch the activity around Prince's stall.

Derek returned just as Sarah finished brushing Prince. She looked relieved when she came out of the stall. "The mineral oil is working. I think Prince is going to make it!" As Sarah walked closer to Derek, her face became more serious. "I've been, like, totally self-centered tonight. You and Bismarck had your first show since you moved east, and I haven't asked you how it went." She paused, looking at him expectantly.

A smile spread across Derek's face. "I hope you won't be too critical," he said, pausing to add some drama. "We won two red ribbons and a blue."

Sarah's eyes widened. "Oh, my god! That's fantastic. What class did you win?"

"It was the class my dad was really hoping we'd do well in, because there were a few bucks involved. We won the last class of the night, Open Jumpers Sweepstakes, with a pretty hefty purse."

Sarah felt like throwing her arms around Derek in a big hug, but she stopped herself in time. She was ecstatic, and her face told it all. "That's awesome! You must have been totally psyched."

"Something like that," Derek said, wearing the smile that melted many girls' heartstrings. "After all the money my folks plunked down to import Bismarck, I was really happy to do well."

Sarah walked closer to Derek. "It's so late—you'd probably

like to go home. Thanks for staying so long. I'll be okay, and I think I'll call my dad before long."

Sarah was turning for the tack room when Derek took her arm and gently turned her toward him. "Sarah, there's something I have to tell you." He hesitated, choosing his words carefully. "I hope I'm not being too pushy at a tough time." He stopped again, wondering if he should go on. After an awkward pause, he said, "I'm not sure why you've kept me at arm's length for a long time, but I got the message. You've sent plenty of signals that you want to be my friend, but nothing more, and you've been pretty clear about that. Then tonight I put my arm around you at a time when all you could think of was your horse. I guess I was out of line."

Sarah was reeling. She was physically and emotionally drained, and now this. He was right—she had kept herself from thinking of Derek as anything other than a riding friend. She looked directly in his eyes, those incredibly blue eyes, and there was a tightening in her throat. "Derek, how can you talk to me this way? Don't you think I know about your girlfriend in Chicago? Why would I be interested in a guy who's already taken?"

Derek's jaw dropped, and for a moment he was speechless. "Girlfriend in Chicago?" he said. "Whatever gave you that idea?"

Sarah shook her head to clear it. Then she remembered learning about Derek's girlfriend from Kayla, who'd been informed by … Rita! Sarah looked back at Derek. "Rita told Kayla she was calling you a lot until you finally spilled the beans. Didn't you tell Rita about a girlfriend named Meredith you dated in Chicago? Didn't you tell her you were going back to see Meredith at Christmas and during spring break?"

Derek shook his head, his teeth clenched. "How could you buy a line that came from Rita Snyder? I don't know any girl named Meredith, and I don't have a girlfriend by any other name either.

I'm not seeing anyone!" He expelled a deep breath. "I did get tired of Rita calling me all the time, and I told her I was busy a few times, but I never mentioned a girlfriend."

Their conversation was interrupted by Gus, who ambled around the corner. Without saying a word, he went directly to Prince's stall and looked in on the horse.

"He's passed manure three times, Gus," Sarah said.

A wave of relief came over Gus's face. With a slight hint of a smile, he said, "Good. But I'll keep looking in on him every hour." With that, he turned and started back to his apartment.

Derek smiled at Sarah. "Yes, I've heard what everyone says about Gus—he takes incredible care of every horse in the barn. Do you feel it's safe to leave Prince now?"

"Knowing that Gus will be checking him through the night, yes, I do."

"Come on, then," he said, taking her hand. "I'll give you a ride home."

CHAPTER 31

Bitter Consequences

SARAH SLEPT LATER THAN USUAL the next morning, waking only when a beam of bright sunlight played on her face. She lay still, her head gradually clearing, as the events of the last few days came flooding back. Wexford Hall, Prince's colic, and Derek. Could she have dreamed any of it? Remembering her late night conversation with Derek, she felt almost giddy. Finally she threw the covers off and got up. She had to go to the barn to check on Prince.

Soon Sarah was pedaling her bike along Ridge Road on her way to the farm. She immediately went to her horse and was overjoyed to find him eating hay in his stall. He took the carrots she offered and lowered his head for her hug. He didn't seem perky, and his eyes weren't as bright as usual, but he was definitely over the colic.

Stepping outside the stall, Sarah speed-dialed Kayla. She wanted to tell her about the nightmare they had gone through and see how Fanny was after Wexford Hall. Kayla picked up right away. "I hope Fanny came out of the event okay," Sarah said.

"Absolutely fine," Kayla said. "She's getting to be a seasoned campaigner." Then Kayla asked about Crown Prince. Sarah's friend sounded horror-struck when she said, "How is Mr. DeWitt going to get to the bottom of this? I think we both have a strong suspicion who did it."

Sarah's brows creased into a frown. "I wish I knew."

"Keep me posted."

Sarah was cleaning Prince's stall when Mr. and Mrs. DeWitt came to the barn with their Jack Russells charging ahead of them. Mrs. DeWitt hurried to Sarah as she came out of the stall. "You poor girl," she said, giving her a hug. "Chandler told me everything you went through last night. What a horrible experience! I'm so relieved Crown Prince came out of it all right."

"I hope you slept in this morning," Mr. DeWitt said. "It certainly was a late night." The DeWitts walked over to look at Crown Prince.

"I guess it's not surprising that he's totally dragging today," Sarah said. "I wonder when he'll be feeling like himself."

Mr. DeWitt studied the horse, who was standing quietly in the rear of his stall with his head slightly lowered. "Crown Prince does look drawn and tucked up," he said, "but he'll be fine in a day or so. The big dose of meds Dr. Reynolds gave him last night to relax him probably hasn't completely worn off. That would partly explain his lethargic manner."

Mr. DeWitt's face was grave when he turned back to Sarah. "I assured you that I intend to find out who acted so maliciously, and I've already begun my own investigation. Gus and Dorothy both confirm that a second key was given to you, so we know that your original key is currently missing."

Mrs. DeWitt voiced an opinion. "I told Chandler that if you say you remember locking the feed room last night, then of course you did. And it doesn't make any sense you would leave your horse's stall door wide open as you were leaving."

"I spoke to Jack this morning," Mr. DeWitt said. "He was absolutely stunned when I told him what happened. He's a light sleeper, and he distinctly remembers hearing Derek's pickup and trailer go by the bungalow on the farm road very late last night. But he also heard a car go by a few hours before that, and not long afterward, a car again passed the bungalow as it left the farm."

Sarah's eyes grew large as she listened expectantly, her mind racing.

Mr. DeWitt read her mind. "Unfortunately Jack didn't see any of the vehicles, so we don't have any positive identification. I'd like to continue my inquiry this morning. Dorothy is planning to ride Medina, and if you can leave your horse for a while, I'd like you to come with me."

Sarah's face clouded, unsure what this meant. "How can I help?" she asked.

"It's your horse that was threatened, and you need to be on top of everything that comes to light. It's possible you'll remember some helpful information as we talk to a few people."

Sarah looked at her horse, who had started nibbling on some hay in his stall. "Okay," she said. "I can leave Prince for a while."

Once they were in his red Blazer, Mr. DeWitt drove out to Ridge Road and turned right toward the beach. They chatted about the Wexford Hall competition as they passed through the Yardley village and onto the road to Winchester. With a lump in her throat, Sarah knew what their destination would be. They were going to see everyone's top suspect: Rita.

A few miles later, they turned by the green-and-white Pyramid Farm sign into the long paved driveway that would take them to the Snyders' estate. Coming out of a grove of evergreen trees, they passed the trout pond, the barn surrounded by white-fenced paddocks, and the hulking indoor arena looming behind it. The Snyders' van and new gooseneck trailer were parked beside the barn. Mr. DeWitt continued along the driveway and pulled up near the portico in front of the pillared house.

"Let's see who's at home this morning," DeWitt said, stepping from the Blazer. Sarah hung back, not looking forward to a confrontation with Rita and her father. Mr. DeWitt paused to glance back at her, his steely gray eyes deeply serious. "We need to do this together, Sarah," he said.

She reluctantly got out of the Blazer, and they walked to the double-doored front entrance. Soon after Mr. DeWitt rang the bell, the door was opened by Judson's wife, Polly, the plump gray-haired woman who served as the Snyders' housekeeper. She looked at them curiously as she dried her hands on her apron.

"Hello," Mr. DeWitt said. "I'm Chandler DeWitt, and if you remember, my wife Dorothy and I were your guests at the party Rita and her father had for the Brookmeade Farm riders last summer. This is Sarah Wagner, one of Rita's riding classmates."

Polly immediately made the connection and nodded, smiling. "Of course," she said. "Mrs. DeWitt was so nice to jump right in and help me serve the buffet supper."

"We'd like to speak to Richard and Rita, if they're at home," Mr. DeWitt said.

Polly frowned. "I'm sorry, but Mr. Snyder left on a business trip yesterday afternoon, and Miss Rita's not here."

Mr. DeWitt drew his lips together firmly. "Perhaps you can help us. Do you know if Rita came to Brookmeade Farm last night?"

Polly's brows were puckered, seeming confused. "Miss Rita had a friend stay overnight with her, and as far as I know, they weren't going anywhere. I think they planned to watch a movie, but I can't be sure. I go to bed pretty early." She pointed beyond them to the Snyders' barn. "The girls were going riding this morning, but maybe they haven't left yet. They may still be in the stable."

DeWitt swung around to look where she had gestured before turned back to the housekeeper. "Thank you, Polly," he said. "We'll go to the stable to see if they're there."

Walking along the crushed rock pathway that led from the house to the large barn, Mr. DeWitt and Sarah saw several horses and a pony turned out in individual white paddocks. There was no sign of Chancellor. *A lot of horses for one girl,* Sarah thought.

The barn's large double doors were open when they approached, and when they walked inside, their eyes were immediately drawn to the large chandelier hung in the entry foyer. The barn was immaculate, with fancy pecan-paneled walls and brass hardware on the stall doors.

At the end of an aisle lined with extra-large box stalls, Rita was grooming Chancellor on cross-ties. When she saw them, a look of surprise registered on her face and she abruptly stepped away from her horse.

Sarah focused intently on Rita as they drew closer, seeing her heavy brows over a sharp nose and thin lips. Had this girl put a plan in action to make her horse colic? Could she be so overcome with jealousy and anger she would plot to *kill* Crown Prince?

As they came closer, Rita had recovered from the shock of seeing them enter her barn. She tried to muster a weak smile as she brushed her dark hair back from her face.

"Hello, Rita," Mr. DeWitt said. He took a moment to survey the stunning black horse. "Chancellor looks well, and he apparently recovered from the Wexford Hall event."

"Yes," Rita said nervously, her eyes darting back and forth between the two of them. "He's fine."

Mr. DeWitt got right to the point. "I wonder if you can tell us how you spent your evening last night. Is there any chance you came to Brookmeade Farm after our boarders left?"

Rita's face flushed crimson, but she stood her ground. She knew something was up and became defensive. "I had a friend sleep over," she retorted hotly. "We hung out here watching a movie. Just ask Polly."

She's so good with her lies, Sarah thought. A vision of Prince thrashing in his stall in agonizing pain flashed through her mind. It had been the night from hell! She could visualize Rita's face contorted in a twisted smile as she worked quickly, unlocking the feed room and swinging its broad door open before turning Prince loose. She might have led the horse directly to the feed room, so he'd be sure to eat enough grain to take his life.

The memory of last night was fresh, filling Sarah with a hatred she had never before experienced. At that moment her temper boiled up inside her, consuming her with rage. Her fists were clenched as she walked toward Rita, shaking with anger. Rita instinctively stepped back until she was braced against a stall wall and could retreat no farther. When Sarah was close enough to see the greenness of Rita's eyes, she exploded. "Don't feed us your lies," she hissed. "You are sick! You were so filled with self-pity and jealously last night, you had to strike out. You wanted to get back at me by attacking my defenseless horse."

Sarah stopped to catch her breath, just as Mr. DeWitt came up behind her and attempted to pull her back. Shrugging his hand off her shoulder, she continued her outburst, her words coming fast. "You would have been so happy if my horse died last night, wouldn't you, Rita. I'm sorry to disappoint you, but your plan backfired! Derek discovered Prince in time to save him."

Rita raised her arms, as if preparing for a physical attack. She stared at Sarah, her mouth gaping, not sure how to react to this withering onslaught. Just then the sound of a door slamming diverted their attention, and whirling around, Sarah saw Kelly Hoffman emerge from a tack room carrying Rita's saddle. *So this is Rita's sleepover friend.* Sarah thought. *I should have known!*

Kelly stopped in her tracks when saw the visitors. As Sarah strode toward her, the anger she harbored toward Rita shifted to a second enemy. For all the drama Kelly had caused and all the lies she had spread about Crown Prince, Sarah had never retaliated. But she wouldn't hold back now.

As Sarah rushed up to Kelly, something caught her eye that caused her to hesitate. A chain around Kelly's neck flashed golden in the rays of sun coming through the barn's skylights. Sarah stopped, rooted to the floor, as she stared at the gold chain. When Mr. DeWitt caught up with her, Sarah pointed to the chain showing at the neckline of Kelly's T-shirt. "Look!" was all she could say, her voice trembling. The chain's significance wasn't lost on Mr. DeWitt, and his eyes widened.

"Kelly, may I see what you have hanging around your neck?" Mr. DeWitt asked.

"Oh, it's nothing," Kelly answered. "It's just a good luck charm I wear."

Mr. DeWitt stepped closer. "Would you please pull the chain up so I can see all of it?"

Mr. DeWitt was an authority figure in Kelly's life, and she couldn't refuse his request. She begrudgingly set the saddle down and reached around her neck to grasp the chain. When she pulled it up, a bronze-colored key flew out, coming to rest on her T-shirt. *Oh, my God,* Sarah thought. *It's the key!* Her eyes met Mr. DeWitt's.

When he turned back to Kelly, Mr. DeWitt said, "It appears you have a key that might fit the feed room door at Brookmeade Farm." His eyes narrowed as he looked at her intently. "Give it to me right now." When Kelly seemed to freeze, he moved as though reaching for his cell phone.

"Here!" Kelly said, as she hurried to lower her head, pulled the chain off, and handed it and the attached key to Mr. DeWitt. Once it was in his hand, Sarah looked down at the key with the familiar scroll pattern engraved on it. The chain was plain and generic, making it hard for her to identify, but she would recognize the key in a heartbeat, even without its buffalo head key ring. She'd used it so many times in the last year!

Sarah nodded to Mr. DeWitt. "I'm pretty sure that's it," she said. Rita had advanced to stand sullenly beside Kelly, both girls watching them closely. Sarah stared angrily at Kelly. "How long have you been hiding that key, Kelly, waiting for your chance to strike? Or did Rita give it to you after she used it last night?"

Rita swung around to stare at Kelly before turning back to Mr. DeWitt. "I suspect this key will fit the lock to our feed room door," he said, "which will prove that you two deliberately set the wheels in motion to harm Crown Prince last night. He's a valuable horse, and there may be serious repercussions from your actions."

Rita turned back to Kelly with a look of shock before slumping and turning her back to them. She covered her face with her hands as she began to cry, her shoulders shaking. Kelly seemed on the verge of tears herself as she put her arm around Rita, trying to comfort her. But Rita pulled away.

Kelly faced Mr. DeWitt and Sarah. "Rita had nothing to do with this," she said in a shaking voice. "It was all my idea, my chance to get back at Miss Smarty Pants. Sarah always thought she was too good to ride with Nicole and me. She got Jack to move her up to the Young Riders class when she didn't even have her own horse! And when Derek Alexander came to the barn, she acted like she owned him."

Kelly pushed her hair out of her face and continued. "It was bad enough that Sarah got a ribbon at Wexford Hall, but then she had to totally flaunt it. She put it on her T-shirt, so the world would know how superior she is. It was enough to make me throw up! I was glad I could ride back with Judson yesterday, just to get away from her."

Mr. DeWitt looked puzzled. "Kelly, are you saying that Rita didn't have any part in what happened last night?"

Kelly met Rita's gaze before continuing. "No, Rita didn't even know about it," she said. "Her father lit into her pretty bad when she got back here with Chancellor, saying he had a good mind to sell the place and take all her horses away. So when I said I'd like to teach Sarah Wagner a lesson, Rita didn't want any part of it. She worried her dad would get wind of it. She was also freaking out about what Jack said to her at Wexford Hall.

Sarah and Mr. DeWitt were shocked as Kelly continued. "When we went out to rent a movie, Rita wanted to drop off some buckets that were left in the big rig at Brookmeade. We were getting back in her car when I told her I'd forgotten to give Jet his supplement. That wasn't true. Rita stayed in her car listening to music when I went back in the barn. I had the key around my neck. I did it all. I first opened the feed room door and then slid Crown Prince's stall door open. I knew he'd find that grain in a New York minute," Kelly said bitterly.

"And the rest we already know," Mr. DeWitt said. He looked at Rita closely. "Kelly says you had nothing to do with her plot against Crown Prince. Is her story absolutely true?"

Rita nodded her head wearily. "I swear," she whispered.

Mr. DeWitt pursed his lips and shook his head before he turned his gaze back at Kelly. "Do you remember what I said to you not long ago? I told you another episode of poor behavior would be grounds for your dismissal from Brookmeade Farm? And it is. Your actions last night were reckless and irresponsible. I haven't decided if the police will be brought in. Do you want to explain this to your mother, or shall I?"

"I will," Kelly said through clenched teeth.

"Very well," Mr. DeWitt replied. "She needs to hear the entire story. I will be sure to confirm that she has. I expect Midnight Jet to be off the Brookmeade Farm property in one week or less, and after that, you will not be welcome there under any circumstances." Mr. DeWitt's gaze came to rest on Rita. "I'm relieved to learn you had nothing to do with Kelly's attempt to sabotage Crown Prince," he said.

Sarah's face was troubled when she spoke up. "I said some pretty hateful things to you, Rita. I'm sorry. I'm just so relieved you didn't do anything to hurt Prince."

"I love horses too much to do something like that," Rita replied quickly. "I know I behaved horribly at the event and treated my horse badly. It has been eating me up inside. I swore I would never hurt any horse again."

* * * * *

Mrs. DeWitt, Jack, and Kathleen were anxiously waiting for them when Mr. DeWitt and Sarah got back to the farm. They gathered in the office with the door shut to discuss what had happened. Mr. DeWitt spoke for all of them when he said it was a relief to have solved the mystery. "There's one thing that's going to happen as a result of this incident, and not a minute too soon," he said. "I'm going to have a surveillance system set up in this barn immediately. It will run twenty-four-seven and will be motion-activated to record all activity in and out of all of our entrances."

Sarah finally excused herself to go to Crown Prince. The

events of the last several days had left her drained, and now she just wanted to be alone with her horse, *her* amazing horse. Prince needed quiet time to fully recover from his bout of colic, and she needed time to rest and reflect.

Prince nickered as she approached his stall, his ears pricked and his large eyes watching her closely. Sarah went to him, stroking his beautiful dark bay head and running her fingers over the white star on his forehead. He reached down to nuzzle her jeans pockets in search of carrots.

Sarah stood close to her horse for a long time and thought of what they both had been through. It would take a while, but eventually they'd put this behind them and move on. She hoped she could ride her horse again soon, and there was so much to look forward to—trail rides with her friends, lessons with Jack, future competitions, and ... Derek?

Glossary

This glossary is designed to help readers better understand various terms that appear in this book. The definitions are short and general in nature, and in some cases readers may wish to consult other sources for a more complete explanation.

Aids Used by riders to give horses directives. The natural aids: hands, legs, seat or weight, and voice. The artificial aids: whips and spurs.

Anglo/Arab A horse with one Thoroughbred parent and one Arabian parent.

Appaloosa A versatile breed developed by the Nez Perce Native Americans, which is commonly known for its distinct spotted coat.

Baker blanket A brand of horse clothing with a distinctive plaid pattern.

Bars The area without teeth in the horse's lower jaw where the bit rests.

Bascule The natural round arc of a horse's body when it jumps a fence athletically, putting its withers at the highest point.

Bat A short crop (whip) with a wide head.

Blaze A white marking on a horse's face that extends from its forehead to its muzzle.

Blemish A mark left from a former condition or injury that may be unattractive but does not indicate unsoundness.

Bone The measure of the circumference of the foreleg below the knee, which is considered to reflect a horse's proclivity toward soundness.

Bran mash A nourishing and easy-to-digest feed for a horse made by mixing bran with warm water, and letting it soak until it expands.

Bridle path A trail intended for recreational use by horses and riders, or the area behind the horse's ears where the mane is clipped short to accommodate a bridle or halter.

Buck When the horse attempts to unseat a rider by leaping in the air with its back arched and its head lowered while kicking out with its hind legs.

Canter The fastest of the horse's three main gaits, which include the walk, trot, and canter. The canter has three beats.

Capped hock A swelling at the point of the hock, which may or may not contribute to unsoundness in the horse.

Cast When a horse rolls against a stall wall in such a way that its legs are pinned and it becomes trapped. This can lead to potentially fatal injuries if the horse isn't assisted to its feet.

Cavalletti Rails placed on or just above the ground in various patterns, which the horse is walked, trotted, and/or cantered over. They are used in the training of the horse in a number of disciplines.

Cavesson The noseband of a bridle, or the headstall with a sturdy noseband commonly used when longeing the horse.

Chaps An article of clothing riders wear over pants when riding to prevent chafing of their legs.

Cleveland Bay A breed of horse originally developed in England for carriage driving.

Cluck The sound a person makes with the tongue commonly used to encourage a horse to move forward.

Cob A small, stout horse of strong build—refers to a body type rather than a specific breed.

Colic Abdominal pain in the horse, ranging from mild to severe and indicating a digestive disorder, which due to the horse's unique intestinal system, can be fatal.

Combination Two or more jumps placed in close proximity with a specific number of strides between each jump.

Conformation A horse's physical form and shape.

Cooler An item of horse clothing used to prevent a hot, sweaty, or wet horse from being chilled.

Coop A type of jump modeled after a chicken coop, which was originally placed over wire fencing to make it safe for jumping on foxhunts.

Counter-canter To canter on the opposite lead from the direction the horse is traveling.

Crest The upper portion of a horse's neck.

Cribbing A vice when a horse pulls against a solid object with its teeth, often while swallowing air.

Crop A small riding whip used by the rider to reinforce the leg aids.

Cross-ties A method of tying a horse, usually in a barn aisle, using ties attached to opposite walls and to each side of the horse's halter.

Curry comb A grooming tool with rows of small teeth used to loosen dirt prior to brushing.

Dam A horse's mother (mare).

Dandy brush A grooming brush made of a stiff material used to remove dirt from the horse's coat.

Diagonal (correct) A way of posting (rising) to the trot so the rider rises in unison with the horse's inside hind leg and outside front leg.

Dispersal sale When an owner puts all his horses up for sale.

Dressage test When a horse and rider are judged on how they perform a series of specific movements and patterns, which demonstrate the horse's level of training.

Dropped noseband A type of bridle noseband that encircles the muzzle to prevent a horse from opening its mouth to evade the action of the bit and is often used on horses that require more control.

Dutch Warmblood A European breed selectively bred as to excel in equestrian sports such as dressage and show jumping.

Eggbutt A type of snaffle bit with egg-shaped (slightly oval) rings to which the cheek pieces and reins of the bridle are attached.

Equitation A type of horse show class in which the rider's form and riding ability are judged.

Equus Scientific term for the species known as horse.

Eventing A three-phase type of equestrian competition in which horses are tested in dressage, cross-country jumping (natural obstacles across varied terrain), and show jumping.

Farrier A person who trims the feet of and "shoes" horses.

Flake (of hay) One measured section from a bale of hay.

Flash noseband A type of bridle noseband used to help keep the bit steady in the horse's mouth and hold the horse's mouth closed, preventing evasion of the rein aids.

Flea-bitten gray A horse coat color that features small splotches of brown and black hairs among predominantly white hairs.

Flexion tests A diagnostic tool often used to test for joint pain (and related unsoundness) by holding the horse's joint (commonly in the legs) in a tightly flexed position for one to two minutes and then having the horse trot off.

Float To remove sharp edges from a horse's teeth by filing them with a rasp, enabling the horse to chew its food more efficiently.

Fly sheet An article of horse clothing designed to protect the horse from insects.

Flying change When a cantering horse changes his lead to the opposite canter lead without slowing to walk or trot.

Forward A term used to describe energetic movement or impulsion in the ridden horse.

Founder A term commonly used to describe the equine vascular disease of laminitis, which impacts the sensitive structures of a horse's hooves. In advanced stages of laminitis, a bone within the horse's hoof can actually detach, rotate, and/or sink, hence the term "founder."

Frame (in a) When a horse is moving forward with energy in response to the rider's leg and seat aids into a restraining hand, often assuming a desirable "profile" or appearance with a rounded topline and the nose positioned just in front of the vertical.

Frog The firm, resilient V-shaped "cushion" that sits in the center of sole of the horse's foot and helps absorb the shock of concussion.

Galloping boots Horse clothing used during exercise to protect a horse's lower legs from injury.

Gelding A neutered (castrated) male horse.

Girth The piece of tack that attaches to either side of the saddle and wraps under the horse's belly, holding the saddle in place on the horse's back.

Going large When a horse is ridden on the outer track of the riding arena around the entire riding space.

Gooseneck trailer A trailer that attaches to the bed of the hauling vehicle, rather than to the bumper.

Green Used to describe a horse in the early stages of training, when it is inexperienced and often lacking confidence.

Half chaps A type of chaps used by riders that begin below the knee and help keep the rider's leg steady as well as offer some protection from chafing.

Half-halt A sequence of aids that ask a horse to adjust its balance in preparation for the rider's request for a particular movement or transition.

Halter A headstall generally made of leather, nylon, or rope used to lead or otherwise control a horse.

Hand The four-inch unit of measure used to determine a horse's height from the ground to its withers.

Hand gallop A controlled gallop, with a speed between canter and full gallop.

Heartgirth The distance around a horse's body when measured just behind the withers.

Homebred A horse whose owner owned its dam at the time it was foaled.

Hot walkers Racetrack workers who walk horses to cool them out following exercise, or the mechanical machines used to serve the same purpose.

Hunter A horse used in the sport of foxhunting (field hunter) or one competed in horse shows (show hunter), where the horse is judged on its way of traveling on the flat and its form over fences.

Impulsion The energy in a horse's forward movement.

In-and-out Two jumps placed in close proximity and jumped consecutively, with a specific number of strides between them.

Interfere When a horse hits one leg against another due to a faulty way of moving its legs.

Irons A common term for the rider's stirrups, which are often made of metal.

Jigging A term that describes the up-and-down movement of a horse between a walk and trot, usually occuring when a horse is excited or nervous.

Jumper A horse competed in classes where the horse's ability to jump fences cleanly in the shortest period of time determines the winner, while its form over fences isn't considered.

Kimberwicke bit A shanked bit with minimal to mild curb action that is more severe ("stronger") in a horse's mouth than a snaffle bit.

Lead To walk a horse with the aid of a rope or lead shank, or the word used to describe the leg extending furthest in front when a horse is cantering. The lead leg is the last hoof to make contact with the ground during each canter stride. The rider is said to be on the "correct lead" when the lead leg matches the direction of travel (for example, the right leg when traveling on a circle to the right).

Leg-yielding When a horse moves laterally, traveling both forward and sideways when cued by the rider's leg, seat, and rein aids.

Liver chestnut A deep shade of chestnut horse coat color.

Liverpool A jump with a ditch or tray of water under it.

Long and low The phrase used to describe the way a horse moves on a long rein with his head and neck stretched out before him; a movement often used to stretch the horse during warm-up.

Long in the tooth An expression meaning "getting along in years," since horses' teeth get longer as they age.

Longeing (lungeing) The exercising and/or training of a horse on a circle using a long lash (longe whip) and a long webbed line (longe line) that is attached to a sturdy headstall (see cavesson).

Martingale, standing A leather strap running from the bridle's noseband between the horse's front legs to the girth, used to prevent the horse from carrying its head too high and evading the rider's rein aids.

Near side The horse's left side.

Never started A phrase often used to describe a horse that was never in a race.

Off A term used to describe a horse whose way of traveling indicates lameness.

Off side The horse's right side.

On the bit When a horse moves forward energetically from the rider's leg into a supporting rein with a rounded topline and the nose positioned just in front of the vertical.

On the flat A phrase describing a horse's ridden performance when it is not jumping.

OTTB An off-the-track Thoroughbred.

Oxer A spread jump featuring the challenge of both height and width.

Paddock boots A low, heeled boot worn by horseback riders.

Palomino A horse coat color that comes in varying shades of gold with a white mane and tail.

Pastern The portion of the horse's lower leg that connects the ankle joint and the hoof.

Pinto A horse coat color featuring mainly white hairs with black or brown patches.

Polo wraps A type of bandage used to protect a horse's legs during exercise.

Pony The term to describe a horse under 14.2 hands high, or a way of exercising a horse by leading it while riding astride a second horse.

Prince of Wales spurs A mild type of spur with a short neck (shank).

Pulled (mane) The term used to describe a horse's mane that has been thinned and shortened by selectively removing the longer hairs.

Quarter Horse A popular breed of horse developed in the United States and commonly used for ranch work, racing, and both English and Western pleasure riding.

Rasp A metal file used to reduce the points on a horse's teeth; also the name for the tool used to file down a horse's hooves.

Revet A way of stabilizing a bank often used in the construction of cross-country obstacles.

Roll-top jump A solid jump with a rounded top.

Run up (stirrups or irons) When the stirrup iron is slid to the top of the stirrup leather as a way of stabilizing the stirrup on the saddle. Usually done when the rider is walking beside the horse, as it prevents a low-hanging stirrup from catching on doors and fences, for example.

Running out When a horse runs to the side of a jump at the last moment to avoid jumping it.

Saddlebred An American breed of horse known for its flashy, animated gaits.

Schooling figures Movements horses are asked to perform on the flat when being trained.

Scribe A person who assists a dressage judge during a dressage test by writing scores and comments on a test sheet as the judge dictates.

Shank The chain on the end of a shank lead, which can be attached over the horse's nose for greater control, or the side pieces of a curb-type bit, or the neck of a spur.

Sheet An item of horse clothing lighter than a horse blanket, usually used in milder conditions or to protect the horse from rain.

Shipping boots An item of horse clothing used to protect the horse's legs when it is being transported.

Simple change When a cantering horse changes his lead after first slowing to a trot or a walk (see flying change).

Sire A horse's father (stallion).

Snaffle The simplest and mildest type of horse bit, which is usually jointed in the middle.

Snip A small grouping of white hairs on the front of the horse's muzzle.

Sound Term used to describe a horse free of lameness or other conditions that would compromise its ability to perform.

Sport horse A horse used for equestrian competitions or recreational purposes.

Spurs An artificial aid attached to the rider's boots to accentuate the leg aids.

Stall walking A vice demonstrated by a horse excessively moving around in its stall.

Stallion A male horse used for breeding purposes.

Standards (jump) The structures on the sides of a manmade jump that support the horizontal rails.

Star A grouping of white hairs on a horse's forehead.

Stocks An enclosure used to constrain a horse, usually used to assist a farrier or vet.

Stride A single coordinated movement of the four legs of a horse, completed when the legs return to their initial relative position.

Sweet feed A palatable horse feed containing various grains plus molasses.

Tack up To saddle and bridle a horse in preparation for riding.

Thoroughbred A breed of horse used for racing at a gallop.

Transition A change from one gait to another.

Triple bar A type of spread fence that includes three sets of standards and rails.

Trot The second gait of the horse's three main gaits, which include the walk, trot, and canter. The trot has two beats, and is faster than the walk but slower than the canter.

Tucked up The phrase commonly used to describe when a horse's flank area is tight and contracted following hard exercise or dehydration.

Twitch A device placed on a horse's sensitive upper lip to restrain it.

Two-point position When a rider lifts his or her seat slightly out of the saddle, leaving his legs and hands in communication with the horse.

Tying-up A muscular disorder occurring in horses usually following stressful exercise or dietary changes, which can cause painful muscle and kidney damage.

USEA The United States Eventing Association.

Vertical jump A jump with height but not width.

Vice An undesirable horse behavior, such as cribbing, weaving, and stall walking.

Walk The slowest of the horse's three main gaits, which include the walk, trot, and canter. The walk has four beats.

Weaving A vice demonstrated by a horse swinging its head and neck from side to side while shifting its weight from one front leg to the other.

Withers The highest part of a horse's back located at the base of its neck.

Wolf tooth A tooth sometimes appearing in the horse's mouth in the area directly above the bars; generally removed to prevent problematic contact with the bit.

Points of the Horse

Croup

Withers

Hip

Flank

Shoulder

Barrel

Crest

Stifle

Elbow

Hock

Poll

Knee

Forehead

Cannon

Pastern

Hoof

Fetlock
("ankle")

Muzzle

ABOUT THE AUTHOR

Linda Snow McLoon was *that girl* who always wanted a horse of her own but had to wait until she was an adult for her dream to come true. She and her horse Bayberry competed in horse shows, dressage competitions, and horse trials. Linda taught young riders as a U.S. Pony Club Affiliate Coordinator of Instruction, and along the way bred and raced Thoroughbred racehorses. She lives in Portland, Maine. You can get in touch with Linda and find out more about the Brookmeade Young Riders Series by visiting www.lindasnowmcloon.com.

ABOUT THE ARTIST

Jennifer Brandon is the painter, illustrator, and graphic designer behind Jaché Studio. Her passion is to share with you a piece of a beautiful moment through the medium of paint. Jen offers original and custom oil paintings, where the personality of each horse, person, or pet is expressively depicted and the energy of the moment is relived through the medium of paint. Visit Jaché Studio on Facebook and view more of Jen's work at www.jachestudio.com.